SECRET AGENT GALS

RICHARD GID POWERS

LIVINGSTON PRESS
UNIVERSITY OF WEST ALABAMA

Library of Congress Control Number: 2023XXXXXX
Printed on acid-free paper
Printed in the United States of America by
Publishers Graphics

Typesetting and page layout: Joe Taylor, Cassidy Pedram
Proofreading: Brooke Barger, Cassidy Pedram,
Savannah F. Beams, Jacob Dial, Dior Wilson, Haina Franco,
Summer Chadwick, and Jessica Meeks

Cover Design: Laura Tolkow

Cover layout: Joe Taylor

6 5 4 3 2 1

SECRET AGENT GALS

Table of Contents

Part 2

INTRODUCTION

to the

New "Big Reveal" Edition of *Secret Agent Gals*

You know the kind of long-lost documents Dan Brown and Daniel Silva are always finding, usually after gunfights, stabbings, beatings, torture, getting dropped out of planes, tossed into a snake pit (I think that was Indiana Jones), the inconveniences Robert Langdon and Gabriel Allon have come to expect before the Big Reveal? Where they come up with the long-lost (but now recovered) document that proves everything we thought we knew about Jesus, the Catholic Church, the Founding Fathers, Pearl Harbor, and the Kennedy assassination was just 180 degrees from the truth. Have I forgotten anyone? Elvis?

Everything we believed (and that Mom taught us) about everything and everybody was just a crock. So now we've got the true gen, as Hemingway would say, kind of a bargain for 20 bucks and a few hours of reading.

This new edition of *Secret Agent Gals* is something like that, with a twist. The first edition — the first nineteen chapters of this version — was a best seller in 1948, the story of how two celebrity art collectors and museum founders, Peggy Guggenheim and Baroness Hilla Rebay, were recruited by J. Edgar Hoover to expose the Nazi spies who infiltrated the painters they helped escape from the Nazis.

Everyone who read that book knows how the Secret Agent Gals won the "Good War" against Hitler and his Nazi ratbastards, not to mention the sneaky Japanese who attacked Pearl Harbor. Also how they kept Stalin's Commie ratbastards from getting the A-Bomb until the heroes of the Strategic Air Command were good and ready to stop the Red Hitler's plans to kill us all. (What I'm trying to say in that last sentence, which got a little confusing, is that Stalin, aka 'The Red Hitler," planned to dump A-Bombs on America, and the G-Girls stopped him. Sorry.)

And everyone knows how Baroness Hilla Rebay built the Guggenheim Museum on Fifth Avenue in New York, and how she and Peggy Guggenheim put together the Museum's great collection of modern painting and sculpture — you know, the kind of art that doesn't look like anything you or I or any sane person would buy and in fact looks like something your five-year-old or a chimp named J. Fred Muggs cudda done. You and I can both see through that kind of crap, but let's not go there. Some people like it and pay big bucks for it, but there's a sucker born, etc, etc.

We *thought* we knew all that. But . . .

Now, because of the declassification of supersecret FBI files in response to Freedom of Information Act (FOIA) requests (really demands) by Fearless Crusading Publisher Joe Taylor, we learn everything we believed about XXXXX and XXXXX and especially XXXXX (no spoilers here, sorry) was just a load of bullshit, and that's putting it mildly.

As Fearless Crusading Publisher Joe Taylor prepared the new "Big Reveal" Chapter Twenty for publication, he had to figure out how exactly to drop this bombshell on you all. He decided that readers should share his (that is, Fearless Crusading Publisher Joe Taylor's) own excitement as he discovered the truth.

And so what you now have is (first) the original first edition, word for word as it appeared in 1948, followed by the author's own suppressed account of how and why the G-Gals embargoed Chapter Twenty, and then . . . the earthshaking revelations of Chapter Twenty itself. And the FBI's desperate attempts to intimidate him (Fearless Crusading Publisher Joe Taylor) from publishing the TRUTH, the truth that will shatter what is left of the Bureau's reputation already in tatters from its Hillary E-mail and Russian Collusion fiascoes. So now the truth can finally be told. But again, no spoilers here! Ya gotta read to the end to get to the good stuff.

As you probably have gathered, we (meaning you) have gotten a little more sensitive to "offensive" reading material over the past seventy some years since the first edition. What you are going to read is not suitable for children under five (or some of you snowflakes) due to filthy language (the s-word, the f-word, and the c-word all over the place) and if you know what those words mean you should stop right now and wash your mouth out with brown soap with pieces of Brillo® pad stuck into it.

There are also scenes in which cigarettes are smoked (which can cause, according to the Attorney of General of Something or Other, serious harm to pregnant women and operators of machinery like snow blowers, chainsaws, or electric toothbrushes), so if you find yourself reaching for a pack of unfiltered Camels® or Kools® after reading this book, don't say Ol' Fearless didn't warn ya.

There is also one scene in which our heroes "black" up with burnt cork, and if your tender little woke hearts can't take that kind of shock you better skip that section (but it was for a good cause, sneaking up on murderous Nazi and Commie ratbastards with flashlights just like John "Duck" Wayne in *The Green Berets* or Leonardo "Leo" DiCaprio in *Inglourious Basterds)*, and if you're so goddamn sensitive, and you don't think trying to stop the Holocaust is worth bending a few rules, Joe Taylor, the Fearless Crusader, wants to know right now if you're willing to admit or deny that the Holocaust did or didn't happen, and that calls for a simple "yes" or "no" answer, you equivocating phony. He nailed ya.

There is also a scene where a Secret Agent guy dresses up like a Secret Agent gal, and if you're not willing to grant "trans" Americans equal rights under the law and equal employment opportunities (and equal pay) you're not the kind of reader this Fearless Guy wants for his crusade.

Okay, that covers all the "trigger" stuff that might give Me-too-ers and "Cancel Everything" vigilantes heart attacks, so you can start reading.

Part 1

CHAPTER 1

The Baroness Hilla Rebay rang the bell, and the door of the split-level ranch in Washington Northeast opened. She found herself staring into the business end of a .45 caliber Police Special. She raised her eyes to the bulldog features of the man holding the gun, J. Edgar Hoover, a face familiar to the millions of kids who belonged to his *Post Toasties® Junior G-man Club* and their parents who believed anything whipped up by Hoover's crack publicity wizards in the FBI's Crime Records Division.

"You must be the Baroness," Hoover said, greeting her with a grin as phony as the smiley face on the welcome mat at Sing-Sing.

"And you must be the gentleman who's gonna get his fucking arm broken if he doesn't put down that gun."

J. Edgar Hoover, reflexes crippled from decades of breathing lead dust while trying (unsuccessfully) to pass his proficiency test at the Bureau's gun range, and slowed even more from years of pounding down martinis with Walter Winchell (his #1 informant) at New York's Stork Club, failed to lower his pistol quickly enough to suit the Baroness. She sidestepped, grabbed his gun arm and twisted hard, sending the hapless hero's sidearm clattering to the parquet floor, and sending the man himself up in the air for a full gainer with a twist.

The Baroness scooped up the revolver as Hoover almost landed on his feet, but lost style points as he slipped on the first banana peel of the slippery yellow trail the Baroness spotted leading to the living room. *The Ol' Trail-of-Banana-Peels Burglar-Baffler*, the Baroness thought, *pretty primitive for the head of a modern scientific law enforcement outfit.*

"That's no way to treat Public Hero Number One," the director blubbered as he struggled to his feet, only to slip and fall on the second banana peel as he bent to retrieve the fedora lost during that first tumble.

The Baroness toyed with the pistol. "This thing loaded?" she wondered aloud, and answered her question by shooting out six bulbs from the foyer chandelier. *I guess it was.*

As Hoover once again struggled to his feet, the Baroness counted the remaining banana peels and calculated eight more pratfalls, somersaults, and other aerial acrobatics, for a total of ten (*Study arithmetic, kids, comes in handy*) before the Crimestopper Commander-in-Chief would make it to the living room couch. So she stepped over the once-again supine (*Supine means flat on his ass, kids. Study your vocabulary*) crimefighter to score a drink on her own.

"Gimme back my gun," Hoover whined.

"You forgot the magic word."

"Magic word? What's that? Oh! How about 'Hocus-pocus'? — No? — 'Alakazam'? — 'Booga-Booga'? — 'Mother May I'?"

"Getting close."

"Aw, come on. Gimme a hint."

"Sorta rhymes with 'police.'"

The Sage of Scientific Sleuthing couldn't think of the Magic Word as he slipped and fell on the third banana peel.

In the living room a well-dressed lady was doubled over in laughter and a tall handsome gent wearing what the Baroness recognized as the G-Man *de rigeur* of three-piece navy blue pin-striped suit, wing-tipped shoes, and a snap-brim fedora was trying unsuccessfully to hide his hilarity by covering his mouth with both hands. He finally gave up and slapped his hands on his thighs and yelled, "You look like such a moron, Boss. I tol' ya that ol' banana skin trick wasn't going to fool any burglar who wasn't already brain dead."

"Like him," the lady added, pointing at the Galumphing Gumshoe, who had just gone down for the fourth time.

The Baroness stuck out her hand to the tall dark stranger, and said, "I'm Hilla Rebay."

"Clyde Tolson, Public Hero Number Two, and best buddy of the boy on his back over there," as Hoover went down for what the Baroness calculated was the fifth time.

"And you I'd know anywhere: Peggy, you slut," she said to the finely-coutured female, as the Director hit the deck for the sixth time.

"Won't somebody help me?" the Nation's Top Cop wailed.

"Why, Hilla, you gold-digger, such an unwelcome surprise. I don't know why we're both here, but I haven't had a drink yet either. Clyde?"

The much-disheveled Law-Enforcement Legend finally crawled into the living room after three more slip-and-falls. "I think that was the last of them," he told them cheerfully as he tried to stand up. "Whoops!" he went down again. "Forgot about that one. I think that was the last of 'em. Supposed to finish off the burglar. The grand finale. Oh well. I could use one too, Clyde."

"'One-two,' quite a way with words," the Baroness

laughed. "And by the way, XYZ."

The Director directed his gaze downward, and sure enough, his fly was unzipped. As he struggled to fix it, Peggy, the heiress and art addict Peggy Guggenheim, said, "Here, lemme help you, you'll never get anywhere with your tie caught in the zipper. Don't worry. I won't touch your willy. . . . There . . . OK now? Good boy. Oh, and ya got yer hat on backwards, Mr. Hoover."

"My friends call me *Speed*," the Director told them.

"OK, Speed," the Baroness said, "And just what the hell is *she* doing here?" pointing to Peggy, who had the same expression of surprise, shock, and horror Hilla would have seen on her own face if a mirror had been handy.

"Why that's your pal Peggy. She just got here. I got something I wanna say to both of you."

"She's not my pal, and whatever it is you have on your mind, you can forget it. I don't wanna be in the same room with that, that . . . woman."

"Aw, lemme have a chance to tell you what I got on my stupid mind. You might find it interesting. So what're you drinking?"

"Gin," the Baroness said.

"Me too," Peggy chimed in. Then, "I didn't know she was coming," Peggy said to the Director. "Whatever you're planning, Speed, I'm sure it's a bad idea."

"Calm down," Hoover told them. "Look around. Make yourselves at home. Clyde, get moving on those drinks. We've gotta cloud the minds of these little ladies. And I don't know what you're both thinking, but just because Clyde lives here with me doesn't mean we're, you know . . ."

"Whatever you say, as long as those drinks get here," Hilla responded. The ladies looked at each other with distaste, then looked around the living room. "Those things loaded?" the Baroness asked, pointing to a brace of submachine guns on the mantel.

"Guns're no good if they ain't loaded," Hoover informed her. *Seems reasonable*, she thought.

The Baroness walked over to Peggy Guggenheim and went face-to-face. Real close. "I've been hearing what you've been saying about me and your uncle. I oughtta paste you a good one."

"Oh, yeah? Go ahead and try."

The Baroness cocked her fist for a right lead, and Hoover rushed between them just in time to catch Rebay's punch square on the nose. "Goddammit, I think you broke my nose. Gimme something to stop the bleeding, Clyde."

The two Public Heroes looked with dismay at the blood on the white plush rug. "Think we can get those spots out, Clyde?"

"I dunno, Chief. You were too cheap to get these things Scotchguarded®. I think we're fucked. Maybe we could burn the place down for the insurance."

"Quit whining," Peggy said, "and how 'bout those drinks?"

"Oh yeah," Clyde said, and he went back to the bar and returned with four highball glasses filled to the brim with gin and ice. "Here's how," he said, raising his glass, as they all tossed down a big gulp. Hoover looked disgusted as a drop of blood from his nose landed in his glass. "Shit! Get me a new drink, Clyde!"

"Aw for Christ's sake, Chief, you won't even taste it. And by the way, I remember there's a blood-on-white-rug exclusion clause in our Homeowner's Policy. Those insurance guys are plenty slick. This'll teach us not to buy our policy from the Tupperware lady."

"It's only a rug, for God's sake," Peggy told him. "And you can gyp the government for a new one. Tell 'em it was ruined during a shoot-out with a Public Enemy who made it past the banana peels. So, what's your big idea, anyway? I'd like to get out of here and go somewhere I don't have to breathe the same air as this slut who's banging my uncle and looting my inheritance to buy her boyfriend's paintings. A boyfriend, by the way, who is a no-talent hack."

"Yeah, well at least he *is* my *boyfriend*. You make *every* painter pass inspection in bed before you'll buy his paintings."

"You ought to try it, you gold-digger," Peggy sneered, and reared back to throw a punch at the Baroness. Clyde stepped between them and this time *he* caught a right to the jaw that dropped him.

"I think you killed my buddy," Hoover wailed.

"It's his own fault. It's the manly art of self-defense, and he didn't defend himself," Peggy explained to Public Hero Number One. "And it's all over town that you're screwing my uncle for his money," Guggenheim told the Baroness.

"Why you liar," the Baroness said, and rushed at Peggy. Speed and Clyde, still groggy from the punches, made a move to get between them, thought it over, looked at each other, shrugged, and sat down on the couch to watch the catfight.

They were pretty well matched, the Baroness with her honey blonde hair in the bob that was the style, Peggy with darker hair, also bobbed. They had both kicked off their high heels as they grappled with each other, Peggy had the Baroness in a headlock on the floor, but the Baroness did an escape and had Peggy from behind, face down. Peggy did the old butt-bump move and had the Baroness pinned, both shoulders to the floor. She looked urgently at Clyde, who got down on the floor to make sure both the Baroness's shoulders were down. Clyde slapped the floor: "One, Two," and was just about to count her out when the Baroness did another escape. She jumped to her feet, picked Peggy up, and slammed her to the floor headfirst. Peggy looked dazed and ready to be finished off. "Got any bridge chairs?" the Baroness asked Hoover.

"In the closet."

The Baroness hastily retrieved a folded bridge chair while

Peggy was trying to gather her wits. She raised the chair over Peggy's head, glancing around at Speed and Clyde to make sure they were watching. Clyde was chanting, "Baroness! Baroness!" and Speed was yelling for Peggy to rally. The Baroness brought the bridge chair down on Guggenheim for the finish, but Peggy twisted aside, escaped, and grabbed the chair from the Baroness. Clyde and Speed were so excited that they started bitch-slapping each other, Clyde cheering for the Baroness, Speed for Peggy. The Baroness was in full retreat, Peggy stalking her around the living room. Peggy backed the Baroness against the fireplace and raised the chair. They were both panting. The Baroness reached to the mantle and grabbed one of the machine guns. She pointed it at Peggy. Peggy retreated with her hands up.

"Whew," the Baroness said. "That was fun," and she lowered the machine gun. "I didn't know you had that much fight in you. Let's do it again sometime." Peggy dropped the chair. "Now let's find out what those two geniuses wanted us here for."

They looked around. The two Ace G-Men were on the floor, Speed sitting astride Clyde, slapping him back and forth across the chops, while Clyde was gesturing frantically to the Baroness to pull Hoover off him. "He's hurting me. . . . Come on, Speed, save that stuff for later when we're alone."

The two ladies sat on the couch to watch, sipping their gin. "If Clyde just pulled up his legs, he could get Hoover in a scissor lock and flip him," Peggy suggested.

"Great idea!" Clyde yelled, as he flipped his boss and began strangling him.

Peggy and the Baroness were comparing manicures and had discovered a common bond in that they both favored Charles of the Ritz cosmetics. "I like the contrast between your fair skin and the bright red lipstick," Peggy told the Baroness. "I go for a little matchy-matchy with a darker lipstick because of my tan."

"I think that's very attractive," the Baroness replied, "but let me fix you up a little. That head slam seems to have dislodged one of your eyelashes. There, that's better."

They looked over at the Lords of Law Enforcement. Clyde tightened his grip on Hoover's throat and had both thumbs pressing on the FBI Director's Adam's apple. "I think the FBI is gonna need a new boss if we let this go on much longer," the Baroness said, as Hoover's face turned red and he stopped moving. She went over and pulled Clyde off Public Hero Number One.

"I had him! I had him! You saw that I had him! Why'd you hafta stop it?" Clyde was so excited he was almost crying. In fact, he *was* crying. "That's the first time I ever beat Speed in a fight."

Speed took a few deep breaths and struggled to his feet. "Two out of three. I only fell 'cause I slipped on one more banana peel that was NOT part of the burglar trap the way we diagrammed it. Maybe a certain hard-boiled dick with a sneaky streak planted that one? Huh, Clyde? Ready to come clean, ya rat?"

"Now, now, boys, calm down. Whaja want to talk about?" the Baroness asked the nation's top spies.

The G-Men calmed down. "OK, here's the deal: You know 'bout this Hitler guy who's taken over Russia, right?" Speed asked.

"I hate to correct the head of U.S. snooping and spying," Peggy told him, "but Hitler is Germany. *Stalin* is Russia."

"Shit, I always get those assholes mixed up."

"Here's the trick. It's easy," Peggy explained. "Use the alphabet and remember it's G H: Germany, Hitler. And with Russia: it's R S, Russia, Stalin. They come after each other when you say your A, B, Cs," she added helpfully. (Got that, kids?)

"Christ. So simple. GH, RS. Whatta great trick. I made that stupid mistake yesterday when I was shaking down the House Appropriations Committee for some more money we needed to save the country. If they weren't so scared of me, they woulda laughed. Now all I have to do is learn the alphabet," he laughed. "How's it go? A, B, C, D, E, F, G . . . Just kidding."

"I know you are, Speed," said Peggy and she squeezed his knee.

"I saw that," Clyde said disapprovingly. "Not that I care."

"The point is, you and Peggy have been bringing in all kindsa radical artists and their stuff from — which is it — Germany? Russia? Germany? Which ones are the Krauts? Which ones are the Ivans?

"You're just pretending to be a *scheisskopf*, right?" the Baroness said.

"Right, whatever that means. Anyway, we want you two to figure out which artists are the Nazi spies."

"I can tell you right now: It's Peggy's Surrealists. Round them up and kill them."

"Hah! Wrong!" Peggy said. "It's your abstract painters that're the spies. They probably put messages in code in their paintings and only the other spies know what they mean. Ship 'em over to me with their paintings and I'll tell you which ones to kill."

"Yeah, ship 'em over and you'll *schtup* 'em," the Baroness told Hoover. "She judges how good painters are by how good they are in bed."

"Hear that, Clyde?"

"I'm getting hot, Speed."

"*She* does the same thing, but lies about it," Peggy said. "Rudolf Bauer, Hans Arp…"

"Hey, I don't sleep with *all* my painters; well, not often, at least not as often as you. I've got *standards*!"

"Standards? Right. They've gotta have two arms and a — wanna start keeping score?"

"Listen up, you two. Here's Clyde's idea," Hoover told them. "Get over here, Big Boy." Clyde slipped onto the couch next to the Nemesis of Ne'er-Do-Wells.

"OK, Sharpshooter, tell the Baroness and Peggy how this Dynamic Duo of Dashing Dames is going to save us from the Reds, the Nazis, whichever buncha assholes we're supposed to catch."

Clyde pulled himself together and addressed the two ladies: "OK. Here's the plan. I'm calling it *Plan 47 with the G-Gal Option*. The two of you are gonna get together and work for us, as loyal Americans — you are loyal Americans, aren't ya?" he asked the Baroness, who reached past Speed and gave Clyde a noogie.

"Speed, did you see what she did?" Clyde complained.

"Man up, Girlfriend," Speed told him. "Now tell them your brainstorm."

"You two could be pals, be on our team," Clyde said earnestly and with fake sincerity that had tricked many a Public Enemy into ratting out his gang. "We'll put you through our Counter-Spy Training Program and you'll learn how to smash Nazi spy rings. Publicity should be good for your museums' images. Nothing wrong with making a buck."

"You mean we have to work together? Hmm . . ." the Baroness pondered the idea. "Before we had that little dustup, I would have said, no way. But now, maybe she's not as bad as I thought. That was a good way to get to know one another. Where'd you learn that spin escape from the pin?"

"Naked wresting at Smith. I was team captain. Dincha do that at your school?"

"Nah. In Germany we went for saber fencing. Like you do here in acting school. See this little scar here?" as she pointed to a nick on her cheek. "That got me dates at the military fraternity at Heidelberg. The guys loved to lick it."

Peggy smiled at the Baroness. "Maybe we *could* work together, Chief," she said.

That made Hoover happy. And Happy Hoover thought, *Let's make everyone happy*. "Let's take a little recess. Clyde, break out those joints."

"Joints, what's that?" the Baroness asked.

Peggy said, "Now yer talking."

"*Nicht verstehe*," the Baroness said.

"You never heard of Reefer Madness?" Peggy asked the Baroness, passing her the joint Speed handed her after taking a deep drag himself. "Here, just pucker up and inhale."

"You mean like I'm smoking a Camel®?"

"That's the idea. You might even get humped." The Baroness looked at her blankly. "That was a joke. I guess you have to be a native speaker to get it."

"Wow," the Baroness said after taking a couple puffs. "This is great. Makes me want to look at a goldfish tank and eat gummy bears, whatever they are. Or listen to whales singing love songs."

"Join our team," Hoover told her, "and I can get you all this shit you want. We've confiscated a ton of it, and it's just for me and Clyde and our pals. We gotta test the stuff if we're gonna arrest someone for having it." He took another hit. "Wow! The guys down in the lab musta put a little extra something in this!" He grabbed a handful of gummy bears from the table. "So, whaddya you think about Clyde's great idea? I just love, I mean *like*, or maybe it's just *admire*, the guy. And ain't he cute? I mean handsome?"

The Baroness ignored Hoover's question and tried to think about how much she used to hate Peggy Guggenheim, but she was high as the Dumbo balloon in Macys® Thanksgiving Day Parade and was having trouble thinking about anything. For her part, Peggy was at peace with the world. "We'll do it," the Baroness said. Peggy couldn't talk, so she just nodded. And grinned. And drooled a little.

"That's it!" Speed yelled. "Yowza! We got 'em!" He slapped Clyde a high five and danced a little jig with his War-on-

Crime Wingman.

"See!" Clyde yelled. "And you said they were *cretins*."

"I never said that. I said, 'great ones,' not 'cretins,'" Speed lied to his two new special agent recruits. He had his fingers crossed where the girls couldn't see them.

CHAPTER 2

Secret Agent School, Day One:

Special Agent Brian Mahony — "and that's with no 'e,' goddamit. I shot the last fucking trainee who stuck an 'e' in 'Mahony'" — greeted his two new recruits on their first day of training. He was big as a moose, and, Rebay detected, smelled like one. "So who do we have here?" Reading from his clipboard, he said, "Hildegard Anna Augusta Elisabeth Freiin Rebay von Ehrenwiesen. It says here you are da *Baroness* Hilla von Rebay or just Hilla Rebay. Well la-di-fuckin'-da. While yer here yer just Agent Trainee Rebay, got it? Thirty-two, huh? Mighty well-preserved for an old dame. Oh, and look at this! Christ almighty, you're not only a woman, which we got no use for here in this man's Bureau, 'cept maybe fer one thing" — he winked at her — "but you ain't even an American! Born in *Strasburg*, hey, isn't that part of Russia, or Germany, or some other lousy Commie country? Maybe *you're* a spy. That'd be just the kinda trick you Commies'd try to pull. Says you're in the art business, run a museum up in

New York. What kinda art you got in that museum of yers? Lots of naked broads, I hope."

"You wouldn't understand, moron."

"Try me. And it's *Special Agent Moron Sir*, to you."

"My museum is called 'The Art of Tomorrow,'" Rebay informed him, somewhat haughtily, "and my paintings are pure spiritual windows into the Fourth Dimension where man's astral selves seek a higher level of consciousness."

"No naked broads?"

Special Agent Trainee Rebay just shook her head. She couldn't make up her mind what to do to Mahony. Some of her ideas risked getting her thrown out of the training program and maybe even into prison. She settled for sticking her tongue out at him, which, fortunately for her, Mahony did not notice as he studied the write-up for Trainee Guggenheim.

Mahony looked up at Guggenheim. "You're thirty-two too. Matched pair. Gotta compliment you, ma'am, not bad look-ing for yer advanced age, although somewhat underdeveloped in the front area. Gotta work on that if ya wanna go undercover as a hooker. Says here you're the niece of some billionaire who lives in the Plaza Hotel. What's the matter? Too cheap to buy a house? And, lemme check, yeah, it says in Trainee Rebay's write-up that she works for this rich homeless uncle of yours. So you're pals, huh. Well, no ganging up on me and no cheating on tests. Yer each on yer own."

"First of all," Agent-to-be Rebay said, spitting out her words and pointing at Guggenheim, "we ain't pals — I mean we *aren't* pals. I guess you could say we're rivals. But now we're trying to get along." She felt herself already sinking to Mahony's level of abysmal grammatical incompetence, something like the one about sleeping with dogs and getting fleas. "Second, I don't work for Mr. Guggenheim. I *advise* him on paintings to buy for our museum collection. We're partners."

"Partners!" Guggenheim sneered. "Do you pay him, or does he pay you? And do you chip in fifty-fifty when you buy those paintings of 'spiritual messages from the other world?'"

Mahony just barely got between them before Rebay could start swinging.

"Easy, girls. It says here, Guggenheim, that you had a museum yourself, but in a foreign country. London? That's in England, right? If I remember fourth-grade geography. And you oughtta know the FBI hates those English pricks. I can't wait until war breaks out and we can burn their houses, rape their women, and sell their kids to the cannibals. Ha-ha. Just kidding. So what kinda paintings did you have in *your* museum? No naked broads either, I spose?"

"A few. Sexual images seething out of the subconscious, art releasing us from the idiotic constraints that fools call civilization. Fools like you, by the way."

"Sticks and stones," Mahony replied smugly. "No need to get personal." *Brilliant comeback*, he thought. *Crushing, even.*

He read on. "So, Guggenheim, says here that you are planning to open a museum in New York. That right?"

This time Mahony was too late to keep Rebay from slapping Guggenheim, yelling, "You bitch! Solly and I will run you out of town before we let you have your own museum."

As he peeled them apart, he asked, "Who's this 'Solly'?"

"That's my uncle," Guggenheim said, "her boss, who this crook is taking for a ride."

"Enough of this, Ladies. Behave. You've signed on to become Special Special FBI Agents. I've gotta train youse to be real G-Gals."

"Wait a minute," the Baroness interrupted. "What's this 'special special'?" Does that mean *very* special?"

"Or *not* so special?" Peggy asked.

"Good question," Special Agent Mahony replied. "I don't

know myself. But I know one thing new special agents gotta learn, whether they are special, very special, or not so special, and that is to keep their traps shut when their bosses are talking to 'em."

"Hey," the Baroness shouted. "I've got no boss 'cept for Solly."

"That's *Mr.* Guggenheim, you gold-digger, *my uncle,* your Sugar Daddy."

"Ladies!" Mahony shouted. "Just shut up!"

The two G-Girl trainees were stunned. Nobody had ever talked to them like that. The Baroness and Peggy were beginning to hate someone else even more than they hated (or at least *used* to hate) each other.

"Here's your schedule," Mahony said, handing them a sheet of paper,

"Day 2: That's tomorrow, cuz today's Day 1. That's the way it goes, 1, 2. Got it? Basic indoctrination tomorrow. You come in knowing the key dates in FBI history and why, right now, in 1941, it is the greatest organization, not just of cop organizations, the greatest organization in *history.* That includes the Elks, the Eagles, the DAR, the Dow Jones, the Boy Scouts, AND the New York Yankees. And you wanna know why it's so great?"

Peggy looked at the Baroness and rolled her eyes. "I bet you're gonna tell us."

"It's because it was founded by the Greatest Man in History."

"You mean Jesus Christ® founded the FBI?" Rebay asked.

"Well, founded by the *second* greatest man then," Mahony said, crossing himself. "No, it was founded by *J. Edgar Hoover.*"

"He's the Second Greatest Man in History?" the Baroness asked.

"Yup. And you have to memorize his birthday, where he went to high school, college, when he joined the J of D — I mean the D of J — the name of his closest friend, well, you've met *him*, which hand he uses to wipe his ass, everything."

"Which hand?" the Baroness asked. "I don't wanna shake it."

"Shake it? What hand?" Mahony said, a little confused. "Oh. That was a joke, dimwit. Anyway, that's your homework for tonight. Here's the handout. Test tomorrow."

"What kind of test?" Peggy asked. "I'm not so good at tests. Flunked out of the best girls' schools in New York *and* Switzerland. So…multiple choice? True-false? Fill in the blank? Can we have our notes handy?"

"Not telling. Tomorrow you learn how to drill — *like at the dentist?* Peggy wondered —then how to send messages in code, then your first class in boxing and jiu jitsu."

"Jew jitsu?" Peggy complained. "Is that an anti-Semitic crack, you Irish thug? Doesn't sound PC, ya bigot!"

"No, it's Chinese dirty fighting. You know, knee 'em in the nuts, that sort of thing. And I'm talking about Chinks, and they ain't got as many lawyers as the Jews, so it's all right. Ain't it?"

"Whatever you say, Boss. This Jew-thing sounds like fun," Peggy said. "I might even use it on you if ya don't watch yer step."

"One minor problem: We don't got a G-Girl locker room yet, so you'll have to wear your work out clothes when you show up."

"Work out? What's that?" the Baroness asked.

"You know, *sports* clothes."

"The only sports I play are golf and horseback riding. Which do you want?" Peggy asked him.

"I don't play golf," the Baroness said. "But I gotta riding outfit. Solly loves seeing me in jodhpurs."

"Jeezuz," Mahony said. "How about the kind of clothes you'd wear gardening?"

"Got it," the Baroness said. "Floppy hat and gardening gloves. Easy. But they're in my country place," she wailed. "This is some kinda fuck-up. What am I gonna do?"

"Fuhgeddaboudit. I'll have my wife put together outfits for youse both. You can change in the Director's office. I don't want any of the other agents to see your pretty little butts. Might distract them from chasing spies." Mahony left the room.

Peggy told the Baroness, "I didn't like you and I guess the feeling was mutual, but we gotta stick together against this idiot. You'll let me copy from your test paper, won't you?"

"Why should I?"

"Because Speed said we're a package deal. Either we *both* get to be Special Special Agents or neither of us does. *Verstehen?*"

The Baroness nodded, and she said, "As long as we're in this together, let's make it Hilla and Peggy between us. OK?"

"Deal."

* * *

Secret Agent School, Day Two:

The next morning, decked out in white middy blouses accented with red, white, and blue neckties and white tennis skirts, provided by Mahony's wife, the two G-Trainees reported for duty on the roof of the Justice Department after taking their tests on FBI lore in Mahony's office. They passed with identical scores. Probably a coincidence.

Lucky for them, it was a bright, sunny day. Their instructor ordered them to stand at attention.

"What's that?" Peggy asked.

"Stand up straight, arms by your sides, feet together, chest out, eyes ahead."

"Peggy's got no chest," the Baroness said, and she giggled. "What's she supposed to stick out?"

"Sir," Peggy protested, "will you tell this bitch to shut up?"

"Who you calling a bitch? I got two eyes. You got not even *klein* boobs; more like *kein* boobs." (*Klein* and *kein* sound alike, kids, but *klein* means 'small' and *kein* means 'none.')

"I've had no complaints, and that's from a lot of men. Including a few who dumped you."

"You mean Hans? He didn't dump me. We're still pals. But he got married. I draw the line at married men."

"Hah! How about my uncle?"

"Flat-chested *dummkopf!*"

"That's enough, Ladies. First, you're going to learn some simple marching maneuvers. When I say, 'Right Face,' you pivot on your right heel and left toe, then place your left toe next to your right foot. OK? Now let's try it: 'Right Face.'"

The Baroness did it perfectly. Peggy got mixed up and turned to the left, got her feet twisted, and fell down. She started to whimper .

"That's OK, Agent Guggenheim. Stand up and try it again. Stand right behind Agent Rebay."

"I'd like you to call me Agent *Baroness* Rebay, please. Back home we string together titles."

"Denied. Now when I say, 'Right Face,' Agent Guggenheim, you wait a second, and look at Agent Rebay's feet."

"At least call me *Baroness* Rebay."

"Dammit, up here you're just Rebay. Now let's get going. Right face." Again, the Agent Trainee Baroness maneuvered perfectly. Peggy watched the Baroness's feet, and this time got it just right. She stopped sniffling. "This is kind of fun. Let's do that again." She shouted, "Right face!" They both turned and wound up side by side again. Mahony beamed. "That was great. You're showing real talent. Now when I say, 'Forward March,' you take a step forward with your left foot, followed by your right foot, then left, right, left, right. Think you got that?"

The G-Girls nodded.

"OK. 'Forward, Harch!'" They stood still.

"Why didn't you start moving?" Mahony demanded.

Peggy said, "We're waiting for you to say, 'Forward March.' You said 'Forward Harch!' Tried to trick us, didn't you? But it didn't work! 'Harch?' That's not even English. We didn't bite."

"She's right," the Baroness added.

"Well," Peggy said to the Baroness, "finally you agree with me! Maybe we *can* get along. Just listen to what I tell you and say, OK."

"Oh, shut up!"

Mahony tried to keep his temper. "'Harch' is the way 'March' is pronounced in Bureau-speak. It's the military pronunciation."

"How come?" the Baroness asked.

"I don't know why. I don't care why. It just *is*. When I say 'Harch' just put out your left foot and start harching. I mean *marching*."

"We got him all mixed up," the Baroness giggled.

"Attention!" Mahony shouted. "Forward harch." The two G-Gals began marching forward, the Baroness goose-stepping, stiff-kneed, with her feet reaching almost up to her waist.

"Stop," Mahony screamed. "Agent Rebay, what in the name of Christ do you think you're doing?"

"Harching."

"That's not how we harch — I mean *march* — in this country."

"Well, that's how we do it back home, and our soldiers been at it a lot longer than yours."

"Well, in this U.S. of A. we don't do that. You ain't a Nazi anymore. Watch Agent Guggenheim. Forward march. I mean *harch*! Goddammit, just do it!" Peggy began striding forward, swinging her arms vigorously, a broad grin on her face. She was making the Baroness look like a jerk and she loved it.

"That's what we call marching *here*," Mahony yelled. "Get it, Agent Rebay?"

"Well, it looks pretty sloppy to me. Like she's out for a stroll in the park. This is marching. Harching. Whatever." And the Baroness began goose-stepping vigorously back and forth. "See what I mean? Looks real sharp. What Peggy's doing looks like *scheiss*."

* * *

Secret Agent School, Day Three:

The next morning, Mahony greeted the Pulchritudinous Proto-Public Defenders. telling them, "Today, Ladies, you get fitted for your uniforms."

"But spies don't wear uniforms, Ace. Why should us counterspies?" Peggy complained. "I've got plenty of nice clothes. More than this so-called royalty," pointing at the Baroness.

"I dress very well. Just not like a slut, like some people."

"If you would just keep your eyes open like real detectives, you'da noticed that all us G-Men wear the same dark blue three-piece suits, official FBI ties, spit-shined black wingtips, and snap-brim fedoras. That's our uniform. Plus, our guns."

"Well, OK. If that's what you call a uniform. I just thought you were all too scared of your boss to wear anything classy."

Introducing the elegantly dressed woman standing beside him, Mahony said, "This here is Claire McCardell. She's going to measure you for your new outfits." The Baroness and Peggy looked at each other. They were finally impressed by something in the FBI. "I love your stuff, Miss McCardell," Peggy said.

"She did her last show in *my* museum," the Baroness informed Peggy.

"*Your* museum?" Peggy scoffed. "That's my *uncle's* museum!"

"We're a team," the Baroness responded angrily.

"Yeah, 'bunkies,'" Guggenheim sneered.

McCardell glanced at Mahony. He shrugged. She showed them a drawing. "These are the drawings of your new outfits, ladies. They will be done in dark blue pin-striped flannel, with a below-the-knees skirt, very fashionable; a cute vest to wear over a white blouse, and a fitted jacket. I've topped it off with a little snap-brim bonnet, a very feminine version of the G-Men's fedoras. If you'll just let me take your measurements: hips, waist, and bust." The Baroness snickered and Peggy glared at her. McCardell whipped out a tape measure, wrapped it around the curvaceous crime-fighting cuties and stepped out the door.

"She's a busy lady," Mahony observed.

"Hey, what about accessories? Looks kinda drab," the Baroness complained to Mahony. He grinned craftily. "We've cooked up something that's really going to fool those spies and crooks." He opened up a little blue box. "All right!" Peggy exulted. "Tiffany's! About time."

"What we've got here is a pair of wedding rings. These are samples because we have to size you. Here's the plan: You wear them so that the Nazi and gangster ratbastards won't hit on youse. Same trick will maybe hold back some of our horny agents who will definitely try to bone ya. And then, and here's the genius part: Say we tell you to sidle up to one of these traitors, you know, romance him, make him spill the beans. Why, you just take off the ring. That's why the rings are gonna be a little loose."

"How far are we supposed to go smooching secrets out of these Nazi animals?" Peggy asked. She didn't look too worried, just curious.

"Just what it takes and no more than it takes," Mahony told her.

The Baroness shook her head. "I'm not playing hide-the-knockwurst with any Nazis," she said firmly. "Or bank robbers."

Peggy appealed to Mahony. "Sorry to say, but she doesn't sound like a *loyal American* to me. Our boys are being drafted. The Nazis are slaughtering the French and the Brits. Least we can do is spread our legs for democracy."

"She's right," Mahony said. "I'm spending my evenings teaching knot-tying and Morse code to the Boy Scouts, so they'll be ready for the big show. You gotta man up too. Er, girl up."

"Oh, OK," the Baroness agreed. "But it's under duress and I'm gonna make 'em wear a rubber. And no extras like the squawking duck. That's only for my boyfriend."

"'Squawking duck'? That sounds like fun. You'll have to teach me," Peggy said.

"Just ask your uncle," the Baroness answered. "It's his favorite."

"I think the Bureau will accept those compromises. I'll bring it up at the next Executive Conference, where I've just been promoted, by the way." He beamed. Peggy gave him a kiss on the cheek and said, "That's swell, Chief."

"You deserve it," the Baroness added.

"I've got a few more surprises." He produced another small box. "This here is an official G-Man Decoder Ring®. One for each of ya."

They let out gasps of surprise. "The same ones that are in the Post Toasties® boxes?" Peggy asked.

"Those are toys. These are the real thing. Here's how they work: Say you get a secret message from headquarters. I've got one here." He showed them a slip of paper with the letters LXQ on it. "Ya turn the ring upside down and turn the jewel until you can see the same letter through it, then turn the ring over and see the letter next to this here pointer. Got that?" They nodded. "It's pointing to 'D.' I'll do it for the next letter, 'X.' The pointer is on 'O.' And now for the last one, it's pointing to 'G.' The secret message is D-O-G. That spells DOG." He looked up triumphantly.

The Baroness and Peggy looked at each other, baffled. "What kind of stupid secret message is that?" Peggy demanded. "'DOG?' What the hell does that mean?"

"Maybe DOG is a code word. Could be it means *beware*. Ya know, like beware of the dog," the Baroness suggested.

"Dammit," Mahony shouted. "That was just an example. Ya think we'd be sending a real secret message to two dames what ain't even gotten their guns yet? And that's what I've got for you now."

He opened his duffel bag and took out two small black handbags. "Yer gonna keep your guns in these, because Miss Mc-Cardell's jackets fit too tight for a shoulder holster."

"Eww," Peggy said. "I can't be seen with a bag like that. Gross. How about Cardin or Vuitton?"

"Negative!" Mahony barked. "Looky here," and he opened one of the bags. Inside were fitted compartments for a pearl-handled pistol, a set of cuffs, ammunition, and a leather FBI badge holder. "Pretty neat, right?"

"What if the purse gets snatched by some mugger on the subway?" the Baroness asked.

"Way ahead of ya. See this strap? It's got a bracelet attached that you put on your wrist. Made of steel cable. They'd have to cut off your arm to get your purse. Here's yours, Agent Guggenheim. And yours, Agent Rebay."

"You're gonna need falsies to fill out your new jacket," the Baroness whispered to Peggy.

* * *

Powers

Secret Agent School, Day Four:

"That was good yesterday, ladies," Mahony told them.

"I liked it better when you called us *girls*," Peggy said.

"Yeah, *ladies* sounds kinda like we're old," the Baroness added. "I really liked 'G-Gals.'"

"Whatever. Now we're getting to the part I like best. I think you will, too. Hand-to-hand combat. First unarmed. Then we'll go to the target range and introduce you to pistols and machine guns."

"You sure we gotta do this?" Peggy asked. "I thought we were gonna be spying on artists. They aren't exactly tough guys. Mostly they're scared of their own shadows. They're sissies."

"She got that right," the Baroness added.

"The Director thinks those clever ratbastards are going to infiltrate some dangerous Nazi agents into those artists you're investigating. If they think you're starting to suspect them, they just might try to kill you."

"Gosh," they said together. "Dirty ratbastards. Guess you can't trust anybody these days," Rebay added.

Mahony walked over to a locker and took out two things that looked like baseball catcher's chest protectors. "These may be a little big for you, but it's the best we got." He walked over to Peggy and slipped the top loop over her head and then tightened a strap around her waist and slipped a strap between her legs.

"Hey, watch it! I don't want anybody fooling around down there who hasn't been invited," Peggy yelled.

"Sorry. Lemme just get this thing strapped on," Mahony told her.

"Don't pay any attention to her," the Baroness told him. "There's been so many guys down there it's like Grand Central Station. At rush hour."

"Shut up, smartass!"

"Touchy, touchy," the Baroness said, and she laughed.

"OK, it's your turn," Mahony told the Baroness.

"Don't worry about strapping her wherever. She's no virgin. She could hide her gun in there if she wanted to," Peggy told Mahony.

Mahony was wondering what he had gotten himself into. But, he figured, the Director must know what he's doing. When he finally had the Baroness padded, he had them watch him make a fist, and then in slow motion, he punched Peggy in the center of the pad. "Didja notice how I turned my fist just before I hit ya? If you don't do that, you'll break your wrist." He slipped a pad on himself. "OK, Agent Guggenheim, punch me right here," and he pointed to the center of his pad. "Hard."

Peggy reared back and punched him as hard as she could. "Ow," she cried. "I hurt my hand."

"Didn't I tell ya? Turn your wrist so the knuckles go level with the floor. Now try again with your left hand."

This time Peggy let him have it and grinned. "Didn't hurt a bit."

"Agent Rebay, yer turn. Lemme see you give me a punch." The Baroness had been watching carefully and slugged him hard, but not in the stomach. In the nuts, neatly turning over her wrist before she hit him.

When Mahony finally got to his feet, still doubled over in pain, he said, "We don't need to do that again. That was great. Ya did that just right." He grimaced, trying to smile as though it didn't still hurt. "Now for the fun part." He took two padded helmets from the chest and slipped them on the two recruits. He stuck tooth protectors in their mouths and put boxing gloves on them. "That's so you don't spoil them pretty smiles. Now I want you to pretend you are a counterspy and you're fighting it out with a Nazi agent. And you don't like each other."

With that, the Baroness landed a straight jab to Peggy's chin, who countered with a low punch to the Baroness's shoulder. In an instant they were flailing at each other, missing as many punches as they landed, until they were both exhausted and stood still panting, arms hanging by their sides.

"Tough work, ain't it?" Mahony said. They nodded. "This time don't swing your punches so wide. Go straight from the shoulder. It's called a 'jab.' I'll tell you when."

The girls put up their dukes. "Agent Rebay, throw a jab to Agent Guggenheim's shoulder." She did what she was told. "Now Agent Guggenheim, do the same thing," which she did. "Agent Rebay, try to punch Agent Guggenheim in the chin. Agent Guggenheim, block her punch with your left hand." The Baroness feinted a jab to the chin with her left and then snuck a powerhouse right to the side of Peggy's head. Peggy went down in a heap and started cursing.

"What the hell, Agent Rebay? Who told you to do that?" he screamed.

"Just doing what comes naturally, Boss. OK if I kick her while she's down?"

"Negative. Can you get up?" he asked Peggy. She nodded, got up slowly, and then charged the Baroness, knocked her down, and knelt on top of her, punching her in the face until Mahony dragged her off. Now the Baroness was screaming.

"What's got into you two?" Mahony yelled. "This was supposed to be a friendly practice. That'll be all for now!" He helped them take off their gloves and pads. The Nazi-hunter-trainees stood glaring at each other.

Mahony thought it was time to let the girls take a break.

"You did so well with boxing, I think we'll skip the jiu jitsu. Just remember that the minute you suspect someone's a spy, just punch him in the face and kick him in the nuts. Instead of jiu jitsu, we'll spend the afternoon practicing knot-tying."

"Knots?" Peggy asked. "What the heck for?"

"When you capture a spy you gotta tie him up, right?"

"'Him?' You think the spies are all gonna be men? How 'bout lady spies like Mata Hari? Remember her?"

"Could be," Mahony admitted.

"Think they'd be trained in boxing, jiu jitsu, all that stuff?"

"Sure."

"They might use poison, too," Peggy said. "Slip us a mickey." She thought she was starting to pick up the lingo.

"Ya gotta be ready for anything. That's why you're getting all this training. Now let me show youse how to put a loop on a rope." He doubled the rope over and secured it with an overhand knot. "Now gimme your hands, Agent Guggenheim. Hold them in front of you. In the real deal you'd make the dirty-ratbastard-crook-spy put his hands behind his back. But this is just a demonstration. Now you put the loop over her hands, Agent Rebay, then slip the free end through and pull tight."

"Ow," Peggy said.

"I bet you're used to that, right?" the Baroness said. "How many times your lover boys tie you up?"

"Don't knock it until you try it. Now untie me and let me tie her up."

"Don't need to. I get the idea," Agent Rebay said.

"Please," Peggy begged Mahony.

"Well, just once. Hold out your hands, Agent Rebay."

"This time let's make it realistic," Peggy told her. "Hands behind your back."

"Do I hafta?"

"Do what she says."

Peggy pulled the Baroness's hands behind her back, quickly passed the loop over the wrists, and pulled tight. She groaned.

"What's the matter, Princess? Dish it out but ya can't take it?"

"Let me loose. You're being mean."

Mahony took the rope from Peggy and freed the Baroness. "That's all for today, Ladies. Tomorrow we learn how to shoot, G-Man style."

* * *

Secret Agent School, Day Five:

"This, ladies, is the beating heart of the FBI. Only a chosen few get to whip out their guns and blast away in the FBI shooting range," Mahony told his recruits. "Now open up your purses and take out your pistols. Don't point them at anyone. If you *have* to point at someone, just make sure it's not me." Nobody laughed. "That was a joke."

"How can we tell it's a joke if it's not funny?" Peggy asked.

"That's not nice," the Baroness whispered to Peggy. "I'm afraid he's too stupid to know what's funny and what's not."

They took out their pistols. "We had these pistols specially made for you by Smith and Wesson®. They have real genuine bona-fide imitation mother-of-pearl handles. They call 'em Lady Smiths®. Nice, huh?"

"Very pretty," the Baroness admitted.

"Now the most important thing with a gun is knowing if it's loaded. Never pull the trigger unless . . ."

BANG!

"Goddammit, Agent Guggenheim, I told you not to pull the trigger. You coulda killed Agent Rebay."

"Would have been an accident. Can't get mad at me for an accident, can you?" Peggy pointed out. "So how *do* you tell if it's loaded?"

"Great question." He took the Baroness's weapon and

said, "You push this button right here and this apparatus called *the cylinder* drops down. It's got these holes in it, and each of these holes can hold a cartridge, which is what we call *these* things," as he tossed one cartridge each to them. "Now watch what I'm doing." He took the Baroness's cartridge. "I'm pushing the cartridge into this hole, then pushing the cylinder back into place. Now I push the button and the cylinder drops down again. If there's cartridges in the cylinder, it's loaded. If not, it's not."

"I don't like these things," Peggy told him. "They look dangerous."

"You bet they're dangerous. But if you know how to use them, they're dangerous to the crooks and the spies and not to you. You'll get to love your gun. Some shrinks have called them 'substitute penises,' and you can guess how much G-Men love their penises. I guess you can think of them as substitute dildos. How's that?"

Peggy smiled widely; the Baroness muttered something about how she preferred a real penis.

"OK," Mahoney said. "Enough of the psychology. Now for the fun part. Let's start shooting." He fitted them with ear protectors, "so you don't lose your hearing," he told them, and he led them down to the firing line. "Now lookee down there. That's John Dillinger, Pretty Boy Floyd, Baby Face Nelson, and Jimmy Cagney. Us G-Men killed 'em all. Well, we haven't killed Cagney yet, but the Director would like to."

"What'd *he* do?" Peggy asked.

"He starred in a movie called *G-Men* the Director didn't like."

"How come he didn't like that movie? I thought it was the cat's pajamas. Saw it three times. One of the reasons I took on this G-Girl gig."

"Because Cagney was a wise guy who didn't follow orders and talked back to his bosses. He was a round peg in a square hole. Here in the FBI, we're all square pegs in square holes."

"Bo-o-oring," Peggy whispered to the Baroness.

Mahony ignored her, loaded their pistols, and led them to the firing line. "You first, Guggenheim. See how many times you can hit John Dillinger."

Bang! Bang! Bang! Bang! Bang! Bang! Click.

Mahony reeled the target in so they could examine it. "Looks like you didn't hit him at all. Were you using the sights?"

"Wottsat?"

"This little thing on top of the muzzle and this little notch at the back of the barrel. You line them up and have the front sight right on the target."

"I didn't know that. How come you didn't tell us? Besides, I had my eyes closed."

"Ya gotta keep them open. Can't even blink. Let me load you up again and this time keep your eyes open."

Bang! Bang! Bang! Bang! Bang! Bang! Click.

"Much better. You put one through his hat and one right in his balls. I'd say his hat and his Johnson are both done for. Nice job. Now most of the time you'll be so close to the filthy skunk that you can stick the gun in his ribs and let him have it. Hard to miss."

"How about letting us see how you can shoot, Chief?" the Baroness asked.

"OK. Watch this!" Mahony turned away from the target, bent down, and squeezed off six quick shots from between his legs. He pulled the targets in, and they could see six holes through Pretty Boy Floyd's heart.

"I'm impressed," Peggy said.

"Now you try it, Agent Rebay," Mahony said.

The Baroness spun the cylinder then quickly turned away from the target, bent down just like Mahony, and fired off six quick shots from between her legs. "See how I did," she ordered

Mahony.

He pulled in the target. "Jesus Fucking Christ®, you nailed Nelson all six times. Three between the eyes and three in the heart. Where the hell did you learn to shoot like that?"

"Back in Chermany, I liked trick shooting. Mostly on horseback. You oughtta let me stand up in the saddle, get the horse galloping, and shoot an apple off your head."

"No thanks, I believe you."

"Chickee, chickee, chickee!"

"She should try that out on a spy," Peggy suggested. "Might adjust his attitude so he'll talk." She gave Rebay a wink. "And if the horse bucks and she misses the apple and nails him, well, he was probably a spy anyway, so what? Who cares? His mommy?"

"There's a suggestion box outside the Director's office, but I don't think he'd like it. He's on a bad losing streak at Hialeah and flies off the handle if anyone even *mentions* horses. But I like the way your mind works. Creative. Outside the box.

"Your next and last lesson for becoming G-Gals will be interrogating suspects. You'll love it. See you tomorrow." Agent Rebay reloaded her revolver and blasted away at Cagney. Five pops into his heart and one between the eyes. She pulled in the target and wrote on it, "With love, from Hilla and . . ." — she looked at Guggenheim — "Peggy."

Peggy beamed in gratitude. "That was so nice. I really think we *can* be pals."

* * *

Secret Agent School, Day Six:

Special Agents-to-be Rebay and Guggenheim presented themselves in Mahony's office dressed in their new Claire Mc-

Cardell suits, their gun purses at their sides. "We noticed the new plaque on your door: 'Assistant Director Brian Mahony.' That's really something. Congratulations!"

"Well, it's only *Assistant* Director," he said modestly. "But thanks. I owe it to you two. You're doing great. The Director is really impressed. Especially how you slaughtered that Jimmy Cagney target. He specifically said, 'Nice shooting,' and he loved the note. He can't wait for you to start kicking the crap out of these phony Nazi spy artists. Real backlog in the lock-up, and they're getting restless. Demanding canvas, paint, crayons, pencils, marble, clay, chisels, and Play-doh®. They're driving us crazy. Some of that stuff can be used as weapons. And the Play-doh® is ruining the rugs. But first you're going to see how we question suspects. So, pay attention.

"The first thing you have to know is that there are three kinds of people in this world: law enforcement, law-abiding citizens, and law-breaking asshole ratbastard criminals. Law enforcement, that's us. And other cops. But some cops are assholes, too: crooked cops. Then there are citizens: not cops, and not assholes. I think I said that. Where was I? Oh, yeah. The assholes: criminals. And spies. Usually you can tell the assholes just by looking at them. They look like assholes: kind of shifty-eyed. Or they talk like assholes: They lie to you. You can usually tell when they're lying. Ask 'em a question and then ask 'em the same question a second time and see if they give the same answer. Usually they're too stupid to remember what they said."

"Makes sense," Peggy said. "I've used the same trick on my husbands and caught 'em every time."

Mahony led them down a hall to a large window where they could see two men facing each other across a desk. "They can't see or hear us," Mahony told them, "but we can hear them."

"That one on the right," Peggy shouted. "He's the spy."

"Why'd you say that?"

"Look at his fingernails. They're dirty. And his tie; the narrow end is longer than the wide end. He's an asshole disguised as a citizen. But I saw through his tricks. The assholes in the movies are never so sloppy. This one was easy."

Mahony was embarrassed. "Goddammit, I keep telling Percy to shape up. What a slob. Actually, that's my assistant, Special Agent Percy Foxworth. Used to be the Director's best friend before Clyde, but now he's on some kind of shit list. I got stuck with him. He's doing the interrogation. But he *is* kind of an asshole, so you weren't too far off, Agent Guggenheim, just not the *crook* kind of asshole. Though, who knows," he said thoughtfully.

"When I push this button, Foxworth will know we're watching, and he'll start interrogating the suspect. Remember, we don't know yet if he's a citizen or an asshole. That's what Foxworth is going to find out. Now I'll turn on the mic so we can hear them."

"You know why we've brought you in, don't you?" Foxworth began.

The suspect said nothing.

"I'm going to ask you again, very nicely: Why did we bring you in?"

("See," Mahony told them, "he's trying to get the asshole to volunteer something. Get him used to talking.")

"I wonder how you feel about capital punishment. Huh, asshole? Are you for it or against it?"

("Not sure what he's getting at here," Mahony said.)

"Actually I've given that a lot of thought," the fucking sonuvabitch traitor ratbastard replied. "It might seem intuitive that capital punishment deters crime, but research shows that most crimes of violence are committed in a moment of passion, so that the poor-victim-of-society murderer doesn't have time to consider whether he (or she) will be executed. Furthermore, comparative statistics on murder in death penalty and non-death penalty states show no difference between . . ."

Foxworth slammed him on the side of his head. "Shut up, you lying sonuvabitch ratbastard Commie Nazi fucking traitor, you fucking . . . Did I say 'fucking' twice?"

"Yes, you did, Chief, and furthermore anybody with a rudimentary grasp of contemporary political ideology would know that it's unlikely that the same suspect could be both a Commie and a Nazi sonuvabitch ratbastard traitor sonuvabitch . . . did I say sonuvabitch twice?"

"Yeah, but that's OK. So I take it that you're against the death penalty? Or were you trying to confuse me with your lying sonuvabitch bullshit academic gibberish bullshit . . ."

"You repeated 'bullshit,' but you got the essence of my conclusion, which is that only a fucking sonuvabitch fucking sadist, sortta like you, would be for the death penalty in this day and fucking age which I hope has advanced from the fucking dark ages. . ."

"You used 'fucking' four times. But here's the bottom line you fucking fucking fucking (nobody can stop me now, I'm on a roll), you're a fucking traitor ratbastard who wants to 'beat the seat.'"

("Beat the seat," Mahony chortled. "Beat the *hot* seat, get it? That's a good one.")

"And despite that somewhat, I have to admit, impressive argument against the fucking death penalty, I still think you're some kind of a moron, you traitor scumbag. Are you a moron? I mean fucking moron?"

The suspect shook his head. "No."

"You're not a moron? Then talk. Prove it. Did you even go to high school?"

The suspect nodded.

"To college?"

The suspect nodded again.

"What college?"

"Yale."

"Yale? Oh. I'm impressed. You must be pretty fucking smart. What'd you study there?"

("That's a great move. Whatever he says, Percy's got him on the ropes.")

"Engineering," the suspect said proudly.

"Well, let me ask you something, Mr. Fucking Smart Guy. If a fucking spy was going to steal the fucking plans for our new fucking ships, what would he fucking study in school?"

The suspect said nothing. He looked nervous. Way too nervous to point out to Percy that he was repeating 'fucking' to the point where it was losing any rhetorical impact. "The Nazis (or the Commies or the Japs) would have you study engineering, right? And you studied engineering, right? Just a coincidence?"

The spy nodded.

("He's got him! He's got him!")

"You're a fucking spy, ain't ya? You're going to get the chair for this, you son-of-a-bitch." Foxworth grabbed the spy by the throat and started punching him. "But first, I'm gonna beat you to a pulp."

Just then the door opened, and another G-Man walked in. "Take a break, Percy," G-Man Number Two said. Foxworth released the rotten sonuvabitch and left the room, panting.

"My pal gets kind of excited," the second agent told the spy. "Last week he killed a spy right here in this room with his bare hands."

The coward fell to his knees and sobbed, "Keep him away from me. I'll talk!"

("See how they did that?" Mahony asked. "The old good cop/bad cop. Ya gotta set that up before ya start.")

"OK, spill, and maybe I can keep ya from getting the chair."

"I'm not a Nazi. I didn't want to spy. It was my girlfriend. *She's* a Nazi spy and she made me do it."

"You willing to testify against her and see her get fried? Are ya?"

"I really love her, and she IS the mother of my three sons, but if it's her or me, FRY THE BITCH! Just don't let that maniac at me again."

"OK, guys, great job," Mahony called out to the agents and the rotten traitor fucking sonuvabitch Commie (or Nazi) spy waved cheerfully to Mahony. "Let's get back to my office," he told the girls.

The girls were bewildered. Why had the spy stood up grinning and waved to Mahony? "That was all an act," Mahony told them. "The spy was one of our guys putting on a demonstration for you. Had you fooled, right?"

When they sat down over cups of coffee, Mahony reviewed what they had just seen. "If that had been for real, would the spy and his girlfriend have gone to jail?" the Baroness asked.

"Nah, both fucking traitors woulda gotten the fucking hot seat. Would have been tomorrow if Ol' Sparky wasn't booked up."

"But Foxworth lied to him. Was that OK?"

"Sure. Everything's fair when it comes to dealing with assholes. Especially Nazi traitors. Now you think you can remember what to do? Because tomorrow we're gonna turn you loose on your first artist. Citizen? Asshole? It's up to you to find out. And I gotta give that great line about 'beat the seat' to Speed to use on his weekly batshit radio harangue about crime."

"What's he got to say about crime?" Agent Guggenheim wanted to know.

"He's against it."

"Really goes out on a limb, huh? But, you know, there's two fucking sides to every fucking question . . ." Mahony was starting to frown. "OK, OK, forget it. See you tomorrow."

Secret Agent School, Day Seven:

"Suspect Number 1," Mahony told Special Agents-in-Training Guggenheim and Rebay, "says his name is Wolfram Merz. That's what it says on his German passport, anyway, but you can't always trust passports. Not stamped "Jewish" — that's a little suspicious. Why's he getting out of Germany since it looks like they're gonna win the war? And he claims to be a painter. That's all we know. He's in the interrogation room. We haven't fed him in two days, and he hasn't had any sleep. Find out if he's a spy. I'll be watching through the window."

Mahony led the two counterspies to the interrogation room, then left. Merz looked scared as the women entered.

"Speak English?" Agent Guggenheim barked at him, a smallish guy dressed in prison stripes and sporting a stupid-looking grey moustache.

"Nein."

"You take over," she told Rebay.

"You say you're a painter?" Rebay asked him in German. He nodded. "What do you paint?"

"Houses."

"What style?"

"Anything you want."

She handed him a sheet of paper and a pencil. "Draw me a picture of a house."

He looked puzzled.

"Come on, a house."

He drew a square, put a triangle on top of it, and a squiggly line on top of the triangle. "Rauch," he told them. ("That means smoke," Rebay told Peggy.) Then just so they knew he had done what Rebay had ordered, he carefully wrote "H-A-U-S" under his drawing.

"Are you thinking what I'm thinking?" she asked Guggenheim. Peggy nodded. "Malevich. One of your boys."

"Draw me a picture of a man," Rebay ordered him. He looked confused. "Come on. Man. M-A-N-N. Man."

"You want me to draw a picture of a man?" He asked in German.

"Yeah, get going."

He shrugged and drew a circle, ran a line down and split it in two for legs. Two more lines for arms. He looked at it for a minute, then put five short lines at the end of each arm. He studied his picture for a few seconds, then asked, "Him or her?"

"Him," Rebay said. He put a rudimentary fedora on top of the head, then two dots for eyes, a slash for a nose, then a line for the mouth. "Mann," he said to himself staring up at the ceiling. Then between the legs he drew a long, thick penis and a set of balls. Studying it a little while longer he scratched in some pubic hair. Looking at it intently, he said to Rebay, "He wants a dog, OK?"

She looked at Peggy and silently mouthed the word, "What?" Taking her silence for assent, he drew an oblong circle, put four lines under it, gave it a circle for a head, drew in some jagged saw-like teeth, and a line from the neck to the man's hand. Then very carefully he gave the dog a collar, and penciled in tiny letters "Ulf."

"What does that mean?" Peggy asked.

"It means 'wolf.'"

"That picture rings a bell, Rebay. Either this guy is fucking with us or that's an homage to Picasso."

"You're right. Your Pablo likes to put words on his paintings, too, just like this guy."

"Let me work him over," Peggy said.

"Good idea," Agent Rebay replied. Peggy leaned over and slapped him on each side of the face. He started crying.

"Ask him what kind of artists he likes."

"Who are your favorite artists?" the Baroness demanded.

Peggy raised her hand and he flinched. Rebay repeated her question. He flinched. "Come on, what artists do you like?"

"Walt Disney?" he offered. "Mickey Mouse? Goofy? Snow White?"

"Ha! Gotcha!" the Baroness yelled. "Mickey, Goofy, and Snow White aren't artists. He's bullshitting us."

"But this guy is a tough nut to crack," Peggy complained. —"He may be just too clever for us. . . . Are you a spy?" she yelled. He shook his head. "Let's just tell Mahony he's a spy and have him executed. Better be safe than sorry."

Just then Mahony raced into the room. "We found out this guy's legit. We just heard from the asshole's sister that he's a *house*painter, not an artist. We've lined up some interior decorators to question him."

"Wasn't Hitler a housepainter?" Peggy objected. "Wouldn't it be just like Adolf to use some of his housepainter buddies for spies. I'd be careful with this guy. He's really tricky. We're pretty sure he's a spy, a real asshole. You're going to be sorry if you let him go. What if he is carrying secret plans to the Japs? If they launch a sneak attack you could've stopped, you're gonna feel like a real chump."

"I'll take this from here, Ladies. We're bringing down another one of these jerks from New York for you."

"I got an idea," Agent Rebay told Mahony. "If you've got all these artists penned up in New York, why not send us up there. Easier on them and us."

"That makes sense. I'll take it up with the Director."

CHAPTER 3

The two very special agents met in front of Carnegie Hall where the Baroness had an apartment/studio. They needed to plan their strategy for interrogating the artists Hoover had dragged off their boats at the Hudson docks and locked up.

Dressed in their natty new outfits, the G-Girls strutted east on 57th Street, their black gun bags swinging by their sides. Turning down Fifth Avenue towards 54th Street, they talked ruefully about their Wolfram Merz fiasco. "One more fuck-up like that and Speed will take away our guns and badges," the Baroness said.

"Our mistake was figuring the guy was a spy before we even started grilling him," Peggy replied. "We gotta remember Speed said that most of these guys are on the level. We're doing our job if we clear them, too."

They turned east on 54th Street. "Yeah, I know. But *finding* spies is more fun." At 24 East 54th they arrived at the Baroness's gallery, The Museum of Non-Objective Art. The current exhibit was "The Art of Tomorrow."

"This isn't my first visit here," Peggy told Rebay. "I

stopped by when I first got to New York in July."

"Oh yeah, whaja think?"

Guggenheim said nothing.

"Oh," the Baroness scowled.

They stood in the center of a dimly lit room. Large paintings in silver frames hung low, almost touching the floor. "What's with how you've got them hung?" Peggy asked.

"It's so you can sit down and have them at eye level. It keeps people from just walking by the paintings. If you don't sit down, you really can't see them. Then once you're seated you have to look at them a long time while you listen to the music."

"That's another thing. What's that music? It's putting me to sleep."

"Why, that's Bach. What's wrong with that?"

"You call this collection, 'The Art of Tomorrow.' That's the music of yesterday. If I have a gallery, it'll be jazz."

"Well, I hope you never have a gallery. At least not in New York."

Peggy smiled and said nothing.

As they walked around the room, Peggy exclaimed, "There's nothing here but your boyfriend Rudolf Bauer's crap. You been spending all my uncle's money on that guy? People are calling your place the Bauer House."

"Rudolf is the greatest genius in the history of painting. That's why we've bought him."

"You're nuts, Hilla. Maybe he's the greatest genius in the history of your bedroom, but that's about it. He's a creep."

"Creep!"

"Yeah, I've met him. I won't say more."

"Met him? Waddya mean?"

"Nope. Lips are sealed." She made a locking motion near her mouth and threw away the imaginary key.

They entered the Baroness's office, its walls decorated

with still more Rudolf Bauer paintings. Peggy groaned, but said nothing. "How do we handle this interrogation job?" she asked the Baroness.

"How about this?" Hilla said. "We ask the painter where he gets his inspiration. If he says it's from dreams, he's yours. If he says it's something spiritual, he's mine. Malevich is mine. Dali is yours. On others, we flip a coin."

"And let's not make the mistake we made before," Peggy added. "Let's figure that most of them aren't spies. But we still oughtta catch a few or else Speed will think we're goofing off."

* * *

When they left Rebay's museum, it was getting dark. The Baroness suggested a German restaurant in Yorkville, so they got a cab and headed to Second Avenue and stopped in front of a *Bier-stube*. As they got out of the taxi, the Baroness grabbed Peggy's arm. "My God®, I know that guy," she said, pointing at a blond young man in a black leather jacket entering the restaurant ahead of them. "That's one of Hitler's guys from the SS. He's interested in modern art, as long as it's not Jewish. If he's not a spy, I'm a Chinaman."

"What are we gonna do?" Peggy whispered.

"I dunno. I think we need backup. How can we get in touch with the Bureau?"

"Didn't Speed say he was gonna be at the Stork Club to-night to get interviewed by Winchell? Lemme get a cab and tell Hoover what's going on. You go in and keep an eye on the spy."

"Might get me in trouble. They don't like single gals at the bar. Think they're hookers."

"Take one for the team, Hilla. Remember, Mahony said we have to brace ourselves and think of America."

"OK, but I don't think I'm going to be very convincing as a whore."

Peggy rolled her eyes. "You'll do just fine, believe me," and she was off in a cab.

In front of the Stork Club the bouncer asked Peggy if she was waiting for her "escort." She rushed by him and asked the *maître d'* where Hoover was. He told her he was in a private room. "I gotta see him."

"You can't."

"National emergency."

"Oh, you're one of those," and he snapped his fingers for the bouncer.

Peggy knew the layout and rushed upstairs and shoved open the door to the private "Cub Room." Hoover was sitting with Winchell and Clyde, relaxing after the interview. "Speed," she yelled, "I think we got a spy."

"Where is he?" Hoover asked excitedly. "In the clink?"

"No, he's in Yorkville at one of those German hangouts. Agent Rebay is keeping an eye on him, but we need back-up."

"Come on, Clyde," Hoover ordered, and Tolson leapt to his feet. "Let's go."

As they rushed out of the club Hoover shouted, "Disguises!" and pulled a pair of sunglasses from his jacket pocket. Clyde did the same and added a Groucho Marx nose and mustache for good luck. "You got your shades?" Clyde asked Peggy.

"No," she wailed. "I left 'em home."

"That's OK," Hoover told her. "Nobody knows who you are. People will think you're just another hooker. Clyde and me, we're celebrities."

Two newspapermen were lounging by the door waiting for celebrities to interview. "Hey Popeye," one said to the other, "Ain't that J. Edgar Hoover and his boyfriend over there in sunglasses? Whaddya think those idiots are doing? And who's the broad? Looks like the Guggenheim chick. What's SHE doing with the FBI?"

"Going incognito, I suppose. What morons. Let's tail them just for fun." They got into the cab that pulled up after Hoover's moved out and had the driver follow it.

When they got to the restaurant, Hilla was in front waving frantically. "He's paying his bill. You got here just in time."

Hoover pulled Clyde and Peggy into the alley next to the restaurant. Hilla stood by the door, and when the German emerged, she pantomimed to them: "That's him."

Hoover called to Clyde, "Plan 7." Clyde crossed the street across from the German. Hoover whispered to Peggy to walk beside the spy, provocatively, like she's looking to turn a trick. Hoover asked Hilla if she had her sunglasses.

"Ja."

"Put 'em on and go up ahead of the rat. This is called a four-man tail. In this case, a two-man, two-gal tail. That's a lot of tail. We can't lose him this way."

The two reporters watched all this maneuvering. "Now what the fuck are those idiots doing?" Popeye asked.

"I think it's the four-man tail routine. In this case a two-man, two-gal tail," his partner answered. "That's a lot of tail."

"Oh, yeah. What a joke!" Popeye laughed. "God®, they might as well be wearing cowbells. Look, he's spotted them."

When their spy entered a liquor store, the G-Men and G-Gals gathered in front, then fanned out along the street. One of the reporters said, "Don't they know enough to check the back door? They're going to lose him." Popeye volunteered to run around the back to see if the guy came out.

The FBI posse waited. Finally, Hoover gave a hand signal and Clyde entered the store. A minute later, he came out. "There's a back door," he wailed. "We lost him."

"Goddammit, Clyde, I knew Plan 7 was no good. Whydja want Plan 7? Why didn't we use Plan 8?"

"Plan 7 was your idea, Chief. I would have said Plan 8. I

hate Plan 7."

"You sure Plan 7 was my idea?"

"Yeah. Right, Agent Guggenheim?" Clyde asked her.

Agent Guggenheim put her palms up and shrugged her shoulders. She wasn't going to get into this catfight.

"I didn't think. I didn't think," Hoover wailed. "If this gets out it'll embarrass the Bureau, maybe destroy it. I gotta blame it on somebody else. How about the girls?"

"That's OK, Chief," Tolson consoled him. "I'll take the rap. Actually, Plan 7 *might* have been my idea. Besides, how's the word gonna get out? It's not like there's reporters watching."

Peggy asked, "Any way I can get reimbursed for my cab ride?"

"Oh, shut up," Hoover explained to her. He was steaming, and Clyde frantically gave a hush sign with his finger across his lips. He had seen Hoover in these moods lots of times, and he was dangerous. Just then Popeye and his partner came running up to them. "I tailed him to a place on First and got the number of the apartment he went in."

"Who the hell are you?" Clyde asked.

"We're with the *NY Post*. Doing a story on the FBI. And, uh, who's the dame?"

"We'll tell you later. Let's go," Hoover yelled and slapped Clyde on the back. They broke into a run following Popeye, the girls racing to keep up. Popeye stopped them all in front of a run-down apartment building. "He's in 4F."

"Good work, boys," Hoover told them. "Hey, ain't I seen you two hanging around the Stork?"

"Yeah."

"Well, go back there and tell Mario your drinks are on me."

"Thanks, Mr. Hoover."

"And let's keep that little mix-up back there quiet, you

know, just among us friends."

"We sure will, Mr. Hoover. Any chance you can put in a word for us with Mr. Winchell?"

"Tomorrow night, get there before his broadcast, and tell Bruno that Speed said Mr. Winchell would like to see you. If you've got something to trade, he will too. Gimme your card. I'll have Lou Nichols call you with a scoop on this case when we're ready to arrest this guy. Or kill him."

* * *

The G-Gals were in the interrogation room at the New York FBI Field Office. An artist or possible spy came in with a portfolio. Rebay leafed through it. She stopped. The image in front of her was a Madonna-like figure floating above a small village in front of a technicolor-tinted blue sky. A house in the foreground had an open window, white curtains billowing, and protruding over the windowsill there was an ultra-realistic rendering of an erect penis, the testicles hanging into the flowerbox. "What is this?" Agent Rebay shrieked.

The painter explained, "It's a dream I had about sleeping with my mother."

"What?" she shouted. "You pervert!" She turned to Agent Guggenheim. "Let's turn him over to the vice squad. He's worse than a spy. He should be castrated."

"Come on, Rebay, all the surrealists have that fantasy. I gotta tell you, whenever I got one of them surrealists in bed with me, they wind up calling me 'Mommy.' I don't mind, though. Kind of exciting."

"I bet they call for their mommies when you start whipping them."

"That too," Peggy grinned.

Just then the phone rang. It was Hoover.

"Glad you called," Peggy said. "We got a painter Rebay thinks is a sex pervert. Waddya want us to do with him?"

"Forget that. You think he's a spy?"

"Nah. Maybe a peepin' Tom."

"Do whatever you want with him. Tell Mahony to slap him around to teach him not to fuck with the Bureau and then turn him loose. I got a new job for you. Really hot. Clyde is on his way. He'll be there in a few minutes."

Tolson crashed through the door, excited out of his mind.

"You're off Operation Painter," Tolson told them. "That Nazi Agent Rebay tagged is definitely dirty. Real dirty. We read him as Hitler's liaison to the American Nazi underground. We gotta get someone inside to see what he's up to. That someone is you," and he pointed to the Baroness. "This is gonna be dangerous. Real dangerous. You might get killed. In fact, I bet you *will* get killed."

"I'm not afraid of anything. Especially not Nazi assholes."

Peggy was awestruck. "Gosh, Hilla. You're a naturalized American hero."

"Aw, shucks," Hilla replied.

Clyde went on. "But as long as you're alive, you've gotta poke around, find out what Hitler is up to in this country. You got your Secret Decoder Ring®?"

The Baroness held up her finger and twirled the ring. "We figure the asshole didn't make you since you were in disguise. Keep those sunglasses handy. You might need 'em again. The apartment where that asshole went belongs to Fritz Kuhn, the head of the American Nazi Party. Works for Henry Ford." He lowered his voice to a whisper. "This is super confidential. Top Secret. We think that any day now we're going to be at war with Germany. This Kuhn will take over the country if we lose the war. And I think we will. Have you seen the pictures of the way the German soldiers goose-step? Makes our parades look like shit."

The Baroness shot a glance at Peggy, who shrugged.

"Here's what's gonna happen. Tonight Kuhn has a reservation for six at Luchow's. Agent Rebay's gonna go there and introduce herself to Kuhn, you know, great admirer, wants to help the cause, that kinda shit, and while she's talking to Kuhn (in German, of course), she makes eye contact with the asshole you spotted and gives him the feeling he makes her hot. Ya gotta figure out a way to get his name. Get a little drunk and tell him you know an FBI agent. That's you, Agent Guggenheim, and Agent Rebay will say she can get you to spy on the Bureau. How's that for a plan?"

"Wow, Clyde. You think that up yourself? Genius!"

Clyde shrugged modestly. "When you work back to back with the greatest man who ever lived (Peggy whispered to Rebay, "or belly to belly"), you get kinda inspired."

"You mean you work with Jesus®?" Agent Rebay asked, quite impressed.

"Well, *second* greatest man. So, it's tonight, eight o'clock, Luchow's. Agent Guggenheim and I will be there for backup. In disguise, natch. Ya know where it is?"

"*Jawohl. Vierzehn Strasse.*"

* * *

Agent Rebay had given a lot of thought to her disguise for this assignment. She had on a green dirndl with a bodice embroidered with a subtle flower design of red swastikas. She had selected a necklace of deer antlers and a matching bonnet of pompoms with silver deer antlers with another swastika in the middle. As a girl her yodeling had been widely admired, so she let loose a practice yowl before entering Luchow's.

Inside, lederhosen-clad waiters clutching foaming steins of beer rushed between the tables while an accordion player pumped out what sounded to her like "My Yiddishe Mama."

Probably wrong about that, she thought.

She spotted Kuhn and The Blond Beast digging into a mound of sauerkraut and sausages at a table near the kitchen. They probably were sitting near a back door in case they had to scram. Pretty sneaky. She took a deep breath, squared her shoulders, and approached the Nazi traitors. "*Heil Hitler*," she intoned, and gave a stiff-armed salute.

"Who are you?" Kuhn asked in German.

"A loyal German who wants to help the cause," she replied.

"And vas ist der *cause*?"

"Right now, bringing National Socialism to this country. And then the world."

"And how you gonna help us?"

She decided it was now or never. "I gotta friend inside the FBI. She can tip us off on their plans, when they are going to raid us, all kindsa shit."

He nodded. "Siddown. This is Wolfgang. Is a personal buddy of der Führer." By reflex the entire table shot out their arms and yelled "*Heil*." One of the waiters did likewise, spilling beer from his clutch of steins.

"*Wie heist du*?" Kuhn asked her. ("That's 'What's your name?' in German for any readers not bright enough to figure that out. You ought to study foreign languages if you make it to high school, kids.) She had given her name some thought and had consulted some of her Wagner LP record jackets for ideas. She liked, "Brunhilda," and for a last name picked Brunhilda's dad. "Brunhilda Wotan," she replied.

"What do you think of this country?" Wolfgang asked her.

"Compared to *der Vaterland*, a complete scheisshole. No culture. Lousy *mit schwartzes* and Jews."

"Tell her some of our plans for fixing that, Fritz," The Beast ordered his friend.

"We're gonna repeal and replace the Thirteenth, Four-teenth, and Fifteenth amendments," he said proudly.

"Does that mean no more beer?" Agent Rebay asked.

"No. That would be the Twenty-first Amendment. I guess you don't know too much USA history. We're gonna leave that one alone. The ones we're gonna get rid of are the ones that freed the slaves. We're gonna bring back slavery, and we've already got thirty-five senators aboard."

"What about the Jews?"

"They're going to be shipped to a new homeland."

"Where?"

"Labrador."

"Where's that?"

"I don't know exactly. Somewhere up north. Principal product, ice. Let 'em make money outta that."

The table erupted in laughter.

"You guys really got it all figured out. Real *schmart*."

"That's not all," a scholarly looking Nazi with a monocle piped up. "We're gonna clean up American literature. Get rid of all them *schwartzes*."

"That'll be tough. There's lots of them in American books. I read *Uncle Tom's Cabin* and *Huck Finn* in Gymnasium. How you gonna fix that up?"

"Easy. In *Huck Finn* we replace Jim with a statue of Hitler that Huck is saving from a Jewish mob and is carrying to a town full of noble German farmers in Texas."

"There are German farmers in Texas?"

"Don't get hung up on details. But why *shouldn't* there be?"

"And if there are, they're sure to be noble," Agent Rebay agreed. "Good thinking. What about *Uncle Tom's Cabin*?"

"More noble Germans being held as slaves by Jewish millionaires. Forced to pick wool out in the woolfields. And get whipped. Makes my blood boil to think of it."

"You might want to check out those woolfields," Agent Rebay suggested, "But I like the way your mind works."

"Now how about this girl FBI agent pal of yours. What's her name?" The Beast asked.

"No can tell. What if you get caught and tortured? Better you not know. I'll be the go-between."

"But we need something from the Bureau so we know we can trust you."

"OK, what?"

"How about a pair of J. Edgar Hoover's underpants?"

"Gross, but otherwise not a problem. Next party of his I'll get 'em for you. That's tomorrow. When can I see you next?"

"Right here, day after tomorrow. And here's a secret just for you:. We got it fixed up with the Japs to bomb Pearl Harbor first week in December. When we win the war, they get the West Coast." He leaned forward conspiratorially and whispered, "But not for long," to a chorus of guffaws. "Dumb Chinks," one of the Nazis laughed.

"Er, I think you mean 'dumb Japs,' not Chinks. The Chinks are Chinese," Rebay couldn't help but pointing out, then realized she may have made a mistake by revealing she wasn't as stupid as her new pals.

"Chinks. Japs. What the hell's the difference? Anyway, what we told you is top secret," Kuhn whispered. "Don't tell no-body." Hilla put her finger across her lips and nodded. She rose from her chair, gave a salute and a "*Heil Hitler*," and left the restaurant, Peggy and Tolson in their disguises exiting a discreet distance behind. As soon as they were across the street, they let out yells of joy and embraced in a group hug.

"Wait'll you hear what I got," Agent Rebay shouted. "All their secrets. And I didn't even have to shtup anyone."

"Let's get a drink," Tolson said. "Celebrate. But maybe

you oughtta cover up those swastikas. And put on another disguise." Peggy lent Rebay a sweater, and Hilla put on her sunglasses. "Wotta team!" he exulted. "Speed is gonna be so proud of me. Of us."

* * *

Two nights later, Rebay was a little flustered. She tried to remember whether she should go into Luchow's in or out of disguise. "*Dummkopf*," she slapped herself on the head. "I want them to recognize me. No disguise." She put away her sunglasses and entered the restaurant. Adjusting her eyes to the dark, she spotted Kuhn and the Blond Beast (a.k.a. Wolfgang). "*Guten Tag*, Fritz and Beast, I mean Wolfgang," she greeted them. "*Heil Hitler*."

She reached into her peasant apron and pulled out a bag embossed with the FBI seal from the FBI gift shop and handed it over to the UnterFührer. He pulled out a pair of red lace panties. "*Donner und Blitzen*," he said, "Hoover wears these things? Just like those S.A. fags."

"Check out the monogram," she said.

He held them up. Embroidered in gold thread were JEH on the ass end and "The Gangbuster" on the basket.

"How do I know you didn't just go to a costume shop and get these made up to fool us?"

"Give 'em the sniff test. He had 'em on yesterday. I got 'em out of his laundry hamper."

The Nazi held them to his nose. "Peeyew," he said. "Really rank. I guess the only way to be sure would be to sniff his crotch and compare, and I ain't going there." Wolfgang snickered. "Listen up. Wolfgang here has come to us with a great secret conspiracy, a plot the Führer dreamed up himself." The whole table jumped to attention and gave Nazi salutes. "It's really just the sort of fantastic plan you'd expect from the most dynamic, the smartest, the strongest, the best-looking guy in the world, the greatest leader the world has ever seen, maybe since Julius Caesar (who was just a dago, by the way), my friend and yours: Adolf Hitler."

"Wow," Agent Rebay gasped. "That's wonderful," she said, as she thought, *and I'm just the gal that's gonna stop it.*

"We got the whole Party getting together in New Paltz tomorrow," he told her. "Why don'cha come along and get in on the fun?"

"How'm I gonna get there? I got no car."

One of the Nazis raised his hand. "I'll give her a ride on my motorcycle. In the *bitch seat*," he smirked. "*Ich heise Fafner.*" Agent Rebay hated motorcycles, but she smiled gamely. "*Wunderbar.*"

* * *

Fafner stopped his motorcycle in front of a log cabin in a public park. "Is this where we're meeting?" Rebay asked.

"Nah. They've got a kind of ravine back of those hills where we can sit in front of a bonfire and sing Nazi songs. Really pretty cool. This is where I stay. You have to stay here too so I can keep an eye on you."

Rebay thought, in for a *pfennig*, in for a *Reichsmark,* and said, "Gee, that's swell."

"Let's get a little rest first," he winked.

Fafner threw his knapsack onto the bed and went into the bathroom. When he came out, he was naked, with a big ol' boner. "Well, hello," the Baroness said, and she laughed. "Just what I had in mind." As she stripped off her leathers and hopped into bed, a sudden thought hit her. She looked again. He was circumcised.

Afterwards, they shared a cigarette, and Agent Rebay asked, "Fafner, that was great, but I gotta ask you something. I thought a foreskin was a *sine qua non* for membership in the Party. Don't all the new recruits have to lay their schlongs on the table for inspection?"

"Yeah," he said, "that did cause me a lot of trouble, but I was born in this country and they slice it off without asking permission. Public health, they call it. Get rid of the community drinking cup and the foreskin. But my folks were pure-blooded Aryans, so I passed muster. I even have an asterisk on my Party card in case anyone raises a stink. The note says, 'Foreskin exception,' so I'll be OK."

"That was nice of them. Good thing you're not a queer or you'd have to show your card every time you hopped in the sack with one of the storm troopers."

"That *would* be a problem, but Hitler got rid of all the homos from the Party when he slaughtered those S.A. fags. So I don't have to worry about that. Although I would do anything for the Führer, even suck a dick."

"You are a credit to the Master Race, Fafner."

"Something I gotta show you, Brunhilda. Lookit this." He showed her a scrap of paper. "I found this in the bathroom. Whaddya think it means?"

Rebay looked at it. Written in pencil was a meaningless line of letters, GRZLB. She shook her head. Suddenly she had an idea. "I gotta take a leak," she said, and headed into the bathroom. She took off her Secret Decoder Ring® and started decoding. *My God®*, she thought, as she read the decoded message: "I'm FBI." She hurriedly coded her own message, "Me too" and scrawled it on the back of the paper.

"Whew," she said, "just made it. That bike of yours is tough on the ol' bladder. Didja notice there was something on the other side of that note?"

"No, lemme see." He snatched the paper from her and headed into the bathroom. A minute later he emerged, grabbed a flashlight from his bag, and said, "Let's get under the covers," building a tent for them on the bed. "I'm afraid they got hidden cameras, so we better have our meetings out of sight and whisper," turning on his flashlight.

"How come I didn't get a flashlight?" she whined.

"Probably not enough room in your gun kit. Anyway, I'm Secret Agent X-9. Who are you?"

"Geeze," Agent Rebay said, "they didn't give me a number. I really got shafted. Probably because I'm a girl."

"Quit bellyaching. Who are you?"

"I'm just Hilla Rebay. Baroness Hilla Rebay."

"I heard that Speed recruited a pair of gals. So, you're one of them? Where's the other gorgeous counterspy?"

"I'm the gorgeous one. She's not. She's roaming around with Clyde. Back-up. Let's get out from under here. It's stuffy."

"OK, but remember," and he put his finger across his lips.

When they got out of bed, Hilla remarked, "Ever since we hit the sack, I been scratching like a hound. You too?"

"Yeah," Fafner replied. "Lemme take a look." Taking a magnifying glass from his bag, he began scrutinizing the sheets.

"Aw," she said, "you got a magnifying glass, too. I suppose you got a fingerprint kit, too."

"Yup," he grinned. He kept looking at the sheets. "Cooties," he said. "Or maybe chiggers."

"We're probably crawling with them," the Baroness said. "Let's get out of here and see if we can find some DDT."

* * *

As Rebay and X-9 entered the ravine, they were handed red swastika armbands. "Give them back after it's over. Anybody caught glomming one is out of the Party." The bonfire was already blazing.

The Nazis stood at attention, and sang the "*Horst Wassel*

Lied," accompanied by an accordion from Luchow's. The singing over, Kuhn strode to the center of the clearing next to the bonfire. "*Heil!*" he shouted. "*Heil!*" the Nazis shouted back. "I just got great news right from the Führer himself." The crowd gasped. One of his Nazi henchmen threw a bottle of gas on the fire to make it blaze higher. "Hitler's got a vital secret mission just for us. Obviously, I can't open the whole can of sauerkraut right out here in the open."

The Nazi horde of fiends nodded in agreement. They loved secrets. "But today we are going to start doing something great to achieve the Führer's beautiful vision of a world where all of us Nazi animals will be outfitted in gorgeous black motorcycle leathers with death's-head chrome medallions, and beautiful Jewish, Negro, and Jap girl slaves will bring us schnapps whenever we snap our Aryan fingers. That'll be *der Tag,* you betcha."

The crowd was growing restless, more so when Kuhn dragged out his dog-eared copy of *Mein Kampf* with Post-It® tabs giving him ready reference to his favorite passages. They knew from past experience that Kuhn was fully capable of droning on quoting the Führer's literary gems until the fire ran out of fuel, the cows came home, and Hector was no longer a pup (in other words, for a long time; and kids, those would have been similes if they had included the word 'like' but in any case they were some figure of speech or other; lemme know if you find out which).

You readers have all had the experience of having to give a speech before a deranged crowd of fanatics packing weapons of all calibers and firing off practice shots just to stay in the mood. And while you are still trying to get to the punch line of your opening joke, you can tell they're not really listening, because they're looking forward to using, not just fondling, their artillery, and you are just getting to the list of all the wonderful folks who made this evening possible. That was Kuhn's problem, and he was just getting to the part of his speech where he was thanking Adolf

Hitler for his innovative racial theories. Now these Nazi scumbags all loved the Führer to pieces, but goddammit, their trigger fingers were getting itchy.

Kuhn was experienced enough running these National-al Socialist black sabbath bonfires to know when it was time to shit or get off the pot, so he wrapped things up with an evil Nazi version of the Pledge of Allegiance to the swastika flag (pretty bad guy, huh?) and then announced, "We are going to the firing range right now for a quick-draw pistol contest. The winner will move onto Stage Two of the plan. How's that? Are you ready, you berserk Nazi maniacs? And you crazy Huns know a compliment when you hear one."

"Let's go. Yay. *Vorwärts*." The Nazi horde headed back to the parking lot. While they were gone, a row of twenty Eleanor Roosevelt targets had been set up a hundred feet from a firing line.

"Here's the drill," Kuhn shouted. "Stuff your pistol in your belt behind you. When I say 'Ready, set,' you take your position, hands by your sides. When I say 'Fire,' you drop down to one knee, pull out your gun and empty your clip into that Commie hag. Only head shots and upper body shots count. Got it?"

Most of the *Übermenschen* nodded, although a few were still confused and asking each other, "*Was ist* going on?" and as you know, having people on the firing line who haven't got with the program is a recipe for trouble, but in this case, ya gotta gun, ya gotta target of the Commie First Lady, how dumb could ya be not to know what yer s'posed to do. "OK," Kuhn screamed, "first twenty to the firing line."

He gave the command and the storm troopers blasted away. Inspectors walked down the line of Eleanors, toted up the fatal shots, pointed out the three winners, and replaced the targets. "Next twenty!" Kuhn shouted, and the eager Nazis lined up quick-ly (*schnell*, that is) and shots rang out.

"I didn't bring my gun," Rebay whispered to X-9.

"That's OK, you can have mine after I've shot."

Secret Agent X-9 moved into the next twenty and was one of the winners. Then Rebay went to the line and got off her six shots. "*Mein Gott, das Hitler Mädchen* popped ER six times in the head. Best shots of the day. Great shooting, lady, but this mission calls for a man."

The Baroness scowled and took her place beside X-9.

"Not fair. I can kill for the Führer as well as any of these guy Nazi assholes," she whispered to X-9.

"Try to remember," he whispered back, "Yer not really a Nazi. Yer an *anti*-Nazi Secret FBI Agent."

"Oh, yeah, I forgot."

Kuhn called the twelve winners to the line. Speaking in a tone of unmitigated evil that sent a chill up the Nazis' devil-worshipping spines (up, down, whatever), he whipped them into a ferocious frenzy, telling them, "This last shoot-off you're going to be shooting at the real Jew Bolshevik we're gonna kill." His assistant stood twelve posters of President Roosevelt up for targets. "That's right. One of you is going to kill that Commie bastard. Hitler's orders. Right after the stupid Japs attack. Now do your *best*." (*Best* means the same thing in German and English. Every once in a while you catch a break with foreign languages.)

Their shots rang out. Kuhn embraced the winner. X-9 let out a curse and stomped back to the Baroness's side.

"I cudda won easy," he whispered to Hilla, "but I had to miss so I can keep spying on these cocksuckers."

"Sure, you could have," Rebay consoled him. "Poor baby. Now let's get that bug powder."

* * *

"I gotta tell ya, Speed, I've got some complaints." Special Agent Rebay was relaxing at Hoover's house with the Director,

Clyde, Special Agent Guggenheim, and Secret Agent X-9. Hoover had invited them to celebrate Rebay and X-9's big win. It was December 7th, the last day of the week that Kuhn had promised a Jap attack. So far nothing. And, no assassination of President Roosevelt, and no big government ceremonies scheduled for the rest of the month. They could relax. The G-Gals were arguing about modern art and each of them still thought the other's favorite artists should be executed as artistic frauds, perverts, and probably spies.

"Surrealism is degenerate," Rebay told Peggy, "and those guys should be put out of their misery."

"You sound like Hitler," Peggy told her.

"Well," Rebay replied, "just because he's a homicidal, genocidal, racist maniac doesn't mean he doesn't have *some* good ideas."

"If you think that stuff Bauer paints is art, you're a gullible fool. Painting the unseen from the fourth dimension, my butt. Next thing you know, your non-objective guys will be painting blank canvases. Nobody can see what they claim to see."

"If you'd just read those theosophy books I gave you on the fourth dimension, you'd see the unseen, too," Rebay said.

"I tried, and they may as well have been in German. Either I'm too stupid to understand that gibberish, which I doubt, or too smart."

"Well they WERE in German. That's probably why you didn't understand them."

"Oh yeah. I guess you're right."

"So what are your gripes?" Hoover asked them.

"To start with, how come Peggy and I didn't get flashlights and magnifying glasses like X-9? And fingerprint kits?"

"Yeah," Peggy agreed. "That's rampant sexual discrimination, and in my case anti-Semitism. If we had an Equal Rights Amendment in this goddamn country, you couldn't get away with that crap."

"Whaddya mean, an Equal Rights Amendment?" a belligerent X-9 demanded.

"It means that us gals get everything you guys get. We can do anything you can do and do it better, and we can go anywhere you go."

"Ya mean ya want to go to the can with us?"

"That's so typical. Shows you're a pervert who should be in jail. It means that I should get the same pay as you. And get a flashlight and a magnifying glass. AND a fingerprint kit."

"You wouldn't know how to use a fingerprint kit."

"I can read instructions, can't I? If a moron like you can do it, so can I. And better."

"Come on," Clyde pleaded. "We're on the same team. There just ain't enough room in them gun bags of yours for any of that other stuff."

"We put our heads together and came up with an idea," Peggy said. "Lookit this." She held up a black handbag with "Mark Cross" on the clasp and a gold chain. She opened it, and it had a holster for her pistol, a slot for her badge, loops for extra ammo, and four compartments built in for a flashlight, a magnifying glass, condoms. and the fingerprint kit. "See, I had a pal at Mark Cross come up with this. It's the first handbag they've ever made. If you let us, we'll pay for them ourselves."

"I dunno," Clyde said doubtfully. "We'll have to have our scientists test 'em to see how fast you can get the gun out. That's the main thing."

"Just one fucking minute!" X-9 shouted. "They get a Mark Cross bag that probably cost fifty bucks and I get this piece of shit." He held up his shoulder bag.

"Fifty bucks?" Peggy scoffed. "Try five hundred."

"Five hundred bucks for a handbag," X-9 yelled. "The whole world's gone crazy. I told you this G-Girl idea was nuts.

Girls just ain't brave like me. They shouldn't get extra stuff that I ain't got. Next thing, they'll want gold-plated machine guns."

"And why not?" Special Agent Rebay retorted. "Wait'll you hear what Secret Agents, I mean Special Agents — why can't we be Secret Agents, too? — Guggenheim and I did last night." She opened her fist and showed the men two gold rings.

"What're those?" X-9 asked suspiciously.

"Take a look." She tossed them to Hoover. He held them up to the light and examined them inside and out. "These are Secret Decoder Rings®. But they're not ours. Where'd you get 'em?" he yelled at Secret — I mean Special — Agent Guggenheim.

"Agent Rebay got invited to a party at the German Embassy and she stole that one, the one with the little swastika design in diamonds. I broke into the Jap Embassy and got the one with the rising sun in rubies. Now we can read all their secret messages."

X-9 was furious. "I cudda done that too if someone had given me the idea. No fair."

Hoover shook his finger and told X-9 to calm down. "You oughtta show some initiative some time, like these dames did. You're still my favorite secret agent and you can get a new handbag just like the girls."

"I ain't got five hundred bucks."

"Don't worry, the Bureau will pay for it."

"Wait a minute!" Peggy yelled. "Why do we gotta pay for ours if he gets his free? This is another fuckin' swindle. See what I mean about an Equal Rights Amendment?"

"OK, you'll all get free handbags."

"I think mine should be called an attaché case," X-9 whined. "The guys will make fun of me if I show up with a handbag."

"OK. We're all pals. Group hug."

"Another thing," Peggy complained. "How come he's got a secret code name," she pointed at X-9, "and we don't?"

Powers

"I guess we never thought of it," Hoover told her.

"Lame excuse. But we've come up with code names for ourselves to save you the trouble."

"Let's hear 'em."

Guggenheim pointed at Rebay. "She's going to be Secret Agent TNA, OK?"

"Fine," Clyde said.

("They don't get it," Rebay whispered to Guggenheim. "The dopes.")

"And I'll be Secret Agent 241. That's 2-4-1. Meaning we're a team. That OK?"

"Great," Hoover said. "Brilliant. Clyde, you shudda come up with code names for the two of us. Something that lets people know how great we are."

"You don't mind that we've promoted ourselves from Special Agents to Secret Agents?"

"No, that's fine," Hoover said wearily.

Just then the phone rang. Speed picked it up. "No shit!" he yelled, and slammed down the phone. "The Japs are attacking Pearl Harbor."

"You mean you didn't warn anybody?" Rebay screamed at him.

"'Course not. If we'da been wrong, we woulda looked like idiots. This way it's the Navy's fault. I always hated those pricks."

"Me too," Clyde said. "We're both in the Navy Reserves. And I shudda been promoted to captain five years ago."

"I wanted ta be an admiral," Speed moaned. "I deserved it."

"Sounds like homophobia to me," Peggy said, stroking her chin judiciously. "Maybe there should be an Equal Rights Amendment for perverts, too."

"Their day will come," Hoover told them, pointing to the

framed portrait of Oscar Wilde over the mantle. "Not that I'm one, of course. But we gotta get to work. Roosevelt said he's going to address Congress tomorrow to declare war."

"Tomorrow! That's when the Nazis are going to kill him!" Rebay shrieked. "Peggy, X-9," she held out her arm and grasped the hands of Special Agent Guggenheim and Secret Agent X-9. "We gotta stop their diabolical plot. One for all and all for one." They repeated after her, "One for all and all for one!"

"*Diabolical*," Clyde said. "I like that. Five syllables! Whole different level of vocabulary from those Irish bogtrotters we been hiring!"

* * *

Joint session of Congress. House of Representatives Chamber. Agents Rebay (Secret Agent TNA), Agent Guggenheim (Secret Agent 241), and Agent X-9, all in sunglass disguises, standing by the speaker's rostrum scanning the crowd.

"Hey," Rebay shouted to X-9, "What're those little boys doing running all over the place?"

"Those're called pages. Every guy in Congress gets one to run errands."

"What kind of errand is that?" pointing at a kid snuggled on the lap of a white-suited Southern senator with flowing silver hair, a moustache and goatee. As she watched in horror, the aged statesman planted a tender kiss on the parted lips of his youthful companion. "Can he get away with that?" she yelled over to X-9.

"Sure, they all have fun with their pages. It's one of the perks, like no parking tickets and free chewing tobacco."

"So, this country is being run by a bunch of pedophiles?"

"Technically," X-9 explained, "they're ephebophiles, not pedophiles."

"What's the difference?"

"Pedophiles like pre-pubescent boys. Ephebophiles like

'em *after* puberty. These kids are all eleven or older, so their boy-friends ain't pedophiles."

"I'd shoot them all. That's too good for them. Castrate them and skin them alive. Or maybe . . . I'll think of something. Do their parents know?"

"Sure. It looks good on their college apps if they been congressional pages. Most Harvard and Yale students have been queered by the nation's highest-ranking public servants. It's kind of a club. And it lets the colleges know the kids will play nice with the professors. Win-win all around."

"What do they do to these kids?"

"You name it. Anal, oral, hands, bondage — to each his own."

"How do you know all this?"

"Aw, the Bureau has hidden cameras in all their offices. But Speed is such a soft touch he just gives them a private show-ing if they get out of hand, like criticize the Bureau. And frankly, I think Speed gets off on watching!"

The Baroness was furious. "I'm gonna stop all that right now." As Roosevelt was being wheeled up to the rostrum, Agent Rebay jumped up and beat him there. "Listen up!" she screamed over the microphone. "Get your hands off them kids!" Nobody noticed her, so she pulled out her gun and let loose a couple of shots at the ceiling. That got their attention. "I want all the kids to clear out. You guys are a disgrace. I'm Secret Agent TNA, and from now on all those pages are fired." She thought hard for a mo-ment. She was stumped. "Anybody got any ideas how to replace them?" she whispered.

The First Lady raised her hand.

"Yeah, you Commie hag, I mean Mrs. Roosevelt?"

She said, "I can get in touch with my pal Phil Randolph and see if the Brotherhood of Sleeping Car Porters can supply retired members to be congressional pages. Old retired Negro porters," she added, "all named George."

The senators and congressmen looked disgruntled and one muttered bitterly, "Who is this bitch?"

"Congress ain't ready for reform!" one senator yelled and raised his hand to throw a half-eaten donut at the First Lady. No sooner did his arm go up than Agent Rebay shot the donut out of his hand. "Ow, that hurt," he yelled. "But I gotta say that was a hell of a nice shot. Glad you're on our side."

"Next one of you perverts who raises his hand gets one right between the eyes!" Agent Rebay shouted, and then, suddenly, "That's him!" She pointed at a dark-suited man wearing sunglasses leading a little boy holding a tin cup on a leash (the boy was on the leash, not the tin cup) moving through the crowd. Agent X-9, Agent Guggenheim and Agent TNA rushed him from three directions. X-9 got to him first and began clubbing him with his pistol while Agent 241 got in some well-placed kicks. Agent TNA held the cowardly lawmakers at bay with her revolver.

"Aw, leave him alone. That's poor ol' Al Gore, and the kid's Al, Jr." a senator yelled.

"Then why's he wearing sunglasses?" Agent Rebay asked.

"He's blind as a bat. He used to be a Senator and now he shows up when we're all together to take up a collection for blind veterans. That's his tin cup and those are his pencils."

"Sorry, Senator," X-9 said, dragging Gore to his feet. He wiped some of the blood off Gore's face and said, "Here's a twenty for the vets," stuffing a bill in the tin cup before heading back to the rostrum.

"Did he really give me a twenty?" Gore asked. One of the senators took a look and said, disgustedly, "Nah, just a single. That cheap bastard."

"Lousy trick to play on a poor blind man," Gore said through his tears.

Back at the rostrum the President was getting annoyed.

Powers

"Can we get on with it? I just wanna declare war and get this over with, get back to the White House, smoke some Camels® and play with my stamps.."

"Hold your horses, Mr. President," Rebay ordered him. "I want to get all them pages out of here before you start yapping. If we don't lay down the law right now, they'll be queering kids again before you can say Jack Robinson."

"Who's she?" the President asked.

"Who knows, but she's right, Franklin," the First Lady told him.

"Oh, all right, but make it snappy."

"Look," Agent Rebay told him, "what's more important, the sexual morality of American youth, who should be out in the woods learning Morse code, how to whittle and tie knots, and practicing bird calls, not getting molested by the entire First Branch of Government (Article I of the Constitution, you know) . . . or listening to you blather about how it wasn't your fault that you let Japs blow the entire Navy to bits in Hawaii."

FDR was insulted. "You're turning this into a day of infamy. Hey, that sounds great. *Day of infamy.* You like it, Eleanor? New start for my speech."

"Fantastic. That'll be the headline tomorrow. You sure can shovel that old shit, Franklin. Kinda makes me hot when you talk like that, too, if you wanta know the truth."

The President did not look pleased at the news that his wife was "in the mood." He had plans for a session with his stamp collection after his speech, if he ever got to give it.

Finally, Agent Rebay turned to FDR and said, "Your turn, Mr. President. But make it quick. We gotta get out of here and chase spies and kill Public Enemies."

As the President gathered his notes and cleared his throat, a black-clad figure in a German military helmet, a swastika armband, and black sunglasses goose-stepped down the center aisle.

"My God®," Hilla whispered. "The sunglass disguise fooled the guards! You'd think they would've noticed the swastika."

The Nazi assassin dropped to one knee, unholstered his pistol, and took aim. A shot rang out. The storm trooper was blasted onto his back, a hole oozing blood between his eyes. Agent Rebay blew the smoke from the muzzle, a pleasant smile on her face.

"She did it!" Someone exclaimed. "What a shot! She's as good as Gene Autry or Roy Rogers."

"Sergeant York."

"John Wayne."

"She's Annie Oakley!" another yelled, and began singing, "Oh, you *can* get a man with a gun."

Agent Rebay twirled her pistol and shoved it back into her holster. "Just doin' mah job, folks."

Roosevelt banged on the mic. "I wanna give my speech. Is anyone listening?"

"Aw shut up, you old bore," a senator told him. "I wanna get this li'l gal's autograph for my kids."

"The hell with it," Roosevelt grumped and threw his speech at the Speaker of the House. "Read it into the record. Declare war or don't declare war; I don't give a shit."

CHAPTER 4

"My code name is Secret Agent TNA, but you can call me Hilla," Rebay told Elmer Davis. Word had gone out to writers, artists, and photographers that Davis was putting together a new propaganda outfit, part of the war effort. Rebay had used Hoover to get an appointment with Davis. She had been sitting in a waiting room all morning to wait for her turn. "Ya know, you've got a roomful of Reds out there," she told Davis.

"How can you tell?" Davis asked her.

"I know a couple of them from around New York, but all you gotta do is look at 'em. Crazy haircuts, squinty eyes — to a trained counterspy like me, they might as well have bombs with lit fuses in their hands. I can spot 'em a mile away. Here's a trick. You know the '*Internationale*' song?" Davis nodded. "Hmm," Rebay murmured, looking at him suspiciously. "Anyway, just be whistling it when they come in. If they come to attention and give that Commie raised fist salute, you've nailed 'em. A real Red can't resist."

"Thanks, I'll try that. Now what can you do for me?"

"I own an art museum called 'The Art of Tomorrow.' Lemme show you the kind of stuff I got." She took out a rolled-up poster and straightened it out. "Lookit this."

Davis contemplated it and scratched his head. He shrugged his shoulders. "What is it? Looks like a triangle with a ball balanced on its tip. How's this gonna help us win the war?"

"This is a painting by the greatest painter who ever lived," Rebay said, "my boyfriend, Rudolf Bauer. If you look at it long enough, a sense of order and balance comes into your life. You lose all feelings of anger and rage. You become a better person. Here's my idea. I just saw a preview of this movie by Walt Disney is working on. It's called *Victory through Air Power*. You seen it?" Davis shook his head. "It's about this Russian named De Seversky or something. He says we aren't gonna beat the Germans or the Japs until 1947 at the earliest, because we gotta drop these big bombs, ten tons each! Thousands of 'em! On the big cities in Germany and Japan. To do that we gotta build some enormous planes that nobody knows how to make yet."

Davis shook his head. "1947? I don't like that. Americans wanna get this war over by the end of the year. Maybe next year. If we say it's gonna be five years from now, they'll say the hell with it. Americans're busy people. Got things to do. Or stuff. Or things and stuff" He yelled at his secretary, "Get Disney on the phone. That's Walt Disney, right?" he asked Rebay, who nodded. "Tell him he can't release that dumb movie of his, the one about the war lasting to 1947. Make him change it to 1943. Lemme know what he says.

"Now whaddya want me to do with the triangle and ball picture, lady? And by the way, you sound like a Hun to me. How'd you get in here?"

His secretary broke in. "I got hold of Disney. He says you missed the whole fucking point. If we win the war in 1943, we won't have time to build the big planes we'll need to win the war in 1947. So, it has to be 1947."

"Why can't he give us a cartoon where we win the war next year?"

"He says you're a fucking dimwit."

"Oh yeah? Gimme that goddamn phone!" He started screaming at Disney, "Put Superman in the goddamn movie and win it this year. . . . Oh?. . . Oh."

He looked over at Rebay. "He says that another studio owns Superman and that Superman just flunked his physical, anyway. He's 4-F." He yelled into the phone, "How can Superman be 4-F?" He listened. "Oh? Oh. Can't he take the test again? No?"

"Of all the stupid . . . oh, this is hopeless. We're gonna lose this war. I can feel it. Superman read the wrong eye chart. With his x-ray vision he was looking at the chart in the next room. Now he's at the bottom of the list to retake it. There's a hundred million guys in front of him. It'll be 1947 before he gets another chance. If I hear anything about 1947 again, I'll take my gun and blow my head off," and putting action into words he pulled out his revolver and shoved it into his mouth. Rebay launched herself across the table and yanked the gun out of his maw, breaking off one of Davis's front teeth. "Oh shit, look what you've done," he wailed. "And I brought peanut brittle for lunch. Get my dentist up here," he shouted at his secretary.

"This is what it's like every day here," he moaned to Rebay. "On top of that, whenever I get a swell idea of how to win the war, like drafting Superman, they laugh at me. Now what's *your* great idea?"

"Remember what I told you about this painting?"

"Yeah, some crap about this boyfriend of yours and how this triangle with a ball balanced on its top makes you feel calm. By the way, I think it would be a better picture if it was a trained seal with a beach ball on its nose."

Rebay contemplated Bauer's picture for a minute and told

Davis maybe he had a point. "Anyway, here's the deal. Instead of waiting until 1947" — Davis reached for his gun — "Sorry, sorry, let's just say a long time; when we start bombing the German cities, we're going to be killing good Germans like me along with the bad Germans."

Davis shook his head. "No good already. It's too hard to explain to the kinds of morons we got in this country subtle concepts like the difference between good and bad anything. They just have to be trained to kill anyone who isn't an American."

"OK, forget that," Rebay said. "My idea is we take millions of copies of this painting and drop them on Berlin and Tokyo. They won't weigh much so we can use those chickenshit little planes we got now. I guarantee you when they see these paintings they'll calm down and stop the war."

"And that's your idea?"

"*Ja*. And I can get you these with a volume discount. Even after paying a commission to my boyfriend, a million will only cost you ten thousand bucks, and you get a complete refund if the war isn't over by 1947." Rebay grabbed his hand before he could get the gun in his mouth, but it went off anyway and shot off the end of his nose. "Christ, look at me now. No tooth, no nose, and I'm supposed to make a VD movie with Mickey Mouse in an hour. I'm starting to hate this war. OK, we'll try your idea but I'm only going to give you five thousand."

"Eight thousand."

"Five thousand seven hundred."

"OK, let's split the difference, seven thousand eight hundred."

"Deal." Davis pulled out a scrap of paper and a pencil and tried to subtract five thousand from ten thousand, got confused and threw the paper into the garbage. "I keep my cash over there in that flowerpot. Take out your seven thousand eight hundred and get out. And don't tell anyone where I keep my cash!"

"Seven thousand nine hundred."

"I thought you said eight hundred."

Rebay shook her head.

"You sure?"

Rebay nodded and grabbed the cash. Just then Secret Agent Guggenheim burst into the room.

"What are you doing here?" she yelled at Rebay.

"Trying to do my little bit to win the war," Secret Agent TNA replied.

"Howzat?"

Davis explained. "We're going to float a million copies of this picture of her boyfriend's down on Berlin and Tokyo and turn the Japs and Krauts into pacifists."

"That'll be the day," Guggenheim sneered. "*Here's* what you gotta do." She pulled out a poster and flattened it out. "Lookit this one." Davis studied it. He turned it upside down and back again. He reached up to scratch his nose before remembering that his nose was gone.

"What happened to you?" Peggy asked. "You look like hell."

"I was talking to this lady here and decided to shoot myself and missed."

"At that range. Pathetic." Peggy pulled out her gun. "Want me to finish you off?"

"No. Maybe later. But this painting of yours. It looks like, I dunno, a bunch of worms or maybe tadpoles. A can of fish bait?"

"No, you imbecile. It's a cauldron of pure, unleashed rage and emotion."

Davis tilted his head and walked around the poster. "You mean someone got mad and did this?"

"More or less. It's by a new discovery of mine. Name's Pollock."

"Isn't Pollock some kinda fish?" Davis asked. The idea of

a fish painting a picture aroused his suspicions. This was the kind of trick a spy might pull to get him confused. "Maybe a monkey could paint that picture," he objected, "but not a fish. Fish ain't got no arms."

"What about an octopus?" the Baroness objected. "They got eight. Or a mermaid?"

"It's by a human being," Peggy countered. "Used to be a janitor at *her* museum," pointing at Rebay. "I gave him paints and this is what he did."

"Shoulda stuck to sweeping floors," the Baroness murmured.

"So, what am I supposed to do with this?" Davis was perplexed. The painting would have been impressive if it had been by a fish. Or a monkey. But for a human, he thought it was definitely disappointing, and even the painter's mom would probably want it to be ripped up and put in the garbage. Certainly not have the family name attached to it.

"Buy a million copies, plaster them all over the country, and it'll turn the entire nation into bloodthirsty, raving maniacs ready to kill every Jap and German you point 'em at."

"You sure this'll work?"

"Yup."

"How much?"

"After paying a commission to the artist, and a little for myself, I can get you a million for $10,000."

"Five thousand."

"Deal," Guggenheim said. Rebay guffawed.

"Take the money out of the flowerpot, and I need both of your posters next week."

"Three weeks," Rebay countered.

"Ten days."

"OK, that's a fortnight," Rebay said.

"Huh," Davis said and yelled to his secretary, "Honey,

what's a fortnight?"

Honey shrugged.

The two secret agents left the office. "You chump," Rebay said to Peggy. "Whydja take his first offer? You cudda got another twenty-five hundred easy. Better let me do your negotiating for you from now on. Twenty percent commission."

"Ten percent."

"Split the difference, eighteen percent."

Guggenheim took out a pencil and paper and tried to subtract five from ten thousand, got confused and gave up. "OK," she said.

* * *

The FBI Laboratory was deep in the basement of the Justice Department on Pennsylvania Avenue. The deepest recess of the Lab was the top-secret lair of Special Scientific Agent MAD-1, the FBI's maddest scientist.

Rebay whispered to Peggy, "They warned us this guy would look crazy. I didn't expect *this* crazy." MAD-1 was wearing a long black robe and, instead of the standard-issue dark blue fedora, he was wearing a conical black wizard's hat decorated with stars, planets, and a photo of Mae West. "But they said he's harmless."

"He gives me the creeps," Peggy whispered back.

The mad scientist greeted them and said, "The Director gave me a rough idea of what you want."

"You really think you can help us?" Rebay asked. "At the rate these so-called artists are showing up, the two of us are going blind figuring out if they are real painters or spies. We need a machine that can do the job so we can get on with our real work."

"What's our work?"

"Psychological warfare."

"Psywar? Gosh darn it, that's what I wanted to do. Not be

stuck in this rotten dungeon coming up with assassination gimmicks our agents are too dumb to use. All they want are old-fashioned clubs and Tommy guns. If the Bureau turned me loose, I'd give 'em psywar that'd make the Japs and Krauts nuttier than fruitcakes. Crazy. They won't be able to handle the kind of crazy I'd give 'em."

"You're starting to scare me," the Baroness said.

"Me too," Guggenheim added. "By the way, what are we supposed to call you? 'Mad-One' sounds a little, well, judgmental."

"My friends would call me Loco. Or just Madman. If I had any friends. Siddown," he said, pointing to a pair of lab stools. He grabbed one for himself and sat down too close for comfort for Rebay, who moved back from him.

"If you don't mind my saying so," Rebay said, saying so anyway, "you don't smell too good."

"Sorry. Formaldehyde. We're trying to bring battle casualties back to life. We call it the Arlington Project. From the Cemetery."

"Geeze," Guggenheim said, impressed.

"Yup, we'll be able to reuse the same soldiers forever. There're a few snags we ain't worked out yet."

"Waddya mean?"

"When they come back to life, the fuckers don't wanna fight. Claim they're C.O.s. But let's get back on track. You want a machine that'll tell you, just what?"

"You gotta build us something any agent can use to tell real artists from fake artist-traitor-spy-ratbastard Nazis. We wanna show some certified, bona fide examples of real art to these bustards and see how they react. We'd like two lights on the machine, one for 'Artist' and one for 'Spy.'"

"And maybe a bell for artists and a buzzer for spies, too. In case the operator falls asleep," Guggenheim added.

"Ya got them paintings with ya?"

Rebay spread two posters out on a lab table. One was that ball balanced on a triangle the psy-warriors were gonna be dropping over Germany. "That's by my ex-boyfriend," she said, putting an emphasis on the "ex." She had just gotten word that Bauer was planning to marry his maid.

The other was Peggy's box of worms. "That's one of my superstar discoveries," she said, "her ex-janitor," putting an emphasis on "ex."

Loco looked puzzled. "You sure this stuff is art?"

"Absolutely. The ball and triangle are from her museum," Guggenheim said, "the other's from the museum I'm gonna start. Maybe."

"Ya mean if you can do this kind of crap, you get to call yourself an artist?" Mad-1 asked.

"Yup. We learned our lesson with that Hitler guy."

"You mean the one that's running Russia?"

"No, you dope. You been down here too long. He's the head of Germany. You know, the one we're fighting. Russia's on our side."

MAD-1 looked confused. "You sure?"

"Yeah, I'm sure. This Hitler was in art school. They flunked him out, so he went into politics, and now he's some kind of a problem. Not anything our Army, Navy, and Psywar guys can't handle, but it would have saved a lot of trouble if they had just let him be an artist. He'd be just your average crazy, homicidal, anti-Semitic lunatic happily painting flowers in the Alps. So now, if a guy says it's art . . ."

"It's art," Rebay completed the sentence.

"Gosh," MAD-1 said. "Maybe I should pay more attention to politics."

"This would be easier if you could visit our museums. They ever let you out of here?"

"Not allowed. The enemy might snatch me and win the war."

"That would be cheating," Rebay said.

"That's the way it goes. We got our dirty tricks, so we can't complain if they got theirs. But give me something more to go on. What're you supposed to feel when you look at this one?" pointing at Rebay's offering.

Rebay answered, "You should be carried into a peaceful, calm, spiritual place; blissful. Oh, let's not beat around the bush: *You should see God®.*"

"See God®, eh?" Loco said thoughtfully. "I've got an idea. How about this one?" he asked Guggenheim.

"Ya get excited, twitchy. Like yer gonna explode."

"She means *hot*," Rebay explained.

"That one should be easy," Mad-1 told them. "We've already got a machine we use to weed out homos from our recruits. We strap 'em down, attach a couple of wires to their pork chops, and show 'em pictures of naked guys. Simple, but effective."

Guggenheim guffawed. "How about guys already in the Bureau? They gotta get their wieners wired up, too?"

"Nope, they get a pass. And we got some pretty sick puppies in this place."

Guggenheim and Rebay exchanged glances.

"I got an idea," Rebay said. "If we think they're spies, can we shoot a few volts into the ol' Johnson and make 'em talk?"

"Don't see why not."

Guggenheim stared at Rebay. "Have you ever thought of picking up some extra cash as a dominatrix? Good money in it."

"Absolutely not. I've got my reputation to consider . . . er, how much money?"

"Plenty. And you'd be wearing a mask. But not much else."

"Worth thinking about," Rebay said.

"But how about my spiritual stuff?" She turned to the Madman. "Seeing God. What's your idea?"

"Not too many mad scientists would know how to handle that, but I'm one of 'em. There's a part of the brain called the Broca area. You can call it the Buddha bump. When someone does something holy, like drop a buck in the collection basket, that region lights up and we can detect it by an electrode on the skull. Of course, you get better results if you drill a hole in the victim's—I mean the *patient's*—head and shove in a silver needle, which I think is kinda cool, but some people don't like having holes drilled in their heads. Don't know why."

"People are so unreasonable," Rebay commiserated.

"I should have this ready in a day or two. I'll test it on some of the zombies I've got back there, but maybe you should bring down a painter for me to try it on."

"I know just the guy," Rebay said grimly, "and I don't mind if you use that silver needle. Or make it a rusty nail."

"Poor Rudolf," Guggenheim laughed. "I think that romance is dead."

* * *

With a grand gesture, a beaming Elmer Davis swept aside the curtain behind his podium and shouted, "There they are! What we're fighting for! The Four Freedoms! By Norman Rockwell, America's greatest painter, except maybe for Grandma Moses."

The crowd of dignitaries — lobbyists, war profiteers, senators, visiting Boy Scouts, and a delegation of Indian chiefs, each chief with a big-breasted hooker supplied by blanket companies' lobbyists — whooped and clapped, while Secret Agents Rebay and Guggenheim, disguised in sunglasses, looked on in haughty disdain.

"Now that's what I call art," a grinning Texas senator said

to one of the Indians. "Ugh," the chief agreed happily, "That papoose picture would look great in my teepee. If I had a flat wall to hang it on." The hooker by his side nodded enthusiastically and whispered, "When do we get outta here? My meter's running."

"See," the Texan said to his new Indian sidekick. "Cowboys and Indians can be friends. All we gotta do is look at paintings together, instead of shooting at each other. Tell that to John Ford. And how's about introducing me to yer friend? She looks like someone who'd be a nice addition to my bunkhouse."

A guy who looked like a university professor was leading the crowd of dignitaries, explaining the art as they proceeded through the Rockwell exhibit:

"*The Four Freedoms: Freedom of Speech, Freedom of Worship, Freedom from Want, Freedom from Fear*," the lecturer began. "Norman Rockwell has stuffed each image with enough sentiment to bring even W. C. Fields to tears." (In fact, Fields himself was on stage, honking noisily into a bandanna handkerchief and crying a river.)

"Wotta great idea it was getting that old ham here," Davis exulted to himself. "Pure gold-plated schmaltz. If that don't win the war, nothing will."

Fields finished drying his eyes, pulled four balls out of his pocket, and waved them at the crowd. "Oh, no. Why's he juggling? Get him offstage!" Davis yelled at his flunkies, who immediately dragged the performer into his dressing room.

The lecturer went on:

"*Freedom of Speech*: A courageous yeoman at a town meeting is speaking his piece on a civic issue vital to his community."

("Yeah, sure," Rebay snickered, adding her own commentary to Peggy. "Probably saying it wasn't his dog that had raided his neighbor's chicken coop. Ol' Shep had nothing to do with killing that bastard's hens. He's only a puppy, and he's being framed. Besides, he only ate one. I think Joe killed 'em himself to cover up that he's married to his sister and his kids have six toes and web feet. I say, string him up." Peggy giggled.)

"Next is *Freedom of Worship*: a congregation of white folks gaze prayerfully toward the Almighty."

(This time, Peggy added *her* interpretation: "They're watching a racetrack tote board just out of the frame; the horses are nearing the finish line. In a second, some of those gambling-addicted fools will be trotting happily to the ticket window to bet again until they've lost their last cent. The rest will slink home to their wives or husbands (as the case might be) who will be waving frying pans (or machetes, as the case might be) at them, 'Don't tell me you lost the grocery money at the track again, you miserable son of a bitch. You better say your prayers, because I'm going to beat you to a pulp.' 'Aw, Ma — or Pa, as the case might be — I almost won this time. What's for dinner?'" Rebay guffawed.)

The lecturer walked them over to *Freedom from Want.* It had a beaming Grampa standing behind his overfed wife as she plunked an enormous turkey down in front of her mob of children and grandchildren.

("What's going on there?" Peggy whispered, and then she answered herself: "Why, that old geezer is probably the town banker giving his Thanksgiving financial report to the family: 'You can thank that retard Sam Jones for the turkey this year. I just kicked his lazy ass off his farm and sent him to the poorhouse with his miserable kids. After I've sold off his animals and family heirlooms and strip-mined his acres, we'll clear a million easy, more if I can sell his daughters to the white slavers and his boys to the army. Waste not, want not. Is this the greatest country in the world, or what? And we can make it even greater if we get that syphilitic Communist cocksucker out of the White House. God® bless America.'")

The lecturer concluded: "Then we have *Freedom from Fear.* See Mom tenderly tucking her toddlers into bed while Dad, holding a newspaper with war atrocity headlines, gazes on loving-ly."

(Rebay had her own gloss: "He's actually gloating that with his connections he should be able to keep his kids out of the Army and get them into Yale. Boola-boola Bulldogs. For him, freedom from fear means his wife not finding out about the fun he is having with his secretary every lunch hour. 'Now if the guy at the motel will just keep his trap shut, I've got freedom from fear.'")

Elmer Davis was beaming. "We're going to plaster these things up in every school, church, and saloon in America and make all our allies put 'em up except in Russia, where Uncle Joe says his people already have all the freedoms they need (and even more) and don't have to be reminded about them again."

Secret Agent Rebay whispered to Secret Agent Guggen-heim, "The boys back in New York aren't gonna like this. We better tell 'em."

* * *

One of the rich widow volunteer docents at the Metropol-itan Museum had provided funds to bring *The Four Freedoms* to New York. The front rows were reserved for her fellow museum patrons, also mostly rich widows, while the rest of the crowd was heavily stocked with artists from Hilla's museum and a mob of Peggy's friends, abstractionists and surrealists, respectively, along with a rabble from the American Abstract Artists Organization.

Mixing these wild-haired artistic wackos in the same room was as bad as holding the cat and dog shows at the same time, same place. By and large, the American artists all hated one another, but the main battle lines were between Rebay's abstract painters — "non-objectivists" in her lingo — and Peggy's surreal-ists, who were, let's face it, pretty close to pornographers, at least in the opinion of Norman Rockwell's fans. The eminent Europeans — Kandinsky, Mondrian, Josef Albers, and Hans Hoffman — sat together looking on and shaking their heads at the Americans squabbling and making fools of themselves.

Fools or not, the artists were in an uproar, and all were in agreement that, as representative examples of American art, Norman Rockwell's *Four Freedoms* WOULD NOT DO! Quite a few of the painters had managed to pound down multiple glasses of the California red served by their red-frizzy-haired docent-hostess. "Lady1" Jackson Pollock yelled, "this wine is too goddamn warm!"

"You don't chill red wine, you moron!" she shrieked.

Things were off to a bad start. The henna-haired hag pulled herself together, smiled sweetly at her opera club friends in the first row, and scowled at the ragged mob of unkempt artists behind them. Reading from a neatly typed script, she said: "*We* are honored to have paintings by America's pre-eminent painter here with us today," looking up to make sure her friends got the point that it really was *this* artist, basically a tradesman, who was being honored by their presence, and not the other way around. One of Peggy's surrealists, Lee Krasner, pretty well plastered, snorted, "Artist my ass. Rockwell's from the fuckin' Society of Illustrators."

"These are beautiful paintings of beautiful people, the kinds of people I would be pleased to have as friends or neighbors, or as servants, doing beautiful things and expressing beautiful sentiments. These paintings are so much more inspiring than the monstrosities I had the misfortune of seeing the other day at Mr. Guggenheim's museum on 54th Street." Rebay glared at her. "I don't imagine anyone here would think of going there, but if you did have such a dumb idea, stay away is my advice. So, I invite you to enjoy these real paintings by a real painter who really knows how to paint. Any questions?"

Hands shot up, and the docent tried to call on one of her friends, but Joseph Albers jumped up, faced the crowd, and said, "Art is a matter of eliminating the unnecessary so that the necessary can speak." With that, he walked over to *Freedom of Speech* with his portable palette board and quickly whited out the background of the painting.

"My God!" the docent screamed, "Guards!"

The artists applauded wildly. "Still not quite right," said surrealist Max Ernst. He walked up and added to the young man's muscular body a fierce erection. "Now *that's* freedom of speech. Says it all."

"Now let's take care of *Freedom of Worship*," Albers continued. He painted over the rosary. "Freedom of worship means freedom *from* religion."

"A good start," said one of Rebay's abstract painters, Wassily Kandinsky. "but God® is pure spirit"; and Kandinsky brushed out the painting completely, leaving a pure white canvas. "*That's* freedom of worship — no religious symbols, no rituals, just the unseen."

"Not quite," said Kazimir Malevich, one of Rebay's non-objectivists. "The spiritual is the fourth dimension," and painted a red-and-black square on the white canvas. "A pilgrim and his pack in the fourth dimension," he said proudly.

"You da man!" the crowd yelled.

Guggenheim and Rebay had to hold back the prune-faced, copper-haired docent who was screaming for the guards, as Ad Reinhardt walked over to *Freedom from Want* with a paintbrush loaded with black. Carefully effacing the entire painting with a coat of the darkest dark, he explained that *Freedom from Want* meant "wanting nothing, and *here's* nothing." The painters began singing, "We got plenty of nothin', and nothin's plenty for me."

Just one was left, *Freedom from Fear*. Quickly overpainting Rockwell's outrage with white oils, Piet Mondrian stuck a checkerboard square in the middle outlined with black tape. "What's behind the nightmare door of politics and religion? *Nothing*," he said. "No heaven, no hell, no God, no devil, no great Oz. Imagine, no government, no religion, no fear." The surrealists began singing "Somewhere Over the Rainbow." The red-haired docent began swinging her fists and kicking in all directions, trying to get at the painters. She wanted to take them all on. Small but fierce. "Where are the guards?" she screamed.

Two guards came running and skidded to a stop in front of the red-headed hoyden, who by then had progressed from hysteria to frothing at the mouth (which, Rebay observed to Peggy, was more of a drool than a froth). "I always wondered what frothing at the mouth really meant."

Peggy pointed out to Hilla that she had heard that it was important, when someone was diagnosed as frothing at the mouth (or projective drooling, if you like), to wrap your fingers in a hanky and take hold of the maniac's tongue to keep him/her from biting it off. "Let's try to save her tongue from herself. I'll hold her down, and you grab her tongue. Be careful. She might have rabies." While Rebay was holding the mad millionairess's tongue, one of the elderly guards asked what was going on. Rebay told him the situation was under control and to get lost. While taking his leave, the guard commented that "The old bitch . . ."

"You mean her?" Rebay said, banging the alleged bitch's head on the floor, "not me?"

"That's the one. She was always throwing scenes and once tried to get me fired for eating an egg salad sandwich in the staff lunchroom. She claimed she had a chicken allergy."

Since the loaded lunatic could manage only strangled and completely unintelligible gasps, she began signaling to her friends, pointing at them and then repeatedly crooking her trigger finger. "Oh," said one of the ditsy dames, "maybe she wants tea and a donut."

The hog-tied heiress shook her head and pointed to her wrists. "Oh, she wants to know what time it is." Like a pitcher who didn't like the catcher's signal, the downtrodden docent shook the suggestion off. She then pointed to her ear.

One of the gals got it: "Oh, sounds like 'O'? This is fun. I love charades." The carrot-topped captive nodded and pointed to the crown of her head. "Sounds like *hair*?" Shake of the head. "*Skull*?" Negative. "*Top*." She nodded. Points to her ear. "*Sounds like* 'top'?" one of the dumpy dowagers said. "Maybe before she was acting out shooting a gun. Who shoots a gun and sounds like a top? Maybe when she pointed to her wrists, she didn't mean a watch. It could have been handcuffs."

The ladies were in a lather. They thought they were getting warm. "Has a gun and handcuffs and sounds like a top." The grounded granny rolled her eyes. One of the bejeweled crones suggested *mop* and was shushed immediately.

While they were scratching their purple heads of hair, Rebay whispered to her fellow secret agent: "I don't think those brainless biddies are ever going to get it. Should I give them a hint?" Peggy nodded. Rebay held up one finger. "First letter," one of the one-percenters shouted. "This is so much *fun*. Better than looking at them stupid paintings." Then Rebay pointed to her eye. "I," one of the lame-brained ladies guessed. No, Rebay signaled. "I got it," one of the hags hollered, "C. Like in 'see.'" Rebay nodded. She put her thumb and forefinger together and, in a horrible example of post-menopausal post-pulchritude, yelled out, "O." Then Rebay pointed between her legs. "Cunt!" one of the silver-haired sisterhood shouted. "That's not a letter, Sadie," she was informed. "Pussy, maybe?" Negative again. "I got it," yelled one of the grizzled old girls, "It's 'P.' Get it? Between your legs. That's where you pee. C-O-P. That spells *cop*."

"I thought *cop* was spelled with a 'K,'" one of the witches complained.

"Nope. My li'l golf buddy down there wants us to call the police." One of the old gals clattered outside in her Uggs to wave down an officer. He came running.

"What's the problem? What's wrong with her?" pointing at the supine septuagenarian.

"She's having a fit," Rebay explained.

"Good work," the first responder responded. "Don't let loose of that tongue."

The bevy of one-time beauties started yelling, all at once. He shushed them and said, "One at a time."

Breathlessly, one finally made herself clear. "That painter," pointing at Albers, "painted paint on that painting."

The trained lawman thought for a moment and, admitting to himself he knew nothing about art, decided to rely on the deductive logic he had learned at Holy Cross that had gotten him through the Police Academy. *Let's see*, he thought. *What was the essence of a painting? Paint on a canvas*, he answered himself. *And before there is paint on a canvas, what is it? It is a potential painting. And who is it who transforms the potential painting into an actualized painting? Potency into act. The painter!* He reached his conclusion, then double-checked it. "A painter who is putting paint on a painting," he announced, "is doing what a painter is supposed to do: painting a painting with paint. *Roma dixit*. Nothing here for me," he said, and made his exit.

CHAPTER 5

"This has gotta be super-secret, Gals," the President told Peggy and the Baroness. "Nobody's heard of this except me and the missus," pointing to Mrs. Roosevelt in her spiffy navy-blue WAVES uniform. The crack secret agents snapped off salutes to the First Lady, who pointed toward a doily-covered plate of *petit-fours* and asked whether they wanted cream and sugar or lemon in their tea. When they both shuddered, the President asked if they would join him in something a little stronger. "Now you're talking," Peggy replied, and Rebay nodded vigorously. Wheeling himself over to the bar, the Commander in Chief asked the secret agents what they wanted. "How about a Grasshopper or a Pink Lady?" and he winked at them.

The girls shuddered again. "Have any gin?" Peggy asked. The President waved a bottle of Beefeater® in their direction. "That's more like it," Rebay said, as he started pouring gin into a pitcher of ice. "Say 'when.'" He kept pouring. "Hey, are you awake? Say 'when'! OK, that's almost the whole bottle. All we got." He stirred the pitcher and poured them each a highball glass filled to the brim. "Maybe I'll have one, too."

"Good for a start, Chief," the Baroness told him. "Maybe you should send out for more. Now what's on your mind?"

Eleanor came over to them and dropped a wedge of lemon in each of their drinks and poured one for herself. "This is shaping up to be a nice party," she said and smiled.

"I gotta little problem," the President told them. "I can't get it through Hoover's fat head that Russia and our guys are on the same side now. All he wants to do is hunt Commies. Claims they're spying on us and stealing the plans for that top-secret bomb we're building in Los Alamos."

"Franklin!" his wife interrupted. "That's supposed to be *entre nous*."

"You mean the A-bomb?" Peggy said. "Speed was right about that. We caught a spy last week, and after Rebay and I worked him over it turns out the Russians know all about it. But they don't have the plans yet. So far, the Baroness and I are the only ones who know they know."

"Hoover doesn't know yet?"

"Nope, we knew this would make you look like a fool, so we've kept it bottled up."

"And the spy?"

The Baroness made an imaginary pistol with her thumb and forefinger and pulled the trigger. "*Former* spy."

"You're my pals," the President told them. "It's top secret that I'm a fool."

"Your bunkies?"

"I'm his bunkie, lady," Eleanor protested.

"The word on the street says not," said Peggy sweetly.

"Anyway," FDR told them, "I owe you one. So far as you know, the only ones who know about the you-know-what in New Mexico (and that I'm a fool) are Uncle Joe, the Reds, and the scientists out there?"

"A lot of the scientists out there are Reds, too," the Baroness told him. "Want us to find out which ones?"

"Can you do that without violating their human rights?" Eleanor asked.

"Sorry, sweetie. Traitors don't have rights," the Baroness informed her. "If we gotta rip 'em a new one, that's what we do. OK with you, Boss?" she asked the President.

"Damn right," he replied. "Makes me surer than ever that Ellie and I had the right idea."

"Which is?"

"We're gonna draft J. Edgar and Clyde and send them to the Pacific to get killed by the Japs. Get them out of my hair."

"Yeah, but who'll run the tours of the FBI headquarters, show kids how we do fingerprints, target practice, all that stuff? Good for morale. Head up the Post Toasties® Junior G-Men Clubs. Not to say watch out for spies."

"The two of you. Eleanor came up with the idea."

"Just the two of us?" Peggy protested.

"Of course not. Eleanor's got it all figured out. You two run the Bureau and organize a G-Gal Auxiliary. It will be like a bullpen as the G-Guys get drafted. Right now, the FBI is just a bunch of draft-dodgers. They should be in the Pacific getting killed by the Japs. Eleanor's already started rounding up gals who know how to march, fight, shoot, and look through microscopes. She's got the Rockettes®, The Girl Scouts® and Brownies®, The acrobats from Ringling Brothers® and Barnum and Bailey®. Women softball players. Eleanor's in tight with a lot of them," and he gave his wife a wink. "We're also paroling female murderers. Some of them are pretty tough. My Mom would like to join up, but I'm afraid she's just too tough —scares the crap out of me."

"I've recruited the field hockey teams from Radcliffe and Smith," Eleanor added. "Those are some tough mamas. Some even into S&M."

Hilla was impressed. "Knot-tying is important. Peggy over here could use some work on that."

"That right, Peggy?" Eleanor asked.

"That granny-knot/square-knot business gets me all mixed up," and she started twining her arms together. "Dammit, I'm stuck already. Baroness, help me out."

"So whaddya think?" Eleanor asked.

Peggy and the Baroness linked the pinkies of their right hands and wiggled the fingers of their left hands behind their heads.

"What the hell is that?" the President demanded.

"That's the Secret Agent howdeedo signal. The way one secret agent recognizes another. Means Rebay and I are on board."

"Gee, that's really neat," FDR told them. "I wish me and the missus had a signal like that. Can you teach it to us?"

"Sure, but there's more to being a secret agent than that. There's a secret password, too. And a Decoder Ring®. Magnifying glass, fingerprint kit. And a gun."

"We get all that stuff?" the President said. "Gosh."

"The First Lady gets all that gear in a Mark Cross handbag. You get an attaché case, Mr. President. Like Webster's Dictionary, it's Morocco bound."

No reaction from the First Couple.

"That's a joke. You know, Crosby and Hope, *Road to Morocco*. Just out. 'Like Webster's Dictionary, we're Morocco bound.' No? Geeze. Tough house."

"Eleanor, tell Elmer Davis to get us a copy of that movie," the President told her. "Gotta be funnier than those VD movies he's so proud of. You girls like to see my stamp collection?"

"Franklin. You promised no more of that until the war is over. Don't fall for that stupid trick, girls. He had me look at them once when I was a sweet young thing. I was never the same."

"Oh, come on Eleanor. It wasn't so bad."

"I hate that stamp collection. Every time I want some special time with him, he's off to play with his stamps. He's not going to be cold in the coffin before I auction that darn thing off."

"Nothing doing, Eleanor. I'm leaving it to the Jungle Room at the Harvard Club. For the members to show their girlfriends. And since when did you start swearing?"

* * *

"Ya mean every other scientist here is a Red?" General Groves, the head of security at Los Alamos, sputtered. He was going over the list of the Los Alamos scientists Secret Agents Guggenheim and Rebay had handed him. "You gals sure?"

They nodded.

"If we get rid of all these guys, we'll never get the 'you-know-what' built," he said, nervously looking around his office. "You think the Commies got this place bugged?"

"Course they do. They have secret meetings every night listening to tapes of you meeting with your cops, yelling at them if they don't make their parking ticket quotas."

"Those aren't quotas. They are guidelines. These geniuses think traffic rules are fascist." He started crying. "Don'cha see. All I'm trying to do is make sure the mechanics who actually are building the bo . . . you know, *the gadget* . . . can get to work. All these Ph.D.s do is scribble on blackboards. I can't make head or tail of it. Lookit this," and he showed them an 8 x 10 glossy of calculations on a blackboard. "This is from Oppenheimer's office last night. These funny-looking s's are called *integrals*. My kid says it means the area under a curve. And this string of numbers, what's that? How am I supposed to summarize this for the file?"

"There's something familiar about those numbers," Peggy said.

"Right," Rebay added, and pulled her Decoder Ring® off

her finger. "Read 'em off, Secret Agent 241."

"SUBENQL289TISFFUTPLIEUCMEWHHQ."

"Got it. It means 'GENERAL GROVES IS A MORON.'"

"That does it!" Groves screamed and grabbed his gun. "I'm gonna kill the sonuvabitch."

Secret Agent Peggy blocked the door. "The Big Guy," as she pointed to the picture of the President on the wall, "said we can't kill 'im until after the 'big noise,'" winking at him.

"I got a better idea," Secret Agent Rebay said: "Psywar."

"What's that?" Groves asked, as Secret Agent Peggy wiped the foam from Groves' mouth.

"It means 'psychological warfare.' Mess with their minds."

"She's right," Guggenheim told him. "Here, write this down," as she started twirling her ring. 'MHJDSP))(*??MSRX-HI[[YTEK"&.' Have one of your goons write that on his blackboard tonight. It'll be the first thing Oppenheimer sees in the morning."

"What's it mean?"

"Simple. It means, 'WE'RE ONTO YOU, YOU COMMIE RAT.'"

"Hey, that's great," Groves chortled. "How about a P.S.?"

"Whaddya got in mind?" Rebay asked.

"Try this: 'Your wife is sleeping with Niels Bohr.'"

"Is that true?" Secret Agent 241 asked.

"Sure. These Reds got the morals of weasels."

"Nothing doing. We can't get these scientists so stirred up they start killing each other. Who's Oppenheimer sleeping with?"

"Who *isn't* he sleeping with? These Commies believe in free love. No morals. And they don't believe in God®." He crossed himself. "'The community of women,' they call it. How about this? We send him a message: 'You've got bad breath.'"

"Does he?" Rebay wanted to know.

"And how. I've got a Smellometer® hidden in his bedroom. I got a daily chart of how bad it is every day."

"Sounds like a total waste of time, if you ask me," Agent Guggenheim said. Rebay nodded. "We tried using it to catch Nazis. Kraut breath. Sauerkraut. Lot easier to just beat the truth out of them. Still, I think the bad breath P.S. can't hurt. Let's do it."

"Is the rat going to be able to figure out what that gobbledygook means?" Groves asked.

"Sure. He's got an official G-Man Decoder Ring®. When Secret Agent X-9 was out here, that big jerk, he lost his. Now we know who got it."

A few days later, Groves was able to tote up a victory for the good guys in Oppenheimer's file. "The SUBINT (*i.e.*, subject of interest) is constantly blowing into the palm of his hand and sniffing his breath. Niels Bohr has been making screwy motions next to his ear and pointing at the SUBINT every time the SUBINT turns his back during lectures. The SUBINT's wife has made a bulk purchase of peppermint LifesSavers® at the PX. I think we're getting to him."

"Now that we've settled that," Secret Agent Rebay said, as she opened a loose-leaf binder, "we've got a plan to turn these Communist ratbastards into patriotic American citizens. Wait'll you see it."

* * *

"OK. Quiet down!" Secret Agent Guggenheim shouted above the hubbub of the assembled scientific geniuses of Los Alamos. General Groves and Robert Oppenheimer were sitting at the head table on either side of the two secret agents, with the rest of the scientists, mechanics, cooks, etc., including the lab's cadre of "comfort women" (in hot pants and tank tops) lounging in the back.

"'Shut up!' I said," Guggenheim repeated. "Everybody

stand up." She dropped the needle on a phonograph on the table in front of her, and the first notes of "The Star-Spangled Banner" blasted out of the speaker. A few of the scientists lazily stood up; the rest stayed sprawled in their chairs. Guggenheim nodded to Rebay, who pulled out her automatic and blasted the coffee cup on the desk of a scientist in the last row, drenching everyone around him and slashing them with sharp shards of china. "Hey, what the fuck?" the scientist yelled.

Peggy shouted back, "Little Miss Sure Shot here can hit the eye of a flea at one hundred feet, and anyone who doesn't stand up now is guilty of mutiny, and we have authority to administer immediate punishment: two pops in the heart and one between the eyes. So get up!" The scientists, auxiliary workers, and whores all jumped up. "Attention," Guggenheim shouted. "Hands on hearts." When the National Anthem ended, Guggenheim ordered, "At ease. Be seated."

"You will notice a few changes around here, beginning right now. Lemme start by introducing ourselves. I am Secret Agent Peggy Guggenheim, and this is Secret Agent Baroness Hilla Rebay." The Baroness waved her pistol as a friendly greeting. "We have been appointed your patriotism counselors, and we're going to turn you into loyal Americans."

"We *are* loyal Americans," a bearded and bushy-haired physicist responded. "We don't need lessons from no storm troopers."

"Why you…" Rebay raced down to the cowering fifth columnist and pistol-whipped him on both sides of his bushy skull. "We're onto you." Waving her gun above her head, she shouted, "This is really Boris Nogudnik, or something like that, and he's the head of Stalin's underground in New Mexico. I would be surprised if he doesn't have a bomb in his lunch pail." She opened it, and sure enough, there was a round black bomb with a fuse sticking up from the top. "Well, I'll be doggoned," a mathematician whispered to his neighbor. "He's the manager of my kid's Little League team. My kid says he makes them keep their fingers crossed in their gloves during the National Anthem. I thought it was for good luck. He was teaching them to be traitors and also how to steal signs. Kill him right now!" the mathematician yelled.

"Not how we do things in this country. First, we torture him to learn all his dirty Commie secrets, *then* we machine-gun him and give him a fair trial."

"Isn't the trial supposed to come before the execution?" a chemist opined. "Just saying. 'Course you ladies know your business better than me. I try to stay out of politics."

"Maybe you're right. See? We've got open minds. You have any suggestions, think up any improvements, just jot them down on a piece of paper … and flush 'em down the toilet!"

Peggy grinned at Rebay, who allowed, "That was a good one, Peggy."

"OK, let's cut the crap. Bobby, hand out their homework." An obviously terrified Oppenheimer checked his breath, then ran down the center aisle passing out sheets of paper left and right. "That's the Pledge of Allegiance. At tomorrow morning's civics assembly, I'm gonna pick out two of you at random, and if you don't know the pledge, it's two times around the football field for everybody."

"What about me?" a crippled wretch in a wheelchair whined.

"Guess you'll have to crawl. No exceptions. Now get outta here. Dismissed." The scientists rushed for the door. "Not you gals," she yelled at the lab whores. "Stick around. I've got special assignments for you."

"How'd that go?" Guggenheim asked General Groves.

"If anyone can turn that gang of Bolsheviks into loyal Americans, it's you two. Even I feel more loyal now," and he walked over to the flag and covered it with kisses. "Maybe we oughtta make 'em do that."

"Good idea. Now lemme talk to the hookers."

* * *

Reading off a typed list, Secret Agent Guggenheim told the little band of bad girls to raise their hands when she called their names. "Bambi."

One of the harlots raised her right hand, crooked her pinkie, and fluttered the fingers of her left hand behind her head. Guggenheim and Rebay exchanged startled glances. "Brandi." Brandi likewise gave them the secret agent howdeedo signal. She ran down the rest of the list: "Sherry." "Knockers." "Lovebomb." "Bliss." Each of them gave the same secret sign.

"Well I'll be goldarned," Guggenheim said. "The whole herd of you are actually secret agents disguised as whores. How long have you been undercover?"

Secret Agent Knockers said that they had been deployed to a Quonset hut brothel at Los Alamos before the first scientists arrived. For a while they had serviced the construction crew "for practice," but since then "these horny highbrows" had been keeping them "plenty busy."

"How much do you charge?" Secret Agent Rebay wanted to know.

"The money's not an issue. They got nothing else to spend it on, since they get free room and board. But if we didn't ration out our carnal consultations, they'd be in the sack with us all day and night, not getting work done on the . . ." and Bliss made an exploding motion with her hands. "So, they have to give us sugar and gas ration cards with their twenty bucks a pop. We can sell the ration cards down in Santa Fe. And the Bureau is OK with that," she hastened to add.

"Not bad," Agent Guggenheim said. "Rebay and I are OK

for cash, but we're short of ration cards, like everyone else. Could you spare us some?"

"Not on your life. You'll have to put out for them like the rest of us."

"Let's hope it doesn't come to that," Secret Agent Rebay told them. "Now what are your assignments, I mean aside from spreading your legs? And which one of you is in charge?"

"That would be me," Secret Agent Knockers told them. "Number one, look out for Nazi and Jap spies. We can practically say for sure there's none of them here."

"How can you be so certain?"

"We have a list of key words to say at specific moments during our *petits assignations*."

"Like?"

"You know, '*Banzai*,' '*Sieg Heil*,' '*Gott im Himmel*,' '*Ichiban* dick you got there soldier': stuff like that. The idea is if they respond in Jap or Deutsch, we gottem."

"Pretty clever. Who thought that up?"

"Eleanor."

"Eleanor! You mean the First Lady is your pimp, or maybe madam?"

"I wouldn't put it quite that way, but I guess you *could* put it that way."

"How did you meet her?"

"We were all getting together with her every week at the Cosmopolitan Club in New York to knit socks for the soldiers and play bridge when she got the idea."

"What kind of secret agent training did you get?"

"Same as you two. We heard of you. Thanks to you we got the same Mark Cross bags to keep our stuff in. But we have to hide our Secret Decoder Rings®. We been told to take orders from you two. So, what do you want us to do?"

"OK, gals, listen up. Rebay and I are turning these pinkos

into patriotic Americans, but it's going to be a tough job, and it's not going to take with all of 'em. Some of them are going to keep spying. Number one: We are pretty sure someone here is making trips to Santa Fe to hand the secrets over to one of Stalin's secret agents. We need to know who it is."

"That's gonna be tough. They go to Santa Fe all the time. They're crazy about the Frito Pies® at Woolworths®."

"What's that?" Rebay wanted to know.

"You buy a bag of Fritos®, then they dump in some salsa and melted Velveeta®. You eat it with your fingers."

"Sounds revolting."

"It's an acquired taste."

"Let's get back on track. We have to figure out who this SUBINT is; oh, let's call him the *courier*. We think he's not a top scientist here, probably just one of the construction or main-tenance guys. But he'd be a leftist, so you can probably trap him with some known Commie key words. Any ideas?"

"First of all," Brandi told her, "we usually don't play hide the wiener with the maintenance guys. They don't wash and are unversed in the gentler skills of sensual lovemaking. Some of them even listen to the ballgame while they are 'doing it,'" in-dicating air quotes. "They claim it keeps them from, you know, finishing too soon, so we can't complain, since one of our selling points is 'anything goes.'"

"Ya gotta take one for the team," Guggenheim told them, "and that's an order."

They groaned.

"But I gotta tell you, this is a win-the-war kind of assign-ment."

The girls all leaned forward in their chairs.

"Here's the deal." Guggenheim's voice dropped to a whisper: "Once we identify the courier, we're going to feed him some bogus secrets, and when he sends them back to Moscow and they use them to build their B-O-M-B." She paused dramatically. "It's . . . going . . . to . . . blow . . . up . . . in . . . their . . . faces."

The girls shouted in delight, jumped up and started giving each other, and Rebay and Guggenheim too, the Secret Agent howdeedo. Knockers was so excited she almost popped out of her tank top. Not almost. Did.

As the harlots ran back to assume their positions in the Quonset hut, Rebay said to Guggenheim, "I think we've got a team of winners here."

* * *

Speed had Rebay on the phone. "I just got word from Roosevelt that he's putting Clyde and me on active duty in the Navy and replacing us here in D.C. with you and Agent Guggenheim. Did you have anything to do with this?"

"Not a thing, Chief."

"Did you know about it?"

"Well, yes, but he swore me to secrecy."

"Come on," Hoover begged.

"Here's what I know. He's pissed because you keep investigating the Commies when they're on our side now."

"So, he's firing me and Clyde and putting you two in charge. Do you know where he's sending us?"

"Affirmative. You're going to the Pacific to get killed by the Japs."

Rebay could hear Hoover wailing, "Clyde, he's going to have the Japs kill us in the Pacific." She heard a crash that sounded like a Number Two G-Man keeling over in a dead faint.

Hoover was back on the line. "Clyde just keeled over in a dead faint. I'll call you right back."

"He's taking it pretty hard," Rebay told Guggenheim. "And the worst part is that he's right about the Commies. If he could just stay alive until the end of the war, everyone will see he was right, and he'll be a hero again."

"Can you think of any way we could bail him out?"

"If they admitted they were a couple of perverts the Navy wouldn't take 'em."

"No good. They couldn't get back in the Bureau."

"We gotta come up with a way for Speed and Clyde to do something so great that the President will *have* to take them back and let 'em run the Bureau again."

"I'm thinking about having General MacArthur hold a reception welcoming them to whatever island he's hiding out on. Then an assassin will break in to kill MacArthur, and Speed and Clyde will kill the sonuvabitch."

"Who could we get to do that?"

"X-9?"

"You think he'd go along with letting Speed and Clyde kill him?"

"Probably not. That's a good point. He's not too bright, but maybe there's a limit . . . "

The phone rang. It was Hoover again. "Clyde's come to, but he's just huddled in the corner sobbing and crying that he doesn't want to die. Poor guy is really sensitive. Did I ever tell you about the time his pet goldfish went belly up?"

"Chief, we gotta come up with a solution fast. Here's my idea. We stage a kidnapping. The Reds snatch you and Clyde. You escape, right into Walter Winchell's car. You give him an amazing story about how you saved the country from a really bad Commie plot."

"What were they planning to do?"

"Dunno. What's the worst thing you can think of?"

"Kidnapping me is pretty bad."

"Yeah, but the logic is no good. Saving yourself from the Reds really won't impress the President. He'd *want* them to kill you. He'd be angry you got away."

"Oh yeah, you're right. He hates me."

"How about this? The Reds are gonna saw through his crutches so that when he hobbles over to the podium at that Madison Square Garden rally next week, he falls on his ass."

"Haw, haw, I'd pay to see that!"

"No, you idiot. You think it's horrible, and when you tell the story to Winchell you sob about how the President is the greatest man in history."

"He is?"

"No. That's just your story. Have you gone brain-dead?"

"Sorry. I'm worried about Clyde. Do you think he might swallow his tongue?"

"You going along with this? Have you understood anything I've said?"

"I think so. We lay low for a few days, then meet up with Winchell, feed him this bullshit story, and the President will have to cancel our orders to get us killed by the Japs. Think it'll work?"

"Yup. We'll send some actors to your office tomorrow to fake the kidnapping. They'll be dressed like secret agents. I'll send Winchell a ransom note from the Reds and have X-9 get to work sawing through the crutches the President's sent ahead to Madison Square Garden. Think you can remember all that?"

"I can if I can get Clyde calmed down. Might be better if he doesn't know about any of this. I'll just tell him you girls are taking care of everything. You're the only ones he trusts. You remind him of his mother *and* his grandmother."

The girls went over to a mirror to look themselves over. "This job is giving me wrinkles," Guggenheim said to Rebay. "Just look at these crow's feet."

"They're not so bad," Rebay replied, "but that grandmother crack was out of line. We need to talk some sense into Clyde," she said, smacking her fist into her palm. Peggy nodded, looking grim as she examined her crow's feet with her FBI magnifying glass.

* * *

Rebay and Guggenheim were grading their first patriotism quizzes. They had decided to do it question by question to find out if anyone was cheating.

1. When they build a second level for the George Washington Bridge:
    a. The upper level will be called Martha and the lower level George.
    b. The upper level will be called George and the lower level Mary.
    c. The upper level will be called Silver Dollar and the lower level Cherry Tree.

"They were all over the place on this one, even though we showed them that porno cartoon of Franklin and Eleanor in bed. And how about this wise-ass: 'Washington cut down the cherry tree with a silver dollar to make his false teeth.' Is he making fun of us?" Guggenheim asked.

"You think?" Rebay replied.

2. The only good Indian is:
    a. A dead Indian.
    b. Tonto.
    c. The one on the nickel.
    d. They are all good, just dangerous when drunk.

"You think they're even listening to the lectures?" Guggenheim complained. "We went to all the trouble of bringing Geronimo down from Taos to tell them about how the white man fucked over the Indians, and then he drank a can of Bud and went berserk and tried to scalp you before you kicked him in the nuts."

"Close call."

3. What color is the flag?

    a. Red.

    b. Red, white, and blue.

    c. Can't tell, could be red or green.

    d. Same color as the hammer and sickle.

"We made a mistake on this one," Rebay said. "Should have taken the flag in front of the room down. This one guy who answered 'c' is color blind. Need to find out if he's the pilot who is going to drop the b**b, and wash him out. And anyone who answered 'd' will be shot right after the test is over. OK?"

4. The Indians taught the Pilgrims:

    a. How to put up a Christmas tree.

    b. How to inhale tobacco.

    c. How to play craps.

    d. To put aluminum foil over the turkey to keep the white meat from drying out.

    e. All of the above.

"They all got that. We ought to tell Cookie what a good job she did with her lecture. Maybe we should always hand out treats."

"Uh-oh! Did you notice how Oppenheimer and Bohr fought over the drumsticks? Those boys don't like each other. Maybe we should give them the 'no *I* in team' lecture. Make a note."

5. The history of America is:

    a. A beautiful story of how we turned an Indian-infested wilderness into forty-eight wonderful states.

    b. A story of how great captains of industry built the greatest economy in history, generously provided working men, women, and children with nice factories to work in and even paid them, and then gave away all their money to build libraries and prisons.

    c.   How they ran a fantastic cotton industry for the benefit of the slaves until some pain-in-the-ass reformers like A. Lincoln stepped in and ruined everything.

    d.   All of the above.

"Copying, cheating. Clear case of copying. We nailed 'em. Lookit this," Rebay shouted. Two cheating bastards had written:

1. The history of the world is the history of class conflict.
2. America is part of the world.
3. Ergo, the history of America is the history of class conflict.
4. Q.E.D.

"That's treason!" Guggenheim yelled. "And look who the cheaters are. Niels Bohr and *Mrs*. J. Robert Oppenheimer. Now we just have to find out which one is the Red and which one is just a chump who didn't know the answer."

"My guess is the traitor is the Oppenheimer broad," Rebay replied. "She's got that crazy Bolshevik hairdo and a wild look in her eye. Bohr just looks like a chuckle-head high school science teacher. Harmless. But we gotta be careful how we torture her. Oppenheimer might complain if he gets her back in pieces. Maybe we should check with headquarters first."

"Good thinking," Secret Agent Guggenheim replied.

CHAPTER 6

Meanwhile, at an undisclosed location in Manhattan (actually the editorial offices of the *New York Times* on 43rd Street) . . .

Hoover and Tolson were being held captive by a gang of Communist desperadoes. "But this is still better than being sent to the Pacific, isn't it, Speed?" Clyde, still slightly hysterical, asked his chief, "to get killed by the Japs?"

"I dunno. There's something funny going on. These guys seem like real Reds."

"Of course they're real Reds. They've kidnapped us and are holding us for ransom. How much do they want? Do you think we can get it from the Agents' Gifts for the Director Fund?"

"Clyde, I'm gonna let you in on a little secret. Secret Agents Rebay and Guggenheim cooked up this great scheme to *fake* a kidnapping. Then we're supposed to escape in three days and expose a plot to make the President look like a dope. He's supposed to feel so grateful that we kept him from falling on his ass in Madison Square Garden that he cancels our orders to get sent to the Pacific to get killed by the Japs, and then he lets us run the Bureau again. Cause we'll be Public Heroes Number One and Two again."

"Gee."

"Trouble is, they had to put X-9 in charge of the plan, and he usually fucks things up. I think something's gone wrong."

"Oh, no. You mean like the time you, I mean me, used that stupid Plan 7 to catch that Nazi and he got away through the back door."

"Something like that. X-9 was supposed to get three of our actors who pretend to be Commies at the FBI Academy so new agents can learn how to outsmart those dirty rats, you know, so agents can see through red doublespeak and their dirty tricks; but something tells me that these *pretend* Commies are actually *real* Commies, so that when the actors pretended to be Commies dressed up like FBI agents to snatch us from our offices, they were actually real Commies disguised as agents, not regular American actors disguised as Commies disguised as FBI agents . . . are you following this?"

"I'm not sure. Are we in trouble?" Clyde started to sob.

"There there, big fella, ol' Speed will figure a way out of this shitstorm."

"How?"

"I figure we're in the secret headquarters of the Party, which is in the back offices of the *New York Times*."

"Oh, no," Clyde screamed. "We'll never get out alive! The fucking *New York Times* hates the FBI even more than they hate the Commies. Wait, actually they love the Commies. Chief, do ya think the *New York Times* and the Commies are the same ratbastards?"

"I'm starting to think so. Look at that steamer trunk over there," he said, pointing to a large black leather-bound box in the corner. "Can you tell what those Russian words on the side mean?"

Clyde was one of the top code experts in the Bureau,

trained in French, Latin, Pig Latin, Morse code, AND Russian. He walked over and peered at the Cyrillic characters closely. "Wish I had my ol' G-Man Magnifying Glass®, but I'm pretty sure it spells out 'Moscow Gold.'"

"Just what I thought," Hoover told him. "And there's no chance the Red rats would be hiding their money from Moscow anywhere but in their most secure headquarters. Which is the *New York Times* building, where they spread their lousy lying propaganda to pollute the innocent minds of American infants *and* adults: Mom, Dad, Junior, Sis, . . . even Fido."

"Oh, I'd like to get my hands on those . . . Wait! You mean they're training Shirley Temple and Mickey Rooney, even Judy Garland, to spread those dirty rotten Commie lies?"

"Right. But calm down, Hoss. That's not the whole story. I'm going to let you in on another little secret. You know this guy William Z. Foster who runs the Communist Party?"

"Sure. We've got pictures of him with a bull's eye on his head at the shooting range."

Hoover leaned over to Clyde, cupped his hands over Clyde's ear, and whispered, "He's an FBI agent."

"No shit. So he'll let us go?"

"Unless one little thing goes wrong. And you know, when there's one little thing that can go wrong, it *will* go wrong."

"And what's that?"

"I've been getting reports that Secret Agent Moscow Mule, that's Foster's FBI code name, may be going native."

"You mean . . .?"

"Yup. Leave an agent undercover too long and he starts seeing things through the bad guys' eyes. Becomes one of them. The reporters are calling it some kinda 'Syndrome.' 'Oslo syndrome,' I think. Or 'Copenhagen syndrome.' One of them South American countries."

"I think they're in Central America, Chief. Like Canada."

"Who cares? They're all just foreigners and they're all spying on us. As I was saying before you showed off how smart you are about geography."

"I think that's geology, Chief."

"Will ya lemme tell you this big secret, for Christ's sake. We think that ol' Moscow Mule, Bill Foster, the FBI agent who's disguised as the head Red, may actually be turning into a *real* Red."

"Oh, no! But this is *still* better than being killed by the Japs."

"Yeah, but I gotta plan. When old Moscow Mule, or Red Bill, or whoever he is now, comes in, just shut up and play dumb. That shouldn't be too hard."

"Speed, that was mean."

"Just a joke, you big lug. Come on over here and let's have a nice big G-Man hug."

* * *

It was time for the two Public Heroes' daily re-education session with the Commies' top psywar experts.

Speed whispered to Clyde, "Plan Double-Cross. Start agreeing with everything he says."

"Huh? But it's all just leftist bullshit. Same as that New Deal crap."

"Nemine. Just play along with me."

The door opened, and three Red rats marched in and took seats behind a long desk in front of the room. Speed and Clyde took seats facing the psywar wizard traitors. The comrades on each side aimed lights in the eyes of the Number One and Two G-Men. They were getting used to this. Routine.

"Have you read your assignments from Comrade Stalin's *History of the Communist Party of the Soviet Union*?"

Hoover raised his hand. Clyde, watching his boss closely, tentatively raised his. "Actually, we have."

"Whadja think?"

"This alienation of labor idea seems … to make a lot of sense."

"You agree, Clyde?" the inquisitor asked him.

"I pretty much agree with the Chief."

"OK, Scourge of the Working Class. You don't mind if I call you that?"

"Not at all."

"Explain that alienation stuff."

"Well, it's like this. Let's say the worker produces products worth a hundred bucks in a day. The boss keeps $90 and gives the worker ten. That $90 profit to the boss is the worker's alienated labor. Right?"

"You got that exactly correct.… Better than we could do!" he whispered to his Red rat right-hand man.

Clyde slapped Hoover on the back. "You really are smart. I couldn't make head nor tail of that Red bullshit."

"You think it's just Red bullshit, Special Agent Javert, I mean Tolson?"

"Well, no, I think it makes sense."

"How about in Russia? We just pay the workers pennies — even when they produce tractors worth thousands for Comrade Stalin's Five-Year Plans, which by the way, haven't worked yet only because of Trotskyite revisionist deviationist sabotage, and anyway will definitely start working one of these decades if we live that long."

"Hah. Thought you tricked me," Hoover chortled. "That's the main point of today's assignment, Chapter 3 of Comrade Stalin's *History of the Communist Party of the Soviet Union*. Under the dictatorship of the proletariat, the worker's surplus value is not alienated because it is held in trust by the Party which IS the working class. So the workers, they still get that $90 or whatever it is in worthless rubles; probably not much, it's just being put to good use for the workers' own benefit because they're too fucking stupid to do it for themselves. It's kind of like when I deduct 10% a month from my agents' pay to go into the Fund for Gifts to the Director because those bastards are too goddamm cheap to do it themselves, even though I know they would want to if they could think for their fucking selves."

"Why isn't that the alienation of their labor?"

"Because they are FBI agents, that is, part of the FBI, and I *am* the FBI, so that when I glom some of their dough, it's really robbing Peter to pay Paul, or Agent Shithead to pay Director Hoover, in this case; and anyway, it makes the whole Bureau happy when I'm happy, and all that loot I get on my birthday makes me happy."

"Well put. You are doing so well with your re-education that Comrade Foster is going to see you tomorrow."

* * *

Speed and Clyde had gotten fresh white shirts for their big meeting with Comrade Foster and had borrowed an iron to get the wrinkles out of their navy-blue flannel suits. Clyde, that big lug, left the iron on the seat of his pants and it burned a mark that made it look like someone had kicked him in the ass. Hoover told him that if he put both hands over his butt when he bent down no one would know the difference.

Finally, the door opened, and the top Red rat entered the room. He was dressed in a nicely pressed pair of Can't-Bust-'em® coveralls, a tee shirt with STRIKE printed on it, and a red bandanna around his neck. All in all, pretty much the Hank Williams drag from his railroad fireman days. Foster took his seat behind the long table and said, "Siddown, boys."

He looked up, raised his right hand and crooked his pinkie. His left hand went behind his Communist cranium and he wiggled his fingers. The G-Men did likewise. "How's the brainwashing going?"

"Great," Hoover answered. "I'm believing the stuff as fast as I can translate it into regular English. I don't think I'm criticizing Comrade Stalin when I say that he could learn a thing or two about topic sentences and punctuation — must be the translator's fault, and I would suggest a bullet in the back of the head might straighten him out."

"I'll take that under advisement. He's my brother-in-law and I am getting sick of the free loading bastard."

"But I got a question for you." Hoover leaned forward conspiratorially. "Are you still a secret agent or have you gone native?"

"Native?"

"'Helsinki syndrome,' or whatever they call it — you know, like the 'Hoover syndrome' when all the agents start thinking like me. Whatever," Hoover continued. "Are you still taking orders from me or have you switched over to," and he pointed at the photo of Stalin on the wall, "him. Whose side are you on?"

"I'm on your side if and when you see the light and put the FBI on the side of the Revolution."

"Hmm. Lemme get this straight."

"Yeah," Clyde chimed in, "I'm all confused too."

Hoover scratched his head. He had learned from long experience that the only way to sort out something this complicated was to use props. "You don't happen to have a set of those Russian dolls on you, do you?"

"Sure." Foster opened his hobo's bag (which went along with the Hank Williams costume, sort of maintaining the unities) and took out a bowling-pin-shaped Russian babushka doll with an idiotically grinning face.

"How about some magic markers?"

"How's this?" and Foster handed over a packet.

Hoover pulled the head off the first doll and shook out a somewhat smaller babushka. One after another he extracted the dolls and Clyde put the heads back on each of them. "See, he's good for something," Hoover said to Foster. Clyde blushed with pleasure.

Speed took the smallest doll, covered the face with white magic marker, waved it until it was dry, then wrote on it in pencil, SAF. "That means Secret Agent Foster. With me so far?"

Stalin's top terrorist nodded.

Hoover then took the next doll, whited out the face, and wrote on it, PTR. "That means 'Pretend Top Red,'" and he fitted the first doll inside it. "So, what we have now is an illustration of how you as an FBI agent are pretending to be the head of the Communist Party. Hmmm. Actually, you *are* the head of the Communist Party, pretending to be a Communist. Gets a little complicated. Maybe I should have had . . . I think I got this a little fucked up."

He erased the P from the PTR and said, "OK, you are the top Red." He took another doll, whited out the face and wrote 'PC.' "That means 'Pretending to be a Communist.' That's right now. See? 'Secret Agent' inside 'Top Red, inside, Pretending to be a Communist.'"

Foster looked dazed. Clyde looked at Speed in adoration, dazzled by his boss's brilliance. *His buddy and chief really was the greatest man in history. (After Jesus®.)*

Hoover picked up the last two dolls and whited out their faces. "Now, what do we put on these two babies?" On one he wrote SG. "That means 'Stalin's Guy.'" On the other he wrote HG. "That means 'Hoover's Guy.'"

"Question is," as he picked up the three nested dolls, "Which one do I put these guys in? Are you Stalin's Guy or My

Guy?" He grinned triumphantly.

Clyde murmured, "My Lord and My God®."

Foster thought for a few moments. "Lemme put it this way." He reached into his hobo bag and took out another Russian doll set and unpacked the five dolls inside. He picked up the smallest doll, performed the whitening routine, and then wrote on it LS. "That means 'Little Speed': you as a kid." He picked up the next doll and wrote on it, TGM "That means 'Top G-Man'" and stuck LS inside it. He picked up the next and wrote POF on it. "That means 'Prisoner of Foster.'"

Hoover and Clyde nodded. Clyde asked, "Could you go a little slower?"

Foster picked up the last two dolls and wrote PTBC on one. "That means, 'Pretending to be a Communist,'" and then wrote RCHI on the other, "and that means, 'Really a Communist, Honest Injun.'"

"Now, should all the Hoover dolls go into this one," waving the 'Pretending' doll, "or this one?" holding out the 'Honest Injun.' "You call it."

"I'm an Honest Injun Commie rat now. A real live traitor to my Uncle Sam, reborn on the first day of May."

"Me too," Clyde added. "Can you let us go now?"

Foster grinned as he put the nested Hoover dolls inside the Honest Injun doll, and picked up the last doll. With a flourish he wrote PHNOA on it.

"Huh?" Hoover said. He didn't get it.

"Public Hero Number One Again."

"Hey great!" Then Hoover's face fell. "But when we get out, the President's still going to send us to the Pacific to get killed by the Japs."

"I don't wanna die," Clyde added.

"Not to worry," Foster assured them. "We're going along with that plan your gals in Los Alamos cooked up, saving the President from falling on his ass in Madison Square Garden. We've got Winchell in a taxi outside. You spill the story to him and you're FDR's favorite boys again."

Hoover and Clyde jumped to their feet. "I can already taste that martini at the Stork Club tonight," Hoover exulted. "Mind if I take these dolls so I can remember which side I'm on?"

"One more thing," Foster said. "Those gals at Los Alamos are closing in on our courier who has been sending us all their secrets. Can you throw dust in their eyes, get them off the case? Comrade Stalin would appreciate it. Maybe a Hero of the Soviet Union Award in it for both of you."

"My badge should be bigger than his," Speed told Foster, pointing to Clyde.

Clyde gave a thumbs-up sign that he was OK with that. *A little Hero of the Soviet Union badge is fine with me,* he thought. \

Hoover was already imagining how swell that badge would look on his G-Man suit. *Oh, boy.*

* * *

Secret Agent Knockers and her 'Poontang Patrol' huddled conspiratorially with Secret Agents Rebay and Guggenheim. The girls had brought their hair dryers with them and had placed them in all four corners of the room, running full blast. "Little trick we learned in Secret Agents' School; in case we're being bugged."

"Kind of hard to hear what you're saying," Guggenheim said. Knockers shrugged.

"Waddya got?" Rebay asked.

"Remember how you told us this Red rat courier would probably not be a scientist?" Knockers whispered. "Probably be one of the maintenance men?"

Rebay nodded.

"Agent Brandi nailed him."

"I have this client, a regular," Secret Agent Brandi told them in an almost inaudible whisper. "I tested this guy. He's no scientist. In fact, he's a class-A moron. I told him I was studying for my GED and couldn't remember the square root of 2. He didn't know it. You don't even have to be a scientist to know that. I asked him whether the sine was the opposite side or the adjacent over the hypotenuse. I mean, my God®. You'd have to be a complete retard not to know those things."

Rebay and Guggenheim had no idea what Brandi was talking about. "Right," Guggenheim said, "What a jerk, everybody knows that."

"And get this. This asshole is always begging for a freebie, so I said I'd give a whole free night to anyone who could explain the quadratic formula to me. He was almost crying. He said he would bring his kid to talk to me. He's taking algebra in eighth grade. Could I give the little tyke a freebie, too? I felt sorry for him, so I gave him a freebie anyway. One for the kid sounded tempting, but I digress. He's our guy. I even found out he has a nickname: 'The Pigeon.'"

"OK, you've established that the guy is no mathematician. But that doesn't mean that he's our spy."

"Wait," Brandi said. "That's not all. He said he was in love with me, so I said I kinda liked him too. He said, what would I like him to do for me. I said I would like to have a romantic trip to Santa Fe, have a Frito® Pie, cuddle in some dark and mysterious places around town at night, and then go to a dreamy hotel."

"Whew, that's romantic all right. I wouldn't mind taking you up on that," Guggenheim joked. "Especially if you threw in a couple Frito® Pies."

"I specified a Frito® Pie picnic. He said it's a deal. But there's more evidence that he's the guy. He says that he takes a trip to Santa Fe each week to drop off a package under one of the river bridges. He says it's just the place for some romantic huggin' and kissin.' How's that sound?"

"Looks like we've got our guy. When's his next drop off?"

"In two days. He said he has to wait around for the 'dues' and then he's heading straight to Santa Fe."

"OK. Tell him you'll go for your love vacation with him then. Say you want to get a big treat for him, tell him you'll wear some skimpy underwear or something."

"Well done, Agent Brandi," Agent Guggenheim said. "How repulsive is the guy? Hardship duty?"

"Here's his picture. Since I taught him how to take a shower, brush his teeth, and use deodorant, he's not so bad. But the Reds have him snowed. He keeps talking about how after the revolution guys like him will be running things. I asked him, 'Won't you have to learn how to read and write to run the country?' He said, yeah, he's planning to get around to that, but he's too busy being The Pigeon for the Party. Get it, *Pigeon*, from carrier pigeon?"

"Not bad. Does The Pigeon have any idea that he's stealing the secrets of the 'you-know-what?'"

"Nope. They just tell him he's delivering Party dues from the Los Alamos chapter to the New Mexico headquarters."

"Very clever. These Reds are no slouches when it comes to dirty filthy rotten spy tricks," Rebay told her. "Now we gotta find out where he leaves off the 'dues.' *And* who picks up the package. Here's the plan. Could someone turn those hairdryers up higher?" The hum rose to a roar.

Down in her basement hideout, Mrs. Oppenheimer gnashed her teeth in frustration. She knew that those rotten secret agent bitches were hatching a plot against her and the Party, but she hadn't been able to make out a word.

She was opposed on principle to capitalist gadgets like hairdryers, but she had to admit that they were a great defense against getting overheard by the fascist enemy. She would request permission at the next cell meeting to buy a couple. Maybe wait for a sale at Woolworths®. Pick up a box of Frito® Pies for the comrades at the same time.

* * *

Back at the White House the President was listening to Walter Winchell's nightly load of bullshit, a tirade directed as always against the 'Communist' New Deal and the Bolshevik President who, Winchell charged, was known to go out in the White House backyard at night to bay at the full moon in a syphilitic frenzy.

"Mr. and Mrs. America and All the Ships at Sea: Breaking News. Your intrepid reporter rescued the Director of the FBI, Public Hero Number One, and his handsome assistant, Clyde Tolson, more or less Public Hero Number Two, and nipped a Communist plot to make the asshole Red in the White House fall on his ass in Madison Square Garden. But first a word from Pepsodent®:"

"The new and improved Pepsodent® contains secret ingredient Choppers #1® that our spies stole from the dirty rotten Nazis who, nevertheless — give them some credit — have the whitest teeth in the world. Now you can flash a blinding white smile, too. And remember to brush up and down and behind your teeth, even the ones in back. So treat them to Choppers #1®. Hopalong Cassidy does, three times a day, and you should too."

FDR checked his teeth and made a note to get this Choppers #1®. The two packs of Camels® he was knocking off daily had turned his fangs as yellow as that Rose those Texan morons were always singing about.

Walter Winchell was back with this late flash: "Three days ago, J. Edgar Hoover and gorgeous Clyde Tolson were abducted from their offices in the Justice Department by three Red rats dressed in the well-known G-Man costume of three-piece suits, navy blue, with wing-tip shoes and snap-brim fedoras. (*For you kids, abducted means being taken away by bad guys. Pay attention to your Mom and Dad when they tell you not to talk to strangers. Unless it's your Uncle Walter. Ha-hah. And by the way, it's a federal crime for anyone except an FBI agent to show up wearing that get-up, just like nobody but a forest ranger can wear Smokey Bear outfit, or nobody but a Brownie can wear the Brownie Scout shirt and hat. So, watch out.*)

"Anyway, like I said, those dirty Red rats — I mean rat-bastards, I told my writers to get that straight; I'm gonna hafta fire somebody — snatched our beloved FBI Director and his cute-as-a-button assistant Clyde. They were held captive for three days until they escaped to my taxi from the Communist front *New York Times* where they were chained up, tortured, and fed the same kind of hideous grub that the war-profiteering Sonuvabitch in the White House sends to our brave troops while he has gourmet goodies like *petits fours*, Camembert cheese, and French champagne. And smokes foreign cigarettes like *Gauloises*. Those two heroic G-Men had indigestion somethin' fierce.

"Your intrepid reporter, that's me, WW, has also learned that the class-traitor President and his ugly wife (you know, I found out they don't even sleep together, take a look at her and you'll see why) had ordered J. Edgar and his beautiful buddy sent to the Pacific to get killed by the Japs.

"Like I said before, while they were captives our heroic G-Men learned of an insidious plot to embarrass the country by having that Commie-loving prick in the White House fall on his ass in Madison Square Garden by sawing through the crutches of that crippled traitor. By the way, did you know he can't walk? That's right. And he took the White House job offa that fit-as-a-fiddle Herbert Hoover. It's a goddamn outrage. And so I, WW, issue a challenge to that tax-and-spend pinko to cancel his orders to have Hoover and Tolson get killed by the Japs *immediately*!

And now, joining me at my table in the super-private and exclusive Cub Room of the famous Stork Club, the New Yorkiest club in New York, are none other than Speed Hoover, as he is known to his friends and admirers, of whom I am certainly one, along with his dashing sidekick, Clyde Tolson. Howdeedo, boys?"

"Not bad, and thanks for helping rescue us from the Reds, Walter. But let me set one thing straight. Me and Clyde, I mean, Clyde and I, are perfectly happy to go to the Pacific to get killed by the Japs. It's just that we are discovering new plots against America by those Commie ratbastards every day, although, you know, *some* of their ideas are not so bad."

"Wait a minute. I don't think I heard you right there, Public Hero. Did you say you *endorse* some of those crazy nutjob Communist ideas like free love and no God®?"

'No, no, that just slipped out. What I meant is that *all* of their ideas are bad. And terrible, un-American, despicable, downright naughty. I should have my mouth washed with soap for making that mistake. Will you issue me a pardon, Uncle Walt?"

"Whew, had me going for a minute. So OK, Moms, Dads, and kids, and even Fido, it's time to send those letters to the Red in the White House demanding that the Sonuvabitch *not* send Hoover and his best boy Tolson to get killed by the Japs in the Pacific. Although as you just heard, the two heroes have already packed their stuff to head to the Pacific to get killed by the Japs. Right, boys?"

"Right."

"This is Walter Winchell — dot-dot-dot-dash-dash-dash — signing off to Mr. and Mrs. America and All the Ships at Sea."

Back in the White House the President ground his yellow teeth in rage, opened up a rear window, and let out a howl at the moon. Winchell and Hoover had outsmarted him again. Then he phoned Admiral "Bull" Halsey somewhere in the Pacific. "Bull, call it off. Tell the Japs those two draft-dodging bastards have managed to get out of their patriotic duty of getting killed by the Japs like everyone else. They're not coming."

* * *

"What's with the hairdryers, Chief?" one of the assistant directors asked Deputy Director Lou Nichols as the roar of the machines all but drowned out his voice at the hastily assembled FBI cabinet meeting.

"Trick we learned from Secret Agent Knockers when we were trying to bug the girls' locker room at the Academy," Nichols answered. "She and her hooker squad always had the dryers on so we couldn't figure out what the horny broads were saying. We did get some pretty good up-skirt shots, though."

Lou headed the Bureau's public relations unit, which in one of his sneakiest moves, Hoover had named the Crime Records Division. Nichols had taken advantage of Hoover's impromptu recuperation visit to the Del Mar Racetrack to call a meeting of the headquarters honchos. "That's why I had all of you borrow your wives' hairdryers. The Chief has all the rooms here bugged, so we gotta play our cards close to our chests. Clever, huh?"

"You mean we're here for a card game? Hot dog," said Assistant Director of General Intelligence Division 5, whose job was spying on everyone, so everyone called him Spy-5. "I brought the cards. Who's got the chips?"

"That was a metaphor," Nichols snarled.

"Huh?" said Secret Agent MAD-1, who we already know is head of the crime labs. "Meta-4? Or is it Met-a-4? Some new kinda code nobody tol' me about?"

"Didja never take an English course in college?" Special Agent Sleuth-1, head of the Criminal Investigations Division, asked. "*Metaphor* means something compared to something else. In other words, Lou was saying that we gotta keep what we are doing secret, just like you don't let the other players peek at your cards. Right, Boss?"

"Pretty much right, Sleuthie. But don't make fun of MAD-1. He was taking those hard science courses at Prince George's County JC while you were goofing off studying art appreciation."

"Yeah, but those art courses came in handy when I had to solve the 'Secret of the Lost Image' case. Remember all those white canvases the Met bought with nothing on 'em but white paint. Turned out it was meant to be that way, 'the abnegation of the subject,' we called it in class . . ."

"Anyway, apologize to MAD-1. Not his fault if he's a simpleton when it comes to anything that doesn't stink or go bang." Round of guffaws.

"Aw, I didn't take it personally," MAD-1 replied, shoving his wizard's hat to the back of his head so he could see. "I did learn how to diagram sentences, even ones with gerunds. Did you know that the gerund takes the possessive as its subject?"

Momentarily distracted, Nichols asked, "How's that?"

"Let's see. Let's say someone steals your gun. You can say, 'I shot him because his stealing my gun got me pissed.'"

"Shit, I'd shoot him, too," yelled one of the other top G-Men. "Me too," they all began to shout. "Can't steal a G-Man's gun and get away with it."

"Someone stealing my gun is as bad as it gets. I'd shoot him inna nuts and then right up his body and leave two for right between his eyes."

"Not the point!" MAD-1 interrupted. "It's whether you use 'him stealing' or 'his stealing.' In this case stealing is a gerund kind of noun, so it takes the possessive. It should be 'his stealing.' Now if you said, 'I saw him stealing my gun,' 'stealing' is a participle, that is a verb, and so it takes the objective case, that is 'him,' because 'him' is also the object of 'saw,' so it's a direct object; in this case it has to be 'him,' not 'his.'"

Several of the assistant directors had pulled out their guns and were drawing a bead on MAD-1, so Nichols had to order them to stand down.

"That jerk reminds me of my high school chemistry teacher," one of them said. "I hated that prick because he gave me a 'D.' Ruined my straight 'C' average."

"Anyway, Boss, to what do we owe the pleasure of meeting with you ON OUR DAY OFF?" asked Secret Agent Sleuth.

"Lemme give it to you straight. I think the Director has turned into a *Red*."

A collective, "Huh?"

"Right. He's nuts, loco, crazy, however ya wanna put it. Ever since he got away from the Commies, he's been acting weird." He dropped his voice to a whisper, almost inaudible over the roar of the hairdryers. "Like he's a Red himself."

"Aw, come on. The Director, a Red? Why, he wrote the book on Reds. When he was practically a yout'," Secret Agent Spy-5 scoffed.

"That's because you didn't hear what he said at the Boy Scouts® Jamboree on the Mall. And that's because I pulled the plug on the feed to the networks. He told them that the history of the country is the history of class conflict. Kind of like the Boy Scouts® against the Cub Scouts®.

"Geesh," Secret Agent Sleuth whistled, and then he said, "That's not good."

"It gets worse. He said that the capitalists are out to get the workers, just like, quote unquote, 'your parents are out to get you.' Then he said, 'You shouldn't take any shit offa your parents, and when you get older don't take any shit offa the capitalists.'"

The Assistant Directors shook their heads in disbelief.

"*Then* he said, 'The FBI has conclusively proved there is no God®. So don't believe in him. Everybody repeat after me: 'I'm an atheist, and proud of it.' Then, 'Religion is the oatmeal of the masses, and is there anyone here who likes oatmeal?' The kids all shouted, 'Hell no!' Imagine that, all those Eagle Scouts shouting dirty words like that. I managed to drag him away from the mic by telling him that the Jap spies we been torturing in the basement are ready to talk."

"Where is he now?"

"He's up in his office, gagged and in a strait jacket."

"Whadja tell Clyde?"

"Clyde is so confused he doesn't know what's happening. I asked him if he was a Red, too, and he said, 'If Speed is a Red, so am I,' and started crying."

"What're we gonna do?" Secret Agent Sleuth asked.

"I've got Secret Agents Rebay and Guggenheim listening to all this on a direct wire to Los Alamos. This calls for psywar, guys, and they're our psywarriors."

"What about me?" MAD-1 objected. "That's science and I'm a scientist."

Nichols ignored him and adjusted the speaker phone on his desk. "Rebay and Guggenheim. Are you there? Did you hear all that?"

"We did," Guggenheim answered. "Frankly, we're not surprised."

"You're not?"

"Nope. We got a call yesterday from Speed. He ordered us to stop chasing Red spies at the top-secret project here. We asked him what we should do, and he said, 'Aw, go chase your tails.' Imagine that! Telling his top-secret agents to chase their tails."

"Nice tails," Secret Agent Spy-5 interrupted.

"Thanks, Spy-5. And we're sure as hell not going to call off our investigations just because some brainwashed dope is trying to stop us secret agents from winning the war. And believe me, we just had a major break on the case, and we've got a plan ready that should win the war for our side."

"Honest? That would be great for the Bureau." The assistant directors all stuck out their right pinkies and fluttered their left hand behind their heads. Big smiles. "That'll mean the Bastard in the White House can't send us all to the Pacific to get killed by the Japs, like he says he's gonna do. OK, gals, what's wrong with the Director, and what do we do with the Commie rat?"

"That would be obvious to any psy-war expert. Right, MAD-1?"

MAD-1 looked bewildered, but nodded vigorously. "That's just what I been thinking."

"Great. We're all on the same page. We're gonna take him to your lab in the basement and strap him down. I want you to set up cameras so out here in Los Alamos we can see what you're doing. Stick electrodes all over his skull. At least fifty. He should look like a porcupine. Then I'm going to read selected pieces of Red bullshit. Every time one of the electrodes lights up, that means it's an area of the brain that the Reds brainwashed. You immediately drill a little hole in his head, stick in a silver needle, and wiggle it around until the light goes off. Then we keep doing it until nothing happens when I sing 'Joe Hill' to him."

"I like the plan," Nichols said, "but by the time we finish, won't he be some kinda . . . *vegetable?*"

"Right. But he'll be a loyal, patriotic, American vegetable. Now get the setup ready for nine tomorrow, our time. We're going to deprogram him or die trying. Either way, better than a Communist running the FBI. By the way, that's him dying. Not us. Notice that in the former sentence 'dying' is a verb, not a gerund, so I didn't use 'his.'"

"Way to go, Secret Agent TNA!" MAD-1 yelled. "You didn't fall into that old trap. It *is* a verb, not a *gerund*. So you are right as rain. You have to use 'him.'"

"Next time we're in town," Rebay told him, "let's read *Strunk and White* together over whatever you're distilling in the ol' lab."

MAD-1 gave a thumbs-up sign to the phone and smiled triumphantly at the rest of the assistant directors, who looked disgusted, he thought, at their being out-grammared. *And notice I used 'their' with the noun-gerund,* he thought happily.

* * *

Meanwhile Secret Agent Gals Guggenheim and Rebay had ordered General Groves to put The Pigeon under surveillance. He was finally spotted sneaking into the boiler room, coming out with a brown paper package under his arm. Groves alerted the G-Gals. Guggenheim and Rebay commandeered a car and waited outside the gates. When The Pigeon left the base, the two crack secret agents were close behind. (But not too close, of course. The Gals knew their stuff and were following Secret Agent Plan 8 for a two-gal tail. Remember what a fuck-up Plan 7 was?)

They trailed The Pigeon to Santa Fe, and when he parked his car, they got out and set up a two-agent tail, Rebay on one side of the street, Guggenheim on the other. Guggenheim had the sunny side of the street; she pointed to the sun and made the secret agent sign for switching sides: crossing her fingers and waving them. Rebay sure as hell wasn't going to get sunburnt, and she replied with the secret agent sign for 'no': two thumbs down. This put Guggenheim in such a bad mood that she almost bumped into The Pigeon as he turned into the Woolworth's® on the plaza. She waited outside until he emerged, dripping Velveeta® on his tee-shirt from his Frito® Pie, the manila envelope under his arm.

He turned south on Washington and walked two blocks to the River, then turned east on the River Trail. Rebay, who was right behind her, waved to Guggenheim and pointed down at the trail of Velveeta drops behind him. She smiled and gave her a thumbs-up. Rebay began thinking about writing an article for *Girl Detectives Monthly®*, maybe "Follow the Yellow Velveeta Road."

Powers

No, didn't scan right. "Follow the Yellow Cheese Road." That had the right sound. Of course, she couldn't disclose that it was a trail leading to the secrets of "the Big Boom."

Just then The Pigeon ducked under the Paseo de Peralta Bridge. When he came out the other side and climbed back onto the River Trail, the envelope was gone. Rebay nodded to Guggenheim, and they split up, Guggenheim shadowing The Pigeon, Rebay ducking under the bridge with her Secret Agent Spy Camera®. She found the envelope under a rock marked "SEKRIT," and she opened her camera ready to photograph what was inside. But as soon as she saw what she had, she changed her mind, put the pages back in the envelope, and stuffed it into her Secret Agent All-Purpose Designer Tote®. A minute later she was back on the River Trail, heading to where Guggenheim was waiting in their car.

"He seems to be heading back to the labs," Peggy said. "If we step on it, we might catch him."

"Change of plans," Rebay told her. "When I saw what was in the envelope, I couldn't let it fall into the hands of the Reds. Lookit this." She took the envelope out of her tote and showed Guggenheim the first page titled, "Complete and Final Plans for the Atom Bomb."

"Holy shit," Peggy gasped.

"It's a step-by-step set of instructions for building the bomb. A child could follow it. And the Reds still have got plenty of children, although Stalin's latest five-year plan is killing them like flies. The last page even says the final paint job should be Benjamin Moore® Red, White, and Blue exterior enamel. And look what's stamped on the front page. 'For patriotic American eyes only. Not for Red spies.' And look what one of those Red rats wrote underneath it: 'Joke's on you, Secret Agent Gals.'"

"And check this out. Sheesh. Cash from the dues. I didn't know the Reds had that much money. There must be over a hundred bucks in here."

"Take any?"

"Tempting, but no. We gotta get back to Los Alamos, round up the rest of the gals, and figure out how we can deal with Mrs. Oppenheimer's gang. By now the Reds must know their plans are missing. And the dues. And we gotta operate on Speed's head in the morning."

* * *

Meanwhile, back in Washington, Roosevelt had Admiral Yamamoto on the phone.

"What happened, Mr. Plesident?" Yamamoto asked. "We had a dear. We kirr Speed and Cryde and you settle this wal befole anyone gets hult."

> *Simurtaneous Egrlish Tlansration: What hap-*
> *pened, Mr. President. We had a deal. We kill*
> *Speed and Clyde and you settle this war before*
> *anyone gets hurt.*

"That's what I wanted, too, Admilar. But . . . ah, it's just a comprete fuck-up, I mean fluck-up."

> *Tlansration: That's what I wanted too, Admiral.*
> *But . . . ah, it's just a complete fuck-up.*

"No, 'fuck-up' is fuck-up in Jap, too. Too bad. If we courd end the wal it would herp me negotiate with the 'Pealr Halbol Widows and Olphans Association®,' and they are prenty tough customels."

> *Tlansration: No, 'fuck-up' is 'fuck-up' in Jap,*
> *too. Too bad. If we could settle the war it would*
> *help me negotiate with the "Pearl Harbor*
> *Widows and Orphans Association," and they are*
> *plenty tough customers.*

"What's the ploblem?"

Tlansration: What's the problem?

"I tord them I was going to give them cash to make up for muldeling theil husbands and sons, and they tulned me down. Said it wasn't the money. It was the plincipre. And by the way, I appleciate you tarking Jap to me."

> *Tlansration: I told them I was going to give them cash to make up for murdering their husbands and sons, and they turned me down. Said it wasn't the money. It was the principle. And by the way, I appreciate you talking Jap to me.*

"My preasuie. I been placticing chop-sticks, too, in case you win the wal. You evel stick 'em up youl nose? Bloke the cabinet up, wlen I did."

> *Tlansration: My pleasure. I been practicing chop-sticks, too, in case you win the war. You ever stick 'em up your nose? Broke the Cabinet up, when I did.*

"Musta been hiralious. Send me a photo. We can use it for a plogaganda postel."

> *Tlansration: Musta been hilarious. Send me a photo. We can use it for a propaganda poster.*

"About them widows and olphens. Ya gotta rot to realn about Amelicans. When Amelicans say, it's not the money, leally it *is* the money. How much did you offel?"

> *Tlansration: About them widows and orphans. Ya gotta lot to learn about Americans. When Americans say, it's not the money, really it's the money. How much did you offer?*

"Fifty bucks per colpse. Or 2.5 million yen, theil choice."

> *Tlansration: Fifty bucks per corpse. Or 2.5 million yen. Their choice.*

The President whistred. "That's a rotta money. How
many did you kirr?"

> *Tlansration: The President whistled. That's a
> lotta money. How many did you kill?*

"2403."

> *Tlansration: 2403 (Little translator's joke)*

"Wow. At fifty bucks a colpse, that's, —— ret's see,
fifteen, cally the one, that makes twenty-one, cally the two, wait,
I'm a rittre mixed up . . ."

> *Tlansration: Wow. At fifty bucks a corpse, that's,
> —— let's see, fifteen, carry the one, that makes
> twenty-one, carry the two, wait, I'm a little
> mixed up . . .*

"Don't bothel. I got it hele. It's $121,500."

> *Tlansration: Don't bother. I got it here. It's
> $121,500.*

"You Japs got that much Amelican dough?"

> *Tlansration: You Japs got that much American
> dough?*

"Lemembel those hundred dorral plinting prates youl
mint rost. We store 'em."

> *Tlansration: Remember those hundred-dollar
> printing plates your mint lost. We stole 'em.*

"Not bad. Ter the plicks $75. They'rr come back with a
countel-offel. That's how you do business hele."

> *Tlansration: Not bad. Tell the pricks $75. They'll
> come back with a counteer-offer. That's how you
> do business here.*

"Okie-dokie. Got anyone else you want us to kirr?"

> *Tlansration: Okie-dokie. Got anyone else you
> want us to kill?*

"Mattel if they'le civirans?"

> *Tlansration: Matter if they're civilians?*

Powers

"Nah. Empelol gave us a new raw that it's a clime not to be Japanese. Death penarly."

> *Translation: Nah. Emperor gave us a new law that it's a crime not to be Japanese. Death penalty.*

"Whatta 'bout me?"

> *Tlansration: What 'bout me?*

"Empelol says you honolaly Jap."

> *Tlansration: Emperor says you honorary Jap.*

"That gives me an idea," the President said gazing at Eleanor.

> *Tlansration: That gives me an idea.*

"Franklin, why are you looking at me like that?"

> *Tlansration: Franklin, why are you looking at me like that.*

* * *

"Boys, I gotta new idea." Rebay's voice boomed out of the speakerphone on a desk next to the Director's supine body tied down to a gurney in MAD-1's lab. A camera gave the Gals in Los Alamos a clear view of the whole scene. "Before we scramble his brains, we'll try something else. Lemme run it by you. You listening, MAD-1?"

"All ears," and he suited action to words by rummaging around in a drawer and putting on a giant pair of rubber leprechaun ears. The Assistant Directors looked at him grumpily.

"Come on, guys, lighten up. Science is fun," MAD-1 pleaded.

"What's this idea, Secret Agent Rebay?" Lou wanted to get on with it, and get Director Veg, as he had started calling him, back to work.

"See if you can follow this. I went back to my psychology

textbook. Any of you take a psych course?" MAD-1 raised his hand. Speed surprised them by fluttering his fingers, all he could move in his strait jacket. "Speed? You took psych?" Hoover fluttered his eyelids. "Rats? Mice? Pigeons?" Hoover grinned, nostalgic for the old days of putting cheese at the end of a maze and running the rats through it. A lot like managing FBI agents.

"It seems he took psych somewhere," Nichols yelled at the Secret Agent Gals. "I think he's sorta conscious."

"OK," she told Hoover. "I want you to follow along, too. You're not looking forward to the silver needles, are you?" Hoover moved his eyes from side to side to indicate "No." He couldn't shake his head 'cause it was strapped down.

"Can any of you pin down exactly the moment when Hoover started acting weird?"

They all looked puzzled. Hoover moved his eyes again, as best he could, meaning he couldn't remember anything.

Then Secret Agent Rebay reminded them: "It was when I told Speed over the phone the President had told me he was gonna send Hoover and Clyde to the Pacific to get killed by the Japs."

As soon as Rebay intoned those words, in a good imitation of Roosevelt's fruity patrician falsetto (except for her slight German accent), Hoover began shaking uncontrollably, and a wet stain spread between his legs.

"Jeezuz," Nichols said, "the Director's pissed himself. Get a towel, MAD-1."

MAD-1 began mopping up the mess.

"Don't rub so hard, MAD-1." Rebay ordered. "We don't want him to get a boner. That would wreck the experiment. He needs to focus."

MAD-1 stopped rubbing and gently blotted up the Director's troublesome release of urine.

"What we have just witnessed, gentlemen, is the involuntary recall of a suppressed trauma," Rebay explained.

"But *none* of us want to get sent to the Pacific to get killed by the Japs," Sleuth moaned. "And we didn't turn into Red rat traitors."

"Or piss in our pants," Nichols added.

"That's because you didn't have Commie psywarriors working you over. What they did was to substitute Red bullshit for Speed's trauma from hearing that Sonuvabitch in the White House say he was gonna send the Ace G-Man and his buddy to the Pacific to get killed by the Japs. Now what we gotta do is dig under the Red crap, uncover the original trauma, and REMOVE it."

"Oh boy," MAD-1 shouted out with glee, and pulled out his pincushion of silver needles.

"Hole on, Hoss," Rebay told him. "Not yet. Take his gag out."

This was the big moment. She and Guggenheim had rehearsed until Peggy could do a perfect imitation of Roosevelt. They had prepared two recordings of Guggenheim doing her Roosevelt impression.

"Everybody be quiet. Now, Speed. I want you to shut your eyes and relax. Take a deep breath. Do you remember what that mean Mr. Roosevelt said to you?" Hoover's eyes filled with tears. "Remember this?"

Out of view of the camera, Peggy dropped the needle on the record and Roosevelt's malevolent voice filled the room: "Hoover, I'm sending you to the Pacific to get killed by the Japs." Hoover went into a spasm like the frogs he had stuck needles into in psych lab. Sweat poured down his face, and a new stain spread from his crotch to his belt. MAD-1 got back to work mopping up the piss and wiping the Director's brow.

"Jeez, MAD-1," Rebay scolded him. "Nice if you used different towels for the piss and the sweat."

"Sorry. Didn't think. Won't happen again," as he wiped his own brow with the towel. "Oh, no! Now I got his piss all over *my* face."

Peggy dropped the needle on her second recording. "Aw, I was just kidding," Roosevelt's voice continued, but this time in a kindly, fatherly tone. "You're my good boy. I just wanted to see how brave you are. And you're very brave. I'm not going to send you to the Pacific to get killed by the Japs. You can stay in Washington helping to save the country from spies, gangsters and the boogey man."

"What a relief," Hoover whispered. "And what about Clyde? Is he still going to be sent to the Pacific to get killed by the Japs?"

"No, Eddy," Peggy ad-libbed. She was getting good at her Roosevelt impression and was on a roll. "Clyde will be right behind you. Or whatever position you'd like him in." (She couldn't help herself sometimes.)

Hoover exhaled. "What a bad dream," he said. "I dreamed I was a Red rat and told the Boy Scouts not to believe in God, or to eat their oatmeal. But it was just a dream. A terrible dream. Untie me, boys, we gotta whole lotta spy-chasing to do."

The assistant directors all tossed their fedoras in the air and did their Secret Agent Victory Dance, forming a circle, linking pinkies and fluttering their left fingers behind their heads.

Peggy and Rebay slapped fives. "Well done, Girlfriend," Peggy told Rebay. "Now let's get back to work on the 'Case of the Red Pigeon.'"

* * *

Rebay and Guggenheim had assembled the Poontang Patrol in their Los Alamos headquarters suite when there was a knock on the door. "It's me. Lemme in."

She looked at Guggenheim and shrugged. "Who is me?"

"You don't recognize my voice? Remember bedbugs?"

"X-9!" Rebay yelled, happily. "You're here? Come on in," and she opened the door. There was Secret Agent X-9 in full Secret Agent disguise. Tan trench coat belted at the waist, sunglasses, and a fedora pulled down over his brow. He stuck out his pinkie and wiggled his left fingers behind his head. "Howdy, Gals."

"This is so great," Rebay said. "We missed you. When I think of the three of us pummeling that poor blind senator, I gotta laugh."

"That was funny," Guggenheim agreed. "What's that about bedbugs?"

"Oh, an inside joke from our undercover work on 'The Case of the Nazi Rally.'"

"Take off your coat and stay awhile," Peggy told him.

"What're we drinking?" X-9 asked.

"Gin. Help yourself," Rebay told him. "What're you doing here?"

"Actually, trying to stay clear of the Director. He's been acting dangerous lately. He was yelling at me and the other secret agents: 'If I'm going to the Pacific to get killed by the Japs, I'm takin' all of ya with me.' Thought it was a good time to get out of town. He's already taken away my job heading up the Post Toasties® Junior G-Man Patrol and he's put William Z. Foster, the top Commie, in charge. You heard about Speed turning into a Red?"

"It's been taken care of. He's himself again. All Roosevelt's fault. When the President ordered Speed to the Pacific to get killed by the Japs, it shook him up a little. I straightened it all out. Me and MAD-1."

"You didn't have to use them silver needles on his brain, did you? I've seen some Red spies after MAD-1 operated on them, and they were vegetables. But *loyal* vegetables."

"Nope. Everything's hunky-dory. But why didn't you let us know you were here?"

"Well, you know I'm the most famous Secret Agent in the Bureau," he said modestly, "except maybe for you two. And it would have gotten the Reds suspicious if someone as big-time as me showed up. So, I stayed undercover. But I was killing some time listening to a bug I planted in Mrs. Oppenheimer's room, and you're in deep shit. I figured I better lend you a hand to hold her off. She's planning an attack. Says she needs to take back something you stole from her."

"Guess we will need your help. What're ya packing?"

X-9 showed them his two shoulder holsters and twin ankle holsters. All empty. Strapped to his back was a holster for a submachine gun. Also, empty. "They searched me before they let me onto the base. Sorry."

"That's bad," Rebay told him. "Lemme introduce you to my working girls."

"You must be Agent Knockers," X-9 interrupted her. "Your reputation has gotten around. And you're easy to recognize 'cause your rack lives up to its rep."

"Thanks," Agent Knockers said, and she smiled. "And these are Secret Agents Brandi, Sherry, and Bliss. All unarmed. They wouldn't let us onto the base with weapons, either. But we do have our S&M whips," and she brandished hers, then used it to flick a fly off the windowsill. "Lemme know if you're interested."

"And whatta *they* got?" he asked.

"Just take a look." Rebay led him to the window. Down below they could see and hear Mrs. Oppenheimer haranguing her Red Brigade of scientists, shaking her fist at the Secret Agents' window, dropping F-bombs, S-bombs, in fact the entire alphabet of four-letter-word bombs. She was whipping her gang of Red traitors into a rage.

"They don't seem to have any weapons," X-9 reported. Just then a Jeep pulled up, and the driver began passing out pitchforks. "Ph.D.s with pitchforks," Rebay said. "And torches. This looks bad. I better let Washington know what's going down." She picked up the phone, listened a second, and then turned to her little band of heroes. "Well, we're on our own, guys. The line's been cut."

CHAPTER 7

Speed was trying to undo or at least blame someone else for what he and Comrade Foster had done to the religious faith of American youth. The worst of it was that not only had America's kids stopped believing in God, but some of their parents had stopped their free-will offerings at church. ("What the fuck," one widely quoted parishioner had told his pastor. "If God® doesn't exist, why the hell should I give him any money. God® played me for a sucker."). And so priests, ministers, rabbis, swamis, the whole tribe of godly charlatans — suffering from nightmares of having to trade in their Caddies for Fords — were clamoring to see the FBI's proof that God® didn't exist so that they could refute it or at least burn the evidence. Worse, they were demanding that the FBI prove that God DID exist.

Even FDR was hounding him. "Edgar, they say there are no atheists in foxholes, so if American boys don't believe in God®, who am I going to be able to send to the Pacific to get killed by the Japs. The Attorney General says it's the law that there can't be any atheists in foxholes. You have to believe in God® to be dumb enough to climb into a foxhole to get killed by the Japs. Am I gonna have to surrender to the Japs *and* to that Hitler fella who's running Russia?"

"That's Germany, Mr. President. Here's the trick. GH= Germany Hitler; RS=Russia Stalin. I learned that from my Agent Gals."

"Oh, that's good. Thanks for straightening me out. I always get those assholes mixed up. But get on it. I want proof that God® exists on my desk by Sunday. If it's not there, I'll be god-damned if I'm going to put a nickel in the basket at church for a God® who doesn't exist."

* * *

"If you don't have proof that God® exists on my desk by Saturday," Hoover screamed at MAD-1, "I'm sending *you* to the Pacific to get killed by the Japs."

MAD-1 raced back to his lab. He was plenty worried. Sooner or later someone actually was going to be sent to the Pacific to get killed by the Japs, and he didn't want it to be him. But as for proving that God® existed, that had him stumped. So, he did what he had gotten into the habit of doing whenever he had a problem that was just plain too much for "this old flatfoot." He put in a call to Secret Agents Rebay and Guggenheim.

And got no answer. Not even a ring tone. He tried General Groves. Same thing. Nothing. By now he was worried.

Number One: He needed the G-gals to show him how to prove that God® existed. Number Two: Something was very wrong out at Los Alamos. He knew that the Reds had discovered we were building a superweapon at Los Alamos. And they would stop at nothing to find out how to build one for themselves. Could they have taken over the whole place?

There was no time to go through channels. He called up the Special Agent in Charge in Santa Fe and told him to get up to

Los Alamos for a look-see.

An hour later he got a call back from the SAC. "Madman, you're not gonna believe what's going on up there. There's gotta be a hundred crazy Reds running around with pitchforks and torches and singing Commie songs. And they've surrounded the building where the Secret Agent Gals have their hideout. I dunno how long those poor ladies can hold out unless we get them reinforcements."

"Any troops available at the army post in Albuquerque?"

"No, they've all been sent to the Pacific to get killed by the Japs."

"So, it's hopeless?"

"I've got an idea. It's just so crazy it might work," the SAC told the Madman.

"I'll try anything."

"There's an Indian named Geronimo down at Taos. He's been boning a Secret Agent named Bambi, one of Rebay's and Guggenheim's hookers. Maybe I can persuade him to round up some of the Taos Indians and head up to Los Alamos to rescue Bambi. Shall I try it?"

"Yes! Great idea! Hurry up."

A few minutes later the Santa Fe Special Agent in Charge was shouting up at Geronimo's adobe hovel, "Geronimo, Bambi's in trouble."

A bleary-eyed Geronimo appeared at the window. "It wasn't me. I always yanked it out in time."

"Not that kind of trouble. A gang of crazy Reds have got her surrounded. They're gonna kill her. Or worse."

Geronimo let out a wild war-whoop of rage. "Those Red animals. Death before dishonor for Bambi. No. Not what I meant. Dishonor is OK. But not death. *We gotta save her!*" He raced around the Taos Indian village yelling, "Saddle up boys! Cavalry to the rescue." Then he stopped. *This could be confusing to my fellow redskins*, he thought. *The bad guys here are called Reds. But we're the red-SKINS. And now we're playing the role of the cavalry. We're homogenizing and blending and mixing up and, even worse, we're culturally appropriating.* He started doing a little war dance in a circle while he tried to figure things out. *This was exactly the time he could have used that anthropologist from Staten Island who'd been nosing round, to help him make sense of these cultural complexities.*

"Come on, Geronimo!" the SAC yelled. "We ain't got much time."

Finally, Geronimo came to a decision. "I hate stereotypes as much as the next woke Indian," he yelled, "but they are useful in a melee to let ya know what side you're on. The Reds wear red bandannas. You don't happen to have any *blue* neckerchiefs we could put on, do ya?"

"No, but I got a box of Junior G-Man Badges® I was passing out at a Cub Scout® rally. Why don't you pin them onto your serapes?" He handed Geronimo a nifty tin badge.

"Perfect! I've always wanted one of these," the grateful Indian said as he pinned the Junior G-Man Badge® on his government-issued Indian blanket. He held them up for his warriors to admire. "Look at these new trinkets the Great White Father is handing out." The Indians lined up to get their handouts. "Now let's rescue that beautiful poontang."

* * *

When Geronimo and his posse reached Los Alamos, the Reds were piling kindling and lumber around the Secret Agents' hideout. "Throw down those A-bomb secrets, or I torch the place," Ma Oppenheimer shrieked, brandishing the aforementioned torch.

"We don't have 'em anymore," Secret Agent Rebay yelled, holding her crossed fingers behind her back so she wouldn't go to hell for fibbing, "The Pigeon stole 'em back from us. Get 'em from him." She winked at her pals, who realized how cleverly she had set up the transfer of the bogus plans back to the Reds if they ever made it out of this trap alive.

Just then Geronimo's Indians on horseback galloped onto the street and formed a line trapping the cowardly Communists between the Indians and the firewood. As the Communists quaked with fear, the Indians pulled their bows from their saddle holsters, and notched their arrows.

Watching from above, Rebay and Guggenheim and the girls, plus X-9, let out cheers of encouragement. Rebay, drawing on her German Catholic training, silently mouthed a prayer to Saint Sebastian, patron saint of death by archery. Secret Slut Sherri remembered a cheer from her high school cheerleading days: "Rah, Rah, Ree, shoot 'em in the knee, Rah Rah, Rass, shoot 'em in the other knee."

Then Guggenheim shook her head. "Uh-oh. Look again."

"At what?"

"The arrows." Rebay looked again. Instead of sharp arrow heads, the arrows were tipped with suction cups. "What the fuck? Is this a joke?"

Bambi explained. "Indians are only allowed to use sharp arrows when they're on the reservation. That was the deal with the Great White Father, and if they violate the treaty, their supply of blankets is cut off. Off the reservation, Geronimo told me, no sharp arrows, so they came up with these suction cups. But these aren't just any ol' suction cups. These are Heap Big Medicine Type Suction Cups®, and if they hit a varmint in the head — man or beast — they suck out his brains."

"Great," Guggenheim yelled. "Let's see the color of these brainwashed Reds' brains."

"No can do," Rebay said, shouting out to Geronimo: "Hold your fire!" She explained to Guggenheim, "We need those

Reds' brains to finish up the bomb. *Afterwards* we can suck out their brains. But not yet. Tell Geronimo not to kill 'em," she told Bambi. "Just round 'em up."

"Hey there, Gerry!" Bambi yelled to Geronimo, rather seductively, in her best 'come hither' voice.

"Hey, baby. You OK?" Geronimo called.

"I'm fine now, you big hunk! You're my hero! But don't suck their brains out. Use your lassos and take them to the corral." The Indians quickly went into rodeo mode, lassoing the hapless Reds, hog-tying them, and dragging them to the corral, depositing them in a traitorous heap, where they spat out threats of what they would do to the lumpen-tribal-tariot "come the Revolution."

Secret Agents Rebay, Guggenheim, X-9 and the Poontang Patrol headed to the corral, where Geronimo gestured to Bambi to join him under his G.I. blanket for a "secret powwow."

"Listen up, Red rats," Guggenheim shouted. "Ya got two choices. Either you finish up work on the bomb, and no more spilling the secrets to Stalin, or," she paused dramatically, "you get sent to the Pacific to get killed by the Japs."

"Don't give in," they heard Mrs. Oppenheimer shriek. "They're bluffing."

"Oh yeah," X-9 told them. He walked over to the stack of socialists and dragged The Pigeon out of the pile. "Groves," he shouted in a command voice that petrified the General, who no longer had a clue about what was going on, "Put this traitor on a military plane to the Pacific to get killed by the Japs."

Groves came running up and threw The Pigeon into a Jeep while Mother Oppenheimer screamed at him, "Pigeon, where'd ya hide those plans?"

"I'll drive him to the airport myself and personally send him to the Pacific to get killed by the Japs," and Groves roared off in a cloud of dust, while The Pigeon screamed back at Ma Oppenheimer something like, "They're in the mail!"

Rebay and Guggenheim gave the Secret Agent Howdeedo to X-9. They loved the cloud of dust bit. "Make sure we get the cloud of dust into our report back to HQ." But Rebay was wondering what the fuck The Pigeon meant by "They're in the mail."

"We still got the plans, don't we?" she whispered to X-9, who had been given the job of hiding them.

"They're in a VERY secure place," he said with a laugh, like he was enjoying a private joke.

Meanwhile the Reds were losing confidence that the Revolution would come soon enough to save them from being sent to the Pacific to be killed by the Japs. They showed signs of wanting to surrender and accept the Secret Agent Gals' conditions.

"They mean business, Mrs. Oppenheimer," one of the Red cowards whined. "I don't wanna get killed by the Japs. I just wanna build bombs and help people."

Seeing she had a mutiny on her hands, Mrs. Oppenheimer called to the secret agents: "OK. What're your terms?"

"Get back to work, but no after-dinner dessert for any of you unless you get A's on the civics tests. And for tomorrow's geography quiz, you better know the capital of North Dakota."

* * *

Secret Agent MAD-1 couldn't sleep. He was developing a stutter. Cold sweats. All he could think about was what was gonna happen to him if he couldn't prove God® existed: Three words boomed in the echo chambers of his crazed mind. "Pacific." "Killed." "Japs." He was waking up in the middle of the night sobbing, "Mommy." No way for an Assistant Director of the FBI to behave. Once the phone lines to Los Alamos had been repaired, he had asked Rebay and Guggenheim what he should do.

He was to follow standard Bureau Secret Agent Procedures to the letter and round up the OBSUS (Obvious Suspects).

In this case, the G-Gals told him, they were the deans of the divinity schools at Harvard, Yale, Princeton, Catholic University, Jewish Theological Seminary, Namaste University, and the Davy Crockett Four-Square Hard-On Baptist God® School. "Lean on them," the girls told him, "hard."

So the Madman informed the nation's leading experts on God® that they were chosen by J. Edgar Hoover, who was practically God®, to prove that God® existed, and to do it in a goddamned hurry. Then he strapped them to gurneys in the deepest crypt of his dungeons, applied sensory deprivation, electric shocks, toenail extraction, and Sunday school film clips of the devil and hell. The next step would be to execute every fourth theologian, to encourage the rest to think faster. He'd gladly execute them all if it would keep Hoover from sending him to the Pacific to get killed by the Japs.

So far, they had come up with nothing but drivel. And they were getting paid big bucks and driving fancy cars telling people to believe in a God® they couldn't prove existed! Even when they were put to the Questions they came up with nothing. MAD-1 loved what the Romans called torture: Putting the Question to the ratbastards. Well, he was goddamn going to put the Question to these pious frauds until they spit out proof that God® existed. Speaking of God®, he wished he could strap the Pope into one of his machines and put the Question to him, good and hard. This was all enough to make him lose his faith. Wait, he already *had* lost his faith.

He had a sudden fit of rage and raced down to his dungeon. He unstrapped the OBSUS from Notre Dame and led him to the blackboard. "You wanna get sent to the Pacific to get killed by the Japs?"

"No! Send someone else!"

"Then put something on the board that will get the Director and the President off my ass."

The Fighting Irishman grabbed the chalk and quickly drew eleven Xs on the board, with eleven Os opposite them. "This guy over here," pointing to an O a little behind the others, "starts counting, hup-one, hup-two, and on hup-three, these four guys, here," he pointed at the four Os lined up behind the other seven, "they shift to the right, like this," and he drew arrows from each over to the right. "And on hup-four *this* guy," he underlined one of the front seven, hikes the ball, but not to *this* guy, but instead to this other guy. Really fucks up the Xs. Now *this* guy stunts over to the right and takes out *this* guy, while *this* guy goes tear-ass down the field, then hooks toward the goal, and *this* guy with the ball either follows his blockers like *this*," and he drew arrows for the ball carrier and the Os in front of him "or he chucks the ball down to this other guy standing all alone in the end zone. Touchdown."

He turned triumphantly to MAD-1. "Can I go home now? We gotta play the Carlisle Indians tomorrow. We can't do that if I'm in the Pacific getting killed by the Japs."

"And that proves that God® exists?"

"Goddamn right. Just ask Michigan what happened to them last week."

"Are you really a theologian?"

"No. I'm Knute Rockne. The football coach."

"Gee. My kid's a big fan. Can I have your autograph? But how come they sent you here? I asked for the guy who can prove God® exists."

"As far as those priests are concerned, I prove he exists every Saturday."

"OK. You can go. Any hints on how I should bet tomorrow?"

"Take the over. Bet the farm."

* * *

"Listen up, the rest of you goddamn frauds: Unless you come up with something better than that, you know what's going to happen to you. Let's start with you, Rufus," and he pointed to the OBSUS theologian from the Davy Crockett God® School.

"I hope this will help. We been kinda shorthanded at Davy Crockett since Uncle Sam's been sending most of the faculty to the Pacific to get killed by the Japs, so I been teaching my own courses on Heaven, Hell, and the Whore of Babylon — that's the Pope. But they've had me handling the advanced math courses too, including algebraic symbolic logic. There's this guy at Princeton, Kurt Gödel, best buds with Einstein, you heard of him? Either of them?" The Madman shook his head. "Geesh, they ever let you out of this place?" MAD-1 shook his head again. "Anyway there are some smart guys who say Kurt has come up with a solid math proof for the existence of God®."

"Hot dog," MAD-1 yelled, and shouted to his two assistants, Secret Agents Igor and Renfield: "Get up to Princeton and bring this guy down here, in chains if necessary. But don't rough him up too bad, and make sure you don't hit him inna head. He's got a lot of 'splainin' to do. Take a break, guys!" he yelled to the captive theologians.

"Can't we have some food?" the Yale OBSUS begged, a fat slob who hadn't missed a meal in his life.

"Hah! If we can't get that proof from this Gödel guy, maybe the Japs will feed you some Chop Suey and Egg Fu Yung."

"I think you may be confusing the Japanese and the Chinese in terms of cuisine," the Harvard know-it-all suggested.

MAD-1 yanked out his pistol and fired a warning shot that took off John Harvard's right ear. "Keep a civil tongue in your head, Matey."

***

The next morning MAD-1 had a terrified Kurt Gödel in front of the blackboard. "OK spill, you rat, or it's to the Pacific to get killed by the Japs." Gödel began scratching away at the blackboard like the Coney Island fortune-telling chicken on speed. He finished and turned to the Madman. "Here it is. No need for any more rough stuff." Renfield and Igor had beaten him black and blue wherever it wouldn't show.

Ax. 1. $(P(\varphi) \wedge \Box \forall x(\varphi(x) \Rightarrow \psi(x))) \Rightarrow P(\psi)$

Ax. 2. $P(\neg\varphi) \Leftrightarrow \neg P(\varphi)$

Th. 1. $P(\varphi) \Rightarrow \Diamond \exists x \, \varphi(x)$

Df. 1. $G(x) \Leftrightarrow \forall\varphi(P(\varphi) \Rightarrow \varphi(x))$

Ax. 3. $P(G)$

Th. 2. $\Diamond \exists x \, G(x)$

Df. 2. $\varphi \text{ ess } x \Leftrightarrow \varphi(x) \wedge \forall\psi \, (\psi(x) \Rightarrow \Box \forall y(\varphi(y) \Rightarrow \psi(y)))$

Ax. 4. $P(\varphi) \Rightarrow \Box \, P(\varphi)$

Th. 3. $G(x) \Rightarrow G \text{ ess } x$

Df. 3. $E(x) \Leftrightarrow \forall\varphi(\varphi \text{ ess } x \Rightarrow \Box \exists y \, \varphi(y))$

Ax. 5. $P(E)$

Th. 4. $\Box \exists x \, G(x)$

The madman glared at him, and the terrified genius stammered, "Let me explain:"

Definition 1: x is God®-like if and only if x has as essential properties those and only those properties which are positive.

Definition 2: A is an essence of x if and only if for every property B, x has B necessarily if and only if A entails B.

Definition 3: x necessarily exists if and only if every essence of x is necessarily exemplified.

Axiom 1: If a property is positive, then its negation is

not positive.

Axiom 2: Any property entailed by—i.e., strictly implied by—a positive property is positive.

Axiom 3: The property of being God®-like is positive.

Axiom 4: If a property is positive, then it is necessarily positive.

Axiom 5: Necessary existence is positive.

Axiom 6: For any property P, if P is positive, then being necessarily P is positive.

Theorem 1: If a property is positive, then it is consistent, i.e., possibly exemplified.

Corollary 1: The property of being God®-like is consistent.

Theorem 2: If something is God®-like, then the property of being God®-like is an essence of that thing.

Theorem 3: Necessarily, the property of being God®-like is exemplified.

Gödel turned to the mad scientist, who was really mad now. "Like it?" he smiled, showing a missing front tooth.

"That's it?" MAD-1 screamed.

"Why? See any holes in that, you dumb cop? Einstein loved it."

"I'll kick your asshole right into your teeth, you phony bastard. I can't go to the Director with that. He never learned the times table past two," and he heaved a chair at Gödel's head, who deftly parried it and fired his chalk at MAD-1, hitting him in the eye.

"Oh, tough guy?" the Madman yelled, yanking out his gun.

Just then the phone rang, and Secret Agent Igor answered. "Don't kill him, Boss. The pressure's off. Congress just passed a law saying there *can* be atheists in foxholes. We don't care anymore if they believe in God® or not; everyone can get sent to the Pacific to get killed by the Japs."

* * *

Meanwhile, Guggenheim and Rebay were working on their lesson plan for the next day's civics class. X-9 was getting ready for what he called a friendly debriefing of the whores. "It's a morale thing. I'm not to be disturbed," he had told them, with a wink.

"You dog," Rebay said, dismissing him with a friendly pat on the ass, giving him the Secret Agents' Howdeedo. "Cheer them up."

Just then General Groves ran into the room. "He got away."

Rebay and Guggenheim were aghast (vocabulary builder time, kids, that means sorta shocked). "What happened?" This changed everything.

"I was halfway to the airport, with The Pigeon hog-tied in the back. I saw a lady on the road with a disabled car. I recognized her. It's that artist from Abiquiu, Georgia O'Keeffe, the one who paints those stupid cattle skull pictures the dudes in New York pay a fortune for. While I was asking if I could help, somehow or other The Pigeon untied himself and went scampering off into the desert. I tried to run after him, but with this gimpy leg — by the way that's why I haven't been sent to the Pacific to get killed by the Japs — I lost him."

"Ya think he might have been in cahoots with this . . . 'artist?'"

"I'd hate to think so, although she is a mite too friendly

with the Injuns than is proper for a respectable white woman."

Rebay scowled. "I think we just might make a call on this artist gal. She's not one of my abstractionists, and she's not one of Peggy's surrealists. She just might be one o' them Rockwell types. She *can't* be trusted."

* * *

Guggenheim knocked on the gate of an adobe house compound that had a sign, "Famous New York Painter. Visiting Hours 10-2 or by appointment. If ya ain't got cash, go away. Critics Will Be Shot."

"Who is it?" a female voice from within called out.

"Open up! FBI."

There was a shotgun blast from a second-story window that carried over their heads. The Secret Agents hit the dirt. "The next one will do damage. Now get lost."

Rebay looked at Guggenheim: "Secret Plan 11."

Guggenheim crawled back to their car, pulled out a milk bottle filled with gas, stuffed a rag into it, shook it a few times, lit it, and lobbed it over the gate. Flash! Bang! Shower of glass fragments! "Next one will be right into a window! Burn you alive and all your lousy ultra-realistic paintings."

"On second thought, let's be friends," the sometimes violent lady inside suggested. "How about some scones and tea?"

"Let's burn her out, Peggy. Who's she think she is, offering us that crap? This bitch is no good," Rebay shook her fist at the hidden hostess who had just made a fatal hospitality *faux pas*. "Scones and tea, my ass, lady. You're going down."

"I've got gin. And ice. And Frito® Pies."

"That's different. . . . Now yer talkin'. When you open the door, I wanna see gin and ice in one hand and Frito® Pies in the other. You only got two arms, right?"

"Wait a minute."

The Secret Agents heard clinking of ice and the mouth-watering sound of CheeseWhiz® being squirted into Frito® bags. The door opened. The secret agents had two pistols each aimed at her head. "Now back up slowly," Rebay ordered. "Let's set up on the veranda."

O'Keeffe set the drinks and grub down on a table and gestured the Secret Agents toward the chairs. "You could sit on the hammock. Or the tire swing."

"Mighty neighborly of you, ma'am," Guggenheim said. "Let's forget that we got off to a little bit of a bad start. We gotta few questions."

"I expect it's about that nice General Groves and his prisoner. I hope he isn't in too much trouble."

"Orders are being drawn up right now to send him to the Pacific to get killed by the Japs."

"Oh dear. Lemme tell you what happened. The General isn't to blame for anything. I was driving along looking for a skull to paint when — bang! — a tire blew. I got out and there were nails all over the road. I smelled a rat. But maybe it was a possum. Not a skunk, though. Ya know when ya run over one of those. And then I remembered the Nancy Drew mystery, *The Case of the Flat Tire?*"

The Secret Agents nodded. It was one of their favorites.

"Same M.O. (and that means *Modus Operandi* in Latin, kids). Tacks on the road. Remember in the book it was a bunch of Communist spies who pulled that dirty trick?"

They nodded again.

"And by the side of the road were a bunch of guys on horses. And they had on RED bandannas. Possible clue that they are Commie ratbastards. 'Course I didn't think anything of it except that the fuckin' flat tire was eating into my painting time, and I got suckers in New York just lined up waiting for that cow-skulls-in-the-desert crap I been turning out like a freakin' painting machine.

"Then along comes that nice General Groves who stopped and asked if he could help, like a real pardner, Western style. He got out and started to jack up the car, when we heard his prisoner scamper toward the cowboys. The General took off in hot pursuit as fast he could manage on his gimpy leg."

"He didn't say anything about cowboys," Rebay objected.

"Why, the poor boy is practically blind. That's another reason he hasn't been sent to the Pacific yet to be killed by the Japs. Besides his gimpy leg. And get this: Can you guess what the cowboys, who I guess were really a gang of dangerous Reds, left behind?"

The Secret Agents shook their heads.

"It was a *book*. That help?"

They started to shake their heads again, when it hit both of them at the same time. The Reds had been copying their plan from the Gals' favorite Nancy Drew, that same *Case of the Flat Tire!*

O'Keeffe nodded. "So that's how they came up with their clever plan. They can't even come up with their own evil conspiracies. Just what you'd expect from the new, brainwashed Soviet man, who's had all impulses of individual thinking and entrepreneurship erased by state propaganda, socialist realist painting, and socialized medicine."

"So, I guess Grove's in the clear," Guggenheim said, holding up her glass and rattling the ice. "Don't suppose you've got any more gin? And if you've got any paintings that aren't of dead cows, how's 'bout giving us a peek? Rebay, here, has a gallery in the Big Apple. And I'm thinking of opening one, too."

"What?" Rebay yelled, whipping out her sidearm and aiming it at Secret Agent 241.

"Just kidding," Guggenheim said. "And point that somewhere else."

* * *

"So, you've got a gallery?" O'Keeffe asked Rebay.

"Sure do. You musta heard of it. The Museum of Non-Objective Art. On East 54ᵗʰ."

"When did you start it?"

"1939. It's a collaboration between me and her uncle," pointing to Peggy, "Solomon Guggenheim. I'm the curator."

"You've got me confused. How come *you* hooked up with him and not *her*?"

"The old Curatorial Couch," Peggy smirked. "It would have been incest for me, doin' it with my uncle. I'm a curator too, but without a place to curate right now. But maybe soon . . . "

Rebay glared at her.

"Looks like you don't like each other."

"Depends on the weather," Peggy laughed. "She's got her likes and dislikes, and so do I. She's got good taste, but kinda narrow. Me? I like everything. Except dead cows."

"How about you, uh, what should I call you?" she asked Rebay.

"You can call me Hilla. Actually, I bought one of those watercolors you sent Stieglitz from Texas in 1916. It's in my museum."

"Nothing since?"

"Uh-uh."

"How about you? You ever buy my stuff?" she asked Guggenheim.

"Nope."

"How come?"

"Well, your work nowadays just doesn't do it for me. It sucks," Peggy said. Hilla nodded.

"The hell you say! I'm the most famous artist in America.

Wanna see my bank account? *Time Magazine* says I am 'American painting's great hope.'"

"Great hype, you mean," Peggy laughed. "Or great dope."

"Why you . . . gimme back that gin," making a lunge for the bottle Peggy was holding.

"Uh-uh," Peggy said, snatching the bottle away. O'Keeffe bull-rushed Guggenheim, who deftly evaded the charge of American painting's great hope (or hype) and pinned her arm in a half-nelson. "You've just assaulted a Federal officer, lady. You know the penalty for that? The hot seat."

"Aw, come on. I was just kidding around."

"Or maybe we draft you into the WAVES as a nurse and send *you* to the Pacific to get killed by the Japs."

"Let me make it up to you. I'll fix you a cocktail. Leggo my arm. You're hurting me. That's my painting arm. It's insured for a million bucks!"

The two Secret Agents looked at each other and nodded. Guggenheim let the Collector of Cattle Carrion go. "Now we're talkin'. What kind of cocktails?"

"Ever had a Corpse Reviver Number Two? Sort of a segue from my paintings of defunct moo cows."

"Sounds interesting," Rebay answered. "What's in it? You ain't gonna poison us, or nothin' like that, are you, just because we don't like your work?"

"Nah. Just watch. Lots of people smarter than you don't like my work. Ever heard of Albert Einstein? He sent me back the painting I did of the cow jumping over the moon. Figured he'd love that allusion to the universe, and to e=mc2. It was a friggin' GIFT! And he made me pay return postage!"

"He's generally considered a smart guy," Rebay pointed out.

O'Keeffe scowled and filled a pitcher with ice, then dumped in gin, lemon juice, Cocchi Americano, absinthe, and a few splashes of orange bitters. The two Secret Agents were drooling. Then the Belladonna of Bovine Bone Boondoggles wet the rims of three lowball glasses, rubbed them in granulated sugar, and poured them all drinks.

"*Prost*," Rebay said, watching O'Keeffe closely as they clinked glasses, looking for any signs that the Countess of Cattle Corpses would reflexively respond with a "*Heil Hitler*." O'Keeffe passed the test, and the two Secret Agents relaxed.

"So that's your secret technique for trapping Nazi spies? Speaking German to 'em to trick 'em into speaking Kraut? *Prost* my foot. Pretty pathetic, if ya ask me," O'Keeffe jeered.

Rebay sipped the Corpse Reviver. "Hey, this is good!" Then she knocked down the rest in one gulp. "*Einmal*."

O'Keeffe looked at her blankly. "Means 'another' in Kraut talk," Peggy told her. "You passed another test."

"So you want another?"

"Me too," Secret Agent Peggy added.

They each swallowed their second Corpse Reviver, and the Cow Pelvis Painter mixed up another batch.

After their third Revivers, the Secret Agents and the Sketcher of Skeletons were lounging on the floor. "You got a helluva nice bod on you for an old dame. Whaddya, fifty?" Peggy asked.

"Pretty close. Wanna see the dirty pictures Stieglitz took of me?"

"Sure."

O'Keeffe brought out a Whitman Sampler® box filled with photos. "Lookit this one," passing Guggenheim a midsection shot that left nothing to the imagination. "Gosh," Peggy said. "I've never seen anything like this. Your, uh, girl parts look a lot like the centers of flowers. Hard to tell the difference, actually. But aren't you a little embarrassed to show this stuff off?"

"Nah. When I get a cowboy here who's a little dense about

what he's supposed to do, I show him this and it gets him off the pot. Anyway, Stieglitz took these, so they're *art*. Among photography specialists, this is technically known as a 'split beaver.'"

"Art, huh? I guess that's to fool the vice squad. But I think they'd figure out that it's a picture of yer . . . oh, never mind. You know, once you loosen up and aren't packing, you're not so bad. But for your own good, give up the bones and go back to that great stuff you did when you were a kid. Or do some flowers that look like this photo. I'd put *that* in my museum," Rebay told her.

"Me too," Peggy said.

Rebay pulled out her gun.

"Just kidding," Peggy said hurriedly.

* * *

Rebay and Guggenheim borrowed horses from O'Keeffe and had her lead them to the spot where The Pigeon had been rescued. They found the place where the Red rescuers had waited. Piles of road apples were a dead giveaway. The trail was easy to follow. The Bolsheviks, brazenly ignoring the laws of God® and man against littering, had left candy wrappers, cigarette butts, and used condoms in their wake. The rubbers indicted that there must have been at least one Commie cowgirl in the rescue party, the gal detectives deduced. Although on second thought, the Gals recalled recent research that suggested that cowboys were not exactly the 'straight' shooters of horse opera legend.

The traitors had taken a beeline toward the Taos ski area, its white slopes beckoning in the distance, and so Rebay began entertaining an increasingly irritated Peggy with stories of searching for fresh tracks at Chamonix with her pals Herbert von Karajan, Princess Juliana of Holland, and James Laughlin, the founder of New Directions Press, who also, she informed Peggy, had started the Alta Ski Resort®.

Peggy told Rebay she wished someone would invent a portable music player so counterspies did not have to listen to *boring* stories about *boring* people nobody cared about, but could divert themselves listening to Ferde Groefe's "Grand Canyon Suite" or Gilbert and Sullivan's "A Wandering Minstrel, I," which the sleuths began to sing as a two-part round while they clip-clopped toward the snow. Before long O'Keeffe left them in order to gather up some cow skulls she spotted alongside the trail.

The secret agents asked the Taos ski-lift attendant if he remembered a dozen horsemen wearing red bandannas coming by earlier in the day. He reckoned he had, and he showed them the literature the Reds had pressed on him, including Joseph Stalin's *History of the Communist Party of the Soviet Union*. He told them that so far he had read how the owners of the ski area had been alienating his labor by paying him a pittance while they made a "whole shitload" of dough for themselves. To teach him to stop mouthing Bolshie Bullshit, Peggy located a bar of brown soap and washed his mouth out. She told him there'd be more where that came from if he didn't watch his step. Then she made him recite the Pledge of Allegiance, hand over heart.

They learned from the chastened proto- or maybe quasi- (I get them mixed up) Communist that their elusive Pigeon had taken the chairlift. "Shouldn't be too hard to track him down. Except for him you're the only folks who've been here all day, and it ain't snowed. He'll leave fresh tracks." He fitted the girls with ski boots and skis. Peggy made him bend over so she could give him a kick in the ass to remember what she had told him about being a loyal American, and then the Secret Agents got on the chair for a ride to the top.

"How we gonna get him back when we kill him?" Peggy asked Secret Agent Rebay. Speed liked to see proof when his agents bagged a Public Enemy.

"Been thinking about that," Rebay said." Seems to me if

we bring back the head and the skin, it ought to satisfy the bean-counters back at headquarters. And I got my Swiss Army Knife®."

"Good thinking. Could I borrow the toothpick? I got some of Georgia's Frito® Pie caught in my teeth."

"There's Getaway Charley's tracks," Rebay whispered to Secret Agent Peggy as they unloaded from the lift at the top. "And lookit that," pointing to a wisp of smoke. "The idiot is making it easy for us."

"Plan 19?" Guggenheim asked Rebay. She nodded. "And would you mind giving me back my toothpick?"

"Hold on a minute. I still got a piece of the cellophane in my fangs." She fished around in her mouth. "There, that got it. Here."

"Weapons check." The G-Girls unholstered their .45s. The original issue lightweight LadySmiths they had replaced long ago as lacking the power to stop a crazed, charging Communist in his tracks. "Loaded. Let's go." Plan 19 was their favorite. They had used it so many times they knew it backwards and forwards. "Just for fun," Rebay said, "Let's do ol' 19 backwards."

"Great idea! Gonna be fun!" Guggenheim replied.

They caught a glimpse of the cabin through the trees, smoke rising from the chimney. Rebay silently circled the cabin so she could crouch by the door. She gave Guggenheim the thumbs-up sign. Secret Agent Peggy began weeping and wailing: "My boots are too tight. My feet are cold. My boyfriend has ditched me. Can anybody help me? Anybody home? Boo-hoo." *Truly heart rending, if I say so myself,* Guggenheim thought. *Now we just have to wait for the gallant desperado to rush out to rescue the frostbitten female before she freezes to death.*

"Well done, Girls. Backwards Plan 19, I believe." The voice came from high up in a tree behind them. "I suggest you holster those guns before someone, and I mean you, not me, gets hurt."

"I guess this is the end of the line, ol' Pard," Rebay said to Peggy. "You sure got the drop on us, you fuckin' Commie."

"Sticks and stones," he laughed. "I hope one of you has a jackknife so I can just bring the heads and skins back to Comrade Stalin."

"How'd you get behind us without leaving tracks?"

"Plan 19, Option 2."

"Hey, how come you know all that Secret Agent shit?" Rebay wanted to know. "Did Speed spill the beans to you when he was a Red?"

"Nothing like that. Turn around real slow."

They followed orders. "Now look up."

Perched on a tree limb was a familiar figure: The Pigeon. Giving them the Secret Agent Howdeedo!

The G-Girls returned the secret signal. "*You're* a Secret Agent, too?" Hilla said. "How come nobody told us?"

The Pigeon jumped down and walked over to them, showing them his Secret Decoder Ring®. "Because I'm not just a Secret Agent, I'm a *Super*-Secret Agent, the Secretest Agent in the Bureau."

"Gosh," the two girls exclaimed.

"And you really fucked things up when you snatched the package I dropped at the Paseo de Peralta Bridge."

"Whaddya mean?" Rebay objected. "I thought we done good. Couldn't let those plans be picked up by the Reds."

"Those were the *phony* plans. The ones for the bomb that was going to blow up in Uncle Joe's face."

"Oh, no!"

"Here's what ya gotta do. Haul ass down the mountain, saddle up, get back to Los Alamos, and set it up so Ma Oppenheimer can get hold of those plans again and get them to Stalin. Got that?"

"Yeah. That's roughly Plan 37 with the Three-Card Monte

Option."

"Right."

"But what about you?"

"I can't go back. I've blown my cover. Got a new assignment: Gonna infiltrate one of the concentration camps where we've penned up the Japs from California and find out if any of them are spies."

"Objection. You don't look anything like a Jap."

"Oh yeah? Watch this." The Pigeon took out a set of false buck teeth, popped them in his mouth, and put on a pair of wire-rimmed glasses with lenses like the bottoms of Coke bottles. "Now take a rook," he said in Japanese. "Can I get away with it?"

"Amazing," Rebay said. "I'd shoot you on sight. You look like Mickey Rooney in *Breakfast at Tiffany's* — is that out yet? Well, when it comes out, you'll see what I mean."

"OK, Girls. Get back to Los Alamos and clean up your mess. Here's how. Take the plans and put them in this." He handed them a large manila envelope. "I've got it all addressed and she knows my Pigeon scrawl." He had written on it:

To: Master Atomic Spy and Top Red Traitor at Los Alamos, Comrade Oppenheimer.

From: Your Pal, The Pigeon

Contents: The Secret Plans for the A-Bomb I Stole Back from the Secret Agent Gals.

Warning to the Secret Agent Gals and Speed: DON'T FUCK WITH THE PIGEON!!

* * *

"Ya still got that package of A-Bomb plans?" Rebay asked X-9.

"Yup. Right under my dirty underwear. Them Reds gonna hafta want them real bad to go digging in there."

"Well, fish 'em out. This is a real clusterfuck. That's the phony baloney plan that's gonna blow up in Uncle Joe's face. We gotta give it back to the Reds."

"How 'bout you gals get it for yourselves. Real rank in there."

Rebay and Guggenheim conferred. On the one hand, it was their fuckup that made it necessary to root through X-9's dirty underpants for the package. On the other hand, they were ladies, and it didn't seem quite *comme il faut* for the big jerk to make them poke around in that odious Stash of Stink. On the third hand, he was a big coward and was likely to start bawling his head off that they were being mean if they made him do it. On the fourth hand . . . "Oh, I don't care how many hands we go through, in the end we're going to have to do it," Rebay said. "Question is, which one of us?"

"I think it should be you," Guggenheim said. "I'm richer than you so I been brought up not to have to do nasty shit like this."

"Good point. But I got a title, and I don't think that in the nobility stud book it says anything about having to root through some asshole's dirty boxers."

"Got an idea," Guggenheim whispered. "Let's let Little Lord Fauntleroy over there choose. That way we'll have a better idea of how each of us stands with the jerk."

"Good thinking," Rebay said. "Hey X-9. Which one of us you think should be the one to stick her fingers in your Dirty Drawer of Doom?"

X-9 had to think fast. If he chose one of them, that one would probably figure he liked the other one better. That might be fatal if they were in a drawdown with gangsters or Reds and he had to count on her to cover his back. Kind of a lose-lose proposition. On the other hand, he sure didn't want to dig into that Stable of Stench himself. So, "I got it. You'll play rock, paper, scissors.

I'll be the judge."

"Rock, paper, scissors?" Rebay wanted to know. "Is this some kind of American game like Spin the Bottle or Pin the Tail on the Ass? No fair. How 'bout a good German game like Pass the Hot *Kartoffel*?"

"Got another idea," X-9 said. "Blind Man's Bluff. I blindfold the two of ya, then you move around the room until one of ya grabs the other one, and that one wins. The other one has to root through the Boxers of Bliss."

Both girls snorted. "All that does is give you a chance to feel us up while we can't see you coming. You think we'll fall for that stupid trick?"

X-9 blushed. These girls were really sharp. "You gals gotta better idea?"

"Yeah," Rebay said. "I'll do it. But you get the yucky end of the stick next time," she told Guggenheim.

"That's my girl," Guggenheim said. "Let's get you ready." She and X-9 ran to gather the equipment specified by the *Secret Agents' Handbook* as protocol for this extraction.

When they returned, Guggenheim took a clothespin and attached it to Rebay's nose, then fitted her with a gas mask and helped her into a hazmat suit. Peggy clamped a clothespin on her own nose, and gave X-9 one. Rebay gave a thumbs-up sign. Then Guggenheim put asbestos gloves on Rebay's hands and handed her a ten-foot pole with a cat's paw at the end. She and X-9 backed into the farthest corner of the room.

Rebay moved slowly towards X-9's bureau, then grasped the drawer handle with the cat's paw and slowly pulled it open. A wave of nauseating fumes staggered Guggenheim and X-9 despite the clothespins on their noses. Poking through X-9's dirty underpants, Rebay felt the package with the ten-foot pole and grasped it with the cat's paw. Moving ultra-carefully, she extracted it from the drawer and dropped it into a metal bucket that Guggenheim had placed next to the bureau after filling it with moth balls, "I Pine Fir Yew" and "Balsam"® air fresheners, and a rag soaked in Clorox®. She picked up the top of the bucket and pressed it down until the can was sealed and then closed the drawer.

She turned around. Guggenheim and X-9 had passed out and were sprawled on the floor. She dropped the ten-foot pole, opened the windows wide, picked up a pair of hair dryers, and pointed them toward the windows, creating a draft. This was the critical moment. She had to revive her pals. She took off her gloves and felt a sting as the acrid air breezed by her exposed skin. Then she pulled off the gas mask, and her eyes filled with tears, and she was momentarily blinded. She climbed out of the hazmat suit. Finally, she pulled the clothespin off her nose. And then, like them, she collapsed. The fumes were still overpowering. She struggled to her feet and groped her way to the unconscious Secret Agents. She slapped them until they groaned and opened their eyes. "Got it." The two supine Secret Agents feebly gave the Secret Agent Howdeedo.

"You're a hero," Guggenheim whispered.

"*Goddamn* right," X-9 agreed. "You're a better man than I am."

"By the living God® that made ya," Guggenheim told Rebay, "you da man."

"Now we just gotta get to a mailbox with this shit," Rebay said, "which is what it smells like," holding the plans an arm's length away from her nose, "and send it to Ma Oppenheimer so she can pass them to Comrade Stalin."

CHAPTER 8

"Great work, gals," Hoover greeted his two Secret Agent gals.

"What 'bout me?" X-9 complained.

"You too."

X-9 grinned contentedly and rested his head on Hoover's shoulder, purring. "That's my good boy," the Director told him as he stroked his head.

The Gals had just gotten word that Ma Oppenheimer had received The Pigeon's "Stalin's Surprise" package in the mail and had passed it on to "Baby Pigeon," The Pigeon's successor as the courier for the red ratbastard traitor spies.

History had repeated itself! The Poontang Patrol, on high alert to identify the "new" Pigeon, had been offering "freebies" to all OBSUSs (Obvious Suspects, remember?) Once again it was Super Slut Bliss who uncovered The New Pigeon, just as she had tricked the Los Alamos barber into giving himself away as a Commie ratbastard traitor when he joined Bliss in a chorus of "Joe Hill" at the climax of their "special moment." To a trained spy-catching whore like Bliss, the Redrat might as well have been carrying a black bomb with a fuse sticking out of it or a badge reading "I'm a Spy." And in fact, when Knockers picked the lock on his lunchroom cubby, there *had been* a bomb with a fuse sticking out of it and an Order of Lenin badge, that said, you guessed it, "I'm a Spy."

This New Pigeon, a perfect embodiment of the "New Soviet Man," lounging in the social safety net of cradle-to-grave socialism, had been robbed by the welfare system of the independent "grab the cash" ethic, the "try something new" spirit, the "yer tomorrow is gonna be nothing like yer yesterday" entrepreneurial spirit of your red-white-and-blue-blooded Wolves of Wall Street, Main Street, or "The Street Where You Live," who are always on the lookout for a profitable scam to foist a new and improved version of breakfast cereal or canned soup on a gullible public. Instead of thinking for himself like a patriotic American spy, The New Pigeon had simply copied the "old" Pigeon's M.O. (Remember your little Latin lesson a little while back, kids? That still means *modus operandi*, and do I have to tell you again how important it is to take high school Latin at least from Caesar to Virgil?) Pigeon Version Two took the "Surprise" envelope to Santa Fe, bought himself a Frito® Pie at the Woolworth's®, left a trail of yellow Velveeta® down the River Trail for Super Slut Bliss to follow, and stashed "the goods" under the Paseo de Peralta Bridge. In due course, under the watchful eye of the Poontang Patrol, Harry Gold himself, the courier for the Rosenberg Spy Ring, picked it up, and a day later it was in a diplomatic pouch to Moscow.

When it arrived, Stalin threw a "We Got the Bomb" bash for his evil henchmen and then executed them all as they picked up their goodie bags of atomic bomb noisemakers and E=MC2 coloring books for their kids. He executed the kids too, along with their moms and household pets. "No people, no problems," Stalin liked to say. And he said it a lot, along with that one about breaking eggs to make an omelet, just about every day, and several times on May Day when the world's workers, ungrateful wretches every one of them, held protest parades yelling shit at the job-creating capitalists who, instead of spending their hard-earned dividends on polo ponies and debutante balls for their beautiful sweet-smelling daughters, built factories for the lower orders where they improved their health through useful work and earned money for booze, dope, and guns, and with their excess profits the factory owners endowed modern prisons where the law-breaking elements could be tossed, and the law-abiding elements could get jobs as guards. A win-win all around.

And if it weren't for the cops (the only thing standing between us and the fucking mobs; remember that, kids), who gun down the Commie rats with their Red flags and armbands (That's the Red rats, not the cops with the flags and armbands. The cops are the ones with guns. Don't get confused) before they can get out of hand, we might have some real situations on our hands.

Where was I? Oh, yeah.

Now Speed had a new case for the Gals.

"That Sonuvabitch in the White House has dropped a little bit of a 'bomb' on us, to stay with the 'bomb' theme of our last case. He's been running his own kinda private secret intelligence service in competition with us, has his own spies, completely illegal as far as I can tell — the big phony oughtta be impeached — but never mind. The thing is that he wants the two of you" — pointing to the babes — "and X-9, you can tag along to make sure they don't get in trouble, to brief this totally bogus spy guy of his about the fourth-dimension. I don't know what the fuck that's all about. Do any of you?"

X-9 shook his head and said, "Sounds like a crock to me, Chief."

The G-Girls disagreed. "We know all about it, Speed," Guggenheim told him.

"Yeah. My gallery is filled with paintings of the fourth dimension," Rebay said. "Very important. We gotta find out why Uncle Joe's interested in that stuff. Could be the big break we've been looking for."

"I feel the same way, Chief," X-9 corrected himself. "I was just seeing if the babes knew anything about it. And I tricked them into spilling their guts. Pretty slick, huh? Fourth-dimension? Oh, yeah. I know all about it. Very important. I'm on the case. And by the way, isn't it 'Uncle Adolf' if she means the guy running Russia?"

"I think you got Secret Agent Know-It-All that time, X-9," Hoover told him. "When'd ya get so smart?" giving him a G-Man hug.

"Here's what I know about the guy. Name is Lanny Budd. He's Presidential Agent 103. Can you beat that? That Sonuvabitch has *at least* 103 Presidential Agents working for him. The money he's paying them should go to us." Hoover began sputtering incoherently and ripping out his hair. Clyde gave him a glass of water to calm him down, and when that didn't work, he pulled out his gun and shot a bullet past the Director's head. The Director pulled out his gun and went into the classic G-Man crouch. "Where are they? Was that a Red or a Public Enemy. Or a New Dealer?"

"That was just me, Boss. You were going off your rocker and I had to snap you out of it."

"OK. Thanks. But maybe next time don't aim so close. Lookit this." He went to a mirror. "I got a scratch on my cheek. And powder burns. Let's see how you like it," and he let loose a shot that nicked Clyde's ear. "Now we're even."

"Chief! I love it! Yer using your gun again. And for you, that was a good shot. Back to yer old self," Clyde yelled, and gave Speed a G-Man hug.

"OK, back to business. What makes this tricky," and Public Hero Number One dropped his voice down to a whisper, "is that I've got reports that this Budd guy is a *socialite*."

Rebay and Guggenheim looked puzzled.

"Did you hear what I just said? He's a *socialite*!" Speed repeated.

"Whaddya talking about, Speed?" Rebay asked. "Peggy and me, we're socialites, too."

"*Christ on a crutch!* We got socialite Secret Agents?" Hoover hollered. He pulled out his gun again. "Clyde, get their weapons. Confiscate their Decoder Rings®. We gotta take them to the basement for MAD-1 to kill. We can't let word of this get out. It could destroy the Bureau. Get all of us sent to the Pacific to get killed by the Japs."

"Come on, Chief, what's wrong with being a socialite? The President's a socialite, too," Guggenheim protested.

"What's wrong?! A socialite is practically a Communist! They want to take away rich people's stuff and kill them. We gotta kill them first."

"I think you've made a very common mistake," Rebay said. "Mind if I go to the blackboard?"

She picked up a piece of chalk and a pointer. "Now watch this." In block letters she wrote S-O-C-I-A-L-I-T-E and then underneath it, S-O-C-I-A-L-I-S-T.

"Following me so far?"

Hoover and Clyde nodded. This time it was X-9 who asked her to go a little slower.

"You will notice that the first seven letters of each word are the same. That's what got you confused." She pointed to the letter T in 'socialite.' "Now if you change that to an S and the E to a T, you get *socialist*. Really close. But completely different." Hoover and Clyde were concentrating so hard that Clyde started crying. Hoover gave him a pat on the back. "That's all right, Slugger."

"Now get this. This is the good part. A socialite is a rich

person, like Peggy and me. And like this Presidential Agent 103, I guess. We're the good guys. It's the *socialist*," she said, pointing to the second word, "who is the bad guy." Speaking very slowly, to make sure that even X-9, who was scratching his head with the barrel of his pistol, could follow, "The socialists want to take the socialites' stuff and kill them. So Peggy and me: We're socialites, and we're OK."

Hoover stared hard at the blackboard. "So, we don't have to take you to the basement and kill you?"

"Nope."

"Well that's a relief. I kinda like the two of you."

"Careful, Boss," X-9 warned him. "Don't wanna get too close to the help. Might have to kill 'em someday. These two are pretty tricky. Lemme work 'em over to see if they're telling the truth."

"Whaddya think, Clyde?" Speed asked his Number Two.

Clyde was still staring at the blackboard, completely befuddled. He went to the blackboard and started drawing dotted lines connecting the letters on the top word with the letters below it. "Are you sure these words aren't the same thing?" he asked Rebay.

"Can't you see? The last two letters are different. That makes them different words."

"Oh, yeah. I'm starting to get it. Sure. It's like she said, Chief. They're two different words. Gotta dictionary?" Rebay flipped a pocket Webster's to him, and he quickly leafed through it, locating 'socialist' and 'socialite.' "It's like she said, Boss, social-ites are OK. It's the *socialists* we gotta kill. But that Sonuvabitch in the White House is both."

"So, it's OK to give the gals back their guns and rings?" Hoover asked Clyde.

"It's OK."

"You're taking a big chance, Chief," X-9 complained.

Rebay and Guggenheim retrieved their guns and rings. Guggenheim fired a warning shot through X-9's snap brim fedora. "We're pals again?" she asked him.

"Pals," he said. "Bunkies," he added, wondering if he could patch the hole with some *Black Jack®* licorice flavored chewing gum.

* * *

The Baroness was in her museum office on East 54th Street when a tall, elegant figure dressed in a green cloth cape and a plaid deerstalker cap, smoking a meerschaum pipe walked in.

"How'd you know I'd be here?" she asked. "I'm usually out chasing spies and Reds and Public Enemies. I just drop in when I'm in town and I got some gallery business. By the way, love the spats. Don't see them much anymore."

"I knew you'd come in because your secretary told you a letter had arrived from the Federal Bureau of Psychoceramics Inspection. It said they were sending an inspector today. The letter was to get you to come to your office. I sent the letter, and I'm the 'inspector.' It was a ruse," he said proudly. "Not bad, huh?"

"Kinda thing a secret agent would do," Rebay said warily. "But I studied ancient Greek in high school (*See why you should study the classics, kids?*) and I know 'psychoceramics' means 'crackpots,' so I knew there was something fishy about you," as she gave him the Secret Agent Howdeedo.

"What in the world are you doing? Have you lost your mind?" the stranger asked.

"Just a nervous tic. Who *are* you?" she asked, drawing her gun and placing it on her desk in easy reach. Clearly this guy was a phony! And dangerous. Kill him now or later?

"That thing loaded?"

"To quote my Boss, the second greatest man who ever

lived, 'A gun ain't much use if it ain't loaded,'" and she demonstrated by flipping a half dollar in the air and blasting away, sending it flying across the room. "Mind fetching that for me?"

He handed the coin to her, which she examined judiciously. "A little off-center. I'm outta practice."

The stranger took a quarter out of his pocket, flipped it in the air, and shot three times, each shot sending it flying up in the air again. "First shot was dead center," he told her as he passed it to her. "The others were on the sides to make it spin."

Rebay pulled a nickel out of her purse, threw it in the air and shot. The coin fell to the floor, neatly sliced in half with an edge shot.

Her guest pulled out a dime and prepared to fling it up like the rest. "Stop. Hold your fire before I need a new ceiling," she told him. "Let's stipulate that if any bad guys throw money at us, they're in mucho trouble."

He grinned. "I'm P.A. 103, that is *Presidential Agent 103*, Lanny Budd; you can call me Lanny. And you're Secret Agent TNA, otherwise known as Secret Agent Baroness Rebay. I've heard all about ya."

"How 'bout calling me Hilla? What's on yer mind?"

"Fourth dimension."

"Fourth dimension? What do *you* know about the fourth dimension?"

"Practically or really absolutely nothing. But I know you know all about it. *That's* what I know. And I need to know more because I gotta secret plan, the 'Fourth Dimension Secret Plan.'"

"Ain't no such thing," Rebay said, after leafing through the *Secret Agent Handbook*®.

"Maybe not in the *Secret Agent Handbook*®, but we got one in the *Presidential Agent Handbook*®."

"You got your own *Handbook*? What about a Decoder Ring®?"

Lanny pulled back his cuff: "Secret Decoder Cufflinks®."

"What about *girl* Presidential Agents? Whatta they got?"

"Secret Decoder Earrings®."

"Nice! And do you have a presidential agent howdeedo?"

He took out a No. 6 Faber® pencil with an eraser, balanced it on his nose, and whistled 'I wanna a girl just like the girl that married dear ol' dad.'

"I like that," Hilla told him. "Just the right touch of corny, goofy, and weird. Now whaddya wanna know about the fourth dimension?"

"Well, before Pearl Harbor, I got to be best pals with one Adi Hitler," he said modestly.

"You're shittin' me. The Hitler who's running Russia?"

Lanny's jaw dropped. "Just kidding," Rebay said. "Kind of a private FBI joke. If I told you what it was, we'd both be in the Pacific being killed by the Japs."

"You had me guessing. When I was pals with Adi, it turned out that he was a believer in astrology. Yeah. Big time. I was able to tap into his astrologers, so now Churchill has astrologers modeling Adi's charts, so he can predict what *der Führer* is planning. We wanna do the same thing with Stalin."

"Does he actually believe in that shit?"

"We don't know. But, or I should say BUT, something about his private painting collection got us wondering."

"*His* collection?" Secret Agent Rebay scoffed. "Heroic tractor drivers. Ladies torturing counterrevolutionaries. Did you know he asked that Sonuvabitch in the White . . . I mean the President, to lend him Norman Rockwell to do the propaganda posters for his latest five-year plan?"

"I know all about that. Those were tough negotiations. Lemme show you the transcript":

FDR: OK, we give you Rockwell. I want that
      figure skater you let Harry Hopkins sleep

with on his mission to Moscow.

JS (Joe Stalin): Too late. I just shot her.

FDR: How about Ivan Magic Fingerski, the Commissar of the Keyboard. Love his version of 'Give Me Stout-hearted Men.'

JS: I wish I had known. I personally put a bullet in the back of his head this morning. Little political disagreement.

FDR: Cheesh. You murder everyone who disagrees with you?

JS: Sure. No people, no problems. Like you done with that Garner fella you fired as Vice President.

FDR: Waddya mean? He's still alive, far as I know.

JS: Big mistake. Guy like that could be a problem. Want me to have Bill Foster finish him off fer ya?

FDR: Lemme think about it. Who can you send me for Rockwell? Anybody still alive over there?

JS: Not too many. I even killed my own wife when she asked me to dry the dishes.

FDR: You did? Killed your wife? And got away with it? Hmmm. Gives me an idea.

JS: How about this? My secret police found that there was a philatelist here in Moscow, and 'philatelist' sounded like he was either a right-wing deviationist or part of a religious cult. (Did I tell you that our scientists have proved that God® doesn't exist, so you ought to get rid of that 'In God® We Trust' on your money.) Anyway I killed him, and it turned out he had a great collection of stamps. You like stamps, right? This guy had every Russian stamp back to the Tsars and get this, I can throw in a page of FDR stamps, that's you, and a page of Eleanor stamps. You know who she is."

FDR: Joe, a philatelist isn't, oh, what's it matter, he's dead. It's a deal. But you can keep the Eleanor stamps. Hate to have my girlfriends staring at those while I'm trying to get them into the mood, if you know what I mean. Haw-haw.

JS: Haw-haw.

Rebay was amazed. "That's amazing. You got the Oval Office bugged?"

"Better than that," he whispered as he leaned over confidentially, and close enough for her to get a whiff of his *Royal Lyme®* aftershave. "I've got a mic and transmitter in his cigarette holder. As far as Rockwell is concerned, he's already been stuffed into a steamer trunk with a Moscow label, so we can look forward to *The Four Communist Freedoms* before Christmas."

Rebay guffawed. "*Freedom One: The Right to a Bullet in the Back of Yer Head.*"

Budd liked Hilla's style. "*Freedom Two: The Right to a Ten-To-A-One-Room-Unheated-Hovel.*"

Hilla kept it going. "*Freedom Three: The Right to One Meal a Day, Every Day — Cabbage.*"

"And last but not least, *Freedom Four: The Right to an All-Expense Paid One-Way Ticket to Siberia.*"

They slapped fives. "So, if Stalin likes that Rockwell shit," Rebay asked, "what's this about the fourth-dimension?"

"He's rounded up all the Dalis and Maleviches in Russia."

"Sure. To burn them. Just like Hitler. 'Degenerate art.' I know his game."

"Nope. That's the funny part. He has them in a private gallery. Just for him. No one else can see them. Something weird going on. I want you to tell me what you think that could mean. He just sent a Malevich and a Dali to Bill Foster. We think they might have secret messages to the Red ratbastards in this country. And who knows what kind of goddamn shit those rotten traitor ratbastards would be up to if they knew what Joe wanted them to do."

"What do you want *me* to do?"

"You *and* me, we're going to break into Foster's stately Fifth Avenue mansion and take a look."

Secret Agent Rebay gave the Secret Agent Howdeedo. Lanny responded with the Presidential Agent Howdeedo, and Rebay joined him in whistling "I wanna gal."

"We're gonna make Secret Agent history," Rebay told him. "007, eat yer heart out."

"Who's he?"

"Still in the fourth dimension," she explained.

* * *

"It's a worldwide phenomenon," Rebay told Secret Agent Guggenheim. "I just heard about it from Secret Agent Knockers."

"What's that mean?"

"Well, 'worldwide' means happening everywhere on Earth. 'Phenomenon' means a fact or situation that is observed to happen. From the Greek φαινόμενον, meaning to appear. In other words . . ."

"For Christ's sake, Hilla. I know what *worldwide phenomenon* means. Although I *am* interested in the Greek roots of words. Did you know I flunked introductory Greek, intermediate

Greek, and advanced Greek at some of the best finishing schools in the U.S. and Switzerland? Pretty well-rounded education, don'cha think?"

"Very impressive," Rebay said. "But we're in a hurry. Do you wanna know what this whatever-ya-want-to-call-it is?"

The Secret Agents were relaxing in Solomon Guggenheim's suite in the Plaza Hotel, which Peggy's uncle had lent them while he was away at his ranch in North Carolina. They had worked their way through a half-gallon of gin and were morosely contemplating having to wrangle another bottle from room service.

"Okay, spill," Guggenheim said. "I know you're dying to tell me, whatever it is. Do you think we could use some more lemons? What did you like better, the *fois gras* or the caviar? I hope Uncle Solly doesn't look at our chits too closely. But he usually does. It'll be another boring lecture from Uncle."

"What were we talking about?"

"You said Knockers said there was a worldwide phenomenon. And I said, 'Whaddya mean?'"

"Okay, Rebay said. "We're on the same page. That's all Knockers said."

"Let's call her up."

"Great idea. Who are we calling up?"

"Knockers, remember?"

"I don't remember anymore whether I'm you or you're me. Musta been a bad bottle of Beefeaters®. OK, I'm on it, call Knockers," Rebay said, slurring her words. "First let's get room service to send up some more vitamins." She dialed. "Listen, I need a gallon of gin, a quart of Cocchi Americano, a bottle of absinthe, and a bottle of lemon juice. Got any smoked salmon? Good. And all the trimmings." She hung up.

"Cocchi Americano? What's that for?"

"It's for that little drink Georgia O'Keeffe showed us,"

Rebay told her. "Remember Corpse Reviver Number Two? X-9 knows all about it. Did you know he went undercover as a bartender?"

"Boy of many talents."

"Poured drinks for the Purple Gang in Detroit. Their killers liked to have a round of Corpse Revivers after a hit. Great sense of humor, those thugs."

"I get it. They kill a guy and then drink a Corpse Reviver. Why Number Two?"

"He says Number One doesn't taste so good," Rebay explained, then . . . "I was gonna do something. What was it? Oh, yeah, call up Knockers."

She dialed. "Knockers, sweetie, how are ya?"

"Hey," she shouted to Guggenheim. "Knockers says I sound funny. Wants to know if I been drinking. Have I been drinking?"

She looked at Guggenheim, who nodded.

"Just a little medicine for a cold," Rebay told Knockers and winked at Guggenheim. "What's this about a worldwide phenomenon? Did you know *phenomenon* comes from the Greek? What, you don't care? Don'cha think a Secret Agent should know things? Things and stuff? No, I am not drunk. Hey Guggenheim, Knockers thinks I'm drunk. Am I drunk?"

Peggy took the phone, "Just a teeny bit," and gave the phone back.

"OK, guilty. Just a teeny bit. Fight a cold, feed a fever. Or is it the other way around? But what was this worldwide whatchamacallit?" — Pause — "No. That's amazing. You sure? All of 'em. And you seen the picture? Hope Super-Secret Agent Pigeon hears about this. It was mostly his plan. It's a big win for our side."

Just then Presidential Agent 103 walked in, X-9 right behind him. "Hey, how'd you get a key?" Guggenheim wanted to know.

"Reception desk guy is another Presidential Agent," PA 103 told them. "We go way back. What're ya drinkin'?"

Room service came in behind them. X-9 gave the bottles a professional once-over. "Oh-ho. Ya got the makings for Corpse Reviver Number Two. Let the maestro get to work," as he began opening, pouring, shaking, and clinking. They all watched, hypnotized, as he expertly wet the rims of four glasses, coated them with granulated sugar, and then filled each to the brim. "Here we go, patriots, sleuths, lock-pickers, nose-pickers, assassins: whatever yer country wants ya to do, we do," and he passed around the glasses.

"Yow," Presidential Agent 103 shouted, "I pity the fool that draws on us," and he pulled his revolver and shot out one of the chandelier bulbs.

"Hey, calm down, Hoss," Peggy told him. "We're just borrowing the room, and I'll get holy hell from my uncle if we trash it."

"Sorry, Peg o' My Heart, but my buddy downstairs will make it all OK."

"Just before you G-Boys came in, I was on the phone with Secret Agent Knockers in Los Alamos. Remember her, X-9?"

"And how. She's got a set that . . . I mean, yeah, I think I remember them. I mean, HER," he told Lanny, nudging him in the ribs.

"By the way," Presidential Agent Lanny said. "Not that it matters, but I'm not a G-Boy. Technically it should be a P-Boy." They all stared at him. "OK, let's stick with G-Boy," he decided.

"Tell them what Knockers said," Guggenheim reminded Rebay, who had just closed her eyes and was starting to snore.

"Yeah, yeah, OK. God®, I could use a little nap right now. Or another Corpse Reviver Number Two."

X-9 took the hint and got busy.

"Now what did you want to know?" Rebay asked. She felt

totally disoriented. *Focus, girl, focus*, she told herself; but the only thing she could focus on was another drink, which at that moment, X-9 put in her hand. "My Lord and my God®," she told him.

"I've always thought so," he replied. "Nice if Speed could hear you say that. He's been holding up my raise. Says it's a waste of money if he's just going to send me to the Pacific to get killed by the Japs."

"So what the hell did Knockers say?" Guggenheim screamed at her.

"Jeeze, Peggy, do ya gotta be so loud? Yer gonna give me a headache. As a matter of fact, I feel one coming on. Anybody got an Alka Seltzer®?"

"Comin' right up," X-9 said, holding two tablets over her Corpse Reviver. "Drop, Drop, Fizz, Fizz, Oh Whatta Relief It Is®."

"Is THAT the jingle for Alka Seltzer? Rebay asked. "I thought it was for K-Y Gel®. You sure? Anyway, you really are a great guy. Remember the good time we had during *The Case of the Nazi Rally*? and she snuggled up to him on the sofa.

"I sure do. And the cooties."

"Mighta been chiggers," Rebay said.

"Mighta been," he agreed as the two Secret Agents closed their eyes. Secret Agent Baroness Rebay was softly snoring.

"We're not getting any more out of her tonight," Peggy told PA 103. "Why don't we go undercover?" as she pointed to the bedroom.

* * *

"I feel great," Secret Agent Rebay informed her Secret Agent gang when she came to in the morning. Her pals were already having a breakfast of Bloody Marys accompanied by more Bloody Marys and Kellogg's Raisin Bran®. "I see you've started the party. Any of that left for me?"

"Better than that," X-9 said. "Hair of the shaggy dog that bit you," handing her another Corpse Reviver (Number Two of course).

"Just what the doctor ordered," as she gulped it down. "But break out the champagne. When I tell you Knockers's news flash, you'll wanna celebrate."

X-9 pulled a Moet® from the fridge, took a saber out of the umbrella stand, and with a flourish neatly slashed off the top of the bottle with a single blow.

"Wow," Presidential Agent 103 said. "Where'd ya learn to do that?"

"The ol' maestro don't give away his secrets. Let's hear it, Baroness."

"Knockers told me that all the Reds at Los Alamos — I mean the dirty-rotten Reds, excuse me, did I say ratbastards? — have shaved off their hair, their eyebrows, and their moustaches. Beards, too. Now you can tell who's a Commie spy a mile away. Or at least a hundred yards away. Maybe a hundred feet. Depends on yer eyesight, I guess."

"Yeah, yeah, but how come," Lanny demanded. "Does this mean if X-9 and I go undercover in disguise, we gotta shave our heads? Gals say this ol' head of hair of mine is my best feature. I mean, *one* of my best features."

Secret Agent Guggenheim shook her finger at him. "Naughty, naughty."

"Ya wanna know why the Communist Party of the USA has gone skinhead? And, Knockers says, all the Reds worldwide, same thing; England, France, Italy, they've all given themselves the new international haircut. That's why it's a *worldwide* phenomenon. Knockers figured it out. She burgled Ma Oppenheimer's office — she's the top Commie traitor ratbastard in New Mexico — and she found the newest copy of the *Daily Worker*, that's where the filthy rotten Red ratbastards get their fake news. And on the front page there's a picture of Stalin reviewing the women's brigade of sanitation workers, and ya don't wanna mess with them broads — a brawny crew."

Rebay paused dramatically.

"Go on," Secret Agent Peggy begged.

"There was Uncle Joe himself. No hair. No eyebrows. And no moustache. A few strands of hair in a stupid comb over that doesn't even reach his forehead. And the top garbagemen with him on the reviewing stand? Same thing: hairless."

"I don't get it," Presidential Agent 103 Lanny Budd said, scratching *his* head with the barrel of *his* revolver, which was what X-9 was doing. With *his* revolver. (In other words, in case that was a little confusing, each of them was scratching his *own* head with his *own* revolver. Clear now?)

"Careful with those things," Rebay told them.

"I get it!" Guggenheim yelled. "Plan 37 with the Three-Card-Conte Option worked! That is so cool."

"Plan 37 with the Three-Card-Monte Option?" X-9 was wracking his brain. "That's the one where you palm off a phony bomb plan on a dirty rat, and it blows up in his face. And burns off all his hair. Talk about a long shot. That makes Stalin look stupider than that Sonuvabitch in the White House, I mean the President, wudda been if he had fallen on his ass in Madison Square Garden because I sawed through his crutches."

"I *knew* you were the one that didn't saw through his crutches," Agent Rebay said.

"Yeah, I was supposed to, but remember, that was when Speed was pretending to be a Red. Actually, Speed *was* a Red. And the plan was for Speed and Clyde to foil my plan to sabotage his crutches, which was just a ploy to stop that Sonuvabitch from sending them to the Pacific to get killed . . . actually, the Gals lost me about halfway through when they told me the plan . . . to get killed by . . ."

"By the Japs, right?" Presidential Agent 103 helped him out. "So, all over the world, that is, 'worldwide,' everyone is yucking it up at the same phenomenon (did you know *phenomenon* comes from the . . . Oh, you did? OK.) because the world's top number one Red looks like Daddy Warbucks. With a comb over." He thought a minute. "Every Red with any self-respect, if there are any, is gonna quit the Party rather than look like a cue ball."

Then the same thought hit them all at the same time. "Does that mean we're gonna be out of work if there's no more Reds for us to catch? Fired? Sent to the Pacific to be killed by the Japs?"

Agent Rebay looked around at her little band of heroes. It was up to her to rally the demoralized troops. "We just gotta keep spying on those Red ratbastards," she told them. "Not let up. A bald Commie is just as dangerous as one with a full head of hair, like 103 here."

She looked at X-9, who was sobbing. Guggenheim was trying to comfort him. "PA 103 and I are going to burgle Bill Foster's stately Fifth Avenue mansion tonight. You two can tag along. We're going to find something there that's going to scare the crap out of the country when we leak it to Walter Winchell. And if we don't find it, we'll plant somethin'."

She stood up. She grabbed Guggenheim's and X-9's hands. Lanny grabbed their free hands and completed the circle. "One for all," she said, and they yelled back, "All for one."

"Now," Rebay said, "a group hug, and then let's get back to counterspying."

* * *

Secret Agent Rebay was calling out the checklist for Plan 10: Breaking and Entry. This was a plan they all knew by heart, since breaking and entering was as much part of the FBI routine as spit-shining shoes and beating the truth out of spies (and other assholes).

"Disguises: sunglasses," she recited.

"Check." The G-Guys and -Girls put on their shades.

"Gumshoes."

The G-Guys took off their wingtips and the Gals their spike heels, and put on crepe-soled shoes for sneaking around silently. (That's why they call them *sneakers*, kids): "Check."

"Blackface."

The Secret Agents corked up: "Check."

"Emergency equipment: cyanide capsules?"

The Agents stowed their suicide pills in their cheeks: "Check."

"Condoms."

The Agents held their rubbers up to the light and examined them for pinholes: "Check."

"Secret Decoder Rings®."

"Check."

"Guns."

The Secret Agents checked that their pistols were fully loaded and took off their safeties: "Check."

"Back-up machine gun."

X-9 cycled through the loading mechanism of his Tommy Gun: "Check."

"Hand grenades."

The Secret Agents loaded their belt pouches with grenades: "Check."

"Entry tools: battering ram."

Presidential Agent 103 and X-9 hefted the battering ram: "Check."

"Burglar's tools."

Guggenheim checked her toolbox: hammer, screwdriver set, socket wrenches, crowbar, gasoline chain saw, lock picks:

"Check."

"Lunch."

Rebay opened her wine cooler: canapes, cucumber and butter sandwiches, coconut and pineapple Jell-O®, wine.

"Hold it," Lanny shouted. "What kinda wine ya got?"

"Chateau Margaux®."

"What year?"

"1925."

"That's a good year. Should be decanted."

"OK. I'll pack a decanter."

"Seltzer?"

"Check!"

"Tablecloth? Linen. Silver? China?" PA 103 asked. "I hate eating offa plastic. And make sure the wine glasses are Riedel®. Good crystal absolutely enhances the taste and bouquet of good wine." PA 103 was in a dream world. "That wine is resonant of tobacco, licorice, and, yes, gunpowder. You're gonna love it. Better pack two bottles. And I like lemons with my seltzer."

"Good idea. Check."

"I think that's about it," Rebay said. "Oh, wait. First aid: stretcher?"

"Check."

"Defibrillator?"

"Check."

"Crutches?"

"Check."

"IV set up for serum and saline?"

"Check."

"Rape kit, in case one of them Reds rapes a G-Girl?"

"Ain't gonna happen as long as I'm around," X-9 boasted.

"Me too," PA 103 added.

"Can't be too careful. Plaster of Paris cast set, in case one of us gets a broken leg?"

"I think we should have enough for eight casts, in case all of us fall down the stairs together in the dark and break all our legs," X-9, who was prone to pratfalls, suggested.

"Good thinking: Check."

"Swiss Army Knife®, in case we have to amputate."

"Check."

"What if we get trapped in there for days and have to re-sort to cannibalism?" PA 103 wanted to know. "Maybe we'll need salt and pepper."

"Good point. Do you think we should roll dice or play cards to see who we eat first? What the hell. Deck of cards *and* a pair of dice."

Just then the phone rang.

"It's Knockers again," Rebay told her team. She listened, then hung up. "She says that all the Redrat scientists have quit work on the bomb and are working three shifts a day on hair-growth creams for Stalin."

"Can't General Groves threaten them? Maybe kill one or two to encourage the rest?" Guggenheim wanted to know.

"Nope. Remember that bald spot he was always trying to comb over? He's thrown in with the Reds. Claims if he has a full head of hair, he'll be able to go to the Pacific and get killed by the Japs."

"What about his gimpy leg? And his eyes? He can't see."

"Claims he can cheat on the medical exam if he gets his confidence back. With some new hair."

"That Agent Knockers has done some *great* spying," Re-bay went on. "Listen to what these Red rats have done. It shows what merciless thugs they are. They've taken a prisoner from the brig, burned off his hair, and then tattooed a ten-by-ten grid on his scalp. They're planning to put a different kind of snake oil in each square. They've got him chained down so he can't scratch his head. They've got almost all the squares filled. Knockers filched the key to the grids so we can follow along. She's going to use Plan 97 with the Dandruff Option to fuck up their results."

"Plan 97," Guggenheim said. "That's where we change the key, so they really don't know what the different snake oils do. Dust in their eyes. Muddy the waters. Great. That Knockers is a real self-starter. If we had a few more like her, we might win this war."

"Yeah," X-9 said. "Brains *and* boobs, big and bulbous. Wow. Mind *and* mammaries, cerebrum *and* C-Cups . . ."

"Are you through?"

"Sorry. When I think of her rack I lose my mind."

"She said the girls are all freezing, and she wants to know if we can send some sleeping bags for the Poontang Patrol."

"What's happened?" X-9 wanted to know. "Poor kid. She can have my blanket. Or we can share it."

"Yer all heart. That's not the one with cooties? Or chiggers, is it?" Rebay asked.

"I sprayed it with Flit®. It's good to go. But what happened to their blankets?"

"The scientists needed all kinds of snakes for their experiments. And where to get them?"

"Of course. Geronimo! And his gang of redskin snake hunters."

"Right. But Indians won't take Uncle Sam's greenbacks. They want blankets. So Knockers says the Reds confiscated all the blankets on the base to pay the Indians, and Geronimo keeps raising the price per snake. It's up to twenty blankets per snake, but the Reds don't care. They never took economics in high school. Not even home economics, they just read that Marx bullshit, so they don't know anything about the supply-demand-price curve and the principle of marginal utility, so the Indians have them over a barrel. Everybody's freezing out there."

"Let me guess: *Except* Ma Oppenheimer."

"Right. And it gets worse. The Indians were having trouble shooting the snakes with those suction cup arrows, so General Groves said they could use real arrows, with points. And when the Reds ran out of blankets, he let them start trading guns to the Indians. And not just pistols and carbines. Anti-tank guns. Howitzers. Bazookas. Armored personnel carriers. A prototype A-bomb. That fuckin' Groves will do anything to get rid of that bald spot so he can get to the Pacific to get killed by the Japs."

"Sounds like ol' Knockers will have everything under control with ol' Plan 97," X-9 said, "once we get her some blankets. Stalin's gonna get a big surprise when he rubs the hair-growth snake-oil onto his evil Commie skull and it takes off those last few hairs he's got, including that stupid comb over! He'll be so pissed he might just execute everyone in Russia."

"That'll be a good thing for us, right?" PA 103 wondered. "Not something that'll get us sent to the Pacific to get killed by the Japs?"

"No problem," Rebay reassured him. "Knockers had some more bad news, which is good news for us. Geronimo is using all those weapons, including his atom bombs with their mule-delivery system, to lead an Indian uprising just like the old Fort Apache days. He's teamed up with all the Plains Indians, and one by one they are capturing the Army forts which are practically unguarded because all the able-bodied soldiers are in the Pacific getting killed by the Japs. Once we get rid of the Reds we'll have plenty of work dealing with the redskins."

"Ugh," X-9 said happily, already getting into character as an Indian fighter.

* * *

The Secret Agents' expedition to William Z. Foster's stately Fifth Avenue mansion had turned into a caravan. They realized there was no way the four of them could carry all that gear from the Plaza Hotel on 59th Street and Fifth to the top Red ratbastard's stately mansion on Fifth and 89th. (*I hope this isn't too much of a spoiler, but that is exactly where that Guggenheim Museum is if you take a little stroll down Fifth these days.*) They requisitioned J. Edgar Hoover's crew of black personal servants (officially listed as agents to help them dodge the draft and not get sent to the Pacific to get killed by the Japs). They'd be the Sherpas, twelve in all: eight to carry the equipment, and four with sedan chair backpacks so the Secret Agents could break and enter in style. Rebay passed out sunglass disguises to the servants and said they could keep them.

"Oh, sure. I see. White folks don't want them shades back if us black folks have worn them, right?" Hoover's gardener complained. "Sounds like more of that institutionalized racism. Or is it structural racism? Sometimes that W. E. B. Du Bois jargon I heard when I was at Harvard confuses the hell out of me."

"I think the point is that institutional racism just means that it is part of the system," Hoover's personal chauffeur offered. "At Yale we were taught that 'structural' means that the system needs the racism in order to function."

"Yeah," Hoover's personal chef explained, "structural is part of functionalist theory. That's how we understood it at Princeton. Durkheim by way of Talcott Parsons."

"That's why Durkheim explains racism better than Max Weber, who can't seem to grasp the difference between mechanical and organic solidarity," Hoover's personal fly-swatter with a degree from Cal Tech pointed out.

"Anyway," Hoover's personal pillow-fluffer from Williams argued, "racism is the reason why us black folks have to carry these white fools around, instead of the other way around, since we are smarter and better-looking than them. And by the way, isn't it cultural appropriation for all them ofays to be wearing blackface?"

"Quit whining and sing us one o' them spirituals," X-9 demanded.

The twelve victims of institutional (or maybe structural) racism launched into a beautifully harmonized version of "Jimmy Crack Corn." They had just started the "Ole Massa's Gone Away" refrain when they arrived at the ruthless Red ratbastard's stately mansion.

"Time sho' does pass fast when we's able to sing together fo the massas, don't it?" Hoover's shoe-tier commented. He had gone to Stanford on a tennis scholarship, just like John McEnroe would, but he *did* go to class. (Unlike Johnny Mac, who claimed his deal with Stanford obligated him to win the NCAA singles championship, which he did, and nothing else.)

"This'd make a nice place for my new museum," Secret Agent Rebay told Secret Agent Guggenheim. "Too bad we'll have to knock down this stately mansion, but I guess the Reds can afford to build more stately mansions."

"Oh my soul, yes they can, if the red Rats ever manage to pull off that revolution they keep yammering about," Guggenheim agreed.

The four Secret Agents dismounted from their sedan chairs and assembled in front of the entrance to Foster's stately mansion. "We need a sign and countersign in case we can't see each other in the dark," Presidential Agent 103 told them. "How about we say, '*Ite missa est*,' and the reply is '*Deo gratias*.' The Reds won't understand it since they don't believe in God® and don't go to church." They agreed that would fool 'em. X-9 didn't understand it either. But he shrugged it off.

While X-9 and PA 103 retrieved the battering ram just in case, Guggenheim and Rebay went to work picking the front door lock, and in a few seconds had it open. "That was easy," Rebay said, "hope it wasn't a trap."

"I'm actually not certain it was even locked, but don't tell anybody."

The Sherpas began piling the burglary equipment inside the door, their grumbling getting on Lanny's nerves to the extent that he yanked out his pistol and let loose a warning shot to get them to "shut the fuck up."

"That was a bad mistake," X-9 told him. "Might bring the cops."

"Sorry," Lanny said. "I just couldn't take it anymore. The singing was bad enough."

They made it to the hallway, facing a wide expanse of marble stairs. To the right was a parlor that caught the Secret Agents' attention.

"For the love of God, look at this!" X-9 yelled. "The Reds got their own bowling alley!"

Secret Agent Guggenheim looked at the apparatus more closely. "Bowling alley *nothing*. This is a bomb-throwing range. Lookit this." She pointed at a stack of round black bombs, each the size of a grapefruit with a string fuse sticking out. "Those are distance markers just like at a driving range. The Reds throw them for practice, and then the bombs roll back for the next toss. Gotta give 'em credit. If they sold this set-up to the Bureau, we could use it to practice throwing grenades."

"Lemme try," PA 103 said, hefting a bomb and then launching it down the bomb alley. "Thirty-five feet. Lemme see you top that," he bragged to X-9.

X-9 picked up a bomb, went into a windup and chucked it down range, letting out a loud grunt.

"Haw-haw! Pretty pathetic," PA 103 jeered, "Twenty-nine feet."

"I used to put the shot back in *Deutschland*," Rebay told them. She picked up a bomb, faced away from the alley resting the bomb on her shoulder, then spun around and launched it.

"My God®, fifty-one feet." X-9 and PA 103 were astounded.

"I cudda done better but I was saving my strength in case we have to fight our way out," X-9 explained.

"Me too," PA 103 added.

"Back to work," Guggenheim said.

"OK," X-9 said, "but you're not gonna tell Speed we got beat by a girl, are ya?"

Rebay grinned and shook her head. "Would we do that to our favwit widdle spies?"

They fanned out through the house, and Rebay let out a yell from the second floor. "Got it. They're up here."

The Secret Agents raced up the stairs. There, behind a massive oak office desk with hammer-and-sickle flags on each corner was a white painting with a blue square and a red square behind it, while beside it was a photo-realistic painting of an erect penis in the grasp of a skeletal hand whose wrist bore a bracelet of interlinked crosses.

"Aha," Guggenheim said. "A Malevich and a Dali. Now we just gotta figure out what they mean."

"I'll take the Malevich," Secret Agent Baroness Rebay said, looking it over closely. "Hmmm, pretty simple, really. Comrade Joe is telling the American Reds that the Communist Party, that's the red square, is supposed to get behind the Democratic Party, that's the blue square."

"Not bad," Presidential Agent Lanny Budd interjected, "but they ain't doing that right now, and Uncle Joe likes his orders carried out *tout suite*."

"Aha, my socialite simpleton. You forget that Malevich is painting in the fourth dimension. In other words, this is supposed to happen *in the future*."

Peggy was helping X-9 set up their picnic and yelled down for Hoover's butler to get his ass upstairs to serve them. He showed up after an ungodly wait with the linen tablecloth and napkins, saying something under his breath as he spread them over the red rat's desk. "What happened to 'Service with a Smile?'" X-9 demanded. The victim of Jim Crow mumbled something else and went back down for the china and silver.

When he had finally laid out the crystal and distributed the pate and sandwiches, Hoover's gentleman's gentleman cut the lead seal on the Margaux®, deftly drew the cork, sniffed it and handed it to PA 103 for inspection. "Which of you gentlemen would care to approve of the wine? And by the way, I will take back all my grumbling if you'll let me have a little sip of this. I've had the '24 and the '26, but the '25 is legendary."

"What the hell?" Lanny said. "Slavery days are over. But mum's the word. I'd have a hard time living it down if the rest of the Presidential Agents heard I been drinkin' with the colored help." Budd took a sip, proclaimed it better than the best at the wedding feast at Cana. He motioned for the wine to be poured all around. The butler drew up a chair and poured himself a glass, filled to the brim, drawing a frown from X-9 who reached over and grabbed the bottle away from him.

"Ha-ha. Give us an inch and we'll take a mile," the rascal guffawed. "Anyway, in my fairly expert opinion, this stuff is THE shit. And you'll be glad to know I hid the second bottle from the field hands who were rummaging through your stuff looking for something to drink. But I'm afraid the cognac and the cigars are *hors de combat*. 'Muzzle not the ox' and all that."

X-9 was feeling, as he put it, tight as a drum and loose as a goose. "Whaddya say we raid this Commie rat's wine cellar on the way out," as he wolfed down the Jell-O® dessert.

The Baroness had fallen asleep, so Agent Peggy nudged her awake. "You were about to say. . ."

"About what?"

Guggenheim snapped her fingers in Hilla's face. "The Malevich. Come on, girl."

"Oh, yeah. Kazimir is painting the future, so that has to be the next election, 1944. And in the fourth dimension, those aren't squares. They're boxes. So, the Reds are not just going to support the Democrats in 1944, they're going to swallow them up. In other words, take over."

"Holy shit," PA 103 shouted. "How they gonna do that?"

"Simple. Vice President Wallace is a complete chowderhead. The Reds can play him like a Hammond organ. He gets re-elected, they do away with that Sonuvabitch in the White House, and they've got their puppet."

"'Chowderhead?' 'Puppet.' You just set a record for scrambling up metaphors," X-9 complained. "Would you care to rephrase that?"

Rebay gave him the finger.

"I gotta warn the President right now!" the Presidential Agent screamed, and raced down the stairs. "FDR's gotta dump that chump before it's too late."

"What about the Dali?" X-9 asked.

"I'll take that one," Secret Agent Guggenheim said, as Agent Rebay snatched Lanny's wine before X-9 or the butler could grab it.

"That ol' Johnson there," she said, pointing at the enormous boner, "is a symbol of s-e-x. Got that?" she said to X-9, who was gazing wistfully at the glass Rebay was draining.

"Think so."

"The wrist with the bracelet of crosses represents religion, holding back uncontrolled, unrepentant sexual madness. But the hand is a skeleton's. So, you know what that means?"

"I get sent to the Pacific to get killed by the Japs?" and X-9 started sniveling.

"No. It means that the Reds are supposed to attack religion by exposing what the priests are doing to the altar boys, so the bony hand of religion will release its hold on that there pork-chop, and a tsunami of free unrestrained sex will complete the moral disintegration of American youth. The moms of America will beg Uncle Joe to take over and straighten their kids out with a few bullets in the back of the head."

"Gosh," X-9 whispered. "We gotta save American boys from going crazy over free pussy. What're we gonna do?"

"Simple. We gotta tell these priests to keep their hands off those altar boys. Clean up their act."

X-9 looked skeptical. "I know those priests. They're plenty horny. Gonna be a hard sell."

CHAPTER 9

To get everyone in the right mood, Secret Agent Rebay had decided to hold her Indian uprising strategy powwow in the Indian Treaty Room of the Old State, Navy, and War Department Building next door to the White House. She had erected a teepee from the Smithsonian in the middle of the great hall for greater security, and the Buffalo Bill Museum in Laramie Wyoming had donated a dozen scalps from its collection, including the famous "First Scalp for Custer" that Buffalo Bill himself lifted from the Cheyenne Chief Yellow Hair he killed to revenge Custer's death in the Battle of Little Bighorn.

Guggenheim and Rebay decorated the interior of the teepee with the scalps, and the Museum of Natural History in New York had shipped over a pair of stuffed buffaloes personally slaughtered by Teddy Roosevelt. They had tossed in a stuffed gorilla and giant anaconda the Museum said were great favorites with visiting grammar school classes. Rebay figured the FBI Executives operated at about the seventh grade mental level themselves. They should react pretty much the same as the kids on class trips. The National Demographic Society had sent over an old Cavalry map of the Western Territories that showed the Indian trails Geronimo was using to attack the Army forts in the West.

To complete the *tout ensemble* she and Secret Agent Guggenheim had daubed themselves with patriotic red, white, and blue war paint, and Secret Slut Knockers was deployed to lead the executives in a traditional war dance of the ridiculous heel-and-toe variety. Secret Agent Baroness Rebay had explained to her how important it was to get the top G-Men fired up before they went on the warpath, so she had agreed to perform her dance topless. Then she led the Executive Council in a prayer chant to Thumper the Rabbit God® asking him to lead the Bureau to victory against the savages. Finally Rebay passed out Phillies Blunts® spiked with loco weed. The top G-Men were now ready for battle. They took off their pin-striped pants and put on the breechclouts Rebay had also gotten from the Smithsonian, and exchanged their wing-tips for moccasins. Some had begun tossing their snap brim fedoras in the air for target practice with bows and arrows.

At this point Lou Nichols, who had polished off three of X-9's Corpse Revivers (Number 2, of course) proposed that if "that fucking Hoover" didn't show up "pretty fucking soon," they should elect Knockers the next "fucking" FBI Director. He had his photographers taking a portrait of Knockers to be hung in every FBI Field Office, firing range, and torture chamber. He had the bare-breasted Secret Slut posing with a Tommy gun in one hand, a whip in the other, and in her third hand . . . better stop at two hands. Nichols yelled that Director Knockers would give "the fucking Bureau" what it needed, "a whole new fucking image." He proposed that Knockers and the Poontang Patrol should work the pom-poms for the Bureau team at the next Washington Civil Service League basketball game.

But Hoover finally limped in. He had pulled every string and poked into every loophole, but the only way he could stop

Roosevelt from sending him to the Pacific to be killed by the Japs was to shoot himself in the leg. Then he chased Clyde around the office and shot him in the leg too.

Secret Agent Rebay let loose a couple warning shots to get their attention. "Geronimo is right here, holed up in Fort Davy Crockett," indicating the spot with a wooden pointer. The G-Men weren't paying attention, so she ordered Super Slut Knockers to cover herself up.

"His men have taken over all the arsenals on the High Plains and down to the Mexican border. That Sonuvabitch in the White House left them all unguarded when he sent the garrisons to the Pacific to get killed by the Japs. The Indians are totally mobile; they've got everything from golf carts to heavy tanks, and of course their ponies. According to General Groves, who's thrown in with them, they've got two atomic bombs strapped to Army mules. He's been giving them advanced military training: left face, right face, close order drill, hut-two-three-four, even Queen Ann salutes. If they win this war, they'll put on a parade down Broadway that will make the West Point drill team look like a bunch of spazzes. Not that there *is* a West Point drill team anymore. They're all in—"

"Yeah, we know," the G-Men all recited together, "in the Pacific getting killed by the Japs."

The Secret Agent Baroness went on: "It's about as hopeless as anything I've ever seen. The Commie scientists have invented secret Smoke Signal Decoder Rings® so we can't figure out the Indians' secret messages, but the noble savages, though ignorant as rocks, can read ours with their stolen Secret Agent Secret Message Decoder Rings®. And the Indians are in tip top shape from performing those inane heel-and-toe dances for the tourists, while the only agents I have to fight for us are 4-Fs who were too crippled to get sent to the Pacific to get killed by the Japs. And then we got the degenerates who've been given dishonorable discharges from the Bureau for disgusting moral behavior too awful for me to mention without getting my mouth washed out with a bar of brown soap mixed with Brillo®. And the out-and-out crazies. They scare the crap out of me. Remember Renfield in *Dracula* who eats flies? We've got some of those. Bestiality? You can't believe the places some of these diabolical devils have inserted their whackadoos. And I've got to go into battle with this gang of cretins, slobs with no table manners, and guys who've never said their prayers. To sum it all up, they aren't the kinda people you'd take home to meet Mom."

"But we got a chance, ain't we, Baroness?" Hoover sobbed. "That Sonuvabitch in the White House says that unless I put down this Indian uprising, he's gonna put me in a basket and drop me out of a plane into the Pacific to get killed by the Japs. Do ya got a plan?"

Secret Agent Rebay held up her copy of the *Secret Agent Handbook®*. She opened to the back cover. There was a sealed envelope pasted to the endpaper marked, "Plan Last Chance: Open Only If the Fucking Indians Have Us by the Balls and It's Hopeless."

Rebay looked at the Director, who was quaking in his wingtips. "It's time," she said.

She opened the envelope and read the plan. She raised her eyes, her face as white as an Irishman's belly in January. "I gotta see that Sonuvabitch in the White House." She declared the meeting adjourned and the FBI Executives scampered back to the Justice Department for their free lunches of baloney and margarine sandwiches at the FBI cafeteria.

* * *

The Baroness had just picked up her free sandwich and was on her way to the White House when Secret Agent Guggenheim came running in yelling, "Real bad news." The Baroness, who was almost out the door on her way to the White House, turned back.

"I got no time for that, Peggy. I gotta save the country from the Indians."

"Hang on. This might be worse. I just heard from Secret Slut Bambi. She got word a Jap spy has been visiting the concentration camps where we got the American Japs penned up, and he's starting a *Jap* rebellion. He's taught them how to make ninja weapons out of their G.I. chopsticks, and they've started murdering the guards, who are half-dead geezers anyway, since all the able-bodied guards are in the Pacific getting killed by the Japs. So now we got the Indians *and* the Japs to deal with. Bambi thinks they might even team up into the kind of irresistible force that would be a challenge for Superman, Batman, the Green Hornet, Plastic Man—"

"I get the idea," the Baroness said. "How much time we got?"

"Not much. The Japs are going to launch their attack on August 7th and march on San Francisco and Los Angeles, which are completely unguarded since the National Guard and the cops are all in the Pacific getting killed by the Japs."

"August 7th!!? Pearl Harbor Day! One of the most sacred days in the calendar, second only to the Director's birthday. Is there no limit to the limitless, diabolical, demented, maniacal, and really unacceptable machinations of the Oriental mind?" Secret Agent Rebay was flying into a rage and before she could stop herself she began slapping the half-crippled Director around like a punching bag.

Secret Agent Guggenheim grabbed Secret Agent Rebay's arms, and X-9 tackled her, and PA 103 grabbed her tongue to keep her from swallowing it. The Madman jabbed her with a needle, and in a few moments she was herself again, able to understand the situation with the fierce focus and resolve that had turned her into a legend, the hero of tall tales around the campfires of Junior G-Men and G-Gals all over the Republic.

"Sorry, Chief, don't know what came over me," as Hoover cowered under the map table.

"Guess there are no limits," Peggy told her, "if your questions about the limits to the diabolical, etc. of the Oriental mind weren't just rhetorical." (*'Rhetorical' means a question you ask, not because you want an answer, since you already know the answer, but just to get people to agree with you. There are lots of great examples in Cicero's First Catilinarian, which you will read in third year Latin if you are smart enough to get that far. But good luck anyway, pueri puellaeque.*)

"And by the way," Guggenheim added, "Pearl Harbor Day is *December* 7th, not August 7th. Maybe yer thinking of August 17th, which is when we've got the Japanese scheduled to surrender in a couple of years? Or August 15th, the feast of the Assumption of the Blessed Virgin Mary? Unless we've decided to celebrate Pearl Harbor Day on the 7th of every month."

"Don't argue with me when I'm this angry," Rebay said, pulling out her .45 and shooting six holes in the Director's framed autographed picture of Man o' War.

Speed grabbed the perforated portrait and screamed for The Madman to see if he could repair his prized souvenir of the horse he loved above all others, but that had, unfortunately, paid only $2.15 on $2 bets.

Rebay was disgusted at how quickly Speed could forget the crisis at hand if something personal came up. "Have we got an I.D. of this yellow-skinned spawn of Satan?"

"Yeah. Bambi says he's got oversized buck teeth and steel-rim glasses with lenses so thick he can't see through them. AND she heard he has that 'left hook.'"

"Are you thinking what I'm thinking?" Peggy asked.

"Of course! Sounds an awful lot like our old pal Super-Secret Agent Pigeon. But why would he turn traitor and lead the Japs against L.A. and S.F.?"

Rebay thought hard. "Wait a minute. Just one fucking minute."

The Baroness raced down to the Bureau personnel division and brought up The Pigeon's file. "Lookit this." She slammed the file down, opened to a photocopy of The Pigeon's high school yearbook. There was his picture as a kid, WITH buck teeth and thick glasses. "He was even voted 'Most Likely to Overthrow the Government of the United States!'"

"So he was really a Jap all along," Guggenheim yelled, The Pigeon's whole unspeakably evil (but she had to admit, pretty fucking clever) plot now completely clear to the two Secret Agent Gals. "He had his teeth filed down and wore contact lenses to get into the Bureau. I wouldn't be surprised if he wasn't the guy who *planned* Pearl Harbor. Gee, I wish we had him on our side now. We could use someone a little smarter than X-9 for backup."

"That was mean!" X-9 protested. He started to cry, and The Madman handed him a Kleenex® from his Secret Agent First Aid Kit®.

Rebay was leafing through the *Secret Agent Secret Handbook®*. "I think we could use *Plan 53 with the Yellow Peril Option.*"

"Yeah. You're right. That one all depends on whether the Secret Agent whores at Los Alamos know how to sew. Lemme ask Bambi right now. And send Knockers out there to take charge. Her two special qualifications will be our two secret weapons."

Rebay finished reading *Plan 53 with the Yellow Peril Option* to Knockers. "You realize," Knockers told Rebay, "you are telling us we are going to do what we have been taught since Secret Agent Training School we must never do, fight a two front war. Now we gotta fight the Japs on the West Coast using the completely untested Plan 53 with the Yellow Peril Option, and on the High Plains we gotta go toe to toe with the entire Indian nation using the equally untried *Plan Last Chance: Open Only If the Fucking Indians Have Us by the Balls and It's Hopeless.*"

Rebay nodded grimly. "Desperate times, etc. Get out there and show us what FBI whores can do when the shit comes to shove, I mean when the push comes to piss, or whatever it is we do when the 'Something A' comes to 'Something B.' If you figure out what I'm trying to say, send me a secret message with your Secret Decoder Ring®. Now get outta here and lemme know when you got the Sluts ready to go. Me, I gotta go see that Sonuvabitch in the White House."

Japs and Indians. Japs and Indians, she pondered. *Was it possible that two cultures, so apparently different in every respect, could actually form an alliance against her and the FBI? The Japanese with their tea ceremony and flower arranging, and their high-tech weaponry that had demonstrated its mojo at Pearl Harbor; the Indians with their tom-tomming and heel-and-toe dancing and their technology that had stopped somewhat short of figuring out the wheel. But there were some similarities. The attack on Pearl Harbor and Crazy Horse's massacre of Custer at Little Bighorn were the two worst defeats in the history of the American Navy and Cavalry. And both the Japanese and the Indians liked to torture prisoners which Americans did only when absolutely necessary. But was there some other connection?*

But of course! The Baroness slapped herself on the side of her head. *The land bridge from Asia! When Alaska and Siberia were connected during the last Ice Age, the Japanese must have sent fifth column squads to infiltrate the future USA to get ready for an invincible red and yellow tidal wave of treachery and mayhem.* It almost (almost, mind you) made Rebay quake in her Manolo Blahniks. *Why hadn't she thought of this before? It would have been so easy to round up all the Indians and put them in (different) concentration camps after Pearl Harbor. Stitch in time (saves nine). Measure twice and cut once. Sin in haste and repent at leisure.*

Fuck, Fuck, Fuck. She was going to have to use Plan 53 with the Yellow Peril Option, *which was bad enough, but now she was also going to have to violate her every moral principle and unleash the dreaded* Plan Last Chance: Open Only If the Fucking Indians Have Us by the Balls and It's Hopeless.

I'm gonna go to hell for this, she thought. *Well then, I'll just have to go to hell.*

* * *

The President sank back in his chair behind the Resolute desk in the Oval Office, his head in his hands. *The American Japs rioting in their concentration camps, the Nazis marching in Europe, Commie traitors spying in Los Alamos, the other Japs sinking his ships in the Pacific, and now this: Indians! How THE HELL was he going to keep his stamp collection out of the careless hands of the enemy, whatever enemy, an enemy that didn't have the slightest idea of how to mount stamps in an album with itsy bitsy glassine hinges. An enemy that might even peel the stamps out of the album and use them to MAIL LETTERS. Why did he ever take this rotten job? And Rice Crispies® had just sent him four new first day covers and a bonus package of 1000 assorted foreign stamps. That had set him back fifty cents and ten Rice Crispies® box tops, and HE HATED RICE CRISPIES®!*

"So it's come to this?" Roosevelt asked the Baroness. "*Plan Last Chance: Open Only If the Fucking Indians Have Us by the Balls and It's Hopeless.* There's no other way? The Indians have us out-gunned and are ready to ride east? You say Chicago and New Orleans are next? And our Japs hate us. And those fucking wars in the Pacific and Europe. And now the Indians. Noth-

216   *Powers*

ing else we can do? What about using my top-secret stockpile of smallpox-infected blankets to give the Indians?"

"I thought of that, Chief. But by now the Indians have so many blankets they're selling the extras to tourists."

"Tourists? Tourists? This is no time for tourists to be buying blankets from the Indians. I want those tourists rounded up and sent to the Pacific to get killed by the Japs."

"I agree, Chief. And killing them with smallpox would be more humane. This is worse. Smallpox would only kill them. This plan will leave them alive but deprived of every trace of their humanity, their noble heritage, and their ability to stop peeing. Horrible. History will never forgive us, but I guess it's this or they steal our stamp collections and rape our broads."

The Sonuvabitch in the White House went white at the mention of his stamp collection.

Eleanor had other ideas. "Do you think they'll rape me?" she tittered.

"I don't think they'll ever get that desperate," Hilla reassured her.

Eleanor was somewhat relieved, but on second thought . . . *was there a compliment in there? Or an insult?*

"Forget about that rape nonsense, honey. But steal our stamp collections! That settles it. Lemme square this with the Pope first. I don't want that backstabbing pious pontifical phony to rat-fuck me for this."

He picked up the phone and ordered the switchboard to ring up the Vatican. "Hi, your Popiness. Yeah, they're hanging just fine. Listen, I'm in a kind of a jam here. The Indians are running amuck, and I'm gonna hafta use that *Secret Last Chance* plan I told ya about. Yeah, I know. I don't like it either. But it's balls to the wall, I got no choice, and I don't want you to fuck me over by telling my goddamn Irish and dago voters not to vote for me. Whaddya want from me? We're grownups. You give me something, I give you something. Oh? Yeah, I can do that. Onay oblem-pray, as you guys say in Latin." He hung up and turned to Rebay. "It's OK. He just wants to exempt priests from the pedophile laws. Seems harmless enough. It's not like these priests are really fooling around with kids, right?"

Rebay didn't reply. "Here's the decision paper, sir. Sign right here and I'll launch the plan."

"Good girl. By the way, how's Edgar's leg?"

* * *

In the FBI basement lab, Secret Agent MAD-1 and his assistant, Secret Agent Igor, had been working round the clock building the prototypes the Baroness needed for *Operation Last Chance*. Finally, they were ready. He requisitioned a dozen condemned prisoners from the FBI dungeon and tested his invention on the hapless guinea pigs, many of them already weak from having the Army test dangerous drugs on them. MAD-1 inspected them in their cages. "How do you feel, you wretches?" he demanded.

One of them stammered, "Real good, Boss."

"Think he's lying, Igor? Maybe he's lying to get us to call off the test."

"Only one way to find out," Igor said, picking up a blowtorch.

"Please, no, not again. I really feel good. Cross my heart and hope to die."

"He didn't say, 'Stick a needle in my eye,' Boss," Igor observed.

The terrified wretch sobbed, "Stick a needle in my eye."

"I didn't see if he had his fingers crossed, did you?" MAD-1 asked.

"It's OK, Boss," Igor said. "I had my eye on both his

hands. No crossed fingers. He's in the clear. I think he's telling the truth."

"OK. Unstrap them from the torture instruments and get Secret Agent Rebay down here."

Secret Agent Baroness Rebay got off the secret elevator to the crime lab and shook her head in admiration. "You've surpassed yourself, Madman. Never, I mean *never*, have I seen a more beautiful Secret Agent Secret Weapon than these jobs. It was worth shooting you in the leg to keep Speed from sending you and Igor to the Pacific to get killed by the Japs. By the way, how's the leg?"

"Healing a little too fast. I think you should shoot me again next week."

"My pleasure."

"Ready to go into mass production?"

"How many do you need?"

"Let's say a thousand, batches of two hundred a week, express shipped to St. Louis. That's where we're assembling our forces for the Plan."

* * *

"Just when you think nothing more can go wrong, something more goes wrong." Presidential Agent 103 was hysterical. "I been listening to that bug I put in that Sonuvabitch in the White House's cigarette holder, and you know what that crazy bastard is up to now? He's been talking to Hitler, offering to surrender.

"The way he sees it, with the Indians roaming the Plains and heading east and the Jap prisoners from the concentration camps marching on the West Coast cities, the only way he can save his stamp collection is for Hitler to send storm troopers to guard the White House from the Japs and Indians once they combine their forces. For days he's been having me search the country looking for someone to guard his stamp collection, and there's no one. They're all in the Pacific getting killed by the Japs."

As always, Secret Agent Rebay was an island of calm in a sea of panic, a pillar of strength in a swamp of fear, a rock of courage against the waves of dread, a mighty fortress of bravery against the storm clouds of cowardice. Et cetera. She pulled out the *Handbook.* "Here it is, Lanny, *Plan 389 with the Spandex®️ Option.* Tell the Sonuvabitch in the White House that he'll have his guards before the day is out. He should pull back the surrender to Hitler. He hasn't signed it yet, has he?"

"Hope not."

"Just follow the plan. I gotta head out west."

* * *

In their Los Alamos squad room, Knockers' Platoon of Prostitutes were putting on their disguises: colorful kimonos, bright obis, and black-lacquered wooded getas. First step in *Plan 53 with the Yellow Peril Option.* Knockers inspected their false buck teeth and steel-rimmed glasses. "Well, ladies, I guess it's show time." They clattered down the stairs to the last two trucks on the base, and shoved off, one detachment heading toward Los Angeles, the other to San Francisco.

Back at the White House, the President heard a clattering coming up the marble stairs to the Oval Office. The door banged open, and a brawny babe clad in a skintight Spandex®️ suit skated into the room. "Who the heck are you?" the President demanded from underneath his desk where he had taken refuge. "They call me the Alabama Jamma," the female human fortress answered, as ten more identically clad Amazons skated into the terrified President's inner sanctum.

"I mean, what are you doing here? Guards!" he shrieked.

"We are your guards, Numbnuts," the Bama Jamma told

him. "PA 103 ordered us here. We're the Brooklyn Bombers from the Metro Roller Derby League. He said something about guarding you and some stamp collection?" as she filched a cigarette from the Presidential supply.

The President crawled out from under his desk and pulled himself together, the sight of all those upstanding breasts and outstanding butts reminding him, as it usually did, that he was a man. "Yes. The stamp collection. I'd like to show it to you. It's over here," and he wheeled himself to a door and indicated to the Jamma that she should precede him. "One at a time, girls," he winked. "Not too much room in here. The rest of you make yourselves at home. There's booze on the bar. Feel free."

* * *

Across the Great Plains, the sons and daughters of the pioneers were huddled in their sod huts, terrified by the relentless tom-tom-tomming of the Indians' war drums. There were dust storms outside and frantic mobs of Okies banging on their doors, begging for water and gruel for their starving, sniveling brats.

But help was on the way. *Plan Last Chance: Open Only If the Fucking Indians Have Us by the Balls and It's Hopeless.* Enormous barges shrouded in cavalry blue tarps were making their way from St. Louis up the Missouri and fanning out along the Platte, Kansas, and Yellowstone tributaries. Finally, all was ready. Within sight of Geronimo's stronghold at Fort Davy Crockett, Secret Agent Rebay's misfits had built a ten-foot fence around an acre expanse, the gate shrouded under a blue tarp. Within it was an enormous cube twenty feet high and eighty feet around. A chill could be felt as the wind rippled past the tarp-shrouded mystery of mysteries.

"Wish me luck, boys," the Baroness Secret Agent told her army of creeps, whom she had drilled into a semblance of a well-trained force commanded by her second-in-command, Hugo the Horse Rapist. She stripped down to her bare skin, plumb nekkid except for her designer G-Gal handbag, took a cylinder-shaped object covered in a blue cloth from Hugo, kicked her heels into Ol' Paint, and broke into a gallop toward the Indian camp. Time to see if *Plan Last Chance: Open Only If the Fucking Indians Have Us by the Balls and It's Hopeless* could work.

Geronimo spotted her first. "Bare-assed white squaw headed our way. What's she want?"

Pulling up Ol' Paint a dozen feet away from the wild-eyed and painted Indians, who were loudly debating whether to kill her first and then rape her or whether it was more seemly to rape her first, "Hey guys!" she shouted.

"Just a minute, White Squaw," Geronimo requested, "We're in the middle of a big pow-wow trying to decide the age-old question of kill-you-then-rape-you or rape-then-kill. You got an opinion on that?"

"I got something even better." She kicked Ol' Paint, who whinnied and reared up on his back legs. "Look what I got," and she whipped the cover off what was... A FROSTY CAN OF BUD-WEISER®. She kicked Ol' Paint into a gallop and sped away.

The Indians broke ranks and jumped on their horses. "That can of Bud's mine," one whooped.

"Didja see how cold it looked?"

"I'm gonna drink it first; we can think about the rape-kill dilemma later."

In vain Geronimo tried to stop his Budweiser®-obsessed redskins from galloping after the Secret Agent, then decided a nice cold brew would suit him just fine, and he joined the chase.

It was working!

* * *

"Whew," the Bama Jamma said to her pals as she emerged from the Stamp Collection Sanctuary. "You ain't gonna believe what that guy's got in his pants. You're next," she said, pointing to Blocker Babs. "You're on deck," she said to Pivot Penny.

* * *

Hugo the Horse Rapist opened the gate for the Baroness, then quickly slammed it shut, leaving the baffled braves milling around in front of the stockade. Hugo nodded to a gate guard, and he pulled the tarp off the gate. It read: "Budweiser, The Big Chief of Beers: Succor for the Thirsty Savage Since 1876®."

The Indians were confused. "What does 'succor' mean?" They didn't like the sound of this. Another white man trick? One of his braves asked Geronimo, who pulled a pocket Webster out of his saddlebag.

"I told you they wouldn't get it," Hugo whispered to Rebay. "Good slogan, but not for *this* crowd."

"Here it is," Geronimo read to his patrol of pitiless scourges of the Plains, "Succor: assistance and support in times of hardship and distress."

"Why didn't they just say so?" another warrior complained. "Are they trying to make us feel bad by using big words? That's really mean."

"Hey," Rebay yelled. "Look here, Indian Nation," and she signaled to Hugo, who pulled a rope releasing the tarp hiding the enormous, mysterious . . . why, it was an eighty-foot-around, twenty-foot-high, pile of Budweiser® six packs. "How ya like that?" Rebay yelled.

The savages began howling and circling in a wild "We want a beer, heya-heya-heya" kinda chant, while prancing around doing that goddamned heel-and-toe dance that the G-Gals had seen so many times it made them sick.

"Calm down," the Baroness ordered. "Here's the drill. For a blanket you get a can of Bud, for a pistol you get a six-pack, for a carbine a case of Bud, for a tank four cases of Bud, and for each atom bomb, ten cases of Bud. And look what else we got for ya."

The Secret Weapon!

She held up a cardboard carton with 'FBI' stenciled on it. "We made these things in the FBI lab just for you." She opened it and pulled out an Indian war bonnet with foam coolers on each side for a can of Bud: The Madman's great invention. "Here's how it works." She put it on the Horse Rapist, then cracked open two cans of Bud, put them in the foam beer can holders on each side of the bonnet, inserted a plastic tube in each can, and stuck the two other ends in the Rapist's mouth. "This way you can suck on your Buds while you gallop after buffalo. It's called a 'Brew Bonnet®.'"

"Geeze, that thing is genius," Geronimo marveled. "I want one."

"One more thing," she said. "You try to attack Fort Budweiser®, and I got it rigged to blow up."

"No, no, we be heap good Uncle Sam's redskins," the Indians promised. "Just give us beer. And make it a Bud."

It was working! It was working!

* * *

The G-Sluts in their geisha girl disguises stood in front of the gibbering army of Japanese concentration camp escapees who were ready for their final assault on a defenseless Los Angeles (whose adult male citizens, remember, were all in the Pacific getting killed by the Japs). Knockers sent a couple of shots over their heads to get their attention. Show time for *Plan 53 with the Yellow Peril Option.*

Far to the north, Secret Agent Slut Bliss was readying the same harangue to the Nisei Army massed on the hills overlooking

San Francisco. The escapees had already captured the cable cars, and all they had to do was slide down to Fisherman's Wharf, capture the town, and start feasting on cioppino. Super-Secret Agent Double (or is it Triple?) Traitor Pigeon (I think it's Quadruple) had a fondness for that Fisherman's Wharf delicacy, as well as owning a reserved table at Tommy Toy's Restaurant®, so he was already licking his evil turncoat chops.

Secret Agents Knockers and Bliss knew the survival of the Republic hung in the balance. It all came down to how well they could put across the do-or-die speeches the two of them had spent days preparing, blue-penciling, re-editing, and practicing in front of mirrors. Each head geisha was backed up only by a pitifully small band of Secret Agent Bad Girls in their kimono costumes, who gave their G-Geisha leaders hopeful thumbs-up signs and nervous smiles. Every one of them knew they were in deepest depths of doo-doos.

"Thanks, Gals," Knockers whispered to her handful of hookers, "I'm going to give it my best shot." In front of her, thousands of revenge-crazed American Japs hopped up and down and screamed rage-filled 'Banzais!' One of the nefarious nips yelled that he was going to fuck Jane Russell and the horse she rode in on. Knockers almost fainted at the thought of such an over-the-top outrage of miscreant miscegenation and brazen bestiality.

The San Francisco Jap army was waving signs, "Free the Alcatraz Three Hundred," meaning that if they had their way Al Capone and his fellow inmate bank robbers, car thieves, counterfeiters, con men, bad check passers, litterbugs, and unreformable exhibitionist masturbaters would be loosed on the helpless citizens of the "City by the Bay," helpless because that Sonuvabitch in the White House had sent their male defenders to the Pacific to be killed by the Japs (*if you recall*).

Knockers grabbed the mic and cleared her throat. In San Francisco, Bliss did the same. (*Let's see if it works . . .*)

* * *

Back at the White House, Roosevelt was his usual full-of-shit self, grinning like the witless wonder he was as long as his stamp collection was safe. He had worked his way through the entire Brooklyn Bomber team, but his true love was the Bama Jamma and he had installed her in the Lincoln Bedroom, along with Eleanor and the new stamp collection he had gotten from Stalin, Hitler, or whoever it was (he couldn't keep those assholes straight). Eleanor had also developed quite a fondness for the Bama Jamma, who had outfitted the First Lady with a wheeled walker and a skintight Spandex® bodysuit (which made her look, in the President's considered opinion, even more hideous than usual) so she could join the girls in their practice sessions.

The Sonuvabitch in the White House (SITWH) had exercised Executive Privilege so that he could ride his wheelchair with the Bombers in their regulation matches against their traditional enemies, the Boston Beaners. He had given the Bama Jamma the Congressional Medal of Honor for foiling a plot by a Commie ratbastard disguised as a Boston Beaner with a gargantuan set of falsies. His beard and mustache had given him away to the eagle-eyed Jamma, and she and the team had run over the ratbastard, who had been planning to put a stick in the spokes of the SITWH's wheelchair. Now the Red Rodent Roadkill was just a bloody smear on the wooden track the President had built in the White House basement.

* * *

Out on the lone prairie, Secret Agent Hilla Rebay's forces were rounding up the last of the drunken redskins to be sent to the Pacific to be killed by the Japs. The Injuns had traded their guns, jeeps, tanks, nuclear weapons, ponies, blankets, tents, squaws and papooses for cans of Bud® and free Frito® Pies. Geronimo had propped himself against the gate of Fort Bud like a cigar store Indian, the two cans of Bud® in his can-holder war bonnet dripping beer into his mouth through plastic tubes, urine running down his legs into his piss-filled moccasins. He was dreaming of the Happy Hunting Ground in the sky, visions of fountains of Bud®. and trees loaded with Frito® Pies. His pony had long ago given up on getting attention or affection from the erstwhile marauding Scourge of the West, and had sidled off to Hugo the Horse Raper, who whispered to the Agent Baroness, "I don't care if I never rape another horse in my life. I'm plumb tuckered out."

"Now, now," she comforted him, patting him on his lecherous lips, "a few weeks back in prison, which is where you should be for life, you sick puppy, and you'll be yourself again, dreaming of Palomino Pussy."

"God, I hope so."

Plan Last Chance: Open Only If the Fucking Indians Have Us by the Balls and It's Hopeless had worked! *But was it worth going to hell for?* the Baroness wondered.

* * *

Back in the hills overlooking LA, Knockers began her harangue. "I have good news, fellow Japs," Knockers began.

"What's yer name, geisha gal?" a fierce representative of the violent horde of vengeance-seeking Nipponese yelled.

"Yokohama Mama," she responded, "last name Suzuki. And I got somethin' to tell ya."

"Make it snappy! We got blood in our eyes and killin' on our minds."

"Calm down, Nihonjin Ninjas, lemme remind you of what this country has done to you. You got shipped over here pretty much as slaves to build the railroads and mine for gold, and afterwards white mobs killed most of you. The survivors carved small farms out of the desert and built schools, churches, and brothels, making a civilized society out of a state filled with the dregs of white semi-humanity. You were model citizens, peaceful and forgiving despite the periodic pogroms launched by lazy ne'er-do-wells who burned down your houses and raped your women and chickens, while you paid your taxes and contributed to the society that your white neighbors were ripping off by going on the dole and demanding free medical care for the STDs they got by sexually consorting with animals like pigs, coons, chickens, snakes, and a horse or two. As relations broke down between America and the Empire of Japan, your boys volunteered for suicide squads to use up the ammunition of those fanatical Jap bastards."

"I think you ought to distinguish between the fanatical Jap bastards in the Japanese Army and Navy, and us fanatical Jap bastards who are loyal, real live nephews of Uncle Sam, one hundred and sixty-fourth or fifth of us were born on the Fourth of July (depending on whether it's a leap year)," one of the Nisei Ranks of Righteousness pointed out.

"I stand corrected. Thank you," Knockers said, with a smile that displayed her lacquer- blackened teeth, an erotic touch that sent a throb through every male Japanese groin (*and some female groins, too, and hey, there's nothing wrong with that, is there? Aren't we long past the day when same-sex attraction, or the 'love that dare not speak its name' has to hide its preference for, well, you know what, in the shadows? The day for gender-specific bigotry is over, and those homophobic bastards are gonna get what they deserve . . . or am I getting off message? Sorry.*)

"As I was saying, what thanks did we get for becoming the model minority of this fucked-up country? The minute war was declared, they rounded us all up, stuck us into those freaking concentration camps in the desert, no A/C, stole our houses and farms and brothels and gave them to those lousy no-good Okies who had been stealing and raping our chickens even before the war. We have been left with less than nothing. Our property has been stolen, our kids have to play baseball with rocks wrapped in socks and broken broom sticks, we are called traitors, and the country won't even let our heroic sons and brothers get sent to the Pacific to get killed by the Japs, you know, those Japs on the other side. We have been treated like shit. Worse than shit. And we got a right to rip their nuts off and stuff 'em down their throats. Speaking of stuffing things down Okies' throats, did I say anything about those Okies' dental hygiene? Disgusting.

"So, let's put all the crimes this country has committed against us on one side, like this," and she extended her left arm out to one side. "On the other side," and she stuck out her right arm, with a piece of paper in her hand, "is this:

"I have put a secret provision in that Sonuvabitch in the White House's Executive Order that rounded us up, stole all our shit, and stuck us in them camps. And it is this: *In fifty years to the day from when we were rounded up, whatever asshole is President is going to issue an official apology to us, saying that the country is sorry for fucking us over.* Whaddya think of that? Pretty goddamn white of 'em, don'cha think?"

A murmur ran through the crowd, which broke up into little groups discussing this amazing development. "That really is *damn* white of them. Far as I'm concerned, this makes it all OK."

"So whaddya think? Call off this rebellion and go back to the concentration camps?"

"*Hai, dozo.* To the rear march." And they turned and headed back to the camps, singing "It's a Grand Old Flag" and "Dixie" as they marched.

Secret Agent Knockers let out a sigh of relief and exchanged the Secret Agent Howdeedo with her little band of sluts. "Time for us to get back to sex work at Los Alamos," she told them.

Same result in San Francisco. The happy, patriotic Nihonjin turned their backs on "The City by The Bay" and started marching back to their concentration camps singing "Take Me Out to the Ball Game," and yelling to each other, "What a Country," and "Ain't ya glad yer an American?" and "U-S-A, U-S-A."

Plan 53 with the Yellow Peril Option worked. The Baroness wondered if, with a few slight modifications, it might work on the country's other troublesome minorities.

* * *

Presidential Agent 103 was lying in his trundle at the foot of the Presidential bed, lulling himself to sleep composing his memoirs filled with true and imagined feats of saving the upper class and their servants from the envious grasp of losers like the Indians, the Japs, the Reds, and the unemployed criminal elements. *Sleep tight, PA 103, and may flights of angels sing thy rest, because this is going to be the last good night's snooze you're gonna have for a long time.*

Part 2

CHAPTER 10

Everyone in the Presidential Bed — the Sonuvabitch in the White House, his wife a.k.a. the Commie Hag, the Bama Jamma, and the stamp collection — were all softly snoring (except for the stamp collection) when Secret Agent X-9 raced into the room, tripped over Presidential Agent 103's trundle bed, and landed on top of the First Lady.

"Hey, what the . . . oh, it's you, X-9. What a nice surprise."

"Sorry, I'm not here for you, ma'am. I'm here for the Sonuv . . . I mean, the President."

"Oh, let him sleep a little bit more. You and I have never really gotten to know each other. Lemme help you off with those pants."

"Ain't got time for that. National Emergency."

"Well, I've got a little emergency I'd like you to take care of. Come on. Please."

"Rain check, ma'am. Mr. President? Mr. President," he whispered, poking him in the Presidential Paunch.

"Jeezuz, can't a guy catch a few winks? And what the hell

you doing on top of my wife? But I guess if you can stand it, so can I."

"You gotta get up. General Ike has called off D-Day."

That got his attention. The President grabbed his stamp collection to get it out of range of Eleanor, who was thrashing around in some kind of erotic fit. "He can't do that. I put a bet down in Vegas that we'd go on June 6. This is gonna cost me money. What's his problem?"

"Kay Summersby has disappeared."

"You mean that Jeep driver he's been fucking."

"One and the same. Ike says he's not invading France, not invading anywhere until he gets her back. And Ike's doctor says that Ike has the worst case of blue balls he's ever seen. And if he springs even a mini-erection in that condition, let alone a reltney, he's sure as shit gonna suffer a penile blowout. You know, let's say a magician at your birthday party (and by the way, Happy Birthday, Mr. President, in case I forgot, or forget) twists a balloon into a make-believe cock and balls, just for fun, and then decides to make it bigger by blowing in some more air, but he blows in too much, and the thing pops. Well, that's what's going to happen to poor Ike's ol' pork chop if he accidentally springs a woodie. I put that in layman's terms since the doctors say you ain't got any more understanding of scientific terminology than a rock, and they don't mean a particularly smart rock. In other words, a fool."

"Well, maybe they're right," the Sonuvabitch said proudly, "But I'm the President and they ain't. And it's top secret that I'm a fool, so keep that to yourself, soldier."

Then he got off his Presidential high horse, metaphorically speaking. (*In other words, kids, he wasn't really on a horse, he was just acting like he was.*) "Oh, no," he whimpered. "What am I gonna do?"

"Silly," his wife said. "Same as every other time you've been in deep shit, you incompetent moron. Call Rebay and Guggenheim."

"Why didn't I think of that? X-9, call Rebay and Guggenheim. But what am I supposed to tell them when they get here?" the Sonuvabitch asked Eleanor.

"That they're going to London!"

"Oh, yeah. They're going to London. What're they gonna do in London?"

"Find Eisenhower's girlfriend, you numbskull," Eleanor told him.

"Right," the Sonuvabitch in the White House told X-9. "That's the plan."

"How about me, Boss?" X-9 wailed.

"You can go, too."

"And me?" Presidential Agent 103 begged.

"OK, you too. But the Bama Jamma stays here."

* * *

Secret Agents Rebay and Guggenheim were huddling with Pierre La Fop, the Assistant Director in charge of the FBI Fashions, Disguises, and Accessories Division. The Gals needed to outfit themselves and the two G-Guys for the trip "across the pond," as the well-traveled PA 103 called it in his infuriatingly insouciant manner. (*Some found this endearing. But they were wrong. There was a twit side of Lanny that would make any red-blooded American want to bash the smug bastard's pretty face in. OK, off track again. Sorry.*)

The Secret Agent Gals had decided to augment their ranks by adding Special Slut Knockers to the team, and she was taking a crash driver's ed course handling the G.I. Jeep, in case la Summersby could not be located. The plan was to dress Knockers up in the same uniform as Ike's departed girlfriend and see if he would notice the difference when they palmed her off on the lovelorn general. Experience had shown that when confronted by Agent Knockers, her face was the last thing the victim noticed.

After scanning the fashion photos in *Country Home®*, the recognized authoritative text on how the Brit fox-hunting set decked themselves out, Agent La Fop had chosen clothes he was sure would allow X-9 and Lanny Budd to pass undetected through British society in their search for Ike's vanished vamp: *de rigeur* tails, white tie, calfskin gloves, white spats, bowler hat, and tightly rolled umbrella, which PA 103 instructed the provincial X-9 to call a "bumbershoot." Assistant Director La Fop had an English saddle mounted on a hobby horse, so X-9 could practice swinging himself onto a horse without grabbing for the saddle horn, a *faux pas* that would get an American disguised as a Brit detected and demoted to the ranks of a gilly. (*That means a servant in Brit-talk, kids*). "What about a lasso?" X-9 wondered. "Or shouldn't I ask?"

"Yes, don't ask."

La Fop then fitted the G-Guys with snap-in sets of British false teeth, so that their smiles could reveal that typical consequence of British dentistry: yellowed rotten fangs, with missing teeth in front. X-9 looked into the mirror and said, "My God®, that's revolting," but PA 103, with the air of a well-traveled swell, assured him that British dames considered rotten teeth a turn-on.

When the G-Guys strapped on their gas masks, La Fop proclaimed them the very model of useless British snobs. "Now work on that accent," Rebay told X-9, whose normal speech ranged between an ignorant Southern drawl and the equally ignorant blather of a tobacco-spitting cowpuncher.

"Tally-ho and yoicks," he replied, to the applause of his three pals.

"By George, I think he's got it," said La Fop.

The G-Gals and the Super Slut were decked out in British Motorized Transport Unit uniforms with baggy woolen underpants, and fitted, like the G-Guys, with lousy false teeth and gas masks. "Why do we gotta wear these underpants?" Knockers wanted to know. "They itch."

"If you take off your clothes and the SUBINT (Subject of Interest) spots silk panties, it's a dead giveaway that you're Americans." AD La Fop knew his stuff, they all agreed.

Speed and Clyde limped out of the Justice Department to see the Secret Summersby Rescue Squad off on what they sadly saw as a suicide mission. He presented each of the heroes with a tightly folded American flag. "In case your plane goes down, or you're about to be executed by those Nazi fiends, you should drape yourselves in these so when we find your corpses they'll be covered by the red, white, and blue. Terrific PR for the Bureau." That was another great idea from Lou Nichols and the Crime Records Division, which had already begun work on turning "The Case of Ike's Blue Balls and the Missing Mistress" into the next great FBI epic. Lou had figured he could come in under budget by using some parts of MAD-1's VD movies, recolored, for the medical episodes of the story and recycling Dillinger "Lady in Red" footage for the sex scenes.

Before their plane began moving down the taxiway at Langley Field, a priest, a rabbi, a minister, and an Indian medicine man passed among the G-martyrs, giving them the last rites of their different religions.

"Isn't this a bit of religious overkill?" Rebay protested. "Whoops. Sorry about using the 'K' word," as X-9 began trembling uncontrollably.

"I'm scared," he whimpered.

When they reached cruising altitude, the co-pilot strolled into their cabin. "If you want to hear what we're saying, just pick up this tube, blow into it, and then listen. Hmmm. Pretty interesting stuff," and he went back to the cockpit.

After lunch, which X-9 promptly puked up, he announced that he wanted to listen to the "pilot chatter," and picked up the rubber tube. He pressed his mouth to the cone at the end, blew into it and listened. He blew into it again. Nothing. "Hey pilot, I can't hear nothin," he yelled.

"Just a minute," the pilot said. "Hey Jack, go back there and see if you can clear the communications line."

Smilin' Jack unstrapped himself from the right seat, took the tube from X-9, unzipped his coveralls and peed like a horse into the "communications" tube. "Try it now."

"Haw-haw, "the pilot guffawed, "I can't believe he fell for that stupid trick."

"Mean thing to do to a guy who's about to die for his country," X-9 whimpered, wiping his lips on his tie.

* * *

As the plane descended through the fog to the Wethersfield Airport, the Secret Agents heard the pilot whisper to the first officer, "We're all gonna die."

Secret Agent Rebay broke out the American flags and passed them out so that their corpses would be found in the patriotic shrouds Speed had ordered.

X-9 began shrieking, "I don't wanna die!" as the plane touched down smoothly.

Guggenheim, somewhat perturbed because they survived after all the trouble she'd gone through with the flags (She had fantasized *New York Times* front-page pictures of the flag-draped cadavers) retrieved the flags, and with PA103's help refolded them into those Boy Scout® prescribed triangles. They stepped out of the plane into a fog so thick that they had to hold onto each other's butts and proceed Indian file as the pilot led them to the base HQ.

"How can we find anyone in these conditions," Rebay asked PA 103. "Is it always this bad?"

"Pretty much."

"I don't think I can find my own ass," X-9 said. "This is hopeless. Let's give up and go home. If Hitler wants this shithole country, I say, let him have it."

Guggenheim hauled off and let the coward have it with a slap right across the chops. "Pull yourself together, man. If we look nervous, the Brits are going to panic and lose the war."

"I don't care. I just wanna go home."

Rebay gave the sniveling jerk another slap that brought him to his knees, and PA 103 showed he was a team player by kicking X-9 while he was rolling in the mud.

"Stop it, stop it," the pitiful fool gasped, "I'll try to be brave. Ouch. Dammit, Lanny, I think you broke my short rib. Now I'll have to be sent home."

"Nothing doing," Rebay said. "We need you for a human shield if we have to storm the hideout of the Nazis, the Japs, the Irish, or whoever has snitched that beautiful snatch (*not bad, huh, kids? Little play on words known as a pun.*) who, by the way, just converted into an American citizen, which makes her kidnapping an official FBI case. I see promotions, medals, maybe we can even be knighted if we pull this off. Well, except for you," she told X-9.

X-9 was covered with resentment and mud. *They had no right treating him this way. It wasn't his fault he was a coward. His parents had dressed him like a girl until he was twenty-five, and he had always liked playing with dolls more than guns.*

Then he had an idea how he would become a big shot again. *If I get the chance,* he told himself, *I will pretend to sell out to the Nazis. I will start letting Hitler think I know the "Rescue Kay" team's every move. Maybe Hitler will give me a medal and one of those black uniforms. Then I'll tell Speed and the guys everything I learned while I was a traitor. That'll make PA 103 and the girls look like the jerks they are. And I would be a hero. That'll teach 'em!* The important thing right now was to stand up so PA 103 would stop kicking him. But he thought his leg was broken.

"Can't anyone help me get up?" he whined. Guggenheim hauled him to his feet and dumped him into a wheelbarrow the pilot had brought over. "Let's get this useless load of shit to the hotel and wash him off," she said. "I need a drink." They dumped their gear on top of X-9 and headed toward the taxi stand, then threw him and their gear into the trunk—"The *boot*," PA 103 the globetrotter corrected them—and headed for London.

Their liaison from MI6 was waiting for them at their hotel. "What's with the coward?" he asked, pointing to X-9 who was on the floor with the luggage piled on top of him. "He's just going to slow us down. Want me to finish him off?" drawing his Webley®.

"Nah, he's kind of a mascot. And good for making drinks. Used to be a bartender in Cincinnati. But lemme see that Webley®."

The Secret Agents passed the legendary revolver around. They even let X-9 heft it. "I want one," he said from the bottom of the suitcase pile.

"Now *that*'s a firearm," PA 103 said, handing it back to the British Secret Agent. "I'm Presidential Agent 103. These are Secret Agents Rebay and Guggenheim, and this is Secret Slut Knockers. The coward down there is X-9," who waved from his somewhat humiliating position. "Who are you?"

"My name is Bond, Jonquil Bond. You can call me Junk Bond. Or 007. Means I gotta license to kill."

"Big deal. And we all got the same license, and not from some cereal box top club, neither, so watch out. Glad to meetcha," Lanny said, extending his hand for a fist bump. "Got any kids?'

"Yes, old chap. Son named Sue."

"Sue? Sue? You've got a boy you named Sue? No! Anything but Sue!"

"Whaddya mean?"

"He's gonna have to fight for his life to defend himself

when they find out he's a boy named Sue. Change his name. Anything but Sue: Joe, Sam, Willie, Ace . . ."

"How about James Bond?"

"Nah. Not manly enough."

"How about Cholmondeley?"

"I like that. Cholmondeley Bond it is. Pronounced 'Chumley.' Chums, for short. 'Bond, Chums Bond.' I like that. Now let's get down to business."

* * *

Back at Los Alamos, Secret Slut Bambi was distraught. She had been heartbroken when she saw what pitiful shape Geronimo was in, the once-fearless brave who had held the key to her heart and the rest of her body. No pony. No bow and arrow. No tent. No blankets.

During the great round-up of alcoholic aborigines, she snuck into the truck that was putting Geronimo and the wretched remnants of his war party on that lonesome trail to the Pacific to be killed by the Japs. She disguised him in one of the Poontang Platoon's minidresses, smeared war paint all over his face until he had achieved something like the tipsy floozy look favored by the Secret Sluts, tied his long hair into a ponytail with a pink ribbon and a bow, then brought him to her room and bed. Under her ministrations—daily Bible lessons, a healthy diet of spring water and canned corned beef, plus a regimen of pushups and jumping jacks-his natural vitality returned. And, as might have been expected, he had fallen in love with love again, that is, with his scantily clad nurse, who also believed that daily sex was required for the health of any boy, particularly a noble savage, who, if anything, needed it more than once a day: twice, maybe three times, and if he was a good boy and quiet in church, four times.

But Geronimo was getting restless, remembering his glory days when he had brought the U. S. Cavalry to its knees and had figgered he'd soon be looting department stores in Chicago and Podunk. He was tired of mincing around the base in his slut disguise of a short frilly skirt, a tank top filled out with gigantic falsies, spike heels, a thick applique of pancake makeup and rouge, and enough perfume to make anybody puke except a cowboy familiar only with the body odors of horses and the stench of pig shit. Worse, word had spread in the labs that there was a new girl in town, and some of the more important Reds were demanding a crack at her. Geronimo was having a hard time warding them off, and J. Robert Oppenheimer claimed he had already gotten to "second base" with the new whore and was bragging that with one more date he would hit a "home run."

"Bambi," Gerry said, "I love you and I am grateful that you saved me from being sent to the Pacific to be killed by the Japs. But I want to be roaming the lone prairie again, dodging the tumbling tumbleweed, eating magic mushrooms, throwing rocks at jackrabbits, and killing buffalo (*American bison, that is, kids, may as well use the right term*) with my jackknife. It's time for me to go. You can't fence me in."

Bambi desperately wanted to keep her Indian brave tied to her apron strings, but she knew he was right. He was a Noble Savage, and he belonged outdoors where he wouldn't be softened by effeminacies like toilet paper and deodorant. But something had come up. Or, more precisely, had *not* come up.

* * *

"Aw, Speed, be reasonable. All we were doing was working on the crossword puzzle and playing pinochle."

The FBI Director and his buddy, sidekick and, according to Commie rats and their pinko pals, his bunkie, were having a little spat in Hoover's Northwest Washington raised ranch.

"Yeah, well how come I caught the two of you naked?"

"It was hot. She said that when she gets overheated, she breaks out in a rash. I didn't want that, so purely as a kind of first-aid remedy I helped get her clothes off, and she said that she felt comfortable but that I was overdressed, so I took mine off. Figured it would make her feel less, well, vulnerable."

"Did you have sex with her?"

"Absolutely *not*. But I used protection. I yanked it out in time. And it was only once. And besides, I won't do it again." Clyde thought he had pretty much dealt with the problem.

Problem was, Speed didn't agree.

Hoover was pacing back and forth in the living room, locking and unlocking his automatic, checking the magazine to see if it had all twelve rounds, then letting off the odd shot at the chandelier bulbs. And missing each time. Then he shook his head. "Nah," he conceded, "this is not the gun for the job." He was a bit frustrated about missing the chandelier bulbs, so he concluded that it was because he was using the wrong weapon. He went to his gun cabinet and pulled out a machine gun. He sequenced it and took aim at Clyde who was hiding behind the sofa.

"Come on, Boss. I gotta grenade back here and I've pulled the pin. You kill me and the whole place blows up."

Hoover was in full hissy-fit mode, but he wasn't suicidal. He calmed down and fired at the chandelier again, this time with the machine gun so he was getting closer. "You know, Sharpshoot-er, no reason why we can't get over this little speed bump. How about putting the pin back in the grenade?"

"OK, just as soon as you put down the Tommy gun." Speed put it down on the coffee table between them. Clyde emerged from hiding, the grenade in one hand, the pin in the other. He held the pin close to the grenade, then slipped it in. In a split second, Hoover lunged for the machine gun, Clyde did the same, and they were rolling on the floor, Hoover holding onto the barrel of the gun, Clyde the stock. They stopped, panting, totally exhausted.

"Maybe what we need is relationship counseling," Clyde said.

"Yeah, but I don't think they got counselors for what we got going."

"I got an idea," Clyde told Public Hero Number One. "That creep in the basement lab, you know, Secret Agent MAD-1, went to college and took a psych course." Clyde was in charge of getting the dirt on special agents, and spent his days looking for things he could use to blackmail those goldbricking lazy slobs, so he knew all about The Madman's educational qualifications. "Let's see if he can schedule us for a mediation session. You know. We write down our favorite colors and look at ink blots. One of my pals said that some of them blots are pretty raunchy. Gave him some fun ideas."

"I like the way your mind works, Clyde. Your body, too. But isn't The Madman the guy who hooks up applicants' Johnsons to some gizmo, then shows them dirty pictures of boys to see if they get a boner?"

"Wouldn't you like to see those pictures?"

"Sure. Who wouldn't? But I don't want to be wired up. My legendary self-control has its limits."

"I'll see if he can skip that electrical part, just show us the pictures."

* * *

"Here's the deal," Junk Bond told the Find Kay Squad. "Let's get down to business. The last time we saw this dame . . ."

"Right," PA 103 interrupted 007. "Blah, blah, blah. Look, before you start boring us with work, it's my pals' here first trip to Old Blighty, and this operation may take days, weeks, months, years. A couple days R&R before we get started isn't going to hurt. In the meantime, nothing is going to happen. Ol' Ike is in his tent sulking. The war is over, far as he's concerned, until he gets back in the rack with Kay. So how 'bout — we're not talking forever — letting us see a bit of London before we get all tied up with this gal hunt. And before this war starts up again. This D-Day thing may be a fiasco. The Reds or the Nazis — I can't keep these assholes straight — may be sacking the country next month. So before we get down to business, as you call it, here's what we wanna do."

"OK, let's have it."

"First, we all want Webleys®. That's one sweet gun you got. We'll pay for 'em, don't worry. Charge it to the Bureau. But we want those guns. All three of us — me, the Baroness, and Guggenheim."

"Me too!" X-9 yelled from under the luggage.

"Aren't you afraid The Coward might throw in with the Nazis?"

"I think he's more afraid of us than them. Besides, if the Nazis take an asshole like him, they're more desperate than we thought. If we GAVE him to them, we'd be money ahead."

"OK, one for him, too. What else?"

"I ain't been on a foxhunt in a long time. Set one up for me."

"No problemo."

"I'll need to borrow some hounds, a horse, and some pinks."

"Right-o, but as soon as you kill and gut the fox, we look for the girl, right?"

"I'd like a picture of me holding up the bloody tail. And can I keep the tail?"

"Sure. Anything. But maybe you can give us some pointers about how to solve a big case like this. So, we can start while you're still having fun. You G-Men solved the Lindbergh kidnapping, didn't you?"

"Not exactly. That was the Secret Service and the New Jersey State Troopers."

"You got Al Capone, though, right?"

"That was the IRS."

"Blimey. What cases did you solve?"

"We recovered 152,678 stolen cars last year," PA 103 said proudly. "And arrested 75 Indians for leaving the reservation without a hall pass. And pulled in one asshole for an unauthorized use of a Smokey Bear costume. And I personally saved the President's stamp collection from the Indians and the Japs."

"Gee whiz. I heard about that one. *The Stamp Collection Caper.* I loved how Peter Lorre played you in the movie for laughs."

"Those wisecracks were all mine. All they had to do was string 'em together and they had a script. I shoulda gotten co-writer credit. But that's Hollywood. Unless you've got a relative in the business, ya get screwed."

* * *

Bambi had decided the time had come. She sat Geronimo down and told it to him straight: "Gerry, the rabbit died."

His heart swelled with pride. His beautiful squaw was now a mighty hunter. "How did you bag the bunny? Bow and arrow? Spear? Rocks? Tommy gun?"

"No, Big Guy. The rabbit drank some of my piss."

"And so that's how you killed it?"

"More or less."

Geronimo was dumbfounded. He realized he did not know all the mores of the more civilized race but hunting rabbits with piss did not seem fair play to him. Not cricket. "I don't know if we can count that one. You're supposed to chase down the enemy, touch him with a stick, then kill him with something that has a point on it. Not piss on him. We Indians show reverence for the spirit of the animal, in this case, Thumper the Rabbit God®. I can consult with my Tribal Council, but I think we may have to wipe this one off the record books. Expunge it. Too bad. But I'm proud of you anyway. Whaddya say we rip off a quick one?"

"No, my tawny Tarzan, you got it all wrong. The rabbit-and-piss deal is a scientific test to find out if a girl is pregnant, you know, knocked up, cake in the oven, baby bump. We're going to have ourselves a little papoose."

"I don't get it. I yanked it out just like you tol' me."

"Evidently not fast enough. It just takes a little bit to do the trick, especially when the boy in question is as potent as you, my Savage Seducer."

"What are we gonna do?"

"First of all, we gotta get you out of here."

"Yeah, but I'm off the reservation without a pass. If they catch me, they'll send me to the Pacific to get killed by the Japs."

"But I thought you were the Chief. Won't they give you some leeway?"

"Don't matter, my Bodacious Bambi. Rez rules. Like with your country: I mean, if your President broke the law, he'd have to pay, right?"

"Er, yeah. Good point. I guess. But I got a plan. You know the tobacco store on the plaza in Santa Fe?"

"Sure. The one with the Cigar Store Indian in front of it. And by the way, that's a whole shitload of racist appropriation of a fucking stereotype for capitalist profit, although it does give the Indians credit for something besides gambling casinos: inventing an addiction that's killing millions of you white bastards every year, although I guess our kid will be one of those white bastards, too. Oh, man, Kemo Sabe. I'm so mixed up."

"That's because you're thinking too much, sweetie. You stick to your tom-tomming and that ridiculous heel-and-toe dance the tourists love, and I'll do the thinking for both of us."

"Wouldn't you think better if we did the nasty right now?"

"In a minute. Here's the plan. We sneak down to the plaza and swap you for the wooden cigar store Indian. Stick a handful of stogies in your fist, and nobody will notice the difference. I got the idea from how you looked when you were propped up drunk against the stockade at Fort Budweiser®."

For an instant, Gerry was dreaming of that great Anheuser-Busch Beer Garden® in the sky, and in a physical reaction immediately comprehensible to anyone who was awake during the lecture on Pavlov in Psych 101, urine began trickling down his leg. But he agreed. Bambi's brilliant plan seemed the only way out.

* * *

X-9 said it wasn't fair for Lanny to go on a fox hunt if he couldn't. That got Rebay and Guggenheim upset. If the guys got to hunt foxes, they wanted in. Now Knockers said she didn't want to be left behind, so Bond would have to round up horses and pinks for the whole G-Man and G-Gal squad when they got to the hunt club.

When they finally arrived, PA 103 took one look and said that the place was not up to his standards. Bond admitted that it was not exactly "top chop, old boy." He had another club in mind, but that one turned out to have members PA 103 knew and didn't like. Finally, Lanny called up a countess he had slept with before the war, and she invited him and his friends to her hunt club. "In return," she said, "you gotta play bury the banger with me."

"How many times?" he asked.

"Every night for a weekypoo."

He explained, "No can do." He was on an important secret mission, he told her, and had to get to work once they had killed the fox.

"What's the secret mission?" she asked.

"If I told you, it wouldn't be a secret, would it?"

"Oh, come on. We're pals."

"OK, we have to find Ike's girlfriend. She's missing. And Ike won't invade France or anywhere else until he gets her back. A real mess. He's got a case of blue balls for the medical journals. We think the Nazis may have her."

"Oh, it's Kay you're after. I may have a little clueyboo that might help you. Let's have a little *tête a tête*ypoo over a drinkypoo after we've renewed out little romancypoo."

Once the G-Gang had saddled up, it became clear that X-9 had never been on a horse before, so he was hanging onto his horse's mane for dear life. "If you lie down on the horse like that," Guggenheim explained to him, "you're on top of your nuts, and when the horse starts galloping (they call it 'loping' here). they're gonna get crushed. Just sayin'."

X-9 was too terrified to understand what she was saying, or sayin', so Peggy shrugged and told Lanny that coward would have to figure it out for himself. They better get the show on the road. Lanny gestured to the Master of the Hunt, who signaled to the bugler, who bugled a blast, and the dogs were let loose in a bedlam of barking, whining, and yelping. The hounds caught the scent, and the hunt was on.

As soon as the horses jumped the first fence, X-9 fell off. The hounds were confused. They thought that he was the fox and began to tear him to bits. The Master of the Hunt used the lash to get them off the hysterical Secret Agent. He calmed X-9's horse down, tossed X-9 across the saddle like a Hefty Bag® full of recyclables *(For some reason the Brits call garbage 'dust' as in 'dustbin' and don't get me going on 'lifts' and 'braces.')*, and tied him down on his horse.

The rest of the hunt was far ahead, and from the sounds of

the hounds' yelping, the dogs had the fox at bay. Lanny rode his horse into the pack, jumped off, and waded through the hounds, his knife unsheathed. Rebay, Guggenheim, and Knockers were out of their minds with excitement. They pulled out their knives and joined PA 103 who had the fox by the throat in one hand while he sawed at the bloody beast's tail. Guggenheim ripped off a front leg, Rebay got a rear leg, while Knockers plunged her knife into the fox's belly and cut out its heart, which she flipped to Rebay, who wolfed it down; then out came its liver which she ate herself in a single gulp; and finally its balls which she forced into X-9's mouth. "Maybe this will make a man outta ya."

"My God®, that was fun!" Knockers yelled. "Let's do it again," she said as they got back to the stable, their lips still smeared with blood.

"But can't we start looking for Kay now?" Bond pleaded.

"Not so fast," the Countess told Bond, as she dragged PA 103 toward a haystack.

"This'll just take a few minutes," Lanny promised Bond, as the Countess peeled the pink pants off the Presidential Agent, "and you promised you'd have someone take my picture with the foxtail as soon as I get my pants back on. And my guys still need to buy souvenirs for their moms. So, you're just going to have to be patient a little bit longer," he said as the Countess pulled him down on top of her. "And isn't it about time for tea?"

* * *

Geronimo's gig as a cigar store Indian was not going as well as he and Bambi had hoped. The neighborhood urchins had figured out he was a real Indian, and they ran down to the tobacco store after school each day to torment him. They stuck straws in his nose, goosed him, grabbed him by the balls, and finally began giving him the hot foot, sticking wooden matches into his moccasins and lighting them. "I can't take much more of this," he told

Bambi.

"You won't have to," she promised. "The girls have been letting me handle a few extra tricks when they're tired, and I've saved enough for a down payment on a Winnebago®. I'll take possession next week. They're giving it an Indian paint job: buffaloes, Bud® cans, and Harley Davidson® stickers all over it. I've got a hookup at the Taos trailer park reserved. Just a few more days, darling, and we'll be in our little dream house."

The two lovebirds shared the dream of living in a trailer park with a soft ice cream machine where they could play shuffleboard with neighbors from the whole forty-eight. Then when the nomadic savage and his squaw felt the wanderlust come over them, they could unhook from the septic line and head to another trailer park, new neighbors, a new septic hook-up, the same wonderful soft ice cream, and this time, maybe horseshoes. And when the papoose arrived, they could hang the little tyke from the rearview mirror and set off after the tumbling tumbleweed.

CHAPTER 11

"You said you knew something about Kay Summersby," Presidential Agent 103 reminded the Countess as they enjoyed a post roll-in-the-hay Benson and Hedges® (Official Cancer Stick Purveyors to their Majesties the King and Queen and the Little Royal Twits). "And are you sure that smoking in the haystack is a good idea?"

"Oh, quit worrying. Next thing, you'll be worrying if I have one of those social diseases."

"Geeze, you don't, do you?"

"I guess you'll find out soon enough," she said, and she laughed with one of those don't-sweat-the-small-stuff chuckles the British aristocracy manage so well, and which made the subjects in the colonies impatient for the day when they could wipe that smile off their fucking faces and smash their misshapen teeth down their throats. And speaking of misshapen teeth, Lanny took advantage of the moment by asking, "When you were a kid, how come your parents didn't get you braces?"

"*Braces*? Ha-ha old boy, ladies don't wear braces! Who

cares if our pants fall down?"

I get it, Lanny thought, *a simple matter of inter-cultural semantic confusion. I'd forgotten that braces in England are suspenders. If people here would just learn to say, "dental braces," instead of just "braces," a whole nation, or at least the upper classes (which are all that matter, right?) would have better-looking smiles.*

"You want to know about Kay?" the Countess asked 103. "I was slumming a week ago (and by the way, anytime I go out anywhere, it's slumming, except maybe when I have tea with George and Elizabeth at BP, (that's Buckingham Palace, kids). I was at this ridiculously garish nightclub in Piccadilly, and I spotted her in the company of two absolutely disgusting-looking American G.I.s. I went over to their table and said I didn't know that a General's lady was supposed to fraternize with the enlisted orders, you know. She said she was doing research on morale in the ranks for the General. I said, 'So, aren't you going to introduce me to your friends?'"

"'Sure,' she said. 'This is Joe, and this is Willie,' and on closer inspection they were even more disgusting than I thought: unshaven, dirty, smelly, really rank. And instead of standing up, they stayed seated and grunted something in what I instantly recognized as an attempt to hide German accents. She thought she was having a pink lady with two American soldiers, but they were really German spies, and I'll stake my listing in *Burke's Peerage* on that."

"I knew it," PA 103 told her. "She's been kidnapped by the Nazis. This is really serious. But foiling Nazi plots is one of my specialties, along with being chickbait and riding to the hounds. And being an ace pilot; did you know that? By the way, did you see my foxtail?" as he waved the bloody fur in her face.

"Very nice. And I like those three gals you got with you. Real savages. You had your way with them yet?"

"Nope. We got this new sexual harassment rule. Violate it and even a hero like me can get his ass handed to him."

"How about you harass me one more time and we'll call it a day?"

"Well, I guess England expects every man to do his doo-dy. Get it, *doody*? A joke, sort of a pun. Another thing: Think you could get my guys a photo-op with the King and what's her name, the Queen? Mean a lot to their moms."

"I'd do anything for you, my Presidential Agent Man. I'll even get them to autograph 'em for you."

"That's my aristocrat."

* * *

Their relationship counseling was going really swell. Hoover and Tolson actually had so much in common. MAD-1 was amazed that they even seemed to see the same thing, more or less, in the inkblots. Where Clyde had seen Ma Barker in one inkblot, Hoover had said, "No. That's *my* Ma."

"Aha," The Madman told him, "that explains why you're always looking for female public enemies to kill. You really want to kill your mother."

"Ya think?"

"Absolutely. You have buried feelings of rage against your mommy. And you probably wanted to castrate your father."

"Nah, Mom took care of that."

"And it helps explain why you get so mad when Clyde, here, strays from what you might call the sissy side of the street and slips it to a woman."

"Whaddya mean?" Hoover and Clyde were fascinated, their jaws hanging open, both of them scratching their heads and looking at The Madman like he was truly The Answer Man, the 'Splainer Guy.

"Look at it this way: When Clyde screws a woman, it's the same as if he was screwing your mom, Speed. In other words, he loves your mom. You hate your mom. You think he should hate your mom too, but instead he loves her, which means" — MAD-1 paused triumphantly — "that he's being disloyal to you. Get it?"

Hoover nodded vigorously. It was all starting to make sense.

Clyde said, "I was following you up to the part where you said I should hate his mom, too. Then you started talking too fast."

"I'll explain it later, Public Hero Number Two," Hoover said, and bumped fists with The Madman. "So, what you're saying," Hoover continued, "is that I am not feeling sexual jealousy when Clyde lays a girl, but rather Oedipal jealousy; that when he shtups a broad it unleashes the unresolved conflict I have with my mom because he's shtupping her."

"Right."

"So, Doc, got any ideas how we could fix this up so I wouldn't get pissed when I catch him doing naked crossword puzzles or playing pinochle with some broad with no clothes on? I guess it all goes back to Mom, right? But what can I DO about it? You know, it's the oldest story in the psychiatric journals: understanding a problem isn't the same as solving it." *(Something to remember, kids, and use on your 'rents when they yell at you for doing something bad.)*

"I got an idea," Secret Agent Madman yelled for Secret Agent Igor, who was lurking outside the door. "Get over to the lab and get me my ditty bag. We're going to engage in some therapeutic play. I've done this with some real perverts, Mr. Director, way worse than you, and they've come out of it wholesome, red-blooded American boys, real Boy Scouts®. I really think you can turn over a new leaf and stop being the sadistic prick you've been up until now."

"Ya really think so?" Hoover was softly sobbing and

holding Clyde's hand.

An hour later Igor handed a black bag emblazoned with silver stars and moons to the wizard, who rummaged around in it and came up with a gray-haired rag doll. "This doll is your mom, Sir. When I hand it to you, I want you to do anything you want to it."

Hoover grabbed it and began ripping off the arms and legs. Then, looking desperately around the room for a knife and not finding one, he pulled out his automatic and emptied it into the doll. Finally he jumped up and down on it, screaming, "Take that, you old hag!" He stood there panting, nothing left of the doll except a rag, a bone, and a hank of hair.

"Feel better?" the FBI's own resident psychoceramicist asked Hoover. This was one for the *Secret Agents and Spies Journal of Deviant Psychology*.

"I feel GREAT!"

"So, from now on, anytime Clyde, you know, gets a little nookie on the side, just grab one of these dolls and let her have it. I've got more where this came from."

"Doc, doc, how can I ever repay you?" Hoover asked.

"I'm getting tired of having to keep shooting myself in the leg so you won't send me to the Pacific to get killed by the Japs. Think you could just mark me down as disabled?"

"That's a lot to ask. That Sonuvabitch in the White House has given me a weekly quota of agents to get killed by the Japs in the Pacific. I'll try to keep you here as long as I can before I cut you loose. But it might come down to just you or me, and you know how that'll play out. In the meantime, I'd advise you to keep shooting yourself in the leg. That's what I do."

* * *

"Ladies, ladies," Junk Bond pleaded with Knockers, Hilla, and Peggy, as they raced around Sloan's® grabbing everything in sight. "Just buy something, anything. We gotta find Kay and get D-Day back on track."

"Watch how you talk to my girls," PA 103 told the upstart limey. "You can't rush American women when they are buying luxury goods. Remember: Happy girls, happy world. Oh, that doesn't quite rhyme. How about: Happy britches, happy bitches. I like that. *Britches*, metonymy, part for the whole, get it? Actually, I think that's *synecdoche*. Britches equals clothes. Hey Bond, you must have studied Greek. Which is it?"

"I'm afraid, despite my plummy accent, I didn't have that kind of education. I was kind of a roughneck," he said proudly. "MI6 plucked me out of the workhouse to polish up the handle of the big brass door and shine the shoes of the swells, and I solved a case when I spotted French mud on the sole of a dirty-rat spy from France who was pretending to be a clubbable gentleman. Filthy wog bastard. I can't wait until we invade and slaughter the lot of them."

"I'd check current state of the alliances, old boy. I think we are supposed to slaughter the krauts and save the frogs. And these days we say 'ratbastard,' not 'dirty-rat,' which is associated with James Cagney, and the Director hates him."

"Really? Damn! Well, nobody told me that the frogs and the Brits are supposed to be friends, and that still doesn't make sense to me, so I'm just going to set my gun to bloody full auto and kill 'em all. Let *Mon Dieu* or *Mein Gott* sort 'em out. I don't want to give myself a headache worrying about it. And do you know what the frogs do for a headache?"

"Take an aspirin?"

"Yeah, but they put the aspirin in a suppository and stick it up the old wazoo, which they call *mon cul*. You know the old jingle: 'The French they are a funny race, they fight with their feet and they fuck with their face.' Actually, I think we're on the wrong side. I've always liked the Germans. Did you know our Royal

Family is German?"

"I think I did know that. And one of the Georges was the German who sent the Hessians to kill and rape us Yanks during the Revolutionary War. But I don't hold grudges. As long as we get that photo-op with the King the countess promised. When is it?"

"As soon as your gals finish up their shopping spree. The King and Queen are holding up their daily walk with their Corgis to oblige you."

"You heard him, ladies. We gotta get a move on."

"Almost done," Knockers said. "We all decided to get the same thing," she said, and they showed Lanny the brown fox stoles they had picked out. "We're going to put some red paint on the tails, kinda like blood. Souvenirs of the hunt. Cute, huh?"

"Not bad. I'm having a wire loop put on the tail of the fox we killed. Hang it from the rear-view mirror of my Duesie."

"Look what I got, guys," X-9 the Coward said. "I know you've been bad-mouthing me to HQ for being a coward, so I'm sending two tins of this stuff to Clyde and Speed. I think it'll square things with them for me. Whaddya think?" He showed them two cans labeled "Gentleman's Relish®."

"What is it?"

"Well, it's a kind of a shitty brown slimy stuff made of puréed rotted anchovies. The idea is to put it on toast in the morning. The bosses'll love it, make them think I really know my way around the *bon ton* here."

"I dunno, 'Niney," the Baroness Secret Agent said, "Seems to me the last guy who sprung something like that on the Chief is in the Pacific right now getting killed by the Japs."

Lanny saw that Junk Bond was leading the G-Gals and their foxes to the cashier. A few minutes later they were outside with their Sloane® shopping bags, getting into the limo Junk had waiting for them.

*　*　*

"That's the King over there," Junk said, pointing to a very ordinary-looking gent in shirtsleeves and braces *(which is what Brits call suspenders, remember. I don't know why either).*

"No good," PA 103 said sourly. "We want the King to look like a king for this picture. Tell him to get his crown and . . . what's that thing that looks like a rolling pin?"

"Scepter?"

"Yeah. Tell him to get rid of that cane, too. Makes him look like a hillbilly out huntin' for possums to bash."

"That's just not done. I just can't tell the King what to wear or what to hold. He's proud of that cane, gift from the King of Siam. Even sleeps with it, so I've heard. If I tell him to leave it home, I might get my head handed to me."

"Well if you can't, I can," and Presidential Agent 103 yelled, "Hey King, get your crown and get rid of that cane and get your scepter. Just for the photo. OK?"

"Must I?" he asked in a plummy but whiny voice.

"You want Ike to invade France or don'cha?"

"I think the Yank means business, your Kingness," Bond told him. "They won't start looking for Ike's mistress until they get their pictures of you. And their moms back home won't believe you're really the King unless you've got the king drag on. Without that stick thingy and with the scepter."

"Yeah, and we want the Queen to wear the Star of India crown."

"Hey sweetie," the King yelled to the Queen, who was holding a brace of corgis on leashes. *(Now this time I'm using 'brace' a third way: Not for teeth and not for suspenders, but to represent a small group of dogs. Confused? Me too. Bloody Brits!)* "Get your crown. The India one. These blokes want us in full costume."

She couldn't quite make out what the King was saying,

and when she cupped her hand to her ear, she lost hold of the dogs and they raced across the lawn toward the King. Acting on instinct, the G-Gals and Lanny opened fire, dropping the yapping curs in their tracks. Like the coward he was, X-9 had hidden behind a tree when the shooting started. When he saw the dogs were down, he sauntered over and administered the *coup de grâce*, a bullet in each of their cute little skulls, proud he had done the heroic thing and put them out of their misery.

"You've killed my babies!" the Queen screamed.

"Can't say how grateful I am, old chap," the King whispered to PA 103. "I hated those little bastards. You all deserve to be knighted for bumping them off, even the Coward over there," pointing to X-9, who was sashaying around striking heroic poses while blowing the smoke from his new Webley®.

"Let's get this shoot over with," Junk Bond said, pushing the King and the sobbing Queen into position. "Gather around them, guys. How 'bout if I pile the dog carcasses in front of you. It's the usual thing after we slaughter animals."

"Oh no," the Queen wailed. "My poor little babies!"

"It's for a good cause," the King consoled her. "Winning the war and all that. Straighten your crown. You look like you're drunk."

Bond had his Kodak Baby Brownie® out. "Let's see. Sun over my shoulder. Looking good. Big smiles. Come on, your Highnesses."

"Just a minute." He rearranged the pile of canine corpses so that he had them looking at the camera too, as *rigor mortis* fixed their mouths in fierce grins.

"Nice touch, that," the King complimented Bond. "You've got a talent for this sort of thing. How 'bout coming to work for me as palace photographer. Lot safer than getting sent to France to be killed by the Jerries. And if Queenie buys any more Corgis, you'll know what to do."

* * *

Bambi's girlfriends in the Poontang Patrol had gotten together with Geronimo's friends' squaws. They had set up a housewarming-party-cum-baby-shower for the couple's new Winnebago® and forthcoming papoose. The Taos tribe was already predicting the brat would be the Great Red Hope who would either free the tribe from the brutal occupation of the Great White Father or else land them a Budweiser Brewery® concession for the reservation.

As the party began to break into small groups, Secret Slut Agent Bliss called Bambi over. "Nice haul you got here. I imagine that the electric tamale maker will come in handy. These Indians eat pretty much the same stuff as the beaners — tamales and salsa and beans — but if you start eating that stuff, you're gonna have a can on you the size of a cow, and I mean a big cow."

"Noted and filed, Secret Agent Slut Bliss. You said you had something to report."

"You seen that new guy running errands for the red scientists? The one with all the hair, looks like a House of David baseball player?"

"I was wondering about him. Somehow seemed familiar."

"And how! Secret Slut Brandi had a session with him and says he has a left hook."

"A left hook? We all know the guy with the left hook."

"Right. The Pigeon. Whaddya think we should do? Arrest him? Kill him? He's got it coming to him, the dirty double-crossing rat. Or is he triple-crossing?"

Bambi thought for minute. "Nope. He wouldn't be here if he wasn't up to something big, even bigger than stealing atom bomb secrets or trying to get the Japs to steal the President's stamp collection. We wait until we figure out what he's got up his dirty treasonous sleeve, and then, and only then, we kill him."

Bambi looked around the Winnebago®. It was just about perfect. Too bad if she had to leave it for another top secret operation to save the country or maybe the world. The girls had given her a framed set of *Winnebago Wanderer®* magazine covers of the National Parks for the walls. The squaws had come up with a papoose backpack with a board for flattening the kid's head, a fashion they had borrowed from the Flathead tribe. She had a painted eagle bone to pierce his nose, compliments of a visiting Nez Perce adobe salesman. She shook her head sadly. Becoming a house squaw would have to wait. The Pigeon wouldn't have risked showing up unless he had an important plot up his dirty rotten sleeve. She better get a message to the Secret Agent Gals.

* * *

"Countesspoo got back to me," PA 103 told Bond. "She went back to the nightclub where she spotted Kay, and the *maître d'* said there was a message for 'three hot girls and a pair of Yank morons.'"

"Huh? Morons?" X-9 said. "I wonder who she could have meant?"

"Let's find out. It appears someone might have been telling stories about us," PA 103 told Bond, and he gestured over toward the Coward. "He may have switched sides. We gotta all get there right now."

When they arrived, the *maître d'* examined the Dashing Delegation from the Colonies and their British companion through his monocle. "I see the three hot broads and the morons, but who are you?" he asked Bond.

"The name is Bond, Jonquil Bond. You can call me Junk Bond. I'm the tour guide," he said, winking at Secret Agent Rebay.

"OK," the lackey murmured, bending over his desk, his left hand behind his back, hand cupped, the traditional gesture of a well-brought-up member of the British Servant Order (i.e., just about the entire class-ridden country) soliciting a bribe. PA 103 took a guinea out of his pocket and dropped it in the hand of the finagling flunky, who said, "And here's your letter."

Bond took a look at it before he passed it to Secret Agent Peggy. "Why, the envelope just has gibberish on it."

"Uh-uh," Peggy said. "That isn't gibberish. That's a Secret Agent secret message. Let's go to the can, ladies, where we can have some privacy. This may take some time," she told the three men, "so you may as well fortify yourselves. And be ready for anything. Underneath all those swell manners, the Brits hate us. Check your ammunition."

Bond pointed to a bottle of gin. The groveling servant brought it to them with glasses and ice. 007 poured them all a glassful, and said, "Here's how."

"How what?" the cowardly X-9 asked. "How can I know how until I know what? And when? And why? And where?"

"It just means something like 'down the hatch,'" PA 103 told him.

"Down what hatch?"

"Just drink up. Haven't you ever been drinking with the guys?"

"Not lately. Guys don't like cowards. Nowadays I generally just have a little drinkypoo with my mom and her friends. They just say 'tee-hee' before they drink. So, 'Tee-hee.'"

The men looked disgusted. "When exactly did you lose your nerve, X-9? You say you were a coward as a kid, but the G-Gals said you were plenty tough during the Nazi Rally case, and Secret Agent Rebay even hinted you were OK in the sack back then. So you weren't always a coward. What happened?"

"Beats me. One day I was the Number Three Ace G-Man,

right after Hilla and Peggy, you shoulda seen me kicking traitors' and public enemies' asses; the next day I was afraid of my own shadow. When we get back I'm gonna drop in on The Madman and see if he has any ideas. Or maybe Shitting Bull can do something for me. One of those magic heel-and-toe dances. Right now the only bigger cowards in the Bureau are Speed and Clyde, and they've got rank. When Rebay and Guggenheim do their next Annual Report on me, I'm afraid I'll be out on my ass."

While the Coward X-9 was letting down his hair, so to speak, Rebay was in the WC, translating the writing on the envelope with her Secret Decoder Ring®. When decrypted, the envelope read, "Eyes Only: Secret Agents Rebay and Guggenheim. From Secret Agent Summersby."

"What is this? Is every goddamn person in the world a Secret Agent?" Guggenheim said. "It'd be nice if someone filled us in on what's going on."

"'Need to know.' That's so if they torture us we can't give anything away."

"You're right," Peggy told her. "My God®, her secret message is two pages long. Lemme take page one, you do page two. Save some time. Those three oafs out there are going to be plastered by the time we finish."

When they were halfway through, Bond yelled through the door, "How you doing? The *maître d'* wants to know who's paying before he cracks open a new bottle of gin."

"Tell him it's on me!" Guggenheim yelled back.

When the two codebreakers were done, this is what they had:

"This is Secret Agent Kay Summersby, on undercover assignment for General of the Army Dwight David Eisenhower, code name 'Golfer.' I have ascertained that the Joe and Willy I have been investigating are not Bill Mauldin's Joe and Willy, who are actually fighting in

Italy. They are the top Nazi spies in England. I can't get them to wash, since they say they have to look like the unshaven slobs in Mauldin's cartoons, so I want 'Golfer' to know that getting intimate with them has been *trés dégoûtant*. Enough about me. Here's the deal: Among their many duties, besides sabotaging gas masks with pin holes, leaving lights on during blackouts, not flushing toilets, and other assorted acts of mayhem, they buy their *Führer* the little necessities he can't get in Germany: the brand of condoms he favors, Old Spice® deodorant, liniment for his riding britches and, get this, hair dye for his hair and moustache. All from Harrods®. That gave me an ideapoo. (I love the way the countesspoo talks.) You know that hair remover the Sluts tricked the Reds into sending to Stalin? I gotta buy the toiletries in three days for Joe and Willie, who can't get past Harrods doorman with their nauseating odor and general shitty looks, so if one of you could meet me at the men's beauty counter on Thursday, 2:00 pm, and pass me the hair dye cans with the snake oil hair remover ingredients, I can slip them to the Nazi ratbastards. Then the Nazi rats will send them to Hitler in a Red Cross pouch meant for his personal political prisoners he keeps on hand for when he's feeling blue and wants to torture somebody. Get cracking on getting that snake oil and get the hair dye cans. It's called Master Race Hair and Moustache Dye. Leave a message that you got the stuff with the *maître d'* here. He'd rape his mother for a guinea. And tell Golferpoo I love him."

"Wow," Secret Agent Hilla said. "Secret Agent Kay is some great spy. Although she could use a little help with paragraphing and topic sentences. Let's get going. I gotta get to a phone."

* * *

The housewarming party in the Winnebago® was just breaking up when the phone rang. Bambi called Geronimo over and asked him to get the folks out of the trailer. "Got a super-secret phone call. Secret Agent Gal Rebay. Spy stuff. Bliss, hang around."

Bliss watched Bambi as her pal took the phone call. She watched as Bambi stiffened. A stern look came over her lovely face, she shook her breasts into "atten-hut," and she saluted as she put down the phone.

"Secret Agent Slut Bliss, the Secret Agent Gals have come up with a plan that just might save the world and get a couple of us promotions. They haven't told Speed yet. Basically it's that same *Plan 97 with the Dandruff Option* we used on Stalin. We gotta steal two cans of snake oil hair remover from the Reds and get the stuff to London by tomorrow. There'll be a transport plane waiting for you and me at the Santa Fe airport. Do you know how we can get our hands on the crap?"

"Roger that. They are all in Ma Oppenheimer's safe, all labeled but only we know which is which. Plus I've got the combo."

Bambi relayed the Baroness's orders: "We are to try to do this the nice way: slip her a mickey and open the safe. But I got orders that we can't let nothin' stop us, so if we have to pistol whip her, torture her, or kill her, we gotta do what we gotta do."

"I never liked that bitch anyway."

"Me neither. And didja tell Rebay 'bout The Pigeon?"

"Yeah. She says she'll get on it."

CHAPTER 12

The Secret Agent Baroness had a pile of shillings in front of her in one of those outdoor red phone booths you see in English movies (but the movies are black and white, so you just have to imagine they're red). This call was going to take a lot longer than the one to Bambi.

"Speed," she said, reporting back to Washington HQ. "Secret Agent Rebay here. Secret Agents Guggenheim and the Coward X-9 are with me, along with Presidential Agent 103. Secret Slut Knockers couldn't quite fit in, if you know what I mean. Pretty cozy in this phone booth. You know the old joke, right, about how many Secret Agents you can fit in a British phone booth? It's a good one, right?

"Anyway, this is a heads-up. We're onto something big. What? You wanna know the punch line? Figure it out for yourself. I ain't got time to explain every fucking thing to every fucking moron — no, I didn't mean you're a moron — I'm the top counterspy in England, and I got other things to do besides explaining jokes. Things and stuff. And if you ask me one more time what the

Secret Agent Gals 265

'D' in 'D-Day' stands for, I'm gonna tell that Sonuvabitch in the White House it's OK with me if he sends you to the Pacific to get killed by the Japs. Stop crying and listen up. Yes, I still like you."

"Here's our big break. Mostly due to Secret Agent Kay Summersby, you know, Eisenhower's honey. Is Clyde on the line? Good. Two heads are better than one. On second thought, maybe not that *particular* second head. Get him off!

"Look. We had good luck with the phony bomb that blew up in Stalin's face. Yes, I'm sure it was Stalin. Hitler's the one in Germany. Yeah, I know. It's confusing. And we had even better luck foisting the hair remover off on Stalin. *Plan 97 with the Dandruff Option*, remember? Made him look like even more of a fool than that Sonuvabitch in the White House. Yes. I'm sure it was Stalin. Think you could stop interrupting? Thanks.

"Listen up. We gotta chance to throw a Hail Mary touchdown pass and win the war. Do you see where this is going? No?

"And who's that. Clyde? You were supposed to get off the line. You don't see where this is going either? Not surprised. Yes, I'm proud of you that you know the 'Hail Mary.' I believe you, stop reciting it … Amen.

"OK. Hold this thought: That stuff the Reds at Los Alamos developed that we used on Stalin is the most powerful hair removal snake oil in history. We need more of it. We're going to reuse *Plan 97 with the Dandruff Option,* but on someone else this time. Got that? Yes, I know what they call football here is really soccer. Or maybe rugby. No, not cricket. 'Hail Mary touchdown' was a metaphor. That means, aw, forget it! Clyde! Get off the line. Or at least keep quiet. You've made me lose my train of thought. Where was I?

"Right. Hair remover. I want you guys to think hard. Who's another guy whose mojo depends on a moustache and stupid haircut. No? Here's a hint: Germany. No, dammit, I told you Stalin's the one in Russia. *Der Führer.* You don't speak Spanish,

Clyde? That's *German*. Don't speak that either? Don't you read the newspapers? Oh, too busy going over personnel files to get guys to send to the Pacific to get killed by the Japs. OK, I understand.

"Well, the answer to the Jackpot Question is *Hitler*. Adolf Hitler. No, goddammit. That's *not* the guy in Russia. And what we're going to do is get Hitler to rub that snake oil into his mustache and hair. *Plan 97 with the Dandruff Option,* and it's pre-tested this time. And get it? His hair and his moustache fall out. And he loses his *mojo*. Don't know what *mojo* is? It's a technical psychology word, means a magic something that makes you into a leader of men. Like you got, Speed. Yeah, *you* too, Clyde.

"It's a great idea. I've already got Special Agent Super Sluts Bambi and Bliss stealing the snake oil off the Reds, and they're going to be on a plane to London tonight with the stuff. Secret Agent Kay has figured out how to get the stuff to Hitler. And one more thing. Brandi thinks The Pigeon has shown up again in Los Alamos, but I think I've given you enough for one phone call. Tell Clyde to make a note that I told you about The Pigeon. I don't want you to blame me when that ratbastard triple or quadruple traitor comes up with another outrageous and evil scheme to fuck the Bureau, the USA, and God®."

* * *

Junk Bond and the Coward X-9 met Secret Agent Super Sluts Bambi and Bliss at the airport. Bambi had an aluminum suitcase fastened to her wrist. Her baby bump was showing just enough for The Coward to begin counting backwards on his fingers to his last motivational visit to the Poontang Patrol. *Could he be the culprit?* "Deny everything, admit nothing, you never knew the girl, and you pulled it out in time." That was the rule for this kind of situation set down in *Secret Agent Handbook's "Plan #9:*

For When the Rabbit Dies."

They drove to Harrods® and 007 sent the Coward X-9 in to buy the Master Race Hair and Moustache Dye®. "And don't forget the receipt."

A few minutes later X-9 was back with the cans in a Harrods® bag. "Got the receipt?"

"I forgot."

"Goddammit, get back in there and get it." Bambi shook her head. "Fucking idiot. Ya wanna get reimbursed, or not?"

They all assembled at the MI6 science lab, where MI6's own mad scientist, Crazy Cuthbert, outfitted in a wizard hat and a black robe, met them. "How's MAD-1?" he asked Secret Agent Rebay. "Still as nuts as ever? Love that guy. Now what do you want me to do?"

"See these cans of Master Race Hair and Moustache Dye®?"

"Good stuff. We use it on the old geezer wizards at Hogwarts."

"Now see these two cans? They're a super-secret snake-oil hair remover. We want you to transfer the snake oil into the hair and moustache dye cans so that it looks just the same, same color, same slimy feel. Think you can do that?"

"Highly unethical, old man. The poor chap who uses the stuff will have his hair and moustache fall out. I'd have to put a warning label on the can."

"Can you keep a secret? Not tell anyone? Except maybe the chaps at your Club?"

"Sure. Mum's the word."

"This stuff is going to Hitler."

"Hitler?"

"You know, *Der Führer*, the homicidal maniac who's running Germany, the guy in charge of the army we're going to fight if Ike ever gets off his ass and invades France."

"I thought Hitler was the one in Russia?"

"No, it's Germany. I'm sure. The idea is that if his moustache falls off, he will lose his mojo, and while the Germans are in a state of panic we invade and defeat them, and *Bob's your uncle*."

"Well, I'm not sure I follow all that. Also, I don't keep up with politics, but it sounds like you know what you're doing. As for my Uncle Bob, most unkind of you to bring that up. He's a pedophile and he's in jail."

Crazy Cuthbert opened up the cans of Master Race® etc. and the cans of snake oil.

"The snake oil and the dye seem to be about the same consistency. I'll just mix some black soot into the snake oil, mix it up a little bit with my magic wand, like this." He did as he said, and nobody could see any difference between the two slimy messes. "Now I just take the Master Race® stuff out of its cans," and he poured the dye into a lab beaker, scrubbed the cans clean, and filled them with the black snake oil. He pressed the lids on the Master Race® cans, then washed the snake oil cans, filled them with the hair dye, put the lids on them, and said, "Anyone want the hair dye? No? Hate to waste it. Mind if I take it to Hogwarts?"

The next afternoon, the Coward X-9 was busying himself at the men's beauty counter at Harrods®. He saw a woman approach in what he immediately recognized as a Secret Agent disguise: sunglasses, trench coat, designer handbag. He gave the Secret Agent Howdeedo, and she did the same. He slipped her the two cans. He couldn't find the receipt. He searched though all his pockets and found the receipt in the last place he looked (old joke).

"You really are a moron," Secret Agent Kay told him.

"You're not the first one to say that," X-9 replied sadly. "And you probably won't be the last. And you hardly know me. I know I don't make a very good first impression, but my friends get to like me, or they would if I had any friends."

* * *

General of the Army Dwight David Eisenhower lowered his pants to show Secret Agent Rebay he had not been kidding when he said he had a case of blue balls verging on terminal. Rebay couldn't actually see his balls. "Do you mind if I just move your weenie a little over to the side? My God®, that's awful. That is really awful. They really are blue! Almost *purple!* Yikes! I've never seen anything like that! Mind if I take a picture of them for the *Northern South Dakota Journal of Gruesome Gonads*?"

"Stop messing around down there," Ike told her. "The doctors said that if I get a hard-on I might have what they call a blowout; the thing might just explode. And what I really need is a good, lovingly applied blow job, and from no one but Kay. She made me promise not to get a blow job from anyone but her. I gave her my West Point ring and she gave me this plastic Post Toasties® copy of her Secret Agent Decoder Ring®, because she needs the real one for work. So ya might say we're going steady. You gotta get Kay back. The doctors say the next stage is purple balls, and they'd have to be amputated.

"Right now if I even think about her, I start to feel a boner coming on. And if I try to do my job and figger out how we're gonna beat the Huns, as a trained warrior I start to get excited all over again. They told me the only thing that might keep me out of trouble is to say the rosary every day and pray to St. Aloysius, the patron saint of impotence. Care to join me in a decade of the Sorrowful Mysteries?"

"Maybe later."

"You really think she'll be back soon?"

"She's just waiting for word that the Master Race Hair and Moustache Dye® has reached Hitler in Berlin. Then she has to kill Joe and Willie. Doesn't want to leave any loose ends."

"Aren't they supposed to get some sort of trial first?"

"It's all on the up-and-up. *D-Day Plan, Subsection 78.* You gotta appoint her a temporary military judge. I got the forms right here for you to sign. Then she shoots them in the legs so they can't get away, reads them their rights, takes their pleas, deliberates, finds them guilty, and finishes them off."

"Sounds OK to me, 'course I'm no lawyer. And then she comes back to me?"

"That's the plan."

"Just so you know I haven't changed my mind: There's not gonna be *no* invasion until we have our reunion."

"You must be pretty proud of her, General. She has been living a life of danger, like a forest ranger, not to mention risking infestation by cooties, chiggers, and any other vermin those two Nazi spy slobs are carrying around with them. Anything you need for your welcome home party?"

"Yeah. You could help me hang this banner. I wanna stretch it across the room."

Secret Agent Rebay took one end and Scotch-taped® it to the arch separating the front and rear parlors. Ike did the same to the other end. "Welcome Home Lt. Colonel Kay Summersby."

"That's a little surprise I cooked up for her. She was only a major when she left. Think she'll like that?"

"Of course. That's so nice. But if you really wanted to mess with Hoover's mind, you could make her a bird colonel, 'cause that's the same rank as Hoover, a Navy captain. And if you *really really* want to fuck with him, make her a brigadier general, 'cause that's the same as a Rear Admiral, and Hoover would saw off his left nut for that."

"Don't mention nuts, if you don't mind." Ike covered up his. "Promotion to brigadier general's got to be reviewed by Congress, but maybe I could call it a battlefield promotion. She will have killed two dangerous enemies at great risk to her life, stockings, fingernails, and make-up. I'll do it. Got a magic marker?"

"Right here, General," and Eisenhower crossed out the Lt. Colonel and wrote in "*General* Summersby."

"Have you given any thought to how you're gonna be dressed when she gets back?"

Ike went to his closet and pulled out a long black silk dressing gown. "Pretty romantic, huh?" He stripped down to his tighty-whiteys and slipped on the gown. "I figure I'll kind of lounge on the sofa here like this when she comes in and, get this" — he took a long-stemmed rose from the vase and gripped it in his teeth — "Ouch. Got to cut off them thorns before I try that again."

"Don't worry, General, I'll take care of that."

"I'll have chilled champagne ready for her, and Gentleman's Relish® on toast points."

Rebay gagged. "You actually eat that stuff? Mind if I bring a can of Cheese Wiz® and a bag of *Fritos®*?"

"Sure. I'll give you a call when Kay and I have finished the welcome home shenanigans. And bring the rest of your gang. Especially Secret Super Slut Knockers. I hear she's got a pair on her that just don't quit. I really want to see them, I mean 'her.' See if my spies were right."

"Your intelligence was correct on that point, or points, General. I hope it's right on everything else."

* * *

Every citizen of Berlin who didn't want to be shot had shown up for Hitler's weekly rally at the Brandenburg Gate. Thousands of goose-stepping Hitler *Jugends* marched by the podium giving the Nazi salute to the Führer, who returned their tribute with an arm half raised. Like he was bored. One of the *Jugends* tried the same lazy salute and was immediately machine-gunned. Point made. What's good for the leader is not necessarily good for the led. *(Something to remember, kids. Just because your dad gets drunk, doesn't mean you can.)*

Tanks rolled by; fighter planes did aerobatics overhead. The crowd had been disappointed to learn that they wouldn't catch a glimpse of their beloved Führer's face. It had been announced that he had a cold, probably sabotage by Jewish Bolshevik traitors who were being tortured to death at that moment — cheers all around — and so he was wearing a surgical mask. (Of course this meant that the masses scrambled to find surgical masks they too could wear, but the stores were all closed for the parade and, besides, only a Jew would cover his face in front of *der Führer*.) The crowd was confused.

Finally, the parade was over, and the crowd, carefully kept in good order by black-uniformed storm troopers carrying the feared German grease guns, was allowed to mass in front of *der Führer*. Then Hitler began one of his trademarked hysterical harangues that so appealed to the German soul. As a berserker frenzy took control of *der Führer*, he began hopping up and down — the crowd loved it — and shaking his head violently from side to side — the crowd shrieked with joy. But when a performer is totally into doing his watusi thing with no thought of consequences, that's when a wardrobe malfunction is most to be feared. And so it was. Just as Hitler reached the point in his speech that the crowd always anticipated with joy, screaming that the Jews and the Bolsheviks would never keep Germany from doing this, that, or the other thing, hard to make out exactly what he claimed the Jews and Bolsheviks were up to whenever he really went off his rocker, the *Führer* shook his head violently — and his hat and mask flew off.

Dead silence. "Oh this," he yelled, pointing to his bare upper lip and scalp, "German scientists have perfected the most advanced hair dyes in the world, and they make hair invisible. *(And for all you kids out there, 'invisible' means you can't see it but it's really there.)* So don't worry, I've still got that cute little Charlie Chaplin moustache you all love, and the same wacky haircut with a disgusting hank of hair plastered to my brow. So don't worry *Herrenvolk*. *(That means 'Master Race')* Your Führer is *ganz gut (means A-OK)*."

By this time in 1944, Germans had gotten used to believing just about any kinda shit Hitler told them, no matter how weird, and so the adults among them just shrugged their shoulders and said, "Wow! Invisible hair dye. That's pretty good. We got some great scientists, best in *die Welt*, especially since we got rid of that phony Jew science like relativity and Darwinism. Well maybe Darwin wasn't exactly a Jew but why take chances because any stuff you can't understand is probably Jewish."

So, the adults were all willing to give the Führer the benefit of the doubt, when a six-year-old boy cried out, in a high-pitched voice that carried over the silenced crowd, *"Der Führer hat keine Haare."* Hitler pointed at the kid, and yelled "Kill that little Jew," and the storm troopers promptly machine-gunned the kid, his parents, and everyone around them. But the crowd had heard. First other kids began yelling, *"Der Führer hat keine Haare,"* then adults picked up the chant. The *Führer* realized he was in danger of losing his *mojo*.

Never one to fart around in a time of crisis, Hitler turned to Goering and said, "Get Rommel and his division back from Normandy. We need to put down this uprising. I'm losing my mojo."

Minutes later Rommel and his division, perched on the cliffs overlooking the Normandy beaches, spun around toward the East and began hauling ass toward Berlin. When the invasion began a few hours later, only one of the few troops left behind noticed the boats arriving on the beach, and when he hollered out "We're fucked" (in German), his commanding officer immediately had him shot.

Two hours earlier, Secret Agents Rebay and Guggenheim had burst into Eisenhower's quarters, where the general was sprawled across his bed, stark naked and sound asleep. General Kay Summersby was on one side of him, and Secret Slut Knockers was on the other side, and each had an arm around Ike who was snoring away with a satisfied smile on his face. Rebay lifted up the sheet and satisfied herself with one glance that his balls were no longer blue. "General, General, the plan worked. Hitler's lost his mojo. And we got a picture of him without any hair and no moustache. A million copies are being dropped on Germany right now. Hitler's ordered Rommel's troops back to Berlin."

The general jumped out of bed and yelled for Kay to get him his Jeep. "We're launching the invasion right now. Get me to my goddamn command post. It's D-Day! And will somebody explain to me why it's *D-Day*. It should be *I-Day*, because *Invasion* starts with an 'I.' What does that 'D' stand for, anyway?"

"At least put on some pants, General," Kay begged him, "you can't lead the invasion with your pecker blowing in the breeze."

"No time for that. Tell everybody I'm wearing an invisible uniform."

* * *

It was turning into "The Good War" for General of the Army Dwight David Eisenhower and now *Major* General Kay Summersby, who were enjoying the spoils of war from liberated Paris — scarfing down frog legs *a l'orange* flown in from Maxim's, refreshing their taste buds with highball glasses of *Chateau Mouton Rothschild®* and picking at desserts of *Gentleman's Relish®* on toast points accompanied by snifters of priceless nineteenth century *Chateau d'Yquem®*.

Not such a good war for *der Führer* in his Berlin bunker. He had pulled his most evil and murderous troops out of the

American and Russian fronts to look for something that would re-grow his moustache and restore his mojo. While he was hopefully checking his upper lip in the mirror each morning for a sprout of hair, he took up watercolors again. Göering organized an exhibit of his paintings in the *Führer* bunker, and the jury— Goering, Göebbels, and Rosenberg, agreed *nem. con. (If you took my advice and studied Latin, kids, translating that is a piece of gateau)* that Hitler's masterful depictions of Alpine flowers made the pathetic efforts of the other major painters of the current unpleasantness, Eisenhower and Churchill, look like pieces of homemade *scheiss*. Göering told the *Führer* that after the war, if they won, he was go-ing to award Hitler top honors at the next Paris Salon, something that came with a full year sabbatical at the *Uffizi*.

That's one debt I'm not gonna have to pay off, the fat *Luft-marschall* chortled to himself.

* * *

Back at the Taos Indian Reservation Trailer Park, Bambi and Geronimo were spending the fall of 1944 waiting out her preg-nancy and listening to the exciting pennant drive of the Cleveland Indian team of 4-Fs and amputees. Geronimo was even thinking of naming his firstborn after "Chief Wahoo."

But now they were having their first little spattypoo. (*I gotta cut out that -poo thing*, Bambi thought. *Might be overdoing it.*)

Her prenatal counseling sessions with Shitting Bull were colorful all right. In fact a visiting anthropologist from the College of Staten Island was in ecstasy, visions of tenure dancing in his little brain as he observed the medicine man and the tribal squaws dancing around Bambi, who was stripped naked with a turtle shell on each breast, and an eagle feather G-string where a G-string — whatever "G" stood for in this particular context — was usually worn. *(That "G" back there in the previous sentence surely didn't mean "Government" as in "G-Gals" and "G-Men." Well, there are some mysteries that won't be solved in this book, but please don't call this one a plot-hole. and come at me with a bad review just because I didn't dot all the i's and cross all the t's. Or is it the other way around? I've got a life to live besides writing these stories for ya.)*

Bambi kinda liked the tom-tomming, the stupid heel-and-toe dancing, the way the fire flared up when Shitting Bull tossed a handful of Mary Jane into the flames. It was just that the midwife looked so unsanitary. She had a nasty habit of picking her nose and eating the boogers, and now she was passing time plucking and gutting a chicken.

"You gonna wash your hands before you start fishing around in me to grab hold of the papoose?" she asked Special Delivery Squaw Minnehooha.

"Nope. I'd just get dirty again. I'll clean up afterwards."

So back at the trailer, Bambi told her favorite fuck-buddy, "You know, Gerry, I really think I'd like to have the papoose in a hospital."

"Minnehooha and Shitting Bull no have visiting privileges at Santa Fe Hospital," he told her.

"Thank God® for that. Such a relief. Do you know anything about the germ theory of disease?"

"Geronimo not know nothing about nothing beyond third grade. Me kill many many buffalo with bow and arrow, no need science."

"OK, I love you dearly, but you're just an ignorant savage, very cute, but you don't have the background to make an informed decision about medical care."

"How come if you're so smart you're just a whore?"

"Good question. That was an undercover assignment. Before that I was a fully trained FBI agent with a nursing degree and a hobby of stamp collecting, just like our President, the Sonuvabitch in the White House. As a matter of fact, I just bought some of his collection, which the Widder Roosevelt filched and put up for auction, some kind of revenge, I guess. Dincha ever wonder how come I never came down with any of those diseases, you know, down there? It's because I know all sorts of what they call prophylactic measures that kept me safe to have a healthy papoose."

"Shitting Bull and Minnehooha no like this. They no covered by insurance. He wants two blankets. She gets one."

"How come no equal pay? I don't like that."

"He's got a graduate degree in medicine man stuff. From other medicine men. It's on the wall of his teepee."

"I didn't see no degree there."

"It's painted on a deerskin. Picture of Shitting Bull hopping around a campfire, with other medicine men whipping him with snake skins and eagle feathers. Very folkloristic. That jerk from Staten Island went nuts over it, took pictures of it. Ask him."

"How about a compromise? I'll give him three blankets, and Minnehooha the same. They don't have to do anything."

"I dunno. The whole tribe will want to see papoose. How about if we let them go through their monkeyshines in the delivery tent and then they go outside with a little Indian doll in a blanket and yell, 'It's a brave?' Then you go to the hospital and have the papoose."

"Think it through, Gerry. What if I actually have a squaw baby and you've told everyone it's a brave? We'd have a lot of 'splainin' to do."

"Let's have Shitting Bull go out and say you've had twins. brave and squaw. Then you go to the hospital. Have a brave, we say the squaw croaked. Other way around if you have a squaw."

"That's brilliant. Only thing that could go wrong is if I have twin braves, or two squaw twins. But that's not very likely.

Lemme see. We had this problem back at nursing school. I think there are four sets of twins per hundred births. One set will be both squaws. One, both braves. Two sets of twins, one of each. So, we are faced with only a two percent chance of both braves or both squaws. If that happens, we dress them both the same, don't let anybody but us look in their diapers, and then move out of town and start over. High-five and fist-bump, Gerry. You *are* smart, for an uneducated savage."

* * *

General Ike — you remember, the guy we last saw wearing an invisible four-star general uniform with a very sharp-looking invisible Eisenhower jacket, getting ready to invade France — used to say that in combat "simple plans are difficult and complicated plans are impossible."

Well, the plan Bambi and Geronimo had concocted to outwit the Taos tribe sure was complicated — bamboozling them into thinking that Shitting Bull and Minehooha had delivered Bambi of twin papooses, while the mom secretly slipped out to the hospital to give birth in sterile conditions as the two savage medicine people cooed over a couple of prototype Chatty Cathy®/Betsy Wetsy® dolls, papoose squaw and papoose brave, one of each.

Well, in words that would one day be immortalized by Nelson Mandela, everything is impossible until it happens, and by God®, IT WORKED. On toppa that, the happy Indian lovebirds didn't even have to report back to the tribe that one of the brats had croaked, which would have touched off a week of howling lamentation and maybe even an attack on Shitting Bull for malpractice, because when Bambi looked down at what was going on, she saw that she had actually given birth to TWINS: a boy papoose and a girl papoose.

I mean, wotthahell? You know what the odds were of that?

Exactly two out of one hundred. And because readers of books like this are probably no mathematical geniuses, I'll simplify it for you. That's one out of fifty. What you do is put the two over the hundred and divide the numerator and denominator by two and you get . . . work it out for yourself. Cast out nines, and you'll see I'm right.

So Bambi, being healthier than the normal slut, was released from the hospital a week after the papooses were born, and she and Geronimo returned to the Taos settlement (the oldest continuously occupied community in the U.S., according to a leaflet put out by the local chapter of Alcoholics Anonymous) for a triumphal homecoming. The twins were dragged into town on a *travois* pulled by two dogs. *(A travois is a kind of Indian stretcher with two sticks tied together at one end, and a G.I. blanket between them, because the Indians, North and South Americans included, for some reason had never managed to invent the wheel. How dumb is that! Or a lot of other things like pop-off cans for beer. They did come up with fire, so give them some credit, for God®'s sake. Although as any Boy Scout will tell you, the rubbing-two-sticks-together method generally doesn't work, especially in the rain. Thank God for Zippos®.)*

* * *

According to a tribal tradition Shitting Bull had learned from the Straight Arrow cards that separated the layers in a Post Shredded Wheat® box, it was his job as a Medicine Man to figger out the true names of the brats in a dream vision. And he had done just that, sitting in a sweat lodge, chewing Wrigley's Spearmint® gum, fasting, breathing in fumes of loco weed he threw on the fire, and pounding down 6-pack after 6-pack of Bud®. When his assistant medicine men dragged him out, he was next thing to dead, but they splashed cold water on him and butt-snapped him with knotted wet towels, and he revived, somewhat the worse for wear.

At first babbling in the Taos language, which was not intelligible to anyone, even the Indians, since Shitting Bull could barely speak English, let alone his ancestral tongue, he revealed that Thumper the Rabbit God® had appeared to him and breathed into his ears many secrets from the Happy Hunting Ground, which the Bull-man seemed to have confused with the Anheuser-Busch Beer Garden® in St. Louis he had visited on a class trip before he dropped out of high school in his sophomore year to join the army and then go to prison.

"The Great God® Thumper himself has vouchsafed" *(The use of the word 'vouchsafed' proves the Bull Shitter actually must have had a vision, since no one had ever heard him utter words of more than one syllable before)* "to me the sacred names of the squaw papoose and brave papoose of our mighty warrior Geronimo and his beautiful Secret Slut Squaw. The squaw papoose will be named Elizabeth Pocahontas Warren Geronimo and the brave will be Johnny Cash Geronimo."

Geronimo begged to know if Thumper gave the holy sachem *(a sachem is a chief, or leader, kids, something to strive for in yer own miserable lives)* any hints about their future. Would Johnny Cash bring us the Budweiser® Brewery we have waited for so long? And what about Elizabeth Pocahontas? Many papooses?

"Yowzah! Do I have surprises for you?" Shitting Bull said, pausing to prolong the suspense, prolonging it so long he dozed off.

Geronimo kicked him awake, and said, "Out with it, you quack."

"The squaw papoose will go to law school, where she will learn how to fleece clients and get away with murder, the boy papoose will go to jail where he will learn useful things like rolling joints and making license plates."

"Jeeze," Bambi said. "I'd rather Elizabeth Pocahontas went to jail, too. I don't want her to be no shyster. Lawyers cause all the problems of the world and just generally fuck things up, and sometimes they even gyp their parents out of their pensions and Winnebagos®. Let her go to jail too. Rolling joints is an important skill for a squaw, and making license plates is a good trade."

"I ain't tol' you the beauty part yet," Shitting Bull smirked. "Harvard Law School is going to make your daughter a tenured full professor just for being an Indian and, get this, she gets to be the first Indian squaw to be a losing candidate for President."

"President of what?" Bambi asked suspiciously.

"Of the U.S. of A. Howdja like that?"

"That is pretty good. And since she loses, she doesn't have to do all that boring shit like pardoning the turkey, hosting the Easter egg roll *(that's a stupid tradition of rolling eggs on the lawn, not the Chinese kind of egg roll)*, and pretending she's sorry when she gets soldiers killed in her stupid wars. Not bad. But how about my boy? What's he do when he gets out of jail? Besides roll joints and make license plates?"

"He's gonna be a rock 'n' roll star like Johnny B. Goode, but more into cowboy kinda stuff, not that he isn't proud to be a redskin, but he develops a feather allergy, so he switches sides. But get this. One of his hit songs is 'Don't Take Your Guns to Town.' One of them songs with a moral lesson for little tykes, because not only does he play with guns, but he starts killing people and gets caught and hanged." *(Well, in Cash's defense, the song is about Billy Joe who gets shot in his first gun fight when he's had [maybe?] his first drink in a bar.)*

"My boy gets hanged? Wot kinda fuck-up is that? Maybe he should be a crooked lawyer like his sister."

Shitting Bull calmed Bambi down by explaining it was the guy in the song who got hanged, not her papoose *(and I myself would say that Bambi and Geronimo have every reason to be proud of the futures in store for their little papoose squaw and brave.)*

Bambi relayed the great news about her papooses' futures to Secret Agent Rebay in her weekly report on The Pigeon, who was staying put and was still trying for a freebie, this time from Bambi herself. "No sale, so far," she reported, "but I'm ready to give it up to save the country. *A sus ordenes*, as the beaners say."

"When duty whispers low 'Thou must come across,'" the Baroness said approvingly, "the slut replies, 'I can.'"

CHAPTER 13

The V-J Day parade a year later was the longest Manhattan's Canyon of Heroes had ever hosted. Tanks. Row after row of WAVES and WACs in their newly shortened skirts, giving an 'eyes right' past the reviewing stands. Soldiers, Marines, Air Force, Coast Guard, all bellowing out their service songs, "Up in the Air, Junior Birdmen," etc. The reviewing stand was a block long, behind it giant X-ed out portraits of Hitler, Mussolini, Tojo, Charlie Chan, Mr. Moto and Fu Manchu.

On the reviewing stand, the President and First Lady Truman and former First Lady Eleanor Roosevelt, along with her ne'er-do-well sons, were sharing the place of honor with the British delegation: Winston Churchill, the King and Queen and her new Corgis, and the Prince of Wales, also known as the Monkey Man because of excessive body hair and his banana jones. There too were His Majesty's Secret Service Agent Jonquil (Junk) Bond and his infant son, Chums Bond, in a backpack. Next to them, so they could hitch a ride to the British Consulate party after the parade, were Speed, Clyde, and Secret Agents Rebay, Guggenheim,

X-9, Presidential Agent 103, and the entire Secret Slut Poontang Patrol led by Secret Sluts Knockers, Bambi, Brandi, and Bliss, and, representing the Noble Savages of the Plains, was Bambi's one and only, Squaw Man Geronimo, in charge of their two-papoose perambulator.

At the end of the magnificent parade, after the military had strutted their stuff *(and why not? they had just won the "Good War")* were floats from General Motors®, Ford®, and Chrysler® with models of the cars that would be in dealers' showrooms as soon as the assembly lines could retool from tanks and planes. General Electric® had a float of new refrigerators and washing machines (which confused Speed since he thought General Electric should be up front with the rest of the generals), and RCA® had a float of new-fangled televisions, with pictures of Goofy, Dumbo®, and Jesus® pasted on the for-now-inoperative screens.

Bringing up the rear was a manure cart drawn by a mule, a Barry Fitzgerald look-alike at the reins (or maybe it was the lovable rascal himself) smoking a clay pipe, a green leprechaun hat perched on his head, while leprechaun-dressed smurfs wielding brooms and shovels cleaned up the mess left by the cavalry horses and the squad of elephants lent by the King of England (a.k.a. Emperor of India) for the great United Nations Victory Parade.

As the manure cart drew up in front of the reviewing stand, Barry jumped off the cart, and sang "Whenever they got his Irish up, Clancy lowered the boom," and he immediately disappeared into the crowd as the manure cart exploded on cue with the word "Boom." The Queen screamed. Junk Bond threw himself in front of the Royal Couple and their Corgis, and received a blast of horse and/or elephant shit in the face. "Goddammit," the King groused, "Why'd he have to save the Corgis?" J. Edgar turned to Truman and told him, "This is one mess we're NOT going to investigate. I'd do anything for my country except dig through that."

"But shouldn't we comb through the crime scene, figure

out what caused the shit to blow up, and recover Barry's body?"

"Barry got away, and I don't think that was Barry. Didja notice he was wearing sunglasses? Sure tip-off that he was someone disguised as Barry. And besides, this could have been a case of spontaneous combustion. Too much manure in the manure pile. Violation of *Manure Cart Safety Regulations*. I believe we can hit the estate of the Barry look-alike with a $25 fine, if he has an estate, which I doubt, since these bog-trotters tend not to have any money 'cause they have to give it all to their priests."

"So, what should we do?"

"Have a couple of Bobcats® shovel the mess into the harbor."

"Sounds good. Do I have any poo on my face?" the President asked Hoover.

"No sir. You're good. But the Queen has it all over *her* face! Frankly, though, it improves her looks. No offense."

"None taken," the King replied with a chortle.

(Now, this is kind of a test for attentive, not to say retentive, readers. Think back on that song, "Clancy Lowered the Boom," that The Pigeon was singing when he blew up the manure cart all over the King and the President and everyone on the reviewing stand, Including Speed, guess where Johnny Cash Geronimo got the tune for his hit song, "Don't Take Your Guns to Town"? Give up? It's the same tune as "Clancy Lowered the Boom." No shit! And by the way, attentive readers, there have been clues scattered all through this book about how this story is going to turn out, which is a good trick, because at this point, I have no idea myself! Happy hunting.)

* * *

The Criminal Division of the FBI wasn't taking the case as lightly as their Director, whose ridiculous spontaneous combustion

286   *Powers*

theory was plainly just a ploy to keep from having to sift through the horse and elephant shit personally, and who could blame him? Since Agents Rebay and Guggenheim had been the closest to the crime scene, they were put in charge of the investigation, which they code-named "The Paddy Poop Bomb Mystery." They sent orders to the field offices for an inventory of the Irish manure carts in their districts, and the results were astounding. There were over five thousand horse-drawn manure carts roaming the forty-eight states, all driven by Irishmen who called themselves Clancy, just like all Pullman porters called themselves George. And when FBI agents visited the horse-cart driving schools in their regions, they discovered an unnerving pattern. Instead of asking to have their first lessons be simulators of little pony carts for kids to ride at county fairs, the Irish trainees wanted their lessons to start with full-sized manure cart simulators. Very unusual, and ominous. And suspicious, too.

An FBI agent in Ireland briefed headquarters on the M.O. for Irish terrorists. (*I've already explained M.O. to you, kids, and I'm not gonna do it again.*) The standard delivery system was to place a bomb (an "infernal machine," the Irish called it) on a cart, then cover it with manure, and park it in front of the target. There were one or two Irish "dirty bombs" every decade or so in England and Ireland. And now the manure-bomb terror had come to America.

Secret Agents Rebay and Guggenheim went through the *Secret Agents' Handbook* and couldn't find a secret plan that fit the current crisis exactly. "We're gonna hafta improvise," Rebay told her squad.

"'Improvise' is my middle name," Guggenheim replied.

"I didn't know that," X-9 whined. "Is it a secret middle name? How come I don't have a secret middle name?"

"How about 'Stupid?'" Knockers suggested.

"That was mean, Knockers!" *He'd show her*!

"X-9, you're in charge of the shit survey. You've gotta give orders to all the Special Agents in Charge to poke into all the manure carts in their areas with ten-foot poles to see which ones have bombs in them."

"I don't have to do any poking myself, do I?"

"Only if a Secret Agent doing the poking gets sick, develops an allergy, or maybe, if he's Irish, goes over to the other side."

"Aw, do I gotta?"

"Yes. Now get to work on those phones."

When the results of the survey started coming in, the FBI had located five hundred manure carts with bombs hidden under the horse shit. The rest were decoys. Rebay consulted with the FBI legal counsel. It turned out that manure bombs were covered by the Second Amendment. Any citizen or resident alien was entitled to a manure bomb for personal defense purposes or, for that matter, as an exercise of his First Amendment right to freedom of speech. (And you gotta admit that blowing up a cart full of shit is one heck of an expression of freedom of speech.) But when a Clancy sets off a bomb, if he survives, the Bureau could treat him just like a public enemy and shoot him dead.

"Doesn't seem like we're doing enough to protect the public," Guggenheim objected.

"Can I get a medal for doing such a good job on the shit survey?" X-9 begged.

"Shut up."

"How come no one ever listens to me when I get a great idea?" X-9 groused.

"I thought of putting a sign on the bomb carts that says, 'Bomb on Board,'" Rebay told them, "but our lawyers said that was interfering with the Clancys' rights to privacy. These rules against effective law enforcement get my goat. Pretty soon we won't be able to beat the truth out of assholes, and that'll be the end of civilization in this country. When the Founders wrote that pain-in-the-ass Bill of Rights, they had no idea . . . I'm getting a little off track here. My other idea is to have a Special Agent follow each bomb cart around, and then clear people away when Clancy parks the cart and begins singing the "lower the boom" song, but we haven't got enough agents."

"How about using the Boy Scouts®? And Cub Scouts®?"

"Good idea."

"What has me really worried," Rebay said, "is that the bomb carts all seem to be positioning themselves close to vital strategic targets: bus stations, porno joints, and Carvel® stands. If they go off, they will totally disrupt the country's transportation, self-gratification, and dessert infrastructure."

"I'll take the porno joints," Clyde volunteered. "I don't want to subject these decent G-Gals or Boy Scouts® to that kind of slime. Although maybe I could take a couple Cub Scouts® along with me, for training purposes."

Hoover overruled Clyde. "Nothing doing. We'll start by covering the Greyhound stations' men's rooms. Remember the good old days when we'd do research on the perverts in those places?"

"If nobody else will do the porno theaters, I'll take them," X-9 said. "Somebody's gotta do the dirty work. I think I could take a few of the Carvel® stands, too."

"You're a real trooper, X-9. Do you still have those sandpaper gloves your mom used to make you wear?" Knockers asked. "And do we have any idea who the Clancys report to?"

Presidential Agent 103 said he had a clue. "There is a Cardinal Clancy in the Vatican, the Pope's Secretary of State. Every Friday he hears confessions in St. Peters, and there is always a long line of Irishmen who look like Barry Fitzgerald. It would be logical that the Clancys of the world are reporting to him in the confessional and are getting orders from him."

"*Bug* that confessional," Rebay ordered. "Brilliant, 103."

"Thanks. I'm on it," Lanny told her.

"What about the Cardinal's First Amendment freedom of religion rights?" Knockers wondered.

"Doesn't apply to foreigners. And it seems to me I've heard of this Cardinal Clancy. Isn't he the one they call the World's Most Evil Man?"

"One and the same."

"This is hopeless," X-9 wailed. "The World's Most Evil Man. WMEM. *(Pronounced WeeMem)*. Five hundred Irish manure dirty bombs. New Irish terror recruits getting taught how to drive manure carts every day. And learning how to sing 'Clancy Lowered the Boom.' And all we got are Boy Scouts® and Cub Scouts® to protect us — We're all gonna die!"

Guggenheim hadn't said much. She had been thinking about the information at hand and analyzing it in the supremely logical manner that set her apart from the other Secret Agents who were prone to shoot first and figure things out later or just panic and run away, if they weren't on lunch break, which they usually were when anything dangerous was about to happen.

"Let's just slow the fuck down. Why are we assuming that these Clancys are Irish?"

"Well, Jeeze, Peggy," X-9 said, looking exasperated. "They're named Clancy, they sing Irish songs, they sit on top of manure carts — which the Irish love to do — and they just tried to kill the King and Queen of England, along with their Corgis and the Monkey Man. Seems pretty fucking obvious to me."

"Yes, but we all know the Irish. They are a traditional folk, proud of their handicrafts, you know, hand-knitted sweaters, small batch Irish whisky, wooden shoes carved from potato crates with a jackknife, and they love to drink that god-awful crap called Guinness® instead of real beer like Budweiser®. They hate the sort of mass production we love in America.

"Irish terror is *artisanal*. Your genuine Irish manure-cart bomb is hand-crafted with loving care using designs passed down from terrorist fathers to terrorist sons for generations. The bomb itself is invariably a milk pail filled with fertilizer from the local feed store. The FBI lab established that the bomb that went off during the parade consisted of high-tech explosives that only trained military personnel could fabricate, and it was a focused device engineered to project the shit only in the direction of the President, the Royal Family, and their hangers-on like us.

"Not at all the Irish style of terror. The manure in the D.C. bombing was the kind of ordinary cow shit they give away at every dairy farm. The manure the Irish use in their manure bombs is dung curated from prize-winning cattle celebrated as the best sperm stock in the world. The D.C. bomb had an igniter programmed to go off when it was triggered by the word 'Boom.' The real Irish manure cart bomb is triggered by the kind of wind-up alarm clock sold in every village general store.

"And furthermore, the Irish have an innate love for the dramatic unities: local fertilizer for the bomb, artisanal manure from a select *terroir*, a unique one-off manure cart reflective of the locale, a hand-raised donkey of a registered bloodline, and a terrorist dressed in farmer garb appropriate to the area. Not like a Hallmark® St. Patrick's card leprechaun.

Would they ever mass-produce five thousand identical manure carts, each with a driver named Clancy? No, each cart would have the distinctive features of the county that produced it, and the drivers' names would reflect the rich variety of Ireland, all those 'Mc's, 'Mac's, and 'O's. (Or is it the 'Mc's or the 'Mac's that belong to the Scots? I always get those assholes mixed up.) But for sure there'd be Padraigs, and Liams and Connors, and there'd have to be a couple of Caoimhíns, and at least one Risteard. You know, unpronounceable names.

"Nope. These terrorists are not Irishmen. They are just *pretending* to be Irishmen to throw fools like X-9 off their trail."

"Gee, I never thought of that," X-9 said. "Sorry I'm such a dope, but it isn't my fault. My friends always said that when they gave out brains, I thought they said 'fish' and hid behind the door. I hate fish."

"It's insulting to tell a joke that old, X-9; that's like expecting us to laugh at a knock-knock joke, and besides, 'brains' doesn't sound anything like 'fish,' you idiot. On the other hand, if you thought they said 'trains' or 'rains' — no that's just as dumb — how about 'stains,' or maybe — I got it, 'pains' — then your stupid joke would have made at least *some* sense," PA 103 told him.

"I don't know. That's what they told me. But I *am* a good shot. See the way I finished off those Corgis at the palace? And what's wrong with knock-knock jokes? If they're good enough for seven-year-olds, they're good enough for me."

"Moving right along," Secret Agent Rebay said, "where's this going?"

"If we eliminate the Irish, that sort of opens things up. But," and Secret Agent Guggenheim paused, "let's look at the rest of this fiendishly clever plot. Whoever is behind this knew enough to take over the manure disposal industry for the whole country. That means he had access to the kind of information nobody but the FBI has. He knew how to disguise his gang in those pathetic Irish costumes, and how to teach them the 'Clancy Lowered the Boom' song. Who knows all about disguises and undercover work? *We* do. Singing, maybe not so much, although we do a pretty good job with 'Happy Birthday, Dear Director.' And we know how to set up a voice-activated trigger on the bomb so the bomber could get a safe distance away before going into his 'Irish Terrorists Got Talent' act. Who knows that much about bombs?"

"That's us," Clyde said. "Of course."

"You mean it's an FBI agent behind this? One of us? What about . . . Cardinal Clancy?"

"Nope. That was just a red cardinal — get it, red herring, but he's a Cardinal, so red cardinal . . . OK, doesn't make much sense," Secret Agent Guggenheim told them. "Or maybe the Pope just has time on his hands now that his pals Hitler and Mussolini are dead and he's plotting some new kind of pontifical evil. No, this guy has inside knowledge of how the FBI works. How our rules and regulations keep us fucking up all our big cases. He knew the locations of our field offices so the manure carts were just out of sight of our goldbricking agents and he knew they never want to get too far from the field offices where they keep their lunches in the gun safe so the secretaries can't steal them. He probably has a Secret Agent Decoder Ring®. So we gotta get new ones."

"So you think our guy is an agent? Or a *former* agent?" Rebay said, and she thought, *Peggy really is smart.*

"There's more. Five thousand manure truck drivers. Clyde, how many of the agents survived that you sent to the Pacific to get killed by the Japs? Go ahead, look it up, Clyde."

"Just a minute." Clyde put on his eye shades, checked how he looked in a mirror, and pulled open a file drawer. "Got it right here. Well, I'll be filleted, breaded, fried to a crisp, and put into a po' boy with lettuce, pickles and a tomato if the answer isn't *five thousand.*"

"So, Clyde, what this fiend in Clancy drag has done is recruited all the agents who survived your chicken-shit policy of protecting yourself and Speed by sending agents to the Pacific to get killed by the Japs. He gave them advanced training as manure-cart bombers, taught them their Clancy song (probably killed the ones who couldn't sing), and is planning to panic the country and then take over the FBI. He's got the decoy manure carts parked right next to our field offices. The agents there have poked into the shit, and since they didn't find bombs, they aren't paying any attention to them, except maybe the smell, which is hard to ignore. So, when he gives the signal, those Clancys will jump off their carts, sing the "Lower the Boom" song, kill the special agents in charge, and take over the offices. So, that Clancy at the parade wasn't trying to kill the King and Queen of England, along with their Corgis and the Monkey Man. He was after *Speed*."

Speed jumped to his feet, yelling, "Ya gotta protect me," and started piling furniture against his office door.

"And who is the one and only former FBI agent who is so low-down, treacherous, treasonous, and, you know, lots of other pejoratives?" *(Pejoratives, by the way, X-9 and all you kids, means bad words).*

"Could you write that down?" X-9 begged Peggy. "I remember words better if I see them in writing."

"There's only one guy that talented and evil," Rebay said.

They all said it together: "The Pigeon."

"And Bambi told me a while ago that a bushy bearded bastard just arrived at Los Alamos, and Brandi says he has A LEFT HOOK! And Bambi says the Black Hearted Pigeon with the black beard was away from Los Alamos during the Victory parade, and then came back."

Peggy grabbed the phone and called Bambi. "Bambi," Peggy yelled, "The Pigeon, take him down. Arrest him, kill him, whatever it takes. He's the Mad Manure Bomber." Pause. "Oh, no." She put down the phone. "He's flown the coop."

"And that," Rebay instructed X-9, "is called *extending the metaphor*. Get it? 'Pigeon,' 'pigeon coop,' 'fly away'? It's a kind of figure of speech."

"I get it," X-9 said excitedly, the way he always felt when he on a rare occasion actually understood something. "Metaphor! Figure of speech! I'll say it three times and have it for life!"

* * *

And ya know, like I said before, just when ya think things can't get any worse, they do. The Widder Roosevelt decided to stick her goddamn nose into a mess that was none of her business, as she now had no official position now except U.S. Ambassador to the U.N., which was about as useless a fucking job as counting the linguine in a pasta box.

And so, droning on in her annoying "My Day" column in the *New York Post*, she wrote:

"My Friends and Neighbors. I take a back seat to nobody in my disdain for the Irish. They are as priest-ridden, superstitious, ignorant, foul-smelling (and did I say dirty? I guess foul-smelling covers that) a people as exists on the face of the earth. In fact, not only do I disdain the Irish, but I also decry them. *(And, kids: 'decry' is a big word that means hate, as in 'I hate spinach!' If you say 'I decry spinach' it will confuse your parents so much they might not notice when you throw the spinach under the table. But I digress. Digress means, oh the hell with it. Ask your teacher.)*

"Anywho, what's happening to the Irish right now is a disgrace to America. Americans are now screaming, 'I don't wanna die,' and running away every time they see an Irish man (or woman, for that matter). Not fair. While I personally would never get too close to an Irish person, it is not because I suspect them all of being goddamn murderous terrorists (although you can be pretty sure they are dishonest, thieving, illiterate semi-humans). No, it's because I find them personally distasteful. And I decry *(use a word three times and it's yours, kids)* the way those Catholic rogues have weaseled their way into rackets like manure hauling, chicken guts disposal, cesspool cleaning, and other jobs that ought to go to Protestants, because this is basically a Protestant nation. (*Read the Classic Illustrated® comic about Myles Standish, for God®'s sake, kids.*)

"But this hatred of the Irish is going too far. They are useful for a lot of things, very simple things, mainly lifting heavy things from one place to another. Now this young Jack Kennedy who's running for Congress in Boston can't even give a speech without people running away screaming, "He's going to explode." And he's a war hero, for Christ's sake!

"As I was going to say, our own FBI, led by that Red-smearing ratbastard J. Edgar Hoover, whom I loathe and detest, even though I believe he is a Protestant — maybe a Methodist or Presbyterian or something, churches not on the same level as the Dutch Reformed, where yours truly is proud to drop a half dollar or at least a quarter in the basket every Sunday. Anyway, as I was about to say, the FBI says there are five thousand manure carts out there and only five hundred have bombs in them. So if my math is right — I did go to the same exclusive Swiss finishing schools as that outstanding FBI Secret Agent Peggy Guggenheim we have all been reading about — right on Peggy, you go girl — the odds are only one in ten that you will be blown to smithereens if you get too close to one of those manure carts, and I for one would take those odds any day of the week, although I still wouldn't want to get downwind from a Clancy. Smells worse than manure (tee hee).

"So the next time you see one of those freckle-faced, carrot-topped little harridans wearing an 'I'm Irish, Kiss Me' badge, instead of running for your life, do this: Out of solidarity with my anti-Irishphobia campaign, just walk up and give her (or him, God® forbid) a kiss, although to avoid infectious diseases I would advise an air kiss, and then give your whole head a thorough scrubbing.

"OK, moving right along. There's this business of Jackie Robinson playing in the white baseball leagues. I'm for it. Although I don't see why anyone would want to play baseball. A good game of croquet followed by an icy lemonade is so much more fun. Now that Harry is President, he ought to quit the Baptists and join a more respectable church, like the Episcopalians. And I think Jean Harlow should wear more clothes. That's it for me today, so until the next time, it's Widder Roosevelt saying, 'Tippecanoe and Tyler too,' whatever that means. And as always, hang by your thumbs and write if you get work."

CHAPTER 14

In his secret cabin hideout on the top of a mountain over-looking the Taos Ski Valley *(You remember that place, I'm sure. That was where The Pigeon bushwhacked Rebay and Guggenheim, after they had beaten up and washed out the mouth of the Pinko lift attendant for yapping some Marxist bullshit, back when Pigeon was just a double agent, not yet a triple agent, and now, for God®'s sake, a quadruple agent!)*, The Pigeon was talking by short-wave radio to his spy in the FBI headquarters.

(And by the way, kids, it's an ironclad rule that in every secret society like the FBI or the Catholic Church — think Judas — there is a traitor. And so if The Pigeon had a traitor working for him in the FBI, you can bet your ass that there is, or will be, a traitor in his Pigeon Coop.)

Back to Pigeon and his treasonous phone call to his dirty rotten spy. "So, they figured out it was me. Goddammit. It had to be that fucking Guggenheim who caught on. None of the rest of those idiots are smart enough to see through my cunning plan of blaming everything on the Irish. I've got a genius idea how I can still kill Hoover and take over the FBI. (*Just you wait and see, Miss Smarty!* he thought.) Any other news?"

He sat back after he hung up the phone. Doin' a little thinkin'. *So, they were going to swap their Secret Agent Decoder Rings® for new ones? His spy was already sending him the new models to pass out to his renegade FBI agents. No problem there. But sooner or later Guggenheim was going to strap all the headquarters agents into MAD-1's torture devices. He knew his spy would break. Hmmm. He drummed his fingers on the table, then mixed himself a double gin martini spiced up with some orange bitters. Man, that was good. One more, maybe. Why not? His spy would have to be put down. He had outlived his usefulness, and now he was nothing more than a loose end. The Pigeon didn't get to be The Pigeon by leaving loose ends.* He cackled evilly. He had been practicing that cackle for weeks, and by now it was *really* evil.

He walked over to his planning table, where he studied a map of the United States with wooden tokens marking the locations of his forces. He picked up a miniature shuffleboard paddle and repositioned a token from New York City to Washington. Time to get into Truman's head. And now to set up Operation Soft Serve. He studied the location of Carvel® stands across the country, then began moving black tokens with "peeyuu" painted on them, one per Carvel®. The key to demoralizing the country was the incremental application of escalating acts of terror. Now to eliminate the spy and deal with Guggenheim. Transfer his base of operations closer to the target. He left the cabin and hung a sign on the door: "DO NOT ENTER, BOOBYTRAPPED, PROPERTY OF THE PIGEON." Then he strapped on his skis and schussed down the mountain like one of those maniacs in a Warren Miller film.

And just in the nick of time.

Bambi had finally figured out, by process of elimination,

that the most logical palace for The Pigeon to hide out was his cabin on top of Taos mountain. She called the kid at the ski lift (called a "lifty") and told him to call her if he spotted a bushy-bearded ratbastard (the FBI had just promoted him from 'bastard"). Minutes later she got a call from the kid. A ratbastard who matched The Pigeon's unkempt description had just left.

"The Pigeon is in flight," Bambi phoned the Secret Agent Gals, *which was not a bad example,* X-9 thought, *of extending a metaphor.*

* * *

"I'm sorry. I'm sorry!" Clyde was strapped into MAD-1's torture machine, which had been set to lie detector mode. The first jolt of 1000 volts had started him screaming: "I didn't do it. I didn't mean to do it. OK, I did it, but just a little bit. I won't do it again."

"What exactly did you do, Clyde?" Hoover asked his Number Two. Hoover was in the on-deck circle, waiting to be tested, and was sweating it. Literally.

"I told The Pigeon everything, how Guggenheim figgered out the Clancys were really ex-FBI Agents, and how Rebay is changing the Secret Decoder Rings®."

"Whydja do it, Clyde?" MAD-1 asked, hitting him with another jolt.

"He said if I didn't help, he'd have me sent to the Pacific to get killed by the Japs."

"Why, you're dumber than me," X-9 told him. "Don'cha know the war is over, all the Japs in the Pacific are dead?"

"When did that happen? And he told me that if I talked, he had another spy in headquarters who would kill me."

"Why that's absurd," Hoover said. "No way there could be two traitors in the Bureau. We got our man; let's call off these tests, Madman. Good work. Now let's go upstairs and figure out how to keep me from getting murdered by this fiend. Or maybe I should see if he'd let me live if we surrender."

"Yeah, but Speed, what are we gonna do with this traitor?" Guggenheim said, pointing to Clyde.

"Aw, now Clyde, you're not going to do it again, are you, big fella?" The Director asked his traitorous Number Two.

"No, no. I promise, hope to God®, cross my heart, pinkie promise."

"Turn him loose, Secret Agent Gal Guggenheim. First offender. And a pinkie promise. We'll put him on probation. If he turns out to be a traitor again, we'll cancel his vacation. Can you live with that?" he asked the sobbing traitor.

"My whole vacation?" Clyde wailed.

"Well, half your vacation."

"OK," Clyde sniffled.

Guggenheim wasn't satisfied. "I really think you oughtta get put through the torture machine yourself, Speed. Everyone else has done it. If we find out that The Pigeon does have another spy here, guess who it'll have to be."

"Nothing doing. And if I was the spy, with my steely self-control I would fool Madman's machine. So, what's the point?"

Guggenheim wasn't convinced, but this was an argument she wasn't going to win. Hoover was plainly terrified of MAD-1's contraption. She thought she knew why.

* * *

Bambi had a hunch.

As soon as she got off the phone with the Gals, she got the chairlift kid at the Taos Ski Area on the phone. Secret Agent Rebay had told Bambi that she and Guggenheim had worked the kid over and if she told the kid there was more where that came from, he might want to cooperate. As soon as Bambi mentioned the two G-Gals and what they had done to him, the kid was eager to talk. Bambi wanted to know how The Pigeon had gotten from the ski area. It was a pickup truck from Los Alamos, the kid said. What direction did they go? Toward Santa Fe, not Los Alamos. Bambi called Brandi and ordered her to grab a car and pick her up at the trailer park. They were going to the airport. "Bring disguises."

The two Secret Sluts stashed their car in short-term parking and put on their trench-coat-and-sunglass disguises. They filled their pockets with pistols, ammo, and handcuffs, and scanned the waiting areas for all the gates. No Pigeon, although they didn't know whether he would have disguised himself as a buck-toothed Jap, an Indian, a bushy-bearded House of David baseball player, or maybe even as one of the Poontang Patrol whores.

Bambi checked the recent departures. A flight to D.C. had just taken off. She went over the manifest. Only five one-way tickets. There was Loco Weed, that one sounded like an Indian, she thought; then there was Banzai Kamikaze, and she speculated that could be a Jap; Lefty Benchwarmer, she'd take a chance that was the baseball player; one named V. D. Pussy, likely a traitor in a whore disguise; and finally, Feathers, likely The Pigeon in some kind of a bird suit.

"Why, the crafty sonuvabitch set up a meeting at the airport with four pals," she said to Secret Slut Brandi, "and from what Rebay told me about The Pigeon's gang, they were former FBI Special Agents and masters of disguise."

She called Rebay and gave her a description of the five scoundrels, but warned her they would probably have re-disguised themselves on the plane. If she had to guess, they would come off the plane as an Eskimo, a Toronto Maple Leaf hockey player, a soprano in a Turandot costume, Abraham Lincoln, and a bird in a big cage. Whether it would be Honest Abe before or after that cute kid told the Ol' Rail-Splitter to grow a beard was anybody's guess.

She also theorized that the four of them might overpower the crew, toss the crew and passengers off the plane to lighten the load, and then fly to a secret airport.

"Any idea where that might be?" Rebay wanted to know.

"Yeah. Boise."

"You're right. Boise, of course." Boise was where Hoover exiled the crookedest, drunkest, most diseased, and generally sorriest excuses for FBI agents, and kept them there until they either straightened themselves out or he had them killed.

Trouble was that Bambi and Rebay couldn't warn the Boise Field Office because those skunks had almost certainly thrown in with the Pigeon. The agents there wanted Hoover dead just as much as The Pigeon did.

Clyde, for once, had what sounded like a good idea. The postmaster in Boise was a fairly loyal American who, for a weekly stipend, was keeping Clyde informed about the Boise agents' shenanigans so he could decide which ones to kill or send to the Pacific to get killed by the Japs. Clyde called the mailman, described the four traitors, and promised him a reward of confiscated weed if the postman killed them and sent their heads to Washington.

As Rebay could have almost predicted whenever she made the mistake of using one of Clyde's stupid suggestions, the postmaster immediately solicited a better offer from the rogue agents and sold Clyde out.

When she heard about the double-cross fiasco, she had Clyde bend over so she, Guggenheim, PA 103, Knockers, and MAD-1 could all kick him in the ass. Rebay suggested it would be more fun if they had a contest to see who could kick Clyde the hardest. They were amazed at how hard Rebay kicked the Dimwitted Public Hero Number Two, lifting him off the ground with each kick by a foot or more.

"Howdja do that," PA 103 wanted to know.

"I'm using the kind of kick we do in Europe, what you call soccer." She demonstrated by taking three steps back from the helpless Clyde, then two steps to the left. Approaching Clyde's butt on a diagonal she booted him, not with the tip of her toes, but with the broad side of the arch of her foot. "Let's see if you can get the hang of it," she suggested. One by one they tried the new style of kicking, and pretty soon each one of them could lift the sobbing Clyde off the ground with each kick.

PA 103 said he was going to teach the new kick to the Harvard special teams in time for the Yale game. "You guys wanna come tailgate with me? Corpse Revivers. Number Two, of course."

* * *

The FBI had sent everyone it could spare to the stakeout at Washington National Airport®, which was still waiting for a President worthy of the honor of having his (or her) name plastered in front of "National." In this case, it was the weekend of the Westminster Dog Show® at Madison Square Garden®, where one of the Bureau's champion bloodhounds, Big Speed, was in contention for Best of Show. The only agents not on deployment to New York to cheer on their K-9 buddy were Clyde and X-9. Dogs have an infallible nose for sniffing out cowards and traitors, and Big Speed was always growling at Clyde and X-9, and for some reason kept trying to bite his namesake, Little Speed, Director Hoover. Even champion bloodhounds can make a mistake sometimes.

Anyhow, Clyde and X-9 had to be left in Washington because their presence seemed to confuse Big Speed and might cause him to run amuck or just give up and start scratching his nuts while his handler, MAD-1, was parading him around the ring and putting him through his tricks: He had fetch, stay, roll-over-

and-play-dead, and bury-a-bone down cold.

So the fate of the nation, the Bureau, and even God rested on the narrow shoulders of the Bureau's two most abject failures as detectives, two buffoons unrivaled in the annals of crime-fighting for fucking up cases, shooting themselves in the foot (or worse places), in short, a disgrace to the sterling image of those wonderful (and heroic) men and women in blue who are all that stand between White Anglo-Saxon America (especially its blond women, delectable, some even virginal) and the "elements." But Clyde and X-9 had been bucked up by a pep talk from Secret Agent Rebay, who told them this stake-out was their chance to "turn their games around" with a "big win" instead of their unbroken losing streak of "fuck-ups."

FBI profilers had given the stake-out team their sketches of what The Pigeon's gang would look like as an Eskimo, a Toronto Maple Leaf® hockey player, Turandot, Lincoln before and after the beard, and a canary in a cage. In case the gang had not changed disguises, they also had furnished pictures of a Japanese kamikaze pilot, an Indian chief, a bearded baseball player, a parrot in a cage, and a whore. As an afterthought, Bambi had suggested a sketch of Clarabell the Clown® with a seltzer bottle. In case the exceptionally tricky Pigeon had thought to take his disguises to the next level, the profilers had included a conception of the entire cast of traitors with sunglasses and trench coats over their costumes.

"I'm scared," X-9 confided to Clyde, as they cowered behind the barricade of beer kegs and cases of Coke® they had built in front of the arrivals gate. "Me, too," Clyde told him. "I wish we had the Baroness or Knockers with us. Them gals know how to shoot."

Finally, the plane taxied up to Gate 4. Clyde had forgotten how to unlock the safety on his machine gun.

"RTFM," X-9 growled.

"What's that mean," Clyde wailed.

"Read The Fucking Manual."

"I left it home. What'm I gonna do?"

"Take out your pistol."

"I forgot that too. I'm gonna die."

"Here." X-9 passed him a can of Coke®. "Throw this at them if they start shooting."

"Underhand or overhand?"

"Which are you better at?"

"Neither. OK if I drink the Coke®?"

"Save some for me."

The first passenger to disembark was a Montreal Canadiens® hockey player, who grinned toothlessly at the FBI agents as he clattered in his skates past them and yelled, "You can call me *Dirty Pierre.*" Clyde wasn't sure what the interlocking 'CH' meant on the jock's uniform, but it sure wasn't Maple Leafs. "Didja ever notice how the plural of 'Leaf' is always 'Leaves' unless it's a hockey team?" Clyde observed pedantically.

"That *is* interesting," X-9 replied. "It bugs me when people screw up tricky plurals. For example, the plural of 'octopus' should be the Greek 'octopodes,' not 'octopi' the way some numbskulls say it. Wait. Here comes someone else."

This time is was Maria Callas, belting out "Casta Diva" at the top of her lungs. "That sure ain't Turandot," Clyde said confidently. "'Casta Diva' is in *Norma*, and 'Turandot' has a crown with lots of beads hanging from it and wears an orange Chinese robe. Some critics consider Callas's 'Turandot' the best ever. Sometimes I feel that way myself, although Tebaldi can give her a run for her money. Callas has her beat on looks and the body. Hey Miss Callas, can you sign my FBI ID?" The diva graciously obliged.

Next was a Luftwaffe pilot, with a leather helmet, goggles, white scarf, and a Nazi armband. "Geeze, that guy's got a lot of nerve. Don't he know they lost the war?" Clyde said, and yelled, "Hey Kraut, I guess Chuck Yeager handed you your ass." The Nazi glared at Clyde and pulled out his Luger, but Clyde sneezed and sprayed him with Coke® so the shot went astray, killing a stewardess. "I'll get you next time," the Nazi ratbastard snarled as he went down the stairs to Baggage Claim, shooting the pilot and first officer on his way out.

Finally, a Royal Canadian Mountie with a pair of huskies walked toward them. "This might be an Eskimo, duded up like Sergeant Preston," X-9 said. "Lemme try an old trick; never fails to smoke out an Eskimo trying to pass as a white man." X-9 walked up to the Mountie and gave him the Nanook of the North Eskimo kiss, that is, he rubbed noses with him. The Mountie doubled X-9 up with a left to the solar plexus and then flattened him with a right uppercut.

"Try a simple handshake next time."

"Hey, that really hurt," X-9 complained. "I'm telling on you."

"Yeah, who you gonna tell, Tattletale?"

"The Queen. I know her, her Corgis, and the Monkey Man. We're gonna get you."

The Mountie gave X-9 the raspberry. The fallen anti-crime crusader struggled to his feet to scrutinize the rest of the passengers. Nothing but lobbyists with their briefcases stuffed with cash, and senators with swag bags for bribes. Except for a man dressed in a pigeon suit who gave them the Secret Agent Howdeedo and flipped a spitball at Clyde.

"Yuck. That was disgusting. And we missed the dog show for this?" Clyde whined. "What a waste of time!"

* * *

"You chumps!" Guggenheim screamed at Clyde and X-9,

who were standing in front of her with hangdog expressions. Rebay, Superslut Knockers, and PA 103 were also glaring at the two hapless Secret Agent failures and cowards. "You didn't think there was something funny about a hockey player in skates clattering off an airplane? Did you ever see anything like that before?"

"No, but you said The Pigeon, or one of his guys, might be dressed like a Toronto Maple Leaf," X-9 blubbered. "And he wasn't any kind of leaf at all — not maple, not apple. He was just a hockey player. And besides, Clyde told me something really interesting. Did you know that except for Maple Leafs from Toronto, the plural of leaf is *leaves*? What kind of spelling do they teach up in Mexico?"

"Toronto is in Canada. Bend over, Clyde," Rebay ordered, then let him have a kick that lifted him two feet off the ground. X-9, seeing the way the wind was blowing, surreptitiously slipped a throw pillow into the seat of his pants, and then stood with a smug expression on his face, ready for anything his furious bosses could dish out. *(Maybe dish isn't the right metaphor. "Whatever Rebay could . . . throw at him?" Weak. "...hit him with?" No good. Damn! Can't come up with anything better right now.)*

She went on. "It was the general concept of a guy in a hockey suit that was important. That was the essence of the deal. The exact uniform was what scholastic philosophers would have called an 'accidental.' You know, like Clyde and you are still jerks even if you change your clothes, let's say from a bowling team uniform to a swimsuit. Changing your clothes doesn't change you from your essential jerkiness. Bend over again."

"It would have been nice if you had told us that stuff BEFORE you ordered us into battle against those dangerous guys," X-9 complained as he bent over. "And besides, you oughtta know Clyde forgot his pistol."

"Is that true, Clyde?"

"Well, yeah, but I did have my machine gun. And what a

damned suck-up X-9 is!"

"But he left the instructions home so he couldn't take the safety off," X-9 chortled, "the big jerk."

"Whaddya say to that, Clyde?"

"A guy can't remember everything. And you're a real pal, X-9! Not! You want me to bend over again?"

"Same thing with Maria Callas. So, she wasn't dressed like Turandot, but she has sung *Turandot*, and you said that when she went for the big high note in 'Casta Diva,' she threw up her arms and you saw that she hadn't shaved her pits. Didn't that make you suspicious?"

"Of what?" Clyde asked.

"That she might be a man *pretending* to be Maria Callas?"

"Should I bend over?"

"I could say the same thing about the Nazi in the Red Baron costume or the Mountie. Especially the Mountie because of the two huskies Sergeant Preston had with him. Don'cha know dogs ain't allowed on planes, unless they're those trained service dogs in those orange day-glo uniforms, which those two huskies were *not* wearing. Those must have been midgets in dog suits. Why didn't you try offering the dogs cigarettes? If they ate the cigarettes, dogs. If they asked for a light? Bad guys. *Little* bad guys."

"Shall I bend over?" Clyde asked.

"Both of you this time."

Rebay delivered ferocious kicks to both of their asses, then yelled, "Goddammit, X-9, do you have a pillow in your pants? Search him," she ordered Knockers.

"Yup, here it is," Knockers said triumphantly, after spending a little more time than necessary with her hands in his pants. "Let's see you lie your way out of this. Boy, you're gonna get it this time," Knockers said, "Let 'im have it. And a second kick for enjoying getting felt up."

"No, you take over. My leg's getting tired."

"Personally," PA 103 told the Secret Agent Gals, "I think you're being a little too hard on the boys. Those were honest mistakes. Besides, they were probably thinking about the dog show. About how our Big Speed got edged out by that silly French Poodle from the State Department. Those sissy diplomats fixed the judging. It was rigged. And I can't get that pink cotton candy out of my hair. I must look like an idiot. I didn't have a very good time."

"Well, maybe I was a little unfair. After all, they're just cowards and fools," Rebay said. "But what about the last one? Even a clown like you," pointing to PA 103, "should have seen something a little off about a guy in a pigeon suit who knows the FBI Howdeedo."

Lanny was a little confused. "You didn't give them pictures of a guy in a pigeon suit."

"We were looking for *The Pigeon*. And a pigeon who would know the Howdeedo. So, when a guy came out in a pigeon suit and did the Howdeedo, shouldn't a light have gone off in X-9's (or Clyde's) pathetic little birdbrain? Hey, *birdbrain,* not bad. X-9, that's called . . ."

"Yeah, I know, 'extending the metaphor.' 'Spose you want me to bend over again." While no one was looking the sneaky bastard had put the pillow back in his pants.

"Nah, that'll be a freebie." Rebay looked at Guggenheim. "Looks like it's time for Plan B."

"Ain't no Plan B," X-9 objected, waving his copy of the *Secret Agents' Secret Handbook®*. "All the plans got numbers."

"By 'Plan B' I obviously meant backup plans in general. Plan B was meant to indicate ALL plans. We call using a part for the whole . . ."

"*Synecdoche*! See, I remembered," X-9 said proudly.

"Good boy. But we had 'em and we let 'em slip through our fingers. Now they're on the loose, probably trying to stir up trouble among the Washington Headquarters Secret Agents. How many agents does the FBI have here in DC?" she asked.

Clyde checked his files. "Geeze, seven hundred thirty-four."

"Let's narrow it down a little. Pigeon will be targeting the agents who hate Speed. How many would that be?"

Clyde licked the end of his pencil, put on his eyeshades, and started doing some calculations on his cuff. Then checked by casting out nines. "That would be seven hundred thirty-four."

"Christ. Every one of 'em. Are you counting yourself?"

"Well, Speed did offer me to The Pigeon to kill if he'd let Speed live. Think I should forgive him? I mean, aside from being a cowardly back-stabbing double-crossing rat-fuck bastard who won't let me have a girlfriend, he's not a bad guy."

PA 103 had an idea. "Can't we warn the guys not to trust anyone who comes to them wearing hockey skates and uniform, or dressed like a Nazi pilot, or looking like Maria Callas or Sergeant Preston, or a Pigeon, not to do what they say, and to write it up in a report? Or just shoot them?"

"Don't forget about them huskies," X-9 reminded them.

"They would have changed their clothes by now, numbskull. They're already in three-piece pinstripe suits, spit-shined wing-tips, and snap-brim fedoras. And sunglasses. Just like you three fools."

"Gee, I never thought of that," PA 103 said.

"All of you, bend over."

CHAPTER 15

Clyde's calculations about the number of D.C. agents who hated Hoover — all of them — was real bad news. When he did the numbers and checked them by casting out nines, he was always right, even if he was a fool and a coward about everything else.

Secret Agents Guggenheim and Rebay knew they were up against it.

"Who can we still trust?" Hilla asked Peggy. "Since you opened up that vulgar gallery of yours, can I even trust you?"

"Let's declare a truce on that. I agree to clear out of New York now that the war is over. The field is yours, but I warn you, unless you give up that wacky idea that your ex-boyfriend has talent, the art world is going to write you off as a grifter, a fool, and a patsy."

"That bad? OK, I still like you, except for your blind spot about Rudolf's genius. So, let's say we can trust each other. Anyone else?"

"The Secret Sluts are all loyal, and they are tough. Bambi

has Geronimo on our side, along with his tribe. And despite the fact that he and the Indians met their match at Fort Budweiser®, now that she's got him dried out, he can get the other tribes to support us. Especially the ones who were paratroopers." *(Why is that? That's a pop quiz kids, what we used to call a Jap quiz, as in a surprise attack, Pearl Harbor. Get it? If you haven't guessed, paratroopers yell "Geronimo!")*

"To the American Japs," Secret Agent Peggy went on, "Knockers is practically a goddess. In fact they call her *Kannon* Knockels. (*Kannon* means goddess in Japanese, kids, and *Knockels* means Knockers. *Didn't think ya'd learn so much reading a stupid comic spy story, didja?*) "They love that apology they're gonna get fifty years from now. In fact, they love it so much that if *Kannon Knockels (Remember what that means? Gotcha! Pay attention.)* can get them another apology, say a hundred years from now, they're cool with getting thrown into concentration camps again and kept there, plus getting their homes, whorehouses, farms, and chickens stolen all over again by their white Okie thieving ratbastard neighbors. Naturally, what they love most of all about her are her *blests* (breasts), both of them. She is pretty sure she can get the whole Nisei nation to come over to our side.

"So, while there's time, there's hope. But right now, we need to see about Secret Agent X-9 and Clyde. Can we count on them? They seem to get stupider and more cowardly by the day."

She had summoned the two men to wait outside the command center she had set up in the anteroom next to Speed's office. Speed himself was still barricaded in his office, perched on top of his "Personal" and "Confidential" file cabinets and sobbing like a little girl whose favorite dolly got chewed up by her doggy, or whose doggy got chewed up by a snow blower. *(Hey, that might make a good country song for Johnny Cash Geronimo.)*

Just then Hoover shouted, "Are they here yet?"

"No, they're not. Won't you come out? We gotta have a

plan."

"I'm scared."

"I don't think he's going to be much use," Guggenheim sighed. "Let's get the guys in here."

They were amazed at the transformation in X-9. Gone was the cowardly, slinking useless piece of shit they had come to write off as worthless in any crisis, in fact useless even when there was no crisis. He strode in the room manfully, his FBI three-piece suit cleaned and pressed, his tie (the universal phallic symbol) falling down stiffly and defiantly to his crotch, wing-tips spit-shined.

"What's come over you, X-9? You look great," Rebay told him, thinking back to the undercover days at the Nazi rally when he had been her hero in bed and battlefield.

"Turns out I just had a vitamin deficiency. The Madman tested me. I only needed a shot of B-12 dissolved in methamphetamine daily. Side benefit: I don't gotta sleep no more."

PA 103 slapped X-9 on the back. "That's my boy!"

Guggenheim looked at X-9 curiously, the fuck-up at Washington National still fresh in her mind. "You look like a new man. But how 'bout your pal? Did the Madman fix up Clyde too?"

"Right. I decided I wouldn't be a true friend if I left Clyde behind, still a coward, so I decided I'd get the Madman to shoot him up too. Wait 'til you see him now!"

He opened the door, and instead of simply entering the room, Clyde raced in, turned three forward somersaults, reversed into three linked cartwheels that ended with a round off, then pulled three pigeons out of his pocket and started juggling them while playing "Clancy Lowered the Boom®" on a harmonica. "That Pigeon ain't gotta chance," he crowed. "The Madman's needle is God."

"This is great," Secret Agent Rebay laughed, and she gave the Secret Agent Howdeedo as her gang gave it right back. She reviewed what she and Guggenheim had going for them: Geronimo and his Indians, Knockers and her American Japs. And now she had two Ace G-Men who *really* looked like Aces again. "You guys got any other ideas? We need more boots and/or moccasins on the ground. *Getas*, too. You see what I'm doing here, X-9?"

"Right. 'Extending the metaphor.' You're the best! I too have a little something up my Secret Agent sleeve. Even during my little, let's call it, chickenshit spell, I kept my hand in with the Post Toasties® Junior G-Men out in Minneapolis. When I got wind of what The Pigeon was up to, I decided to expand my authority just a little. The kids were always pretty good at figuring out secret messages with their Decoder Rings®, slapping the cuffs on each other, putting on disguises; but they were lacking in offensive weaponry. Pretty much strictly defensive. Not proactive."

"Come on, X-9, ya didn't give them guns? For Chrissake, they're just kids, six, seven, eight years old. Howdja get that past their moms?"

"'Course not. I got 'em sling shots. And goggles. That way they can shoot out the terrorists' eyes. New costumes, too. Sort of Buster Brown® versions of FBI three-piece suits, little navy blue pin-striped blazers, snap brim Cub Scout® caps and black Keds® with shiny plastic toes. They're raring to go. I was just wondering, what about giving them the Madman's B-12 shots? Just an idea."

"Let's hold that in reserve. You might think about passing out Daisy Red Ryders®. Those lever-action babies. Fantastic work, X-9."

"I've got a little something, too," PA 103 said. "Been talking to Eleanor. She's reassembled the Bama Jamma and her girls. And that Kellogg's Raisin Bran® Junior G-Girl Patrol that she's been running in Battle Creek, Michigan is ready to go. If the Pigeon's guys are stupid enough to get tricked into Double Dutch, they're toast with sprained ankles. (I know, I know, X-9, I mixed my metaphors.) And as for aggressive tactics, can you imagine what a thousand pre-teen girls sound like when they get to shrieking, yelling, and generally making a racket. That's psywar at its most inhuman. Let's get the hag in here."

Harry had been letting Eleanor stay in the White House Guest Cottage just down the street, and in a few minutes the Widder Roosevelt skated into the room wearing her skintight Brooklyn Bomber® spandex uniform, a sight that made them all avert their eyes.

"I hear you and your girls are ready for war, right?" Rebay asked her.

"Betcher ass," she said, giving Clyde an elbow to the chops that would have reduced the pre-B-12 Clyde to a sobbing, cowering wreck, but the new Clyde kicked her in the stomach, then followed up with a rabbit punch to the back of the Widder's neck.

"Wow, I'm impressed," Eleanor said, as she got up from the floor. "Where's the sissy-boy we all used to make fun of?"

"Sissy Clyde, he died," Clyde replied, smiling at his clever rhyme and flexing his muscles in a Charles Atlas® post-97-pound weakling pose.

Rebay gathered her heroes around her. "Now let's talk about what we're gonna do next. I got a plan."

"First we smoke out the traitors in the Bureau. We already caught Clyde, but now he's a reformed traitor. Right, Clyde?"

Clyde gave her a thumbs-up.

"Clyde says that all seven hundred thirty-four Washington agents hate Speed. Add to that The Pigeon and his four pals, and that makes . . ."

"Seven hundred thirty-nine." Clyde was not only quick on his feet now; his brain was clickin' like a steel trap that had just clamped down on the balls of a bank-robber, Commie spy, or car thief. "Back when I was a sissy, I had a stupid idea, which was to ship all the traitors to Boise and bring X-9's kids to headquarters. Especially now that he's armed 'em with sling-shots and maybe

Red Ryders®. But now that I'm a mighty man again, I know we gotta come up with something better. And I have an idea."

"You know, hang onto that Junior G-Man idea. We might need it. What's your other plan?"

"You're gonna love this. You know how it was a vitamin B-12 deficiency that turned me and X-9 into chickenshit cowards and idiots?"

"Sure. Go on."

"Well, I been talking to the Madman, here, and he's come up with a shot that GIVES people vitamin B-12 deficiency."

Stunned silence. "They oughtta have some kind of genius medal for you," Eleanor said. "I know these rich MacArthur idiots who are just dying to give their money away to useless fucks whose only skill is writing grant applications. I'll talk to them."

"You mean General MacArthur?" Clyde asked.

"Hell no," Eleanor shot back. "That cheap war-mongering bastard wouldn't give a dime to a cripple if he got a quarter in change. You're a *real* entrepreneur, Madman, like Richard Simmons and Hugh Hefner, who figured out how to make money off things people used to do for free, like jumping jacks and masturbating. You're the real genius."

"God," the Baroness exulted. "After they get their shots, just the seven of us will be able to beat all seven hundred—what was it, thirty-nine?—97-pound, B-12-deficiency weaklings at the annual Special Agents' tug-of-war. But how do we get them to take the shots? They're so scared of hypodermics they might quit before we can dose them."

Knockers raised her hand. "Piece of cake. All seven hundred thirty-four of the cheap bastards — not sure about The Pigeon and his traitors — check in every day for a free lunch at the Secret Agents' Cafeteria. Baloney on white bread with margarine and mayo. Because as anyone running a restaurant around here knows, you can't compete with free. So here's what we do: We put out a story that there was a deadly virus in the baloney sandwiches, and they're all gonna die unless they come in for shots. And we'll say we gotta new kinda shot that doesn't hurt. That's a joke. Might be even better if we had a few agents die to encourage the rest."

"Have we got a few agents in the brig that the Madman could kill?" PA 103 asked.

"It just so happens that Speed threw a dozen of them in jail for not sending him a birthday card. And they've still been getting their baloney sandwiches," Clyde told them.

"Get Lou Nichols in here," Rebay ordered.

Lou Nichols, the FBI's head flack, lumbered into the room, a dead ringer for Boris Karloff.

"My God®, you look just like Boris Karloff in *Frankenstein*," PA103 gasped. Nichols made a quick move to strangle Lanny, who quickly added, "but you ain't got no stitches. My mistake."

"Listen up Nichols, and how about standing at attention." Nichols' sloppy slouch annoyed Secret Slut Knockers.

Nichols straightened up and gave the Secret Agent Howdeedo. "Sorry. I'm developing that kind of neck osteoporosis old ladies get. I think I inherited it from my grandmother. Or maybe my aunt. Anyway, I'm gonna be stuck in that position in a few years according to the Madman unless I get an operation, but I'm going back and forth on that. On the one hand, I'd like to look like a sharp agent again instead of a pathetic hag. On the other hand . . ."

Rebay pulled her gun, fired a shot past his ear, and asked him to shut up. "Not interested in your pathetic neck. I've gotta question for you. And look me in the eye and don't lie or I'll kill you on the spot, so help me the Great God®, Jehovah."

"I lie for a living. The motto of the Crime Records Division is 'Why Tell the Truth When You Can Lie.' But I'll do my best. But remember, I might still lie out of habit. How about figuring the opposite of whatever I say is true?"

Rebay didn't reply to that nonsense, and Guggenheim walked over and slammed him on the side of the head with her pistol. "Turn around," she ordered, and slammed him on the other side of his head.

"Here's the question. And hold your hands out. No crossed fingers. Are you still loyal to Speed?" Rebay demanded. All the agents pulled out their weapons, cocked them, and aimed them at the head of the hapless horseshit slinger.

"Yes, absolutely, the sonuvabitch has files on me that would get me executed, and that would be letting me off easy. Plus, I got this two-hundred-acre pecan farm I bought with money Speed let me steal from the Special Agents Welfare Fund, and the cocksucker (sorry ladies) put his name on the deed. I'm on his side forever, or at least until I manage to kill him."

"OK. Here's what you gotta do. We wanna put out a story that the baloney sandwiches in the cafeteria were infected, maybe bad margarine, and all the agents who ate there yesterday have to come in and get a shot."

"But that's, what is it, seven hundred thirty-four of our tight-til-they-squeak agents? That's a lot. I keep track of 'em all so I can deduct the meals from their pensions. They don't know about that yet . . . and Speed lets me keep half. Another reason why I love him as well as hate him. *Odi et amo.*"

"Huh? Yeah, same to you, buddy. Anyway, to make it easy for you, we're killing the prisoners in the brig and we'll lay their bodies out in front of the Justice Department. You take pictures of them. We'll have MAD-1 make them die in horrible pain so they'll have terrifying grimaces on their mugs."

"I like that," Nichols said, his crooked mind already spinning the story and coming up with creepy captions for the pictures. "How's this for the headline: 'Deadly Delicatessen, Dozen Dead

Detectives'? I wish the cafeteria wasn't so cheap and had fancy food, because I could have done something really good with 'Poisoned Pastrami Puts Public in Peril' or, get this, 'Life-Threatening Liverwurst Leaves Luckless Losers Lifeless' or 'Public Heroes Perish from Putrid Heroes,' or 'Salami Slays Sleuths,' or 'Mighty Men Meet Murderous Margarine' or—"

"Enough already. You're on the right track. Get to work. X-9, go down to the lab and help the Madman kill the prisoners and get the bodies out front."

* * *

Nichols came running back to the command post. They could still hear Speed moaning and sobbing inside his barricaded office: "Have they come for me yet? I'll do anything they want. They can even have my dogs."

Nichols reported: "I got new figures on how many agents ate the sandwiches yesterday: seven-hundred thirty-nine."

Rebay made a mental calculation and gasped. "That means that murderous ratbastard traitor Pigeon is still too cheap to pass up a free sandwich. Just goes to show you, you can take the agent out of cheap, but you can't take the cheap out of the agent. No, that doesn't make sense."

"I think I might fix that up for you, Secret Agent Baroness," Nichols said. "How about, 'You can take the agents out of the cheap seats, but you can't take the cheap seats out of the agents'? Something like that? I guess it needs a little more work."

"That's pretty good, though. I can see now how you managed to spin all Speed's fuckups into big wins. You took that lucky tip from the Chicago cops' whore in red that killed Dillinger and turned it into a triumph for FBI fingerprinting: 'Against science, crime has no chance.' Right? It shudda been, 'Against dumb luck and good public relations, crime has no chance.' What a load of manure, and it fooled everyone."

"Yeah. Kinda proud of that one."

"Anyway, we've got a chance to trap The Pigeon before he can cause any more trouble. He'll most likely try to sneak in with the rest of the agents to get his shot. How do we get him?"

* * *

"This might be a trap," the Pigeon told his little band of ratbastard rotten-fuck traitors.

"Yeah maybe, Boss, but do you think Speed would kill a dozen of his agents to bait a trap? Isn't that kinda drastic?"

"It's what I would do. But we can't take a chance. Didja see the looks on those cadavers? I don't wanna die like that. We gotta get those shots. But how without getting caught?"

The Pigeon sent a scout to check out the Justice Department and reported that there was already a long line, hundreds of agents in front of the building, stepping over the corpses and waiting for their shots. And Clyde, X-9, Knockers, Rebay, Guggenheim, and PA 103 were standing by the door, scrutinizing the agents as they entered, Clyde with a cabinet full of personnel files beside him.

The Pigeon and his ratbastard etc. traitors began scheming, running through their list of disguises. They quickly discarded all the costumes they had worn on the plane, since X-9 and Clyde had seen them. Likewise, Clyde would have their pictures in standard G-Man drag in his files, and he would recognize them. Knockers had seen him in the buck-toothed Jap disguise, and Rebay and Guggenheim had seen him in ski clothes. They were stumped.

But then the hockey player, who was practicing his slap shot against the wall of their hideout, had an inspiration. He looked at his ice skates hanging on a hook on the wall. "Skaters," he said. "That's it."

"Whaddya mean, moron? We've already shit-canned that idea. Besides, there's no ice."

"Not ice skaters. *Roller* skaters!"

Pigeon didn't get it.

"The Bama Jamma and her team. We lure them out of the line with a ruse, chloroform them, tie 'em up, slip into their uniforms, put on their skates, and get in line. Most of them look like bull dykes so we'll pass easy. Little bit of blusher, eye make-up, lipstick, and falsies and we're in. Have to strap our pork chops down in our pants tight and that'll hurt, but it won't last long."

"Let's try it. It's do or die."

* * *

"I don't get it. We gave out seven hundred thirty-nine shots, and there were only seven hundred thirty-four agents, so the Pigeon and his gang must have gotten theirs. How come we didn't spot 'em?"

"Wait a minute," Clyde said. "What about the Bama Jamma and her four gals who were gonna get fake shots, because we didn't wanna turn *them* into cowards? With them the count should have been . . ."

"Seven hundred forty-four, if The Pigeon and his gang slipped through," X-9 yelled. "So the Jamma and her four gals must have *been* the Pigeon and his gang in disguise. I mean his ratbastard gang in disguise."

"Oh, no," Rebay said. "And that means they got fake shots. And didn't get turned into cowards. This time it's all my fault," and she bent over. "Give it to me good and hard."

"What do you mean?" Guggenheim asked.

"I should have had the Commie hag with us at the door. Eleanor would have seen that the Jamma was really The Pigeon.

Owa tana sami. (That means "Oh what an ass am I," in commie gibberish.) Go ahead." she moaned in another of her foreign languages along with Classical Greek and Latin and German. "Kick me, someone."

Just as the Secret Agent Gal had feared, two D.C. cops came up to the Secret Agents, leading the Bama Jamma and her team wearing nothing but their sports bras and panties, carrying a pile of FBI suits and shoes. "We found these gals in a dumpster. They say they been drugged."

"Well, at least all those Hoover-killing agents are now chickenshit Hoover-killing agents. But The Pigeon and his turds *(pun, get it?)* are as dangerous as ever."

* * *

"I feel great," Pigeon said.

"Me too, boss," bragged one of his ratbastard swine gang. "That shot worked. If those free baloney and margarine sandwiches had poisoned us, we'd know by now. Let's get back to figuring out how to kill Hoover and take over the FBI. And go back for another free lunch."

* * *

"What do we do now?" X-9 asked.

Rebay told them her idea. "Back when Peggy and I were still looking for Nazi painters, the Madman came up with an automatic spy-catcher machine. Basically, it's a kind of lie detector, but way more sophisticated than the one that caught you, Clyde."

"I bet I could beat it now that I'm not a coward anymore."

"Me too," X-9 added.

"Same for me," PA 103 chimed in.

"Yeah, yeah, but remember that all the Washington agents are certified Vitamin B-12 deficiency cowards now. And mostly simpletons, which'll make my trick easy. Show 'em the gizmo,

Madman."

The FBI's maddest scientist, decked out in his wizard's hat and black robe, held out a little plastic tube with metal mesh on each end. The tube was, he pointed out, just the right size to put two forefingers into, one on each end.

"Now here's how it works. We make all seven hundred thirty-four D.C. agents sit down in the big auditorium. I don't think The Pigeon's flock will show up, so I'm not counting them."

"Beautiful example of an extended metaphor, Madman," X-9 told him. "Didja like that one, Baroness?"

"Not bad, Madman. Now go on."

"Backing up a little, we have all the agents stick their pointer fingers into each end of the Chinese handcuff, which is what I call this thing."

The Madman had dragged a still-live (for the moment) prisoner up from Speed's personal enemies dungeon, and he jammed the rat's fingers into the contraption. Then MAD-1 pulled a cloth off a six-by-six-foot control panel with a grid of light bulbs. "There's eight hundred bulbs here, so we have a few spares in case we want to test Speed's crew of black personal servants. Now for the test."

The Madman flipped a switch and all the lights flashed, from number one to eight hundred. "Seems to be OK. Watch bulb Number One. That's for this rat. Now I ask him a question: Do you hate J. Edgar Hoover? Yes or no."

"Yes," the rat shouted, and the bulb flashed green.

"See. That means he's telling the truth."

"Now listen up, Rat. Anyone who wants to kill the Director, we kill on the spot," and he pulled out his gun. "Yes or no: Do you want to *kill* J. Edgar Hoover?"

"No!" the rat shrieked. The light flashed red.

"See. That means he's lying. Now try to pull your fingers out, Rat."

The rat tried, yanking with all his might. "They're stuck! Omigod!!!"

MAD-1 released the rat and had his guard take him back to the dungeon. "Give him a baloney sandwich for being a good sport." The agents all guffawed.

Rebay took over. "Good show, Madman. We're gonna get all the agents to stick their fingers in the 'Treason Tester' and ask them those same two questions. They'll all say they hate Hoover, because they all do. If any of them tests out that he don't hate Hoover, we fire him for being stupid. Then we ask them if they want to kill Hoover. The ones who say 'no' and are lying are stuck in the trap. We ship them to Boise. The ones who are telling the truth that they don't wanna kill Speed, they get their fingers back and those are our boys. They'll be on our side when we fight The Pigeon."

"I just have one little suggestion," PA 103 said. "A little suggestionpoo."

"What is it?"

"Instead of putting their fingers in the gizmo, how about making them stick their peckers into it. Might give a more sensitive reading, cut down on false positives and negatives, and we'd still have 'em by the old pork chop if they're traitors. Added benefit: We would be testing them two-by-two, save time and money."

"Hmmm. Not a bad idea," Guggenheim said. "Be a great photo-op, too: all the agents belly to belly with their peckers stuck together."

"I'll give it some thought," MAD-1 said. "Maybe save the pecker idea for the next version of the gizmo, but we gotta go with this one now. No time to make a switch."

CHAPTER 16

On such a day as this, the *Pequod* sailed serenely through the balmy warmth of the Pacific, at peace with the world, its crew fondly exchanging glances of brotherly love (to put it mildly), a lookout on the highest mast thinking Platonic or at least Emersonian thoughts, captain and crew alike blissfully unaware that a hundred fathoms below lurked a white whale planning to rip them limb from limb and timber from timber, leaving only one to tell the tale, namely that useless jerk on the topmast who wasn't paying attention to anything except, metaphorically speaking, his navel.

On such a day as this the Archangel Michael looked benignly over the heavens flexing his muscles and waving his vorpal blade (*That's a kind of a sword, kids, good for killing Jabberwocks*), admiring the billowing folds of his white cotton robes and flicking specks off his sparkling wings, not dreaming that in the morn he and his heavenly host would have to face down a rebellion led by the Prince of Darkness against the Almighty (God®️ that is) and that Michael himself would be obliged to cast into hell Satan and the other evil spirits roaming the world seeking the ruin of souls, a tale that would be told in an endless and reader-less poem, full of spectacular visual effects, although written by a blind man. Go figure . . .

On such a day as this Desi would wave goodbye to Lucy and head off to band practice with nothing on his mind except rehearsing some new mambos, sambas, and maybe limbos, never thinking that by the end of the day he would have to rescue Lucy from another goddamn mess she'd gotten herself into, shrieking, yelling, carrying on; and she'd have a lot of 'splainin' to do.

On such a day as this, let's call it December 7, 1941, the sailors at Pearl Harbor were catching a last few winks before rev-eille, dropping their cocks and grabbing their socks, expecting an-other perfect Hawaiian day, a few hours polishing their brass belt buckles, shining their shoes, a couple of hours peeling potatoes or weeding the captain's lawn, and then a trip to the bar and the whorehouse, rinse and repeat.

And it was on such a day (as those poetically described in the above lines) that the Stars and Stripes (and in some places the Stars and Bars) were flying over a happy land, nothing but blue skies up above, everyone in love, no reason for the executive, legislative, and judicial branches of national, state, or local gov-ernments to concern themselves with anything except looting the public treasury and staying out of jail.

The country rested secure in the knowledge that protect-ing them against the evils across the seas and south of the Rio Grande was the Greatest Organization in the History of the World, led by the Greatest (next to Jesus®) Man Who Ever Lived, J. Ed-gar "Speed" Hoover. If all else failed, the FBI's Secret Agents would guard the nation's honor, the virtue of its females, the integ-rity of Little League baseball, the two-car garage, the barbecue out back, a turkey at Thanksgiving, chocolate eggs at Easter, milk and cookies for Santa, to say nothing of the true Christian religion and those minor sects for the most part tolerated by most Christians and, oh yes, *God®*. (Don't want to leave *Him* out.)

No reason at all to suspect a dark and desperate conspiracy was about to erupt, something like that white whale mentioned above (or, since this isn't the kind of book likely to attract English majors, like Freddie Kreuger in *Friday the 13th*). Whichever metaphor makes the most sense to you, something evil would be ripping and rending the fabric of the nation, leaving citizens of a once-happy land dazed, confused, worried, and maybe even clinically depressed, or even dead, wandering in the wilderness like foreign refugees, no longer sure which was their ass, and which was their elbow.

Against this mighty and, let's face it, really scary gosh-darn malignant force of ratbastards the once-invincible-but-now-severely-depleted FBI was really up against it, sort of like a kids' pickup sandlot team against Babe Ruth, Lou Gehrig, and the rest of the 1927 Yankees, or Charlie Brown against the New England Patriots (when they were a good team, which was a long time in the future since they didn't even exist in 1947; and neither did Charlie Brown). Or maybe, hey, here's a thought: like David against Goliath. I like that. David won, didn't he?

Because don't the underdogs always have a chance? Guys (and gals) with grit, determination, clean hands, healthy habits, good hygiene, straight teeth or braces (And I do NOT mean suspenders. This is America, where we call a lift an elevator, goddammit!), and a bottomless bag of nifty and crafty tricks learned in Boy Scouts®. And a scrappy never-say-quit kinda determination that coach taught them in gym class.

So, the Secret Agent Gals gotta chance. Maybe.

* * *

Secret Agent Rebay was trying to figure out if they really *did* have a chance. With the foresight that set her above all other Secret Agents (except Secret Agent Peggy) who seldom looked into the future any further than their next meal and bowel movement, Secret Agent Baroness Hilla Rebay was figuring out her options in the upcoming battle (to which she had given the code name *Armageddon*).

"But won't the shots wear off?" she asked MAD-1, "and as soon as they do, those vitamin B-12-deficient yellow-bellied piles of shit will be trying to kill Speed again. Even quicker, if they figure out what's wrong and get new B-12 shots. And we're gonna have a mess on our hands out in Boise. Besides the twenty-five misfits and semi-criminals Speed sent there for rehab or execution, we've shipped four hundred eighty-nine new ratbastard traitors there (because exactly two-thirds of the seven hundred thirty four agents the Madman tested were lying when they said they didn't want to kill Hoover). And if they ever get those Chinese handcuffs off their fingers, they're gonna come back here and join ranks with The Pigeon."

"Hah," the FBI Magician answered. "You think your ol' Wizardpoo didn't work all that out? I got your back, honey, and your front, and your top and your bottom, and your—"

"Enough! Enlighten me."

"Just a minute. I feel a spell coming on." The Madman shut his eyes, then started humming like a sex toy run amuck. Strange words burbled from his mouth, along with an unsightly amount of saliva. He keeled over on his back, his limbs spread out wide, twitching. He opened his eyes. "I'm OK. Help me up. I just had a vision of Armageddon. Scary."

"Do we win?"

"Can't quite tell. I need help. If I had Shitting Bull out here, I think we could work together to figure out the future and cast spells that'd help our side."

"Knockers. Tell Bambi to get the Bull Shitter out here. Tell her we need him. And you, put on your Yokohama Mama disguise and head out to the Jap concentration camps. We need you in-country and in-position."

Knockers snapped off a quick Secret Agent Howdeedo, clicked her high heels, did an about face, and marched smartly out of the room.

"God, I like that broad's style," Rebay said happily. "A model for us all. And I'm glad Geronimo is such a good papoose sitter. OK, Madman, as you were saying."

"First of all, my anti-B-12 drug won't wear off so soon. I don't know yet when it will wear off. Maybe six months, maybe a year, maybe never. And if they get B-12 shots, it won't help. Make them worse, mattera fact. B-12 will produce more anti-B-12 antibodies, and they'll be even more cowardly. My prisoners in the basement shriek every time they see themselves in the mirror. Anyway, no need to worry about those agents in Boise. They'll be chickenshit cowards long past Armageddon."

"Any chance it was the methamphetamines that did the trick for Clyde, X-9, and PA 103, and not the B-12?"

"Huh. Ya think? Damn. Never thought of that. And anyway, the only way they'll get those Chinese handcuffs off is for me to push a button on the control board, like I did for that poor wretch in the dungeon."

"Can't they cut them off?"

"Let 'em try. They'll have to cut their trigger fingers off."

"Maybe they can learn to pull the trigger with their middle fingers."

"Maybe, but you know what they say about an old dog and new tricks."

"No," X-9 said, "can't say that I do. What do they say?"

"Shit, how should I know? I never said it. 'They' said it."

That stirred X-9 to bark, "Come on, extend that metaphor.

You can do it."

"You're like a dog with a bone," Rebay told him.

X-9 grinned happily. He loved these guys.

She continued: "And if you lie down with a dog you're gonna get fleeced."

"Fleeced," X-9 said. "Like a sheep? Don't you mean *fleas*?"

"Hmm," Rebay said. "Maybe it is 'fleas.' Damn." Then she brightened up. "Or is this a pun opening the path to a new, but related metaphor. Get it?"

"Talk about reaching into a pile of dogshit and pulling out a shearling slipper. Not bad, Baroness!"

"Come on, kids," Guggenheim fired them up: "We got *work* to do."

She sent Clyde to the blackboard. "Let's do the math, Clyde." He put on his eyeshades, picked up a fresh piece of chalk, examined it critically and, from long experience, rejected it, chucked it into the wastebasket and chose another piece. "Much better," he said.

Rebay began rattling off the figures. There were seven hundred thirty-four D.C. agents who got the shot and so were rendered gormless. *(That means 'stupid,' kids. Try it out on the playground next time you get bullied. That will stop 'em.)* Plus, The Pigeon and his four ratbastard traitors. Put the seven hundred thirty-four on one side and put the Pigeon Five in a separate column."

"Can't you tell me that before I start writing," Clyde complained. "Now I gotta erase and it looks sloppy." He got to work erasing. "OK, got it."

"Now there are the four hundred eighty-nine would-be Speed-killers the Madman's Treason-Tester caught that are out in Boise trying to learn to knit with their toes."

PA 103 and X-9 sniggered. "That's a good one," Clyde chuckled. "That's gotta be hard. Can't wait to put that into the agent training curriculum."

"So how many we got here?"

Clyde subtracted four hundred eighty-nine from seven hundred thirty-four and came up with two hundred forty-five. "Lemme check by casting out nines . . . Yeah, looks OK."

"So, we got two hundred forty-five hate-Speed-but-not-wanna-murder-Speed agents on our side. But remember, they are all B-12-deficient cowards. Plus, we got Eleanor, the Bama Jamma, and her four thugs. That makes?"

"Two hundred and fifty-one," Clyde said quickly. "Want me to cast out nines?"

"Wotthahell, sure. Can't afford to make mistakes now."

Clyde reported back that the calculations were checking out so far.

"Then there are the four of us, plus the ten sluts in the Poontang Patrol."

"Two hundred sixty-five," Clyde reported back. "Checked and accurate, Ma'am."

Rebay inspected Clyde's calculations. "But of the two hundred seventy-four, two hundred forty-five are cowards and only twenty of us got the right stuff."

Baroness Rebay shifted gears. "On the other hand, whatta *they* got? There's the Pigeon Five, the four hundred eighty-nine coward traitors we sent to Boise, plus the twenty-five career criminals at the Boise Field Office. Ya got all this, Clyde?"

"I'm writing as fast as I can. Slow down."

"Add to that the five thousand Clancys. We know they all hate Speed and wanna kill him because he sent them to the Pacific to get killed by the Japs to save his own skin."

"Got it."

"Here's the hard part: How can we figure out how many of the other agents out in the field wanna kill Speed?"

"Kinda thing I do for a living," Clyde told her. "Lemme

check how many agents there are out in the field." He pulled out a file folder. "Eleven thousand forty-nine. Now of the seven hundred thirty-four D.C. agents, the Madman's gizmo proved that four hundred eighty-nine wanted to kill Speed. That is, 66.66 %. I'd usually round that up to 70%, but things are bad enough, so I'm gonna work with two-thirds. Okay with that? If I apply that percentage to the eleven thousand forty-nine agents, we come up with seven thousand three hundred sixty-five point twenty-six agents who want to kill him, and we can round that down to seven thousand three hundred sixty-five. The answer is seven thousand three hundred sixty-five. Ya want me to add that to the other guys who want to kill Speed, right?"

"Go ahead."

"Lemme cast out nines. The answer is we're up against twelve thousand eight hundred eighty-eight agents who wanna kill Speed. 'Course four hundred eighty-nine are cowards with their trigger fingers stuck in MAD-1's trap, so should we count them?"

"We gotta. I figure The Pigeon will drive the cowards and the guys with their fingers in the Chinese handcuffs ahead of his main forces, you know, cannon fodder to exhaust our ammo. How many we got on our side?"

"Two hundred seventy-four, with only twenty-nine not vitamin B-12-deficient cowards. Against twelve thousand eight hundred eighty-eight."

"Remember Leonidas and the three hundred?"

"Yeah. They all got killed."

* * *

The Pigeon was also trying to calculate the odds, which he was pretty sure favored him. But he was losing it. "God® damn these numbers to hell. This is why I wanted Clyde on our side.

He's good at math if nothing else. I can't figure these things out. See if you can get him to switch sides, will ya? After all, he was a traitor once, why not again?"

"Nah. You're doing fine, Boss," the hockey player told him. "Start over."

"OK. We've got the four-hundred-and-something cowards in Chinese handcuffs the Baroness sent to Boise, so I guess we can use them for human shields. So, them and us together, it's four hundred and, oh shit, something over four hundred cowards. Plus, there's the five thousand Clancys, and what is it, the twenty-five thugs from Boise? And then there's around ten thousand agents in the country and they're on our side too, right?"

"No, Boss. You gotta calculate the percentage of agents at headquarters who didn't want to kill Speed against the ones who did, and then use that percentage to figure out the field agents we can count on."

"What the fuck? I could never work that out. Can't I say we get half, he gets half?"

"If you want to, but remember: Clyde will have these figures down to two decimal places, and he'll cast out nines and..."

The Pigeon pulled out his gun and shoved it against the forehead of his faithful lieutenant. "You just utter the words 'cast out nines' one more time and I'll pull the trigger."

"Gotcha, Boss. Just saying."

"Don't say nothing. Way I see it we got about ten thousand and they got a couple hundred, maybe three hundred."

"Remember Leonidas? He won. You better get those numbers right."

* * *

PA 103 picked up the phone. "It's for you Clyde."

Clyde listened. "It's The Pigeon," he told the Baroness. "He says he can't figure out the numbers for the big fight, and he wonders if I'd tell him what I came up with. Says it's only fair. Not right if we know how many are on each side and he doesn't. Shall I lie to him?"

"Ask him what he came up with."

"He says he couldn't do casting out nines, but he thinks he's got ten thousand and we've got three hundred."

X-9 guffawed. "Whatta dope! He's way off."

Rebay said, "We gotta tell the truth. After all, we're the Good Guys, and Good Guys don't lie, usually. Right? Just say we're way stronger than that, but he's gotta figure it out himself."

Clyde listened and hung up. "He said that's not fair, and he called you a bad name. Me too. Then he asked me if I would come over to his side. He'd make it worth my while, he said. Otherwise I'll be a shit sandwich."

"Don't worry, Clyde," X-9 reassured him. "When we catch him, we'll wash his mouth out with soap."

"Brown soap," Clyde said, "with pieces of Brillo® in it!"

* * *

Rebay and Guggenheim had been counting on the Pigeon's B-12 deficiency to slow down his timetable. So much for that. The Assistant Directors (ADs), led by Lou Nichols, were kept loyal to Speed by the stuff he had on them in his blackmail files. Next they needed to find out if they could count on the FBI bosses around the country, the Special Agents in Charge (SACs). Like the ADs, the SACs had also been cut in on the swag by Clyde and Speed, so Clyde figured most of them would stay on the team to keep the gravy flowing. But they had to be sure. Clyde had them fly to Washington for what he billed as a workshop session on using the new Secret Decoder Rings®.

"Ok, guys," Clyde told the fifty-five SACs taking their ease in the Executive Lounge. "Before we get to the hard stuff figuring out the new rings, we're gonna play a little game." He passed out the Chinese handcuffs. "It's kind of a refresher quiz on FBI history." The guys exchanged knowing glances. They were always throwing pop quizzes at their men on FBI lore: important stuff like the Director's Mom's birthday and Clyde's college frat song ("Tiny Bubbles"). They were ready.

"These little gizmos help me record your answers. Stick your trigger fingers in each end. Now I'm gonna ask you a question just to test the machine." He looked at the Assistant Directors to make sure they were ready, with their free hands on their guns. "You can answer all at once. Here's the question. 'Do you hate the Director?'"

There was a chorus of 'no's. Clyde scrutinized the control panel. "This is pretty interesting. Fifty of ya said you did not hate the Director and you were telling the truth. Joe, Ed, Sal, Vinnie, and Brad, you said you didn't hate him, but you were lying. How come?"

"I got confused," Ed said. "Lemme try it again. I can beat those things." The other liars also wanted a second chance. "Hey, how do you get these things off?" one of them yelled, pulling at his Chinese handcuffs.

"Madman, take these five down to the lab and do an extensive debriefing. But not too rough. We want 'em to look good if their widows ask for an open casket."

MAD-1, with the help of Secret Agent Igor, led the Chinese-handcuffed wretches down to the dungeon.

"One more question, guys. This is easy. Kinda hate to ask, but it's part of the drill. Here it is, yes or no. 'Are you planning to *kill* the Director?'" There was a chorus of 'no's. Clyde looked at the Madman's machine. "One of ya is lying! Christ almighty, Maxie, it's you! You're planning to kill the Director!"

Maxie was struggling to get out his gun, but with his fingers caught in the Chinese handcuffs he was just making a fool of himself.

"How come, Maxie?"

"The Pigeon said that if I killed Speed, I could have Clyde's job as the Director's best friend and bunkie."

"How'd you make it through the Madman's HomoMeter?"

"I beat it. I thought I could beat this one too. I just kept thinking about baseball while I was looking at those photos of nekkid boys."

"Well, ya didn't get away with it," and all the ADs emptied their pistols into the rat-traitor-assassin-killer-homo bastard.

PA 103 objected. "I'm gonna have to report on all this to Truman, so I think we should give Maxie a trial."

"You're right," Clyde said. "How many of you guys think he was guilty?" All forty-nine hands went up. "Should have been executed?" Again, unanimous. "Does that take care of the formalities, Lanny?"

"I'm not exactly a lawyer, but neither is the President. Seems OK to me."

"Who's this Pigeon that Maxie was talking about?" an SAC asked, as orderlies dragged Maxie's body out to be donated to the medical students. "We've been hearing rumors."

"This is the toppest of top secrets," Rebay told them. "A renegade agent code-named *The Pigeon* is going to try to kill Hoover and take over the FBI. He's hiding here in Washington with four of his gang, but we've clipped his wings."

X-9 gave a fist pump and mouthed a 'Yes!'

"But even with only one wing," Rebay went on (X-9 was so ecstatic he nearly peed his pants), "he's the most dangerous enemy the FBI has ever faced, worse than Dillinger, Ma Barker, the Joker, the Penguin, Cagney, and that former Sonuvabitch in the White House put together. We all gotta fly as a flock," she said, winking at X-9.

"What can we do? Have we gotta chance?"

"Of course, we gotta chance. We're the FBI," and she turned on a quick film clip of Jimmy Cagney machine-gunning public enemies, while over the gun blasts the soundtrack played the FBI march, 'Men of the FBI,' which brought the SACs to their feet at attention.

"At ease," Rebay told them. "Job Number One: Keep your men from nesting with The Pigeon." X-9 gave her a thumbs-up. "The Madman's going to be sending you the Chinese hand-cuffs and instructions on how to trap the ratbastard traitors in your offices. In the meantime use the buddy system. Every agent has to have a buddy, and every hour ya gotta yell 'buddy up' and you'll all have to find their buddy and hold up his arm. That way no one traitor can fly off by himself."

"What about if two traitors are buddies? And they decide to fly away together?" one of the SACs asked, winking at X-9.

"The Madman is going to give you hypodermics and a secret drug he invented. Amazing stuff. What you do is to give a shot to one buddy in each pair, remember, only one. That will turn him into a sniveling coward, so that even if his buddy wants to fly off, he will be too scared to join him even if he would like to. That's the best we can come up with until you can run the Chinese handcuff test. Anyone who flunks the handcuff test, you kill him or send him to Boise. Or both, for really hard cases. And dock him his vacation."

"His whole vacation?"

"OK, *half* his vacation."

"And remember the manure carts? And the Clancys?" Rebay asked Guggenheim.

"Oh, yeah. We almost forgot about them."

"As soon as you get back, report on where they are. We have guards around the Carvel® stands. We think that's where The Pigeon is going to strike first. But he may launch a second wave of attacks synchronized with his attack here on Headquarters."

The SACs were shocked. "So, his plan is to take over the FBI office here in the Justice Department, trap Speed in his office, and kill him? That's awful. What a dirty ratbastard!"

"You said it. And the worst part is, the FBI Headquarters is so full of kids and tourists who come here to watch our sharpshooters on the gun range, the scientists holding up test tubes of stuff in the lab, Boy Scouts® getting tips on code-breaking and knife safety, and ordinary citizens volunteering to be fingerprinted or used for target practice, and asking if we really have Dillinger's dork in a giant bottle of formaldehyde ("Do we?" X-9 interrupted) that we won't be able to use guns to defend ourselves or we'd slaughter all our fans who crowd into the building to worship our Greatness. We won't have the tools to do much more than ruffle their feathers."

X-9 collapsed in extended-metaphor heaven.

* * *

The guards were gone. The gates were open. But the Japanese-Americans who had been rounded up and stuck in the concentration camp had nowhere to go.

Their homes, their farms, their businesses had been grabbed by their Okie neighbors and they weren't giving them back. But the apology Knockers, disguised as Suzuki-San, the Yokohama Mama, had extracted from whatever asshole would be president in fifty years had more than made up for the way the Japs had been screwed. So actually all Agent Knockers had to do was show up, stand, and smile, and the Nisei would do anything she wanted.

So, when Knockers appeared just at the finish of the camp's Japanese Lutheran Church's Bingo Game and *Ikebana* Competition, everyone erupted in cries of joy at the sight of their benefactor, some would say *savior*, and her *blests* (remember your Japanese?) : "Suzuki-San, selfie prease," the grateful but penniless and half-starved ex-prisoners begged. "Yokohama Mama-San, you *ichi-ban*, number one. You OK! Got chewing gum?" It so happened that Knockers had a van full of Juicy Fruit®, Black Jack®, Doublemint® and everyone's favorite, Bazooka® with the Nancy and Sluggo® comics. *"Sruggo wa suki desu,"* they crooned as they squatted down, Japanese style, to try to decipher the inscrutable Occidental jokes.

It took a while for Knockers to kiss all the babies held out for her admiration, and to greet the men hoping to cop a quick feel from the woman many had raised, as you know, to the status of "*Kannon*," with effigies of the buck-toothed Yokohama Mama in wire-rimmed glasses propped up in the shrine nooks in their homes, fronted by candles, joss sticks, and sacrificial flakes of crack cocaine.

When she managed to calm the crowd, Knockers prepared for her big reveal. "You all know me as Suzuki, the Yokohama Mama, but that's not all I am. The reason I was able to get you that apology that has made up for all the crap ya had to take from those California Okies and Yahoos and, let's face it, sonuvabitchin' criminals, is because I am also" — as she shucked the false teeth out of her mouth, threw off the glasses, dropped the kimono, and stood before them in a skin-tight mini-skirt that tried but failed to conceal her thong, and a tight tank top that would have contained the average female's mammaries but not hers. She kicked off the *getas* and slipped into a pair of silver six-inch spike heels, generally known as *Come-Fuck-Me-Shoes* — I am also "Secret Agent and Super Slut Knockers of the FBI!"

The crowd was stunned to silence which was finally broken by a hoarse yell almost strangled by unrestrainable, but nevertheless strangely reverent lust, "H-O-R-Y shit, wirr ya take a rook at that lack."

Knockers held up her arms to restore order, but the sight of her exposed armpits provoked the male half of the ex-prisoners into such an uncontrollable burst of passion that a tidal wave of rampant manhood would have engulfed Knockers had not a minister jumped between the Super Slut and the rapacious throng, holding them at bay with a cross. "Gentremen, gentremen, mind youl mannels. Miss Agent Srut Knockels is oul guest. Be porite. One at a time," and he spun around unbuttoning his pants. "Me first."

Knockers realized that the fun was getting out of hand, so she pulled her gun and fired a warning shot, at the same time kicking the minister off the stage into the mosh pit.

"I'm here because I have a favor to ask. I need your help."

"Anything," they yelled back, "anything. Oul filst boln? A vilgin? I think thele's one alound hele somewhele. We ain't got much erse. Them fuckin' Okies store evelything erse."

"Lemme tell you what I need."

* * *

Nobody had to worry about Bambi. She was getting the Indians ready for the Pigeon war. With her twin papooses in a double backpack, the Super Slut had set up a training camp. She had the warriors from Taos and other nearby tribes lined up at the archery range, practicing with suction-cupped arrows at targets with Pigeon bullseyes.

MAD-1 from D.C. arrived at the Taos Reservation with Shitting Bull for an inspection. "How are they doing?" he asked her.

"Geronimo is weeding out the winners from the losers," Bambi told them. "The guys who can't hit the target can stay home and help the squaws load the dishwashers, you know, household stuff to keep the home fires burning while their guys are off killing, scalping and stealing liquor. Anyway, why are you out here? Checking up on me? Shouldn't you be back in D.C. casting spells or something?"

"Got a little invention-poo," the Madman said with a smirk.

"Heap powerful medicine," the Bullshitter added, doing a little heel-and-toe dance with a hop-step added, to the tune of "Shrimp Boats are A'Comin'."

"You gotta teach me that one," Bambi told him. "Something to get the brats to stop screaming."

"How about this one?" and he launched into "Let's Take an Old-Fashioned Walk," while beating out the rhythm with a tom-tom, soft shoe, and the occasional war whoop.

"I like 'Shrimp Boats' better. That war whoop is likely to stir them up just when they're nodding off."

"Good point."

"Back to the reason for your visit," Bambi said. "As you can see, we're pretty busy. The Baroness wants us deployed to the Carvel® stands tomorrow, backup for the Junior G-Men."

"Got some good news there: X-9 has managed to requisition Supersoakers® for the kids, and he thinks he can get 'em cap pistols. But wait . . . you're gonna *love* this."

He set a gallon can on the ground and opened it. "You don't happen to have a pile of manure around here, do you? Any old pile of shit will do."

"We got nothing but. How about that one over there?" pointing to a noxious mound behind her Winnebago®.

"Great. Can you get Gerry to come over here? With his bow and arrow."

The Madman dipped a rag in the can of magic stuff, tied it to the business end of Geronimo's arrow, lit it, and said, "OK, Chief, can ya hit that shit pile over there."

Bambi's Indian brave notched his arrow, drew it back

to the feathers, and let fly, striking the manure pile dead center, which immediately burst into flames. In a second the whole pile was burning, and a few minutes later there was nothing but a pile of ashes, and they smelled pretty good.

"What the hell was that?" Geronimo said, amazed. The Indians gathered around, scratching their war-bonneted heads.

"This stuff I came up with turns manure into napalm, and on top of that, Shitting Bull blessed the magic manure slop with one of his dances, which makes it even more deadly. You're all gonna take some of this with you when you head out to the Carvel® stands. You take your orders from the boss Junior G-Man who'll be wearing the Pigeon Buster badge. One of the older kids, probably a nine-year-old. That's how you'll recognize him. He's got the battle plan."

* * *

"Louder, girls," Eleanor screamed above the deafening din of three thousand Junior G-Girls, ages six to ten, at their Jamboree in Battle Creek, Michigan. Most of the high-pitched yelling seemed to be about what they wanted for lunch, or "If you pull my doll's hair, I'll pull yours" and "I gotta go to the potty." It was going well. The hag (really more of a progressive leftist than a Commie, if truth be told) was almost losing her mind having to listen to the racket. And she was a seasoned leader of Brownies®, Camp Fire Girls® and Future Homemakers of America®. The Pigeon's guys didn't stand a chance. The girls were looking forward to guarding the Carvel® stands from the Pigeon's manure wagons. Sounded like fun.

The girls had already passed their tests on making beds, sweeping toward the center of the room, not into the corners or under the bed, and the exceptions to the five-second rule. They knew how to use their Secret Decoder Rings®, and how to fingerprint their dolls. If they yelled loud enough at the Penguin and his traitors, the Widder Roosevelt had promised them they could have their photos with the Bama Jamma, their hero. For a test run, the Widder had taken the girls to the Ford Plant at Willow Run, and in five minutes they had shrieked the assembly line to a halt, and Henry Ford had decided that making cars wasn't worth all this noise and had sold out to the goddamn Wall Street bloodsucking bankers he had always hated. "Let them listen to this racket, it's what they deserve," he moaned.

"What do you do when you see the bad guys, girls?"

"We run up to them and yell, 'Go away! Mommy won't let me talk to strangers!' and then yell some more!"

"And if the bad guys say anything?"

"We start crying!"

"Now I haven't told you one little thing, girls. I hope you take this in the right way. When you go the Carvel® stands, there are going to be Indians."

The girls were awed. They had never seen real Indians. They were jumping up and down with excitement.

"And one more thing. There are going to be *boys*."

"Oh no. Eww. Boys. They stink. They'll ruin everything. Why do *they* have to be there?"

"They are Junior G-Men, and they have BB guns."

"Aw. Do we have to share the ice cream with them?"

"Yes. But never mind. Before we split up to go guard the Carvel® stands, we are going to have a campfire party. With marshmallows."

"Yay. Do we get our own sticks?"

"They are already cut for you."

The girls had a terrible thought. "Will there be boys?"

Eleanor nodded.

* * *

And out in Minneapolis, the Junior G-Men were practicing field-stripping their Daisy Red Ryder® lever-action BB guns and Supersoakers®. X-9 was giving them last-minute instructions: They were NOT to shoot the Indians who would be sharing Carvel® guard duty with them ("aww"), they were to aim for the Clancys' faces with the BB guns, and they were to save the Supersoakers® in case the exploding manure trucks set the stands on fire. They were also warned not to eat any ice cream with black specks on it.

X-9 had saved the bad news for last. "There's one more thing. You're not going to like this. There are going to be *girls*."

"What? They're going to ruin everything. How come?"

"These are the Junior G-Girls and they know all about making beds and cleaning up. They'll be a big help."

"No fair. Do they have guns too?"

"No, they don't have guns. Their job is to yell and scream and confuse the Clancys."

"OK, but they're just going to get in the way. And do we have to share the soft ice cream with them?"

"Yes."

"Aw."

"Tomorrow we all get in buses and we're gonna have a campfire to roast marshmallows."

"Great. Where do we get the sticks? Can we cut down trees with our hatchets?"

A happy bunch of kids. Guns. Supersoakers®. Indians. Hatchets. Marshmallows.

Then a terrible thought.

"Wait a minute. Are the *girls* going to be *there,* too?"

X-9 didn't feel like breaking it to them, but there was no way out. He nodded.

A command center had been set up in the waiting room outside J. Edgar Hoover's office, the Director still barricaded behind doors blocked with furniture. As far as they could tell, he was still perched on top of his Official and Confidential file cabinets. They could hear him sobbing, moaning, and yelling, "Have they come to get me yet? I surrender. Let them have Dillinger's dork." Clyde had to keep reminding him that they really didn't have the giant dork, that it was one of Lou Nichols' lies to increase tourism at Headquarters.

Rebay and Guggenheim were reviewing the situation with their general staff: Clyde, PA 103, X-9, Knockers, Bambi, who had just arrived from Taos, along with the Madman and Shitting Bull, and Bambi's papooses.

"Make our job a whole lot easier if we could get Speed out in front of the troops. A lot of them still remember when he was a mojoed-up hero and not the pathetic loser he is today."

"I heard that," Speed yelled from behind his locked door. *"Nobody likes me anymore."*

"I still like you, Speed," Clyde shouted, "but for God® sakes, we gotta situation on our hands and I for one don't see why you don't just strap on your guns and get out here with the rest of us. It's balls to the wall, man."

"But we're gonna lose," Speed sobbed. "What is it, 300 of us and 12,000 for The Pigeon? We ain't gotta chance. Let's give up and make a deal to let me live if he can kill the rest of you."

"Come on, Speed," PA 103 said, shaking his head. "What kind of deal is that for us?"

"You people are so selfish! After all I've done for you."

"Do we really *need* him?" PA 103 asked.

"It would be a big help. He could broadcast messages of encouragement to the troops before they go out to get killed by

The Pigeon. Remember those nice mimeographed note cards he gave to the agents he sent to the Pacific to get killed by the Japs? 'Dear Secret Agent Whatsyername: Yours is not to wonder why, Yours is but to do and die. RIP. Yours truly, Your Personal Friend, Director J. Edgar Hoover.' Just the right touch. He could do something heartfelt for us like that now."

"I think that with the Bullshitter's help, I can put Speed under," the Madman said.

"Whaddya mean, 'under.'"

"Hypnotize him. Make him open the door. Then give him the old meth/B-12 shot, enough to make a dead horse hop around like a jackrabbit."

"Can you do it through the door?"

"Not exactly. Shitting Bull has a spell that can levitate me into his room, where I can cast a spell on him. Then we got him."

"That true, Bull Man?" Rebay asked.

"Wizard no speak with forked tongue. Bullshitter got Right Stuff."

"OK," Rebay ordered. "Go for it."

Shitting Bull began dancing around the room, moaning and groaning in a sort of out-of-step march beat. Then he stopped still, extended his arms in front of his body, and advanced, eyes shut, toward the Madman, grabbed him by the neck, and smashed MAD-1's head into Speed's door like a battering ram. The Madman fell to the floor unconscious, blood running from his ears, eyes, nose and mouth.

"What the fuck, Bullshitter, I think you killed him," X-9 said, looking distraught.

"Little White Idiot no understand how Shitting Bull's medicine work. My wizard pal's spirit went through the door and is now doing his own monkey business with the big boss. Look. Door opening."

Sure enough, the door opened and Speed himself walked

into the command post, knees stiff and arms waving at random by his side, exactly, precisely, like Frankenstein's monster getting out of bed to take a leak. At the same time they saw MAD-1's corpse twitch, then come to life, sit up, wipe off the blood, and say to Shitting Bull, "That's one for the books, Bull Baby. His case of the heebie jeebies was so bad I had to use Love Potion Number Nine® on him."

"Love Potion Number Nine®, huh," Shitting Bull said thoughtfully. "I would have advised Formula 409® or maybe Grecian Formula 16®. Trouble with Love Potion Number 9® is he's gonna fall in love with first person he sees when he comes to. Maybe we ought to have ol' Clyde in front of him when you snap him out of it."

"OK with that, Clyde? Come on, take it for the team," Knockers said, snuggling up to him.

"OK," Clyde said. "Desperate times, desperate measures. But how about a few kisses from the gals before I say goodbye to you gorgeous pieces of tail forever, unless Speed's not looking." Rebay, Guggenheim, and Knockers lined up to give some wet kisses to their pal Clyde, who then said, "Before we bring him to, let's have a little fun with him. Hey, Speed, get down on all fours."

The Director did as he was directed.

"OK, now bark like a dog."

"Arf, arf."

Now lift your leg and take a leak into the wastebasket. That's a good boy, here's a Milk Bone®," and gave him a pencil to chomp on. Now chase your tail."

That trick got them all guffawing. "Lemme get a picture of that," PA 103 said. "Truman hates the bastard and would love to see it."

"Enough," Guggenheim said. "We got a war to win. Madman . . ."

The Wizard pulled out a hypodermic the size of a horse

needle and plunged it into Speed's butt, and he began growling viciously. Then the Madman said, "Stand in front of him, Clyde, and give him one of those come-hither looks. Wet your lips. That's it." MAD-1 snapped his fingers and said, "You are J. Edgar Hoover, Crusader Against Crime, the Scourge of Spies and Satan, and Poison to Pigeons."

Hoover squared his shoulders, looked at Clyde and said, "Later, big fella," then gazed sternly at his commanders: "I want a full and detailed report. Order of battle. Disposition of the troops, ours and the enemy's. And *lunch*. I'm starving."

CHAPTER 17

Speed was behind his desk finishing up his sandwich, Boars Head® baloney with Kraft® American cheese and Hellman's® mayonnaise on Wonder® bread washed down with milk (generic). "I could really use a Drake's Devil Dog®, Clyde. Think you could see if any were left over from my birthday party last year? They should still be fresh."

"No time for that, Speed. Let's listen to Rebay go over the battle plans."

Secret Agent Rebay was holding a long pointer in front of a large wall map of the U. S. of A. Speed was scarfing up a few crumbs from his sandwich. She rapped the pointer on his desk to get his attention. "These red dots are the locations of Carvel® stands across the country."

"Sure are a lot of them," Junk Bond said. "Must be really good stuff." He had just arrived with a planeload of 00Xs from Blighty, 001 through 0040, all with their standard bowler hats and thin, black, tightly rolled umbrellas.

"Haven't you ever had any?" X-9 asked him.

"No. My wife's holding out for a new car. Oh, you mean the Carvel® stuff. I heard it was something like *blanc mange*."

"What's that?"

"A dessert made from congealed lard and library paste."

"Nothing like that," X-9 informed him. "It's a kind of ice cream that comes out of a tube attached to a machine that looks like one of the iron lungs those March of Dimes® kids live in. In fact, Frank Carvel, who is an American success story like Einstein and Bronko Nagurski, began by using war surplus iron lungs for his machines. He started as a humble aluminum storm and screen-window replacement flunky. He got the idea from those caulking guns they use to seal the windows when they manage to bamboozle a sucker into buying those useless pieces of crap.

"He was amusing himself during a lunch break by squirting the caulk into a Dixie® cup. He had the urge to taste it. When he managed to cut his lips free, he thought, *Hey, I bet if I squirted something that tastes good into a cup, I could get kids to buy it. Or maybe into a cone. How about half-melted ice cream I could get cheap from the A&P®? I'll just clean out one of these caulk guns, fill it with the soupy ice cream, and I'll be in business.* —The rest is a Harvard Business School case study."

"Think Frank would let me franchise a stand in England? 'Soft Ice Cream Purveyor to His and Her Majesties the King and Queen of England, Ireland, the Falklands, and Emperor of India'?"

The Baroness hated to interrupt a conversation that might lead to the first business success story to come out of England since the invention of gin and butt paddling, but she rapped the table with her pointer and said, "Boys, we were going over the battle plan, remember? Like I said, the red dots are the Carvel® stands." She paused. She was getting irritated. Bond and X-9 were excitedly whispering about plans for a Carvel® Empire in England. "If you boys don't quiet down, I'm gonna have to separate you."

"Sorry."

"The dots with circles around them are the Carvel® stands where we've found a Clancy with a manure cart within striking distance." She motioned to a new addition to the gang, a boy who was impatiently waiting to talk. "This is little Ronnie Howard who is the chief intelligence officer (G-2) of the Junior G-Men, and he's going to explain the battle plan."

Little Ronnie Howard, a cute little freckle-faced, red-headed tyke, walked over to a whiteboard propped up on a tripod that stood taller than the little feller.

"This is a typical set-up. Here's the stand. In front you got the two windows, each with a kid in a soda jerk's cap handling the order. Two more kids handling the machines. The owner is in charge of the cash register, making sure the little crooks keep their fingers out of the till. Nothing special there. In back you have your dumpster. That's where the Junior G-Girls will be hiding. The Indian is in the john."

"Quick interruption, Ronnie," Rebay said. "The Indians wanted to light their flaming arrows using the traditional two sticks fire starter, but that usually doesn't work, so Shitting Bull issued a fatwa that flint and steel would be OK, so we've given them all Zippos®."

"Smart move," Speed said, nodding approval of Rebay's initiative.

"If I may continue," Ronnie said, getting exasperated at the way these old fools couldn't sustain a coherent line of thought, "when our Clancy gets ready to steer his two-mule-power manure cart into the parking lot — see where I got the 'X' right between the road and the entrance to the parking lot? — that's the point of attack."

They all nodded. Even Junk Bond seemed to be following, once he figured out that it was OK for the manure cart to be on the wrong side of the road.

Ronnie went on. "As soon as Clancy slows to make the

turn into the lot, the Junior G-Men — they've been hiding behind the bushes and up in the trees on the sides of the parking lot — let him have it with stones from their sling shots and BBs from their Red Ryders®. That should at least slow him down. The G-Girls come yelling and screaming at the top of their lungs and surround him. At the very least this will confuse him, maybe panic him. And listen to this, this is really great — I thought of this myself — one of the Junior G-Girls is really a Junior G-*Man*, yup, that's right, in a dress, and he's got a Junior G-Man Jackknife® and he cuts the mule loose. So, the Clancy is basically helpless. Sorta like a freighter when the engines conk out. Or in this case, maybe a barge fulla shit."

X-9 nodded approvingly. Little Ronnie didn't quite have the hang of metaphorical rhetorical consistency and extension, but he was getting there.

"As soon as the mule runs away, the Junior G-Man gives the signal for the girls to run back to the dumpster."

"What's the signal?" Clyde was jotting down the bullet points of the plan since he was a stickler for details.

"Remember that Frankie Laine song, 'Mule Train'? That's it. He goes, 'Muuuuule Teeeraiiin,' and that's the signal. The Indian has been listening, and as soon as he hears that 'Muuuuule' he lights his arrow, runs out of the crapper, nails the manure cart with a flaming arrow, and it starts burning. The boys drop their BB guns and sling shots, pick up their Supersoakers®, and hose the shit off the stand and extinguish any grass fires. And that's it, except I think the kids should get a round of free soft-serve, but that cheap bastard Carvel is only offering half price."

"Ya still gotta learn something about free enterprise and the sanctity of private property, Ronnie," Clyde explained. "When you grow up, you'll understand that it's Frank's legal responsibility to his stockholders to squeeze every last fucking penny out of his customers, and that includes kids."

"Well, OK, I guess, but it still seems like a raw deal to me."

"Think maybe we could chip in a little something toward the kids' ice cream from the Director's Birthday Fund?" Clyde asked his boss.

"I'll think about it," Hoover said, which was the signal to Clyde that the Director didn't think much of the idea and not to bring it up again.

"What do ya think of the plan?" Clyde wanted to know.

"Not bad," Hoover replied. "Just one thing: Don't you think the kids might shoot the Clancy's eyes out with those BBs and rocks?"

"That's the whole idea," Ronnie yelled. "You really are as dumb as they say."

"Shaddup kid," Speed growled. "Remember, Clyde, the Clancys are ex-FBI agents, even though they turned into dirty rotten ratbastard traitors out to kill their favorite director, me. I think I can have the Madman reprogram them when this is all over, you know, that silver needle in the brain trick, and they can work for me again. I've invested a lot of money in their training, and besides, we need their dues for the Director's Hialeah Expense Fund. The Madman has been telling me about a new betting system he's worked out for me, but he says it takes a lotta dough to make it work. It's called doubling down on your losses. Ever hear of it?

"Anyway, I don't want the Clancys to be blind when I reprogram them back onto the force. Get me The Pigeon on the phone."

Clyde quickly dialed the pay phone in the convenient phone booth Speed had set up in his office to extract spare change from his goddamn freeloading agents. "Hey Pigeon, just wanted to give you a heads-up. Make sure your Clancys are wearing eye protection. No, can't tell you why, that would be a spoiler. So what if eyeglasses don't conform to the stereotypical bog-trotter image you are striving for? Forget about preserving the dramatic unities. Just have them wear glasses. Goodbye."

Ronnie was behind his command switchboard, listening on his headset. "Yeah, yeah, great," Clyde signed off. "Keep me posted."

Ronnie grabbed the phone and began feeding it nickels. "The war has started at the Bull Run Carvel® stand," he yelled. "Yeah, I know. Where Civil War reenactments usually start, traditionally. And close by. If we had had enough warning, we could have organized a picnic excursion for the congressional wives to watch the battle."

Ronnie went back to the phone.

"Wow, wow, wow!" he crowed. "It's over. Exactly according to plan. The boys stopped Clancy before he could turn into the parking lot, then the girls ran out and drove him crazy with their screaming, and our guy-in-drag cut the mule loose. Clancy panicked and ran. He stopped for a minute and tried to sing his song, but nobody could hear him over all the screaming. Gotta hand it to those girls. I thought it was a bad idea having them, but they were great. Some of them even started skipping Double Dutch, and that got them shrieking even louder. The mule lay down and covered his ears with his hoofs. The Indian — I got his name; he's Chief Ford F-150® — scored a bullseye with his arrow and the manure burned. Just a few flakes of shit on the Carvel® stand which are being washed off with Supersoakers®."

The FBI top command was dancing around Hoover's office giving high fives (or, in the case of Little Ronnie, low fives). Ronnie ran back to his switchboard.

"This is big. Chief Ford F-150® jumped on his pony, chased Clancy down, and lassoed him. I didn't even know Indians could lasso. I thought that was only for cowboys."

"Nah, they work together at rodeos," Clyde explained to Little Ronnie, "and when they're shorthanded the Indians have to put on Stetsons® and the cowboys have to feather up. All part of professional show business."

"I guess I'm never too old to stop learning," Little Ronnie said. "And they brought Clancy back for a kind of enhanced interrogation I came up with. They tied him to a chair and then all the girls shrieked at him. He cracked. Turns out we were right; the bombs are song-activated. When the perp sings 'Whenever they get his Irish Up,' the bomb is activated; and when he sings 'Clancy lowered the boom,' the bomb goes off at the word 'boom,' just like we figgered."

"Oh, boy!" X-9, yelled, "It's time for us all to start crowing. We've got The Pigeon by the . . ." he ran out of inspiration and looked at Rebay for help. She shrugged and tossed him a Roget's Thesaurus®.

Speed's phone rang. "Oh, no," he wailed, "that idiot. Just when everything was perfect, he had to fuck things up."

"What's wrong, Boss?" Clyde asked, very worried. He knew that when Speed was this angry, he was going to get a boot in the ass, so he walked over and bent down.

"Frank Carvel went on the Jack Benny Radio Show® and announced a special two-for-one sale on Tutti Frutti/Spumoni (generic terms, not subject to copyright) Swirl. Now every non-lactose-intolerant man, woman, and child in the country is heading to Carvel® stands looking for that great deal."

Ronnie looked up from his switchboard. "Lines are already winding twice around Carvel® stands across the country. Parking lots are full. Traffic jams for miles. If a Clancy manages to blow up one of those manure carts, it's going to be a shitstorm like this country has never seen. Worse than Pearl Harbor, the Wall Street crash, and the Black Sox scandal rolled into one."

"The dirty rotten lying press is going to blame me," Hoover wailed. "It's Fake News! Any way I can make 'em believe it's your fault, Clyde?"

"Could be. Let's put Nichols to work."

* * *

Back at his Command Coop, The Pigeon was beating Dirty Pierre over the head with a hockey stick.

Pierre had his helmet on, so he was willing to let the evil criminal vent if it would make him feel better. "Goddammit," The Pigeon screamed. "Will you take off that fucking helmet? I want to beat your brains out."

Pierre pretended he didn't hear The Pigeon, and just grinned toothlessly at him and shrugged, pointing to his ears.

"I had everything set up perfectly," the Pigeon howled, punctuating each phrase with a blow to Pierre's head: "We're all set to take out every goddamn Carvel® in the country" — another blow to Pierre's head — "but that fuckin' Frank Carvel" — crash, bam — "had to spoil everything." He varied the blows with a kick to Pierre's ass, cushioned by Pierre's hockey shorts — "with that two-for-one Tutti Frutti/Spumoni Swirl promotion." The Pigeon was on the verge of tears. "Who can resist that?"

He yelled at his heavily bearded communication director, who had slipped back into "something a little more comfortable" (i.e., his whore disguise): "How many Clancys are still driving the bloody manure carts?"

"None, boss," the scantily clad villain said, practicing his seductive falsetto, "they've all lined up for their soft-serves."

"I told you to stop talking like that," The Pigeon screamed, chasing him around the command post with the hockey stick.

"Here, better put this on," Pierre told the slut, tossing him his helmet.

The Pigeon knew it was time for an executive decision. Out of spite he ordered a manure truck to head to downtown D. C. to blow up the Greyhound Station men's room, Clyde and Speed's old hunting ground. "That'll get their attention," he cackled evilly. He then ordered the Clancys, once they had picked up their Tutti Fruitti/Spumoni Swirl bargains, to redeploy to the porno movie theater nearest each FBI field office where agents liked to spend their lunch hours. Once there, the Clancys should await further orders.

* * *

Back at FBI headquarters, PA 103, X-9, and Junk Bond had just returned from enjoying their lunch hour at the porno house on 9th Street. Bond was saying he was struck by how well American porn starlets adopted the Stella Adler/Stanislavsky method technique, as opposed to the English actresses who "declaimed" their lines like "Harder, harder," in a Shakespearean manner with a superior touch of Oxbridge irony.

X-9 slapped himself on the side of his head, and shouted, "Of course!"

"Of course what?" Speed asked him.

"Of course I know where The Pigeon is going to strike next."

"Where?"

"Where can you find every Special Agent in the country every lunch hour?"

"Just like us, down at the local porno house, playing 'choke the chicken.'"

The same thought struck the Director. "That's it!"

He went over to Little Ronnie Howard. "Tell the Indians and the Junior G-Boys and -Girls that they should get ready to redeploy."

Rebay was already on the job. "I've plotted the tracks of the manure carts that are on the move, and they are all on course to intercept theaters near FBI offices that show dirty movies. It'll be easy to have the kids and the Indians shift their posts from the ice cream stands to take up positions at those Commercial Cathedrals of Corruption and Carnality."

"Great word choice, Agent Rebay!" X-9 exclaimed. "I love the repetition of consonants. That's called *alliteration*. Did it just come to you on the spot? Wow!"

Rebay blushed and walked over to Little Ronnie's switchboard. "I'm going to give you the new coordinates where I want you to relocate your teams. They're going to be stationed in and around movie houses. Work out the new battle plans."

"What kinds of movies are they showing? Can us kids get in for free?" Ronnie asked.

"Never you mind what kind of movies; and no, you kids *can't* get in for free. And the kids that are inside the theaters are not allowed to look at the movies or Speed'll catch hell from their moms."

"Not me," Speed protested. "This is all Agent Rebay's fault if anything goes wrong."

A lascivious leer spread across Little Ronnie's cute little kisser. "I think I may have to carry out a little field inspection."

* * *

Speed and his executive cabinet were waiting for reports from the porno houses. Each Theater of Filth was defended by an Indian warrior and a team of Junior G-Boys and Girls. Their orders were to let FBI agents in with their lunches, no one else. The boys had their slingshots and BB guns, the girls were practicing their Clancy-terrifying screams and yells, the Indians had their arrows dipped in the Madman's secret sauce, Zippos® flicked open, ready to light. What could go wrong? Huh? The plan was perfect. Speed's boys and girls and Indians were all battle-tested. Speed and Clyde had their game faces on. This was just like the Dillinger Days.

Clyde had set up the blackboard to keep score. He had chalked a line down the middle of the board, and on the top of each half he had written, in the usual FBI Circus serif font, "Home" and "Visitors." He had drawn a line across the bottom for the "Totals" so he could record the scores as they came in: wins in the FBI column for the FBI, wins in the Pigeon column for The Pigeon.

Speed had never been more confident. Not even when he had surrounded an unarmed and handcuffed Pretty Boy Floyd with five hundred machine-gun-toting agents with orders to open fire if Floyd moved. One agent swore he had seen Floyd move his pinky and they all opened fire. The rest was FBI history. That was a BIG win.

Speed saw no reason to prolong things. "Why not save time and put a big fat zero on the total line for the Pigeon?" he chortled to Clyde. "The old bagel. Pigeon is going to get the *schneid*." Clyde had already put a slash mark in the FBI column for the win at Bull Run.

Rebay was at Little Ronnie's switchboard, since the little feller had not gotten back yet from his field inspection tour. "I'm getting the first report. It's from the porn house near the Richmond field office. That's the one Ronnie was inspecting. He probably got *them* to put on their game faces, just like Speed and Clyde." She listened and then reported to Clyde, "Don't think you need to put this on the scoreboard, but the movie was *Debbie Does the Harvard Ultimate Frisbee® Team*: Ever think of adding Frisbee to agent training at Quantico?"

She suddenly stood up in shock. "No! How could that be?"

She put down the phone. "*Complete win* for The Pigeon. No one came out of the theater to stop Clancy. He parked the manure cart right under the marquee, jumped out, sang his song, and the bomb exploded. The lobby is nothing but a pile of bovine excrement now, and the Fire Department is waiting for their special

ShitMat suits before they can go in to look for survivors."

"I don't understand it," Clyde said, as he put a chalk mark in the Pigeon column. "We were absolutely ready for them."

The Madman had been thinking. "Next time we do this, I could build an automated electronic scoreboard that could give off a buzzer sound each time a score came in, and the totals could be figured out by a computer, no chance for Clyde or whoever is handling the arithmetic to make a mistake."

"Good idea," Clyde said. "As soon as more scores come in, I plan to check the math by casting out nines, but as long as it's just one to one, I'm making an executive decision that it's not necessary."

"Good thinking," Junk Bond reassured him.

"Ronnie's on the phone now," Rebay told them. "What? Oh no. You didn't. They didn't."

She put down the phone slowly. And she explained: "When Ronnie showed up at the theater, he didn't see anyone, so he went inside. All the Junior G-Men and Junior G-Girls were watching the movie. The Indians had moved in with a bunch of FBI agents and they were all doing something. When Ronnie asked them what was going on, they said something about 'Choking the chicken,' and that Ronnie should mind his own business. So, I sat down to watch the movie, since I thought it might help me get my 'Adult Behavior' merit badge. Did you know all the places you can put your—"

"Yes, I do! Then what happened?"

"Shit happened. I heard someone singing, 'Whenever they got his Irish up, Clancy lowered the boom' and the place just exploded. We all got covered with shit. I'm hosing myself off with a Supersoaker®. Am I in trouble?"

"Tell the kids that the stuff they saw in the movie is a big secret and they can't tell anybody what they saw, and not to talk to any bad people called reporters or else their mommies and daddies will get angry at them. No, tell them their mommies and daddies will be *shot* if they tell anyone what they saw in the movie. And then get back to Headquarters. We need help at the switchboard."

Clyde said, "I guess that's a clear win for The Pigeon," and he checked to make sure he had the slash mark in the win column for the Visitors. "That's OK. I never counted on Richmond," trying to cheer up Speed. "Wait'll the returns from the heartland start coming in. Those kids out there are wholesome, Christian, clean-livin' young scamps, the Indians too. They're not gonna get distracted by *Debbie and Doofus Do the Nasty*."

Rebay put down the headphones. "More bad news. Wichita, Kansas City, and Billings just called in. Three more wins for The Pigeon. A Junior G-Man told a reporter that now he knows what Mommy and Daddy do in bed."

"That's four for The Pigeon and just one for us. Totals, four for The Pigeon and one for the home team. Casting out nines, totals check out. Four to one."

The returns were coming in faster now. Four for The Pigeon, nine for The Pigeon, ten, twenty for The Pigeon. Finally, the calls stopped. "What do we get, Clyde?" X-9 asked.

"Just a minute, nine, carry the one, that's forty-eight for The Pigeon and one for us. Lemme cast out nines. No, there's a mistake somewhere. Lemme add it up again. Forty-nine for The Pigeon, one for us. Those are the final returns, and they all check out," Clyde said proudly. "Nice job, huh?"

Speed was distraught. "Nice job, nothing! Worst disaster in FBI history. Our reputation is shot. Whose plan was this, anyway?"

"No such thing as a failed experiment," the Madman reminded them. "What went wrong? We knew how horny our agents are, but we forgot how horny little kids are. You know, playing doctor and nurse, 'you show me yours if I show you mine,' that sort of stuff. But I'm surprised that the Indians turned out to be such smut hounds. Reputation as Noble Savage, and all that. Crying because someone littered. If we ever do this again . . ."

"Do this again?!" Speed screamed. "When word of this gets out, we'll be lucky if they let us do anything again except go to jail. This is even worse than the time I told the Boy Scouts® there is no God®. Fuckin' ministers are still giving me crap about that. We gotta come up with a big win to get the shit off our faces."

X-9 was rooting for the Director to extend the metaphor. "Come on, Chief, you can do it!"

* * *

"We gotta come up with something new for the agents to do on their lunch hour," Clyde was telling Speed and X-9. "They're gonna miss choking the chicken now that their porno houses have all been shit-bombed," Clyde said. He was, after all, in charge of Bureau morale.

"How about making them all wear the Madman's Chinese handcuffs. That'd keep their hands away from that chicken they keep choking," X-9 suggested. "Or X-9's sandpaper mittens?"

"What about if they hafta shoot it out with The Pigeon's gang? Didja think about that? They'll need those hands." Speed said. "Impractical, but I think the general idea of having agents handcuffed except when they're bumping off spies or SUBINTs (*Remember, kids? SUBINT means SUBject of INTerest. That's Big G-Man talk, but you should practice sounding like big G-Men*) is not bad. Also keep 'em from stealing cash from the Director's Mom's Birthday Fund. Future project, Clyde."

"I was thinking something more along the lines of a lunchtime office rosary," Clyde told him. "It would be uplifting, and fingering the beads will build up the finger strength they'll lose now that they're not choking the chicken. They could be looking at holy cards of The Little Flower or Saint Aloysius, protector of those struggling against the solitary vice, or maybe Blessed Oliver Plunkett — any of them would be a heck of a lot better for their souls than watching *Debbie Do Whatever and Whoever She Does.*"

"We took a big hit when The Pigeon exploded his shit bombs into our guys' favorite skin-flick shops, but maybe some good can come out of this," Speed said, doing some fast G-Man thinking. "Maybe we can volunteer our guys to be altar boys at the 6:00 am Mass. Good PR. Our recruiting posters can have our agents on their knees sticking out their tongues for Communion instead of machine-gunning spy or gangster suspects. A kinder, gentler, *holier* FBI."

"Hold that thought, Chief," Little Ronnie Howard whispered. "More bad news. You remember how we were planning to redeploy our Junior G&G teams and their faithful Indian companions to Greyhound® stations, once we repulsed the threat to our guys' porno palaces?"

"Oh, no!"

"Oh, yes! The Pigeon beat us to it. Reports are coming in, but it looks like the Pigeon exploded four hundred fifty of the manure cart bombs at Greyhound® stations. Nobody's going to Grandma's house this Thanksgiving, and our soldiers aren't going to be able to spend the holidays with their lovely and pure fiancées. They're gonna hafta rip off a piece at the base whorehouse."

"What about the D.C. Greyhound® station?" Speed asked, his heart, as the cliché has it, in his mouth. (Which doesn't make much sense, even for a cliché. 'Bout time to retire that one.)

"Gone. For some reason the Clancy drove the manure cart right into the men's room there, like he had something special against that place."

"That's where Clyde and I met," Speed sobbed. "It had special sentimental value for us. We endowed matching 'His and His' brass plaques over those two special urinals. The Pigeon must have known that and was being especially mean. *This is getting personal. It's me against him. Okay, Birdbrain — Bring it on.*" Speed was raging. Clyde was trying to console him.

"We need a spy in The Pigeon's inner circle. But how?" Rebay wondered. "Anybody?"

"I got an idea," Knockers said. "Back when we didn't know which of the Red ratbastards at Los Alamos was the courier, I put the girls onto it, and Brandi was the one who caught The Pigeon with his pants down. And he was really sweet on her (and off her), always begging for a freebie. Maybe she can get to him again. I'll call her."

"Yeah," Speed said. "She can cuddle up to him and break his heart like he broke mine." He was snuffling again. Guggenheim passed him a Kleenex®.

Knockers put down the phone. "We're in luck. Brandi says that the Pigeon has never stopped sniffing around her snatch. In fact, he just sent her a two-pound Whitman Sampler®. 'Course, sneaky ratbastard that he is, he ate all the ones with cherry centers and replaced them with Milk Duds®. And," Knockers told them, "he enclosed a note, *If you're ever in D.C., your Pigeon has a special treat for you, and it won't be 'Pigeon feed.'*"

"Pretty lame metaphor, if you ask me," X-9 said authoritatively, "since 'pigeon feed' doesn't have either romantic or sexual connotations. How about something like, 'You sure do stiffen my tail feathers, baby'?"

"Not bad. Maybe Brandi can work something like that into her reply."

"But how does she tell The Pigeon she's on her way?" X-9 asked. "If we had e-mail already it'd be easy, but I'd give that another sixty, seventy years. Did he send her a return address?"

"Lemme ask." She spoke to Brandi, getting more excited by the second. "Yup. He suggested the Beltway Overpass at Rock Creek Park. She should leave a chalk mark and he'll put a hotel key there the next day."

"That ratbastard," Speed yelled. "That's what Clyde and I did when we were dating. Same spot. He's really getting under my skin. I'm getting my Irish up." He stops and thinks. "And how does the Pigeon KNOW all this stuff about Clyde and me, unless Clyde . . . No. Not possible."

Clyde was looking at Speed kinda funny. *He hadn't said anything about that to The Pigeon. The Second spy . . . could it be . . .?*

* * *

"Oh boy, oh boy," The Pigeon chortled to Dirty Pierre. "Wait'll you see this babe. So sweet, so nice; knows how to cook, how to clean up — this place is getting to smell like a real pigeon coop — and how to make a man happy!! Oh that Brandi! Goes great with a cigar, too."

"She'll make her man happy, all right. You mean she'll mow the lawn and take out the garbage and wax the car? Remind her to take off her rings when she's doing the car. Wow! Don't let her get away. *And* you'll get rid of these blue balls soon. They're keeping you from concentrating on our plan to kill Hoover and take over the FBI. All you think about is poontang. We got eleven thousand of our guys on the way, not to mention four and a half thousand manure carts. And no bombs for them manure carts, kinda useless if ya ask me. And how about the five thousand guys that got them Chinese handcuffs on their trigger fingers. Got a plan for them? When's she arriving?"

"Not to worry. The old Maestro still has a few tricks up his sleeve. *(I know! I know! Lousy metaphor for a pigeon)* I gotta take a shower. For some reason Brandi always makes me wash up before we do the nasty."

"I been meaning to say something about that, Boss, but I

guess she beat me to it."

* * *

"Brandi's picked up the hotel key. We've got X-9 and PA 103 tailing them, Junk Bond for backup," Clyde told Rebay and Guggenheim. "Standard three-man tail."

"You know, I'd feel better if Peggy or I just kind of tagged along. Somehow, I get this weird feeling of a fuck-up hiding in the woodpile. (If X-9 were here he'd have me trying to extend the metaphor, and I kinda like the challenge.) Anyway, you or me, Agent Guggenheim?"

"You take it. I better keep my eye on Speed and Clyde. They seem a little emotional. You know, thinking with their hearts — or whatever — instead of their heads."

Brandi was waiting for The Pigeon in the Robin's Nest Bar at the Willard. She was thinking that X-9 would like the connection: 'Pigeon,' 'Robin's Nest,' a metaphor practically auto-extending. Then, out of the corner of her eye she saw X-9 who grinned and gave her the thumbs-up, doubtless also happily thinking about metaphors.

And, hello, will you get a look at The Pigeon, she thought: *Black silk shirt, opened at the collar, somewhat clumsily tied FBI emblem cravat (little irony there,* she thought*), harem pajama bottoms, a white silk bathrobe, gold lamé slippers, and, oh no, a rose in his teeth. Well,* she thought, *can't say he isn't making a statement about our next stop.*

"Brandi," he shouted. "Brandy for Brandi," he yelled to the barman. "Am I glad to see you," he said as he slipped onto the barstool next to her. "Check it out," he said, glancing suggestively toward his crotch. She did check it out, and indeed, he *was* glad to see her. He hoisted his snifter. "Here's to happy takeoffs and landings," he said as he toasted her. She clinked glasses, and glanced over at X-9, hoping he had heard the avian imagery.

* * *

"Good thing I'm a pro," Brandi reported to Rebay, "or that boy woulda worn me out. He ain't had any in a long time. But I got what we need. His full forces are arriving day after to-morrow. For some reason he isn't loading the manure carts with bombs. Says Hoover's gonna be up to his ears in shit. He got the idea from some book called *Danny's Infirmary* or something. Sorry, I ain't much on literary allusions. He's planning to use the agents with the Chinese handcuffs as battering rams to get into the doors you've boarded up. I'll let you know if I get anything else. Gotta get back upstairs. If I know my fine-feathered pal, he's gonna want some more."

* * *

"Knick of time," Knockers said, when she heard the new timetable. "My guys from the Jap internment camps are arriving tomorrow. "

"How many? What weapons?"

"We gotta thousand sumo wrestlers. Really big ones. Fat like you can't believe. And two thousand *kendo* fighters."

"What's that?"

"Kids with big, long sticks. Unless you been trained to fight 'em, they'll bust yer head with the first blow."

"Bambi's Indians are already here. They're looking over the American Indian exhibits at the Smithsonian and can be here in minutes across the Mall. Unless they get all nostalgic about the artifacts that the Government has stolen from their reservations. Or unless they join the protesters outside the building who are accusing the Smithsonian of appropriating their culture. Anyway if all goes well, they'll be with us. They've all got their ponies."

"Great. They got their flaming arrows?"

"Aye, Aye."

Little Ronnie Howard piped up in his endearing squeaky voice: "Brandi says she doesn't know how she did it, but The Pigeon's finally worn out. She's seen his tabletop war game battlefield. She says watch out for some big towers. He's got four of them, and they're six stories high. Got something up his sleeve. Or under his wing."

"Nice. Remember that for X-9."

* * *

Speed's reinforcements were pouring in. Indians, sumo wrestlers, *kendo* fighters, Junior G-Boys and Girls, the Widder Roosevelt and the Bama Jamma's girls. The SACs from around the country had sent all the non-treasonous agents they could spare. Clyde had requisitioned 20,000 meals ready to eat and 10,000 folding cots. The Madman had the great idea that all the FBI fighters should be in disguise, so he had gotten hold of 20,000 black sunglasses, trench coats and snap-brim fedoras. Nobody had trench coats big enough for the sumo wrestlers, so he sliced theirs open down the back, but they still looked great up front. "And after all, our guys never retreat, so no one will see their asses sticking out," he explained.

The troops were being bunked in every room of the Justice Department. The Attorney General yelled to Clyde that there was no room for him in his own office, now that the Junior G-Girls were in there, driving him crazy with their screaming.

"Right," Speed told him curtly. "Get out of that office. We need the space!"

The Indians had decided to lodge themselves at the Smithsonian in its collection of antique teepees. Geronimo had pulled babysitting duty, and had the twin papooses on his back, Elizabeth Pocahontas Warren and Johnny Cash, each with a chaw of tobacco pacifier dribbling sickening yellow drool onto Geronimo's Government Issue Indian Blanket®. He had stationed himself on the roof of the Old Post Office where he had a clear view of the prospective battlefield and could issue smoke signal commands to the Indians. Shitting Bull had issued another fatwa that the two-way wrist radios the FBI had borrowed from Dick Tracy® violated Indian rules of war, so they were stuck with the smoke signals. But it turned out Chief Remington Rand had developed a system of speed smoke-signaling, the equivalent of touch-typing, so nobody figured that was a problem, and adhering to traditions would keep Thumper the Rabbit God® happy.

The Madman had constructed a scale model of the Justice Department and the surrounding streets and avenues. He had made miniature lead Indians, sumo wrestlers, *kendo* fighters, Junior G-Men and G-Girls, the Bama Jamma's Roller Derby Girls, the Poontang Patrol, and of course the loyal agents, all in their sunglass disguises. He had placed them in hypothetical but logical positions throughout the model Justice Department and had explained how each group should respond to possible attacks.

The next morning dawned, and Speed's general staff could see that The Pigeon had positioned a giant tower covered with heavy cloth a short distance from each of the four sides of the building. MAD-1 was ready with his scale models, and placed models of the towers in the proper positions.

"What is he up to?" Rebay asked.

Guggenheim shrugged. "Let's send out a reconnaissance in force: Jamma's girls and the Junior G-Men with their slingshots. And let's see what happens." Peggy nodded and called for X-9.

From his lookout post on the roof, Speed could see something in the distance moving toward the Department from the four principal points of the compass. *(Since it is foolish to assume readers of this kind of book know anything about anything, that would be north, south, east, and west.)*

Whatever those things were, they looked like long segmented snakes covered with something like tarps. Impossible to guess what was under those covers. "What the hell do you suppose that is?" Speed asked Clyde.

Guggenheim put X-9 in charge of the reconnaissance expedition. "Here's the plan. We charge out with the Jamma's ladies in the lead, and they skate towards the tower. You boys let loose a barrage from your slingshots and follow the Jamma's girls. Make noise. If you reach the tower, hold it, and we'll send an expedition of the sumo wrestlers to take control. If they counterattack, retreat. We'll hold the door open until you get back inside."

X-9 clapped his hands and opened the doors, and the pack of Hoover loyalists ran out screaming and yelling and firing and reloading their slingshots as they ran.

When they had almost reached the tower, a hundred Chinese-handcuffed traitor-agents hidden behind the tower charged, swinging ropes from their cuffed hands, screaming "Pigeon, Pigeon, He's Our Man" and "Fuck Speed," scattering the G-Kids and the Bama Jamma's spandex-clad skaters. The G-Kids and the Roller Derby broads fought their way back to the Department just in time for X-9 to slam the door in the face of the furious ex-agents. One dirty-ratbastard traitor was too close behind them to turn around before the door closed. He was immediately set upon and thrashed by the G-Kids before being hauled to the lab for debriefing by the Madman.

* * *

"Well, we just lost another one," Clyde said, grabbing a chalk to ring up another win for The Pigeon.

"That one doesn't count. Erase it," X-9 protested. "Don't you know anything? That was a reconnaissance in force. We found out what we wanted. The towers are defended. We captured a prisoner and he'll spill his guts to the Madman. They all do. So, chalk that up on our side."

"You sure?" Clyde said doubtfully. "I don't think that was a win. How about a draw. One half point for each of us?"

"Fair enough," X-9 conceded.

Madman dragged in the broken and bleeding captive. "Seems The Pigeon is playing this one close to his breast. All this rat knows is that The Pigeon's men with free hands have all been issued shovels."

On the roof Hoover could see the long procession drawing nearer, single file, each segment separate from the rest, moving in a herky-jerky motion.

* * *

Speed and The Pigeon were feeling each other out over the phone, figuratively speaking, of course, *out*, not *up*.

"What's the matter, Speed? Wanna give up? Scared?" The Pigeon jeered.

"Give up? Are you nuts? We've got you right where we want you."

"Sure you do!" *(That was what you'd call sarcasm, kids)*. We've got you outnumbered. And half your guys are children."

"And half *your* guys have their hands cuffed together, you jerk," Hoover sneered.

"I'm a jerk? You're a bigger jerk."

"You're the biggest jerk. You need to outnumber us three to one for an attack to win against a defended position, and you ain't got that. Basic Offensive Warfare 101. Ain't ya read *Military Tactics for Complete Dummies©*? I think it's Chapter Three."

"Huh? I didn't know about that. You sure?"

"Absolutely. Plus, we got a Superpower that will stop your secret weapon."

"Well, we got a Superpower that will block your Superpower. Waddya think about that?"

"Geeze," Hoover whispered to his Executive Cabinet. He looked defeated. "He's got a Superpower that can block our Superpower."

The Pigeon chortled, "No answer to that, huh? Mr. Soon-To-Be-*Ex*-Director. You has-been."

Knockers leaned over and whispered into Speed's ear. He smiled, as they say, ear to ear. "Yeah," Speed said. "That's great. For real?"

"Cross my heart," Knockers assured him.

"Hey, listen to this, Pigeon, I've got a New Superpower that will stop your Superpower from blocking my Old Superpower. You loser. Now *you* wanna give up?"

"What is it? What is it? No fair. I thought each side only got one Superpower," The Pigeon wailed. "You're lying. AND you're cheating! You *always* cheat. By the way, how did you score that little squirmish earlier today, Clyde?"

"Hey Clyde," Hoover yelled over to his buddy. "Pigeon wants to know how you booked today's fight. Oh? . . . Clyde ruled it a draw," he reported to The Pigeon, "half a point to each. You saw it that way, too? OK, see you on the battlefield tomorrow."

Guggenheim and the rest of the cabinet yelled, "Goodbye Pigeon."

"My guys say goodbye," Speed told The Pigeon.

"He says his guys say goodbye too," Hoover told *his* guys. "Nighty-night."

CHAPTER 18

The forecast had been for rain, and Speed and The Pigeon had agreed to postpone the battle in case it was too wet for The Pigeon's secret weapon to work, and the FBI Executive Cabinet agreed that was only fair, especially since the Madman wasn't sure his flaming arrows would work in the rain, either. But, you know, meteorology (*That's weather forecasting, kids*), like any kind of forecasting — stocks, horses, whether the fish will be biting — is not an exact science, and it turned out to be a beautiful day.

Geronimo had his campfire going on top of the Old Post Office and he sent off the "Ready to Transmit" smoke signal. Shitting Bull, who was in charge of the Indians at the Smithsonian, sent off two puffs on his peace pipe. That meant, "We're mounting up." The Indians had gotten special permission from the park rangers to let their ponies graze on the Mall, and they looked ready to go. Some of the Indians were amusing themselves and the tourists by playing a game of mounted lacrosse, a variation they had learned at Dartmouth®.

From his lookout post on the roof, Speed and the G-Gals

could see some movement behind the mystery towers, and then—OMG! The towers began moving forward toward the walls of the Department. Knockers was ready for this, and she had the sumo wrestlers oiling up and tossing ritual salt over their shoulders and under their armpits. *Pee-yew*, she thought, *but you gotta respect these age-old customs of Japanese culture. It ain't all flower arrangement, sister*. She ordered the doors opened, and the sumo wrestlers charged the towers, putting their shoulders against the tower bases. But wait! They were getting pushed back. Slowly, but surely, the towers were winning. Some of the wrestlers were getting crushed under the towers, others were trampled by the wrestlers behind them. Knockers picked up her bullhorn, and shouted, *"Minasama, letleat."*

When they had retreated back to the Department, Knockers had to cheer up her despondent fat boys. She told them the story of John Henry and the steam steel-driving machine. They didn't quite get the exact meaning, but they got the point that it hadn't been a fair fight since they were pitted against some sort of engine that was not in the standard sumo rule book. They shouldn't feel too bad, and they didn't have to cut off their ponytails, the standard punishment for defeat. The Pigeon got Clyde on the phone, "That's a clear win for our side. Agree?"

Sadly, Clyde chalked up another win for The Pigeon.

* * *

The towers were now close to the four walls of the Justice Department, and then they began to lean forward, until the tops of the towers were actually dangling over the roof itself. Speed still couldn't figure out what the fuck was going on. There was a grinding noise, a clanking, and a huge bucket emerged from the top of the tower, made a turn, and then headed back down. IT WAS AN ENORMOUS CONVEYOR BELT. So were the other three, all clanking and banging. But what were they going to convey?

The Director had a horrible thought. He rushed to the edge of the roof and looked past the base of the towers. There was a line of mules dragging manure carts as far as the eye could see, but the manure, if that's what it was, was covered with dark gray tarps. He ran to the side of the building toward the Old Post Office and began jumping up and down to get Geronimo's attention, making bow-and-arrow gestures.

Geronimo looked at Speed completely puzzled. *What the hell was the old fool trying to say?* The Indian pointed at his ear. Speed nodded. He got the idea. He held out his arms in a circle shape. *Sounds like 'o,'* Geronimo thought. *'Row?' 'Sew?' I get it, 'Bow!' He wants to borrow a bow."* He held up his bow and pointed it at Hoover, indicating that he would send one over. Hoover shook his head and ran from one end of the building to the other, his arm describing a long, wide arc. *He wants me to shoot an arrow at him? Doesn't make sense. He can't want to commit suicide by Indian. Are things that bad already?* Hoover was pointing down at the manure carts. Geronimo's momma didn't raise no dumb papoose, and he got the picture. *He wants us to shoot our flaming arrows at the manure carts,* and he rushed to his campfire and began swinging his blanket over it, sending out a long and complicated message with complete plans for the Indian attack. Shitting Bull sent back a signal from his pipe that the message was received. The much-respected and pretty-impressive medicine man pointed toward the Justice Department with his battle spear, the Indians let loose their terrifying war whoops, and they charged toward the conveyor belts, letting loose wave after wave of flaming arrows, all of them aimed perfectly at the manure carts. AND THEY BOUNCED OFF THE CARTS, HARMLESSLY.

The Indians were amazed and looked up at Hoover on the roof. They spread their arms out helplessly, as if to say, "Some fucking pathetic Superpower, Madman," and trotted back toward the Smithsonian. "Let the white men settle this themselves," Shitting Bull told his hangdog bunch of losers. "We've done our part."

Hoover understood. "That was The Pigeon's Superpower, some kind of flameproof covering for the manure carts. His Superpower blocked my Superpower."

"Don't worry, Chief," Rebay assured him. "We still got one Superpower left."

The Pigeon had Clyde on the phone: "No doubt about that one. Another win for The Pigeon."

Clyde had to agree as he slumped his way over to the blackboard, where he picked up his chalk.

* * *

Peering through his binoculars, Hoover could see the first manure cart move up to the base of the conveyor. He could see a trap door open, and the manure slid down, out of the cart where The Pigeon's shit shovelers shoveled it into a hopper at the bottom of the belt, where one bucket, then another, began picking up the cow turds and lifting them toward the Justice Department roof. Hoover watched, paralyzed with fear, as the empty buckets clanked toward him one after another, until the first bucket full of cow pie made the bend, dumped its load on the roof of the building, and headed back as another dumped *its* load. He looked around. The other three conveyors were doing the same thing. He finally got it. The conveyors were going to transfer an unending load of reeking, stinking cow pie all over the roof of the Justice Department.

But could the roof stand the stress? Would it collapse? He yelled to his staff, "We got anybody who can figure out how much shit this building can take?"

Knockers replied, "Secret Slut Sherry was an architect before she signed up as a Slut."

"Get her up here."

Sherry showed up with a slide rule tucked into her mini-dress, ballpoint pens in a pocket protector clipped to her sequined bra.

"Our data is that there are 4,500 manure carts out there," Speed told her. "That rat-bastard Pigeon is going to send it all up here. What's gonna happen to the building?"

Sherry asked Clyde to lend her his eyeshades and she got to work. "Let's see, is that dry manure or wet," leafing through her engineers' *Strength of Materials Handbook*®.

"Figure wet."

"OK, let's figure six tons per cart, and you said 4,500 manure carts, that would be 27,000 tons. Let's multiply that by 2000 pounds per ton, and that gives us 54 million pounds of shit. The roof is roughly 200 by 200 feet. That would be 40,000 square feet. Divide 54 million by 40,000 and you get 1350 pounds per square foot. Casting out nines, it all checks out."

"Can the roof hold up?"

"Well, Commando Against Crime, let's say you just had 1350 pounds on one square foot, and that's all. Sure. No sweat. But there's gonna be a weak point where the roof will buckle. As the depression deepens, all the shit will flow toward that point, which we can call the point of entry, or POE. Inevitably there will be a breakthrough, or BT. The shit will pour towards the POE and through the BT onto the floor beneath, which is not constructed with the strength of the roof. There will quickly be another POE and a BT. So, the crap will be pouring from floor to floor, each floor buckling in turn, until the entire Justice Department will be full of shit."

"I know that this is no time for levity, but that's what some of us have been saying for a long time," X-9 said.

"So, we're totally fucked," Clyde said. "Shall I call The Pigeon and tell him to stop the shit, that we surrender?"

"Not yet," the Secret Agent Baroness told him. "There's that last Superpower I told you we have. Been saving it for a surprise."

* * *

The Pigeon was giving Secret Slut Brandi a tour of the battlefield. He pointed at the conveyor belt and told her how there was one on each side of the Justice Department, each one transporting shit from the manure carts to the roof.

He started bragging to her. "We got, how much, I forget . . ." He got Clyde on the phone. "I figure we got 53 million pounds of shit here. What did you come up with? 54? Huh? Which edition of the *Strength of Materials Handbook*® did you use? Last year's? Check this year's? Either way, your roof can't take it, right? Correct. There'll be a POE and then a BT. All the way down to Speed's dungeons and the Madman's torture chambers. OK. Talk to you later. I got the beautiful Brandi on my arm right now, while we watch what I am already calling The Pigeon's Playground, that is, the FBI Headquarters, get filled full of shit. Like you and Speed ol' boy. Bye-bye."

"The idea of using last year's *Strength of Materials!*" the Pigeon cackled evilly. "That Speed is so cheap. Ya gotta update your reference books if you want to stay ahead of The Pigeon," he bragged to Slut Brandi. "He even buys day-old Wonder Bread® for those baloney and margarine sandwiches. Though they are delicious."

Brandi was jumping up and down, her breasts in motion. "Can I see how that big machine works?" Brandi begged, pointing at the conveyor. "Things like that always get me hot. They're so big and strong. Like you," as she goosed him.

"Sure, sweetie. And afterwards, I wanna show you the dressing room trailer I got for you. It's got a star on the door and your name, which is . . . uh, I forget . . . Ha-Ha! Just kidding."

He led her to a platform at the base of the conveyor right over the hopper where the manure carts were dumping the shit, one after another, and the shovelers were shoveling.

"Lemme see how that works. You are *so* smart," Brandi said. She walked to the edge of the platform and leaned over the boiling sea of manure in the hopper to get a better look.

"Don't get so close, honey," The Pigeon warned her as he grabbed her arm to pull her back. But Brandi, using a jiu-jitsu move she had learned from Mahony at the FBI Academy during agent training, pulled his arm forward as she jumped back, catapulting him into the hopper full of shit, where a bucket scooped him up and sent him up the belt.

"Stop the belt, the boss is in the shit," Dirty Pierre yelled, lunging for the panic switch. Brandi yanked out her pistol and shot off his finger just before it hit the button. "There's more where that came from if anyone moves toward that switch."

"I never should have quit hockey," Dirty Pierre moaned. "And now I've been shot by a girl. And where was she hiding that gun? She's hardly wearing anything."

"He's on the way up," Brandi yelled into her Dick Tracy Two-Way Wrist Radio®. (I don't think it's registered, but why take a chance?) "Get the net ready!"

On the roof, Speed and Clyde spread a wide mesh net where the shit was pouring from the conveyor belt.

"You know, when you get used to it, this stuff don't smell so bad," Speed told his wing man.

"Know what you mean. Reminds me of my mom's rhubarb garden. We had a farmer dump a load of this stuff on it every fall. Boosted production."

"I'm thinking, maybe we could make this the official scent of the FBI. Have the Madman come up with shit smelling body rub, after shave, deodorant, make the Junior G-Kids buy it."

"Let's think big. It could be the fragrance of the entire

government. You could call it the Scent of Sam®, you know Uncle Sam. *(And by the way, I have already registered that Scent of Sam® name, in case any of you crooked readers are thinking of ripping me off).*

"Look, here he comes!" Clyde yelled.

And there was the Pigeon, covered with shit, sputtering and waving his arms and legs like a newborn babe (if the babe were a full-grown ratbastard traitor covered in shit) and he plopped into the net Speed and Clyde were holding. They quickly gathered the loose ends of the net. They had him, The Pigeon, the guy who laughed about how he was gonna kill Speed *(Who's laughing now?)*, all wrapped up in a big ball of shit. Not such a big shot now. Attaching a rope to the net, Speed and Clyde dangled him over the edge. "We got The Pigeon," Hoover shouted over his bullhorn. "Stop the machines."

"Stop the presses, I mean, stop the belts," The Pigeon screamed. "Do like Speed says. Put me down. I hate heights."

"Some Pigeon you are," Speed laughed. "You never guessed Brandi was my last Superpower, didja?"

"I coulda if you'da given me a hint."

Speed waved to get Geronimo's attention and then got down on all fours like a horsey. Geronimo got the idea right away and sent a smoke signal to the Indians who raced to the towers to take possession of the controls and stop the carts from dumping their loads. Knockers sent out her sumo wrestlers who sat on the few traitors who still had any fight left in them.

"I guessed you'd have to call this a win for us," Speed told The Pigeon. "Chalk it up, Clyde."

Pigeon mumbled something. "I hope that wasn't something rude, Pigeon. This would be a great time to mind your manners. I'm still thinking about your punishment, *after* I wash your mouth out with soap," Speed said grimly.

"With Brillo® in it," Clyde added. "That's gonna be fun."

CHAPTER 19

"Howdeedo, gals," Harry Truman greeted the Secret Agent Gals as they entered the Oval Office.

Ever since Secret Agent Rebay had saved President Roosevelt's life back in 1941, Truman had been using the two G-Gals for super-sensitive assignments. Now they had asked to see him. "Anything new on that cocksucker you work for?" he joked, but he did not look hopeful. "Like I told you, if you could get me a candid shot of that bastard going at it with his boyfriend, I'd put you two in charge of the Bureau. It doesn't have to be him swallowing the sausage. Even a little kissy face would be enough to get rid of that prick," he guffawed. "Edgar and Clyde, sitting in a tree, K-I-S-S-I-N-G. Some damn fine people in that outfit, except for those two and their flack, Lou Nichols. I hate him, too."

"Sorry, Mr. President," Secret Agent Guggenheim replied, "Ever since you tipped off Dorothy Schiff about him and Clyde, she's had reporters from the *New York Post* staking out his house 24/7. He's been extra careful. I think I'd have to hide in his closet to get the pictures you want."

"Cudja? Cudja?" the President pleaded.

"Really too risky, Mr. President. He's got a torture chamber in the basement that he and Clyde use for their private parties. If they caught me, I don't think I could stand it when they turned on the blowtorch."

"How 'bout you, Secret Agent Rebay?"

"Same goes for me. Can't stand pain. I have my dentist put me under for teeth cleaning."

"No problem. I could give you these here cyanide pills. Keep 'em in your mouth, and when the pain gets too much, just bite down and you'll come to Jesus®."

"Mighty thoughtful of you, Mr. President, but I think we'll pass."

Just then, Truman's daughter Margaret entered the Oval Office. "Time for my piano practice, Daddy. Who are these impressive gals with their Chanel® gun bags?" she asked. "If I'm not mistaken. that's the little dead-eye who saved FDR the day after Pearl Harbor, right?"

Rebay nodded modestly.

"You know, if Daddy had become President, then he had a plan to end the war with no fuss. Turned out the psywar boys had these paintings they were going to drop on Tokyo and Berlin that would have turned the Japs and Krauts into pacifists. Wouldn't that have been wonderful? Did you hear anything about that? FDR put the kibosh on the whole idea. He wanted the Navy to win the war."

Rebay grimaced. So *that* was what had happened to their posters. But at least they got paid, so it came out all right.

"Well, I'll let you get back to business with Daddy. I'm going to practice some Chopin for my concert at the DAR Hall next week."

She began playing a few scales and then launched into Chopin's *Prelude Number 4.*

Rebay listened attentively, and then turned to the President. "On second thought, how about one of those cyanide pills?"

"Got one for me, too?" Secret Agent Guggenheim asked.

"Not enough for all of us," Truman answered. "I want to keep one for myself."

Margaret looked up angrily.

"Just kidding, honey. Sounds great." The trained eyes of the two Secret Agents did not miss seeing the President stuff cotton into his ears. Rebay snapped her fingers and pointed at herself and Peggy, and the President passed them the cotton.

"Well, Gals, what's this all about?"

"Ya must've heard, Mr. President, about the little dust-up we had at the Bureau with that super-villain called The Pigeon."

"The Widder Roosevelt told me something about it, when she visited me wearing some kind of skintight spandex onesie. I felt sick for a week. Anyway, I gotta say I was rooting for The Pigeon, but I guess I gotta face the facts: Speed won, and I'm gonna have to put up with him until I get out of this rotten job. Which I now have for four more years. I was hoping I'd lose."

"Everybody knows you're a good sport and not a sore loser. It's one of the few things they like about you."

"Ouch," the President protested.

"Whatever. We're gonna have a big victory parade down Constitution Avenue all the way from the Capitol to the Washington Zoo. Hoover, Clyde, and all the gang: X-9's Junior G-Men; Eleanor's Junior G-Girls; the Bama Jamma's roller derby team; Lanny Budd, you know, Presidential Agent 103; all the Super Sluts from Los Alamos; Geronimo's Indians; Knockers' sumo wrestlers and *kendo* fighters; and us, of course," indicating herself and Guggenheim, "all wearing our FBI black sunglasses disguises. We're gonna be followed by the four shit towers towed by Army tanks, the four thousand five hundred manure carts with the Clancys on top of the manure in chains; and then, at the end of the parade, The

Pigeon himself *in a cage*. We're passing out stuff for the crowd to throw at him, kinda like a Mardi Gras parade in reverse."

"And you're asking me for permission to let you stage this outrage? Making that Red-smearing bastard and his gestapo out to be national heroes? Hell no."

"Too late for that, Harry. It's by popular demand. Get in the way and you'll get run over, or impeached. We've got a space for you on the reviewing stand. You gotta practice holding a salute for the whole parade. Should be about three hours. Remember how Aaron had to hold up Moses' arm in the Bible? Might want to look into that. Maybe Ike or General MacArthur will help out."

"I don't trust those guys. So, you say I got no choice? OK. What's this about the zoo? What's going to happen there?"

"Big surprise. If I told you, it wouldn't be a surprise. Right?"

"I guess."

Just then the door opened, and here *was* a surprise. Liberace came in, flashed them all a grin that left them blinking, and sat down on the piano bench next to Margaret. (He hadn't yet achieved the popularity he would later find on TV, but he certainly had the glam look his fans loved.)

"Hey, Larry," the President greeted the Sequined Sweetheart of the Senior Sisterhood.

"I hired him to polish up Margaret's act," he explained to the G-Gals. "I'm gonna give you a special treat right now." He nudged the two Secret Agent Gals and winked.

"Give me the intro, Larry. Instead of a speech for the State of the Union, I've been rehearsing a song. It goes a little bit like this," and he began shouting out "Unchained Melody," employing all the major and minor scales at once, definitely one for *Ripley's®*.

As he rounded the bend of "Lonely rivers flow, to the sea, to the sea," and got to "Wait for me, wait for me," he hitched up his britches, and strained for the high note on "me," missing it by a million miles. Rebay and Guggenheim were already out the door, white-faced and shaking.

"That was, that was . . ." Rebay gasped.

"There are no words," Guggenheim agreed.

* * *

Every time Harry lowered his salute, the parade ground to a halt. At first Liberace helped prop the President's arm up, but then he got tired and explained he had to play at a party that night for Frank Sinatra and the Rat Pack. Little Ronnie Howard was on the reviewing stand, and he took a turn holding up Truman's arm, and when he got tired his pal Don Knotts took over.

Finally, The Pigeon's cage passed by the President, who wearily tossed a dead cat and a rotten tomato at the disgraced traitor. "If I hadn't won the election," the President promised himself, "which was some kind of unlucky miracle, I was gonna have Hoover killed, if it was the last thing I did. Now I'm stuck with him," as he dragged his sorry ass back to the White House.

The agent driving The Pigeon's manure cart laid his whip onto the mule, and finally they arrived at the National Zoo. "Time to find out your punishment, Pigeon," Rebay told him, as they put the cage on a dolly and rolled it into the Monkey House, where they shoved him into a cage full of gibbering apes.

Facing the cage was Pigeon's jury, and quite a jury it was: A roster of tough guys from the sleazy sidewalks of Grauman's Chinese Theater in L.A., John Wayne, Edward G. Robinson, Jimmy Cagney, Lee Marvin, Jack Palance, and Richard Widmark.

Speed was wearing a judge's robe and white wig, and he addressed The Pigeon, who was frantically trying to ward off the monkeys who were pelting him with their feces. "Are you ready for sentence to be pronounced and to get your punishment?"

Speed asked, and began reading, "You ratbastard, Commie, Nazi, disgrace to the Bureau, squaw-man — where'd *that* come from? — and defiler of Super Sluts," pointing to Brandi, who had a stern but cute and modest expression on her face, which, on the balance, rendered *almost* chaste the outfit she was wearing of *almost* nothing, just a coupla red, white, and blue strings. Hoover finished reading the charges: "arson, mad bombing, and baloney sandwich freeloading."

"Hey, Speed, how about a trial first!" The Pigeon shouted. "And how 'bout one a them sandwiches?"

"Not a chance, Scumbag. Now, would you like to address the jury?"

Something strange happened just here. I cudda sworn I saw the Pigeon winking at Speed, and Speed winking back! Nah.

The Pigeon took out his brief, and opened his mouth to speak, whereupon John Wayne said, "Waall, Pilgrim," and he made that dramatic pause that became his trademark.

The Pigeon couldn't stand the suspense, and screamed, "For God®'s sake, Duke, spit it out. I ain't got all day. I'm supposed to be executed in an hour."

"Shut-up Pilgrim . . . and it's *Duck*, not Duke. As I was . . . about to say before you say another word — hey, wait a minute *'Duke,'* I like that. They started calling me 'Duck' because of that stupid way I walk, and I never liked it. Maybe . . . Okay . . . I'm gonna be 'Duke Wayne' from now on, ya hear that Morris?" and Wayne's agent, William Morris, yelled back, "Got it Duke, I mean Duck, ya got me confused. Which is it, 'Duke' or 'Duck'?" and to make sure Bill Morris remembered, the Duke *(or is it the Duck? . . . ya got me confused too)* shot off one of Bill's ears.

Back to the script.

"Waall Pilgrim . . ."

The Pigeon let out a groan, and the Secret Agent Baroness interrupted. "I don't think you can just start calling yourself a Duke just because it sounds good. Duck was OK because you walk like one, but to be a Duke ya gotta do something so great that the King or the Pope or the Emperor decides to 'ennoble' you and make you a Duke or a Baroness or something."

"Oh yeah, little lady, and just what did you do that was so great?"

"How about saving that Sonuvabitch in the White House's life by shooting that Nazi assassin right between the eyes from fifty yards. How about sending a bomb to Stalin that blew up in his face and burnt off all his hair? How about stealing Hitler's mojo by making his moustache fall out? How about figgering out this fucking Pigeon's plan to kill Speed and take over the Bureau? How about . . .?"

"Ah, big . . . deal . . . Pilgrim . . ."

"Goddammit, Duke or Duck or whoever you are, spit it out," the Secret Agent Gal yelled. "Ya got some kinda goddamn speech impediment or something?"

"Why, you . . ." and the Duke/Duck pointed his Peacemaker at her, but before he could draw a bead on her she shot it out of his hand.

"Ow, that hurt. But pretty goddamn good shot . . . for a . . ."

"I suppose you're gonna say 'girl,' so let me finish your sentence for you before the prisoner dies of old age instead of the horrible fate I've dreamed up for him. But if ya really wanna know, I'm a Baroness because one of my ancestors rescued the Holy Foreskin from the Moslems, and gave it back to the Pope, and the Pope made Great-Great-Great . . . and so on, Granddad a Baron because without the Holy Foreskin of Our Lord and Savior the Catholic Church has no mojo, and what's happening to the Church right now (actually the Secret Agent Gal was peeking into the future a little bit) makes me believe the Pope has misplaced, lost, or had that foreskin stolen, which explains why the Church is in such deep shit: It's got no mojo. Got all that?" she yelled at me standing in the crowd, where I was trying to take down her every word for this book.

"All except how many grandfathers back all that was," I yelled back, "and where is the Foreskin — that's the Sanctum Praeputium — right now?"

"It's either in a jar of formaldehyde in a Columbia University lab, or on the key chain of some camel jockey's ratbastard son, and I'm gonna find it if we ever get this execution back on track."

She pointed to the Duke/Duck who recognized his cue and started up again. When the Pigeon opened his mouth to try to talk, the — let's just call him 'The D' — said, "That'll be jest about enough out of you . . . Pilgrim . . . (The Pigeon began making 'get on with it' gestures with both hands) . . . we find you guilty and sentence you to be shot like the rat you are," picking up his Peacemaker from where it had fallen after Miss Sure-Shot had blasted it out of his hand.

If Clint Eastwood had been born yet, he would have pulled out his Magnum Force cannon, and sneered at the Duke (or Duck), the vein on his forehead throbbing, "You call that a gun? *This* is a gun."

And likewise, if Crocodile Dundee had been there, he would have brandished his weapon and yelled, "And *this* is a knife."

Edward G. Robinson, who *was* there, groaned, "Mother of God®, is this the end of The Pigeon?"

Jack Palance dropped to the floor and began pumping out one-handed push-ups, saying "Someone tell me when to stop."

Then The Pigeon noticed James Cagney. "Cagney, Cagney," he yelled. "Anybody got a grapefruit for him to smash in my face? A picture of that'll almost make it worth getting executed."

Baroness Rebay, prepared as always, handed a half grapefruit to Cagney who rammed it into The Pigeon's face, leaving him licking rind and seeds off his lips. "Thanks Jimmy, I'll remember that as long as I live."

Humphrey Bogart lit a cigarette and started to mumble something about how a guy's supposed to do something when someone kills his partner, and how this might be the beginning of a beautiful friendship, but The Pigeon cut him off. "We ain't got time for that now, Bogey. I gotta get executed TODAY."

Richard Widmark gave The Pigeon one of those sneers that scared audiences to death, and said, "You know what I do to squealers? I let 'em have it in the belly, so they can roll around for a long time thinkin' it over. And by the way, everybody hated me in high school because I was so popular."

Lee Marvin gave The Pigeon a look so mean that two monkeys dropped dead of fright.

"Waall, Pilgrim . . ." the Duck or Duke began again, and paused. A long time . . .

"Jesus Christ®, Duck," The Pigeon screamed, "say what ya gotta say and kill me. Please!"

"For the last time, Pigeon" — Pigeon was tearing his hair out — "It's *Duke*, and . . . ya got any last words?"

Rebay stepped in front of the Duke/Duck: "No. Don't kill him now, Duck. Might hurt the monkeys."

The Duck fired a shot past Rebay's ear. "Care to rephrase that . . . little lady?"

"Oh, yeah, *Duke*, *Duke*. Don't kill him now, *Duke*, we got something better. The Big Reveal. Put a leash on him and drag him out," Rebay said, pointing to the door.

She led the jury, the Pigeon, and his handler in a solemn procession, with music: Secret Agent X-9 on his accordion with the "Dead March" from *Saul. (That's from a Handel Oratorio, kids. You know, classical music? Ever heard of it?)* Presidential Agent 103 was keeping them in step with the cowbell, Clyde improvising cadenzas on the comb kazoo, and Knockers twirling and tossing a gold and silver baton with red, white, and blue streamers. The dignity of the proceedings was marred only by The Pigeon, who for some reason was grinning right and left and holding his fists over his head like a prize-fighter entering the ring for the World Championship of Traitor-Ratbastards. But that shit-eating smirk was wiped off his face *tout suite* when he saw where Rebay was leading him: TO THE LIONS' DEN!

"How do ya like this, Pigeon?" the Baroness yelled, pointing to a pride *(That means a bunch, kids)* of lions who hadn't been fed for two days, and were so hungry they were eating themselves and each other. They were looking at The Pigeon and licking their chops. "Toss him in, boys," and two zookeepers hoisted The Pigeon over the cage and dropped him next to the pride *(remember, kids?)*, which began moving purposefully toward the Pigeon.

"Nice lions, nice lions," The Pigeon pleaded. "Remember how I pulled a thorn out of your foot? Oh, that was another lion. I thought you only ate Christians. I ain't no Christian. In fact, I worship the Lion King. I lionize lions. *(Kids, 'lionize' means he likes them a lot.)* Come on, lions. Gimme a break."

The lions got closer and closer until their noses pressed up against him. Then . . . they all turned tail and ran, fleeing to the farthest corners of the den.

"What the fuck? What's the matter?" Rebay yelled. "Come on. I expect every lion to do his duty."

"It's no use," one of the zookeepers told her, "if there's one thing lions can't stand it's the smell of manure — cow manure, horse manure, don't matter. And *that* guy there just reeks of it. Ya gotta take him out, hose him off, and then try again."

"That right? OK, let's clean him up!"

"No fair, no fair," The Pigeon shouted. "That's double jeopardy. Can't be punished twice for the same crime. Ya gotta let me go."

The Baroness waved at the Duke or Duck and begged him, "Come on, 'D' *(not to make a mistake)*, shoot him, shoot him."

"Overruled," they heard from behind them. It was Speed. "Put away your gun, Duck. The Pigeon is right. Can't execute him for the same crime twice."

"But Jesus, Speed," Rebay pleaded, "he's committed so many crimes it'd take me an hour to say 'em all. All day if we gave the job to the Duke. And I don't think it's quite legit for him to promote himself into the nobility. Although I think I could do it for him if he'd introduce me to Katherine Hepburn, who is a big favorite of mine. Let's kill him for one of his other crimes."

"Overruled again. Hose him off and turn him loose."

The crowd murmured, but Speed quieted them by announcing, "I'm gonna rehabilitate him. Turn him into a good American, a good Christian and a great Special Agent of the FBI again."

Duck/Duke shrugged. "Waall, Pilgrim . . . looks like this time ya just got lucky. . . . This time."

"Oh," The Pigeon bleated, "Thank you, Speed. You're a saint. I was lost but now I'm found. We should all get down on our knees and worship you. I think I'm gonna swoon." And he swooned.

Speed pulled off his white judge's wig and sidled over to The Pigeon. Holding his nose to ward off the stench, he touched him tenderly on the cheek and whispered, "How about meeting me at the Robin's Nest for a drinkypoo after we get back. We have to discuss your future."

Publisher's Note:

As Fearless Crusading Publisher Joe Taylor readied the 1948 edition of *Secret Agent Gals* for publication this year, a nagging thought kept buzzing around in his brain, sorta the way a housefly *(musca domestica)* or a skeeter or such tries to get out a window in the winter when the sun wakes it up, or like, well, you can probably come up with a better metaphor yourself. The story just had too many loose ends, too many plot holes.

There seemed to be a big secret missing that would explain everything. For example, and this was kinda sneaky of Powers, remember how he called our attention to the curious fact that the tune of "Clancy Lowered the Boom" was the same as the tune of Johnny Cash Geronimo's hit song, "Don't Take Your Guns to Town?" And then he just about gave the game way when he wrote, "And by the way, attentive readers, there have been clues scattered all through this book about how this story is going to turn out, which is a good trick because at this point I have no idea myself? Happy hunting." Shouldn't everyone have started wondering then and there what the fuck he was up to?

Then there was the phony-baloney way The Pigeon lucked out in the lions' cage, when Speed "accidentally" forgot that lions hate the smell of shit, something every grammar school kid learns in his jungle zoology class. And the way Speed and The Pigeon were flirtatiously winking at each other during the trial in the Monkey House. And made a date to meet at the Robin's Nest.

Yup, Fearless (and Crusading) Publisher Joe Taylor thought, *something seems to be missing. Maybe . . .*

. . . a lost last chapter.

Even an author as incompetent (and clueless) as Richard "Gid" Powers had to notice how fucked up his story was, and besides . . . nineteen was such an odd number of chapters. Any damn fool writer, even one, as Taylor had noticed, as incompetent (and clueless) as Powers would have figured out a way to make it twenty chapters.

But where was that Chapter Twenty? The chapter that would have tied up all those loose ends, filled in all those plot holes . . . maybe, just maybe, the FBI had held back that last chapter for its own sneaky nefarious Bureau reasons. Because . . . it might make the *Bureau* look bad. If it is ever possible to make the Bureau look bad! *(That, kids, is sarcasm.)*

So Taylor unleashed his team of crack lawyers to force the FBI to disgorge everything in their Secret Agent Gals file, and after legal squabbles too many to count (but not too many to bill), the Bureau finally coughed up that missing Chapter Twenty that had "the rest of the story" that prescient (as well as crusading and fearless) Joe Taylor KNEW had to be there.

So here it is . . .

CHAPTER 20

"The Rest of the Story"

(Written in 1948, by the cowardly Powers, but just now seeing the
light of day)

    I can't tell you how much shit I've taken for that ending
you just read back there in Chapter 19. And the protests weren't
just from my target audience, 11- and 12-year old boys. Some of
the kids even quit the Junior G-Man Club and sent ME back their
Secret Agent Decoder Rings®, along with secret coded messages
that I can't say here, or I'd have to wash my mouth out with brown
soap and Brillo® pads. Where do kids pick up that kind of foul
language? From their parents, right?

    Their parents started writing me, too. "Listen you ratbas-
tard fool, how can you let The Pigeon get away with it. 'You do
the crime, you gotta do the time' (which doesn't just mean jail
but *does* include getting eaten by lions or getting a humane lethal
injection). Now, because of your shitty book, my kid don't believe
in capital punishment no more, which is the cornerstone of the

Christian Religion ('Do unto others as they would do unto you if they had the fucking chance,' to paraphrase the *Baltimore Catechism®*.) Or just check out a crucifix. (If that ain't capital punishment, nothing is.) If you know what's good for you, you better stick a new ending on your goddamn book where The Pigeon gets what he fucking deserves."

"And another thing," — this from an irate mom — "you left so many fucking loose ends in your stupid story that my little girl says she's never gonna read another book if they all end without explaining why anything happened. She figgered there had to be some secret — even if you didn't know what it was, ya dumb fuck — that tied together all the parts of your stupid story: that interrogation of the phony spy at the training school, the Blond Beast at Luchow's, the way the Baroness was the only one who recognized the Nazi assassin who was going to kill that Sonuvabitch in the White House, those Russian dolls Speed and that Commie ratbastard Foster were playing with, Ma Oppenheimer (who reminded my girl, who knows her G-Man history, of Ma Barker), Ike's blue balls, the fuck-up at the porno houses — my little girl is asking me embarrassing questions about where Debby and her friend were putting their whatevers wherever, where Secret Slut Knockers could hide her gun if she was wearing practically nothing (she made me try hiding *my* gun in my thong — doesn't work, BIG plot hole).

"And even you gotta admit that all those plots or subplots or whatever the hell you wanna call them in *Secret Agent Gals* were just stuck together, no connections between them, like they had never met each other. Didn't make any sense. Anyway, to make a long rant short, if yer gonna write a book, ya oughtta have some goddamn idea of how it's gonna end so that a poor little kid can put it down without having to ask her mom a million stupid questions she can't answer because you were too stupid to answer them for her, ya dumb shit. Finally, in case no one has told you yet, you are a fucking idiot who can't write."

* * *

I was feeling pretty bad that I had let down all my little tyke readers and their mommies and daddies too, but what could I do? I just called 'em the way I saw 'em. My characters just did their stuff, and I wrote 'em down. I'm not God®, am I? I can't make them do things if they don't wanna. Nope. I am a camera, to coin a phrase I am sure some writer better than me will turn into the title of a book that *does* make sense. But there wasn't much I could do about it, and here's why:

One day in 1948 I was sitting in my nowhere office on a nowhere street in a nowhere part of town, preparing the book for publication, when there was a knock on the door. A gorgeous blond woman a little on the sleazy side, with a sensational rack, walked in. I hoped she might have a sensational bank account to match that rack, or at least some unmaxed-out credit cards, the sort I hadn't seen in a long time.

"It's me again," she said, like she expected me to jump up and say, "Where ya been, baby?"

"Do I know you?"

"Maybe you will now," she said, as she pulled off the blond wig. It was none other than Hoover's sidekick and Public Hero Number Two, Clyde Tolson.

"What the fuck," I said in one of those eloquent turns of phrase readers have come to expect from me, "What's with the wig? What's with the make-up? And put the wig back on. You looked GREAT!"

Quite fuckable, I thought. But I shouldn't be thinking dirty thoughts like that about a man, even if he/she looks great in that hot babe disguise. As William Buckley liked to say, "One time a philosopher, two times a pervert."

"You in drag for me or Speed?"

"Speed and I have gone pfft."

"You mean pfft as in, no longer bunkies?"

"I've been replaced," and she started to sniffle.

"Who's the homewrecker? Want me to kill him for ya? That'd be a hundred bucks a day plus expenses for food, booze, and ammo."

"It's The Pigeon. He's Speed's silent partner at the Bureau and in his heart. And in his bed. They tried to keep it a secret, but he was always acting like he had someone else on his mind when we were together. Then one day I was leafing through the *Secret Agent Director's Handbook®*, the one he never let anyone else read, and there it was. The loose end that let me unravel the whole awful, evil, unpatriotic, maybe even unconstitutional, and definitely sneaky way Speed pulled the wool (credit for extended metaphor, please) over all our eyes." She paused.

"Come on, spit it out, what was this dark, dread secret. You take as long to get to the point as the Duck. I mean Duke."

"Here, read it yourself." She passed me a page she/he had evidently ripped out of that top secret *Handbook* she was talkin' about.

I spread the page out on my desk and noticed that there was a diagonal watermark across the page, "For the Director's Eyes Only."

"Can I get in trouble for reading this?"

"Go ahead. Like you once wrote, 'Ratbastard traitors got no rights, not even to privacy.'"

At the top of the page was the title:

SECRET DIRECTOR'S PLAN NUMBER 34: THROW HIM INTO A LION'S DEN COVERED IN SHIT. *(THAT IS, THE RATBASTARD, NOT THE LIONS OR THEIR DEN, COVERED IN SHIT.)*

To be used when you have to pretend to execute a ratbastard double agent who has been fucking up the country with evil plots but is really your double-agent (might be triple, but beyond that, what the fuck difference does it make?). This procedure should save yer ass.

1. *Cover your double agent with shit. Precise variety of excrement is up to you, but cow manure seems to work best.*

2. *Starve your pride (that means a pack, or a bunch) of lions for two days until they are so hungry they are starting to eat each other or themselves. Makes the whole thing more dramatic.*

3. *Put the double agent on trial. Cut him off if he tries to say anything and sentence him to death. When outraged Hollywood stars want to execute him on the spot, tell them, or better yet, maneuver one of the G-Gals into saying, "Hold off, there's something worse in store for him than a bullet between the eyes."*

4. *Lead him to the Lions' Den. Have the double agent ratbastard put on a show how brave he is, but when he sees the lions he starts acting like a coward. That'll fool 'em.*

5. *Toss him in the lion's den. Lead the crowd in cheering: "Lion, Lion, he's*

our man, if he can't eat him (meaning
your double agent) no one can."

6. *Act surprised when the lions get close*
    enough to smell the shit on the double
    agent, then run away.

7. *When one of the fools says, let's hose*
    him off and let the lions at him again,
    say

8. *"No can do. Double jeopardy. We got-*
    ta let him go."

9. *Have a secret meeting with him (Rob-*
    in's Nest Bar is a good place) to give
    your guy his next sneaky rotten mis-
    sion.

10. *Good to go.*

"So," I said, when I finished reading, "what's your point? What's this got to do with anything?"

"Just *think*, asshole, if you can. Don't you see? Speed followed Secret Plan 34 step by step to fool us all into thinking he was really going to execute The Pigeon, but he was really planning to let him go."

I looked Plan 34 over again. "I see how you *could* read it that way, if you wanted to. There's a *superficial* resemblance between Plan 34 and what happened at the end of the book, but maybe it's just a coincidence. Maybe it's just that you wanna make Speed out a bad guy because he jilted you. You know, a woman scorned and all that. But look at step five, the one where the crowd chants 'Lion, Lion, he's our man, etc.' That didn't happen. So I guess that blows your theory all to hell."

"They *did* chant it. You were just too far back trying to cop a feel from the Poontang Patrol to hear."

"You saw that, didja?"

Clyde seemed a little pissed off at me. "Okay, so maybe you missed that one. But what about the other nine steps? Ya gotta admit they all happened just like in the *Secret Plan 34*."

"How about step nine? You don't know that Speed met The Pigeon at the Robin's Nest, do ya?"

"Do too, do too. I went to the Mayflower and got a copy of their chit. They both signed, because the Pigeon put the bill on his card, but that cheap bastard Speed took a copy so that he could bill the Bureau for drinks HE DIDN'T EVEN PAY FOR." He handed me the chit.

"Well, seems to me you *might* be able to get him for fiddling his expense account, but who doesn't? Is this all ya got?"

"All I got!" she/he said sarcastically, which I overlooked instead of pistol-whipping him/her which is what I usually would have done to an asshole who got fresh, because I was going to ask him/her for his/her number and see about a date, once she/he got off his/her chest (some chest!) whatever the hell he/she was trying to say, which I had lost track of because I got distracted by his /her gigantic set of falsies.

"Lemme run through the whole megillah," Clyde summed up, "which is Jewish for telling you everything."

"I didn't know you were Jewish. You don't look Jewish."

"Any law against plastic surgery, you bigot?"

"Does that mean if we go out you can't have kielbasa and a chocolate shake, my favorites?"

"You got a long way to go before you get a date with me, buster. First you gotta listen to the . . ."

"Yeah, I know, the whole whatchamacallit. Go on." And what a McGill thingy it was!

I still wasn't buying the Plan 34 thing, because it was fulla holes. But I wanted her at least to think I was listening so that she'd go out with me after she finished telling me her whole ridiculous stupid theory, so I asked him/her to go back and start at the beginning.

But I didn't know the beginning would go back that far! And it was already lunch time, which if she/he hired me I was going to bill her for (lemme just stick with her, because that's how I was starting to think of . . . her). So I settled in for the long haul.

And Clyde had really done some digging! He/she had gone back to Agent Training School and had shown Mahony, now Assistant Director Mahony, a picture of The Pigeon. Mahony had played dumb at first, but when Clyde batted him around a little and stuck Mahony's thumbs in one of the Madman's Chinese handcuffs, he had admitted that the agent who had pretended to be a Nazi spy in that little scenario with Percy Foxworth did look an awful lot like The Pigeon. When Clyde tightened up the handcuffs and used them to suspend Mahony from the ceiling, he admitted that Speed himself had sent The Pigeon to put on that show for the G-Gals.

Then there was the Blond Beast, Hitler's messenger to the American Nazis. That was The Pigeon again. Speed staged the whole thing, trolled the Beast/Pigeon past the two Gals, and they bit. Why? Hoover knew the Sonuvabitch in the White House, who hated him, was going to send him to the Pacific to get killed by the Japs when the war started, unless he did something that would make him a hero. So he had the Gals in place in Congress when the Nazi patsy, whose gun was loaded with blanks by The Pigeon, showed up while the Sonuvabitch in the White House was trying to declare war. Same thing with the fake kidnapping.

The Commies who pretended to be FBI Agents were really The Pigeon's boys, FBI Agents from the Bureau's "School of Dramatic Arts and Tricks for Fooling Assholes®." Speed and The Pigeon staged the whole thing, including tricking X-9 into thinking he was supposed to sabotage the Sonuvabitch's crutches so he'd fall on his ass in Madison Square Garden. The Russian Dolls:

from Assistant Director La Fop's prop trunk. And can you believe it? Comrade William Z. Foster was really The Pigeon again, wearing sneaky Commie make-up.

And Pearl Harbor. Another ploy by Speed to make himself a big shot. The Pigeon was in cahoots with Admiral Yamamoto long before Speed's phone call that PA 103 had intercepted. When the G-Gals learned about the plans for the attack, he didn't forward the news to the Navy. Why? Because he wanted to start a war so he could send disloyal agents who hadn't contributed to the Director's Birthday Fund to the Pacific to get killed by the Japs.

What about the Red Ratbastard traitor spies at Los Alamos? The Pigeon was Speed's contact with Ma Oppenheimer, and they had done a triple switch of the bomb plans. Yeah, Stalin got the real bomb because Speed wanted the Russians to have it so that the public would panic and make Hoover Spy Catcher Number One now that all the public enemies had been killed or died of old age.

Joe and Willie and Kay Summersby? Joe and Willie were double agents for The Pigeon and Speed, and they didn't even know it. Pigeon used them to get the hair remover to Hitler AND to kidnap Kay. His plan was to get the FBI credit from Ike for having the G-Gals rescue Kay and for stealing Hitler's mojo. That way he could control Ike when he became president. He would kidnap Kay anytime Ike didn't do exactly what Speed told him. Once the blue balls set in, Ike would panic and come running to the FBI to get her back.

And then the Clancy thing: After the war, all the demobilized disloyal agents were coming back, and Hoover knew they'd be out to get him for sending them to the Pacific to get killed by the Japs just to save his cowardly ass. So he and The Pigeon came up with the manure plot to get all the cheapskate agents who not only didn't contribute to the Director's Birthday Fund, but wouldn't help him when the Madman's Doubling Down on Yer

Losses betting system was proving much more costly than they thought (although the Madman swore that in a thousand years give or take a few centuries, the math said they would break even.)

But Speed and the Pigeon didn't even have to think up Clancy and the Manure Bomb Plot by themselves. Clyde showed me another Secret Plan in the *Secret Agent's Director's Handbook®:*

> SECRET PLAN 53:
>
> *USING CLANCYS ON TOP OF EXPLODING MANURE CARTS TO GET ALL THE DISLOYAL AGENTS IN ONE PLACE SO THE MADMAN CAN STICK SILVER NEEDLES IN THEIR BRAINS SO THEY WILL LOVE THE DIRECTOR AGAIN AND GIVE HIM MONEY TO COVER HIS GAMBLING ADDICTION.*

That, I had to admit, *also* bore a *superficial* resemblance to the Clancy McGill something. Sure, *Plan 53* gave the specs for the carts, phone numbers for renting mules and buying cow shit, sheet music with lyrics for "Clancy Lowered the Boom," blueprints for building the conveyor towers, the secret formula for the blue tarp superpower, and details of the costume he should wear for seducing Secret Slut Bliss. Yes, it was all there, but surely a criminal genius like The Pigeon could have come up the plans himself without needing to crib from *Secret Agent Director's Handbook®*. But so what? More coincidences that didn't prove anything, let alone that Speed had been a bad guy.

I still didn't see the connection between what Clyde was telling me and the plot(s) of my book — nothing that would satisfy the 11- and 12-year-old readers of *Secret Agent Gals* and their pissed off parents. There was no way anyone would swallow Clyde's crazy story that everyone's hero, Public Hero Number One, J. Edgar Hoover, was the brains behind The Pigeon and had planned every major disaster in late twentieth century American history. Not even if Speed had been ratted out by his best friend and ex-bunkie Public Hero Number Two Clyde Tolson. Anyone could see Clyde was just a romantic loser with a broken heart and an insane itch for revenge.

They wouldn't believe it unless . . . unless . . . they heard it from the ONLY two people in the world everybody trusted.

* * *

A day later I got the call I was waiting for. I was to go to the Robin's Nest Bar at 3:00 that afternoon. I should wear a tan trench coat, a snap brim fedora, and sunglasses.

I was in a corner banquette, nervous as hell. Something like Woodward off to a secret meeting with Deep Throat, in this case two Deep Throats, let's say Ms. Deep Throat Numbers 1 and 2.

I had moved past Martinis (two was my limit) and was onto my second Gibson when I felt a tap on my shoulder. I looked up and there were two figures in full G-Man disguise like the one I was wearing, trench coats, gal versions of fedoras, and sunglasses. Yes. It was it was them. The Secret Agent Gals.

They sat down. "Take off your disguises," I asked. "I have to be sure it's really you."

They took off their glasses and hats. It was Secret Agent Rebay and Secret Agent Guggenheim, all right.

"Did you read Clyde's wild story I sent you?" I said.

"We did. What did *you* think of it?" Rebay asked me.

"I thought it was nuts, that he was crazy. And I didn't think his story had any connection to what was in my book. Sure, there were some matches here and there, some slight resemblances between the Lions' Den plot and *Secret Plan 34*, and between the Clancys on Top of Shit Wagons Plot and *Plan 53*, but those could be explained away as coincidences. It couldn't be true that your hero and mine, Speed Hoover, 'The Man Who Killed Dillinger,' or least 'The Man Who Hired the Man Who Killed Dillinger,' could have been the ratbastard boss of The Pigeon, a dirty rat Nazi Commie, ratbastard traitor (I think I said that), the guy who planned Pearl Harbor with the Japs and gave the A-bomb to Stalin. Who'd believe any of that?"

"Why do you think Clyde made it up?" Guggenheim asked.

"Simple. He was just on a rebound from a failed love affair, a jilted lover. It wouldn't take a Henry James, let alone a Mickey Spillane to see that Clyde's story was the raving of a lovelorn madman, although I must say a very attractive lovelorn madman when he puts on his hot babe disguise and that set of falsies."

"What we have to say will shock you," Secret Agent Guggenheim said.

"That's right," Secret Agent Rebay added. "Every word of what Clyde told you is true. Clyde *is* a very unhappy man (or woman), and we agree he makes a much more attractive woman than man, in fact Peggy and I have gotten some good make-up tips from him, but he is not a nutcase. When she/he came to us with her story we brought her down to the Madman, and he put him/her through his lie detector, his homo detector, his traitor detector, every torture device he had and some he borrowed from an S&M store in Greenwich Village, and every part of his story checked out.

"We decided that we had to intervene to rescue the country from these two crazed ratbastards who had captured the FBI and were giving every sign that they intended to launch an attack against God® and the USA, which would have been bad for the stock market and our pensions.

"We invited Speed and his 'New Clyde,' who we now knew was that master of disguise, the Pigeon, looking exactly like the 'Old Clyde,' to a meeting in Madman's lab. The pretext was to discuss shortfalls in the Director's Trips to Vegas fund. We strapped them into straitjackets. clamped iron masks on them and took them to a maximum security prison for the criminally insane, a place called Chock Full O' Nuts. They will never be a threat to God® or democracy or the stability of the dollar again. I understand they are making good progress weaving gimp lanyards and making potholders out of cloth loops. Two actors from the FBI Studios of Dramatic Arts and Ruses to Fool Assholes have taken their places, and will be, as far as the public is concerned, Speed and Clyde for the rest of the century.

"But for the good of the country, the Christian Religion, the FBI, and all the boys and girls in the *Post Toasties Junior G-Man Clubs®* who believe that Speed and Clyde are heroes, you cannot publish a word of what Clyde told you until everyone in the story is dead. Let's say seventy some years. You can publish *Secret Agent Gals* now, but without this last, what do you call it? CHAPTER 20."

"We knew that Clyde, the 'Old Clyde,' was a loose cannon, so we put out a contract for the Madman to shoot him full of that scaredy-cat serum and ship him off to a madhouse, but he fooled us by putting on that very attractive disguise as a magnificently stacked sexpot and slipped away. But we finally caught him. We got a report last night that a woman with an amazing rack was drinking right here, and once we had made sure Knockers wasn't on the loose, we picked him/her up."

I could hardly believe my own two ears, but if ya can't believe the Secret Agent Gals, who can you trust? But then, if what Clyde had told me was true, I was getting a super raw deal. I was going to have to print a crock of shit as the true story, and the truth couldn't come out until, (and I did some math, cast out nines) 2023. "But that means for seventy some years, that's almost a century if you round up and cast out nines, this country is going to be believing a bunch of lies, in other words, bullshit, about

Speed, Clyde, and The Pigeon. And about youse gals and X-9 and PA 103."

"It's for their own good. They can't stand the truth," Secret Agent Rebay said. "But at the end of seventy years, you or your pathetic heirs can publish and be damned. All of us will be dead, you can't hurt anyone with that 'truth,' and no one will believe it anyway."

She made it clear that if I didn't accept what she blandly called her "offer," that the Gals already had a place booked for me at Chock Full O' Nuts where I could share a room with my new girlfriend. Clyde was already in transit to that Conservatory for Crackpot Criminals.

"So, whaddya say? Are you gonna keep your trap shut and your fingers off the keyboard, and just publish the first nineteen chapters, or is it gonna be a one-way ticket to the funny farm?"

I recognized that she was parroting my way with dialog, whether as an homage or a parody *(Almost a pun there, kiddies, parroting/parody)* I wasn't quite sure.

"If yer having trouble making up yer mind, we brought some muscle to help make it up for you."

She pointed to the end of the bar, where PA 103 and X-9 grinned and waved a pair of butterfly nets in my direction, and MAD-1, in his black wizard's robe and pointed black hat with the moon, the stars, and 'I'm a G-Madman' badge pinned to it, held up a giant hypodermic and mouthed the words, "Happy juice."

"Yer not leaving me much choice," I told them. "It's a deal. But does the Chock Full O' Nuthouse allow conjugal visits? I have a 2 pound *Whitman Sampler®* I'd like to give Clyde."

"Once he's settled in, and we've adjusted his medication, I think that'd be okay."

"And how 'bout picking up my bar bill?"

"Not a chance. Bad habit, mooching drinks from girls in bars. 'If ya drank the Bellini, pay the billini,' and in your case,

'If ya drank the martini, pay the tabini,' or 'Ya had the Gibson, so . . .'"

"Let's see ya rhyme that one," I challenged her, and X-9 yelled over, "Extend that metaphor, Secret Agent Rebay, you can do it!"

But she couldn't, and she glared at me as she left.

And so our disastrous (to my career) meeting ended with that one small pathetic win for my side. I do get my date with Clyde, and if he's still in a straitjacket when I visit him at Chock Full O' Nuts he/she won't be able to resist my advances. I'll have to see if Clyde wants to keep score, which I calculate as one for the Gals, one for me, but we haven't checked by casting out nines yet. I'll leave that to Clyde, who'll look so cute when he's in a pair of pink heels.

And so, until somebody manages to pry that last chapter out of the Bureau's clutches, readers are going to be stuck with a bunch of lies instead of the REAL story of the Secret Agent Gals and Speed Hoover.

* * *

And that someone, of course, who managed to pry the last chapter out of the Bureau's feverish clutches was none other than Crusading (and Fearless) Publisher Joe Taylor. So now you have had, as the old-time radio newscaster Paul Harvey (b.t.w. a real blowhard) used to sign off, "The Rest of the Story."

The End

Richard Gid Powers (call him RGP) and the other novelist Richard Powers (call him RP) are not related as far as they know, although both were born in Illinois (which is a big state). The RGP you got here is the son of the Science Fiction Hall of Fame illustrator Richard M. Powers, call him RMP, who also wrote stories that have the same surreal quality as his science fiction covers, which is a roundabout way of raising the possibility that RGP inherited his own wayward imagination (as in *Secret Agent Gals*) from RMP. (Whew! That's a sentence!) RGP spent his writing career until about ten years ago writing absolutely non-fictional studies of the FBI and their famous bad guys and teaching the future leaders and followers of America the difference between right and wrong (there *is* one, you should know) at the College of Staten Island, City University of New York. He is also a pretty good skier and tennis player FHA (For His Age) and hopes there are no more writing Powers lurking around to make things even more confusing.